Who hasn't thought Pride and Prejudice could use more dragons?

Praise for Maria Grace

"Maria Grace did a wonderful job spinning a tale that's enjoyable for Austen lovers who do and who don't typically delve into the fantasy genre because she does a great job balancing the dragon world she has created alongside Austen's characters." **Just Jane 1813**

"Grace has quickly become one of my favorite authors of Austen-inspired fiction. Her love of Austen's characters and the Regency era shine through in all of her novels." **Diary of an Eccentric**

"Maria Grace is stunning and emotional, and readers will be blown away by the uniqueness of her plot and characterization" **Savvy Wit and Verse**

"I believe that this is what Maria Grace does best, blend old and new together to create a story that has the framework of Austen and her characters, but contains enough new and exciting content to keep me turning the pages. ... Grace's style is not to be missed." **From the desk of Kimberly Denny-Ryder**

D1158837

Longbourn: Dragon Entail

Maria Grace

White Soup Press

Published by: White Soup Press

Longbourn: Dragon Entail
Copyright © 2017 Maria Grace

For information, address
author.MariaGrace@gmail.com

ISBN-10: 0-9980937-3-4
ISBN-13: 978-0-9980937-3-4 (White Soup Press)

Author's Website: RandomBitsofFaascination.com
Email address: Author.MariaGrace@gmail.com

Dedication

For my husband and sons.
You have always believed in me.

1
Chapter

Getting what one wants may not be as important as wanting
what one has.

A CHILL BREEZE cut through the garden, rattling dry, withered stems. So lonely and barren. Elizabeth pulled her cloak against her chest a little tighter and turned toward the house.

Soon the evergreen cutting party would return, and she would be pressed into service decorating the house. The Gardiner children's contagious enthusiasm offered a balm to her soul ... something to look forward to even more than tomorrow's Christmas dinner, the first major Christmastide celebration of the season.

Mama had invited all of the officers to join them. They, along with the Gardiners and Mr. Collins, should make for a very full dining room and a very merry party. The more company Mama—and Lydia—had, the merrier they were.

Was there any way she could claim a sick headache and skip the whole affair?

How Mama would scold to hear such a thought.

April peeked out from Elizabeth's hood and rubbed her fluffy, iridescent blue head against Elizabeth's ear. "I am cold."

"Then cozy up in my hood, you silly featherpate. There is no reason for you to be out in the wind. Why did you even come out with me if you hate the cold so?" Elizabeth pulled her hood up over the dainty fairy dragon.

"You have not been acting like yourself. We are all worried."

"So that is why I am always accompanied by a draconic entourage?" She glanced over her shoulder.

Rustle nodded at her from his post on the garden gate and flapped his wings in a cockatrice greeting. She clutched the edges of her cloak and fluttered them back at him. He squawked a happy note. He was a dear, even if an unsubtle one.

A fuzzy, warm body bumped against her ankles.

"Mrow." Rumblkins blinked up at her as he wove between her feet. He was so much longer than an actual cat, she stumbled a bit in the effort not to kick him.

How fat and glossy he had become since he had come to be Mrs. Hill's particular Friend.

She crouched to scratch his ears. "You too—checking up on me?"

The tatzelwurm purred, rearing up a bit on his serpentine tail. He did so love to have his head petted. "You are acting strange, even for a warm-blood."

"You are very sweet, all of you, but there is nothing to be concerned about. A touch of melancholy is to be expected on occasion. Many considered it a rather poetic trait for a young woman to possess now and then."

Particularly when she had been forcibly separated from a dearly loved baby by a cruel, unjust man.

Gracious, that sounded almost gothic!

Rumblkins chirruped and stared at her. "Stuff and nonsense. Come inside. There is hot cider." He caught her hem with his thumbed paw and pulled her toward the house.

"I like hot cider." April nipped her ear softly.

"Very well. But only a spoonful for you lest you are rendered flightless and silly."

April squawked, but did not argue.

If it had just been the family about, a little overindulgence would hardly have been a problem, but in the company of Mr. Collins, everything was different. He was resolutely dragon-deaf and not fond of pets. Birds and cats, according to him, did not belong in the house. What would he say if he discovered they were really dragons?

Somehow, it was perversely fitting that he should be resolute in that opinion, immune to draconic persuasion.

Vexing, troublesome man.

He probably disliked dogs too.

Of course, Mama would find him all that a young man should be—at least all that a young man worthy of Elizabeth should be. Jane, or even Lydia, deserved so much more.

At least Aunt Gardiner understood Elizabeth's reluctance. That helped. Jane was far too caught up with

Mr. Bingley to have much attention to spare for such sisterly confidences.

And Mary—how was it that she did not find Mr. Collins nearly so odious? Was it her saintly patience, or just that she had a far more realistic expectation of men? Or perhaps, not facing life as Mr. Collins' wife made things look very, very different.

Once inside, Elizabeth accepted a cup of cider from Hill and sat near the kitchen fire. Rumblkins jumped into his hearth basket and purred until Hill stopped what she was doing to scratch under his chin. She looked so very content petting her devoted ratter, with no idea at all that he was a dragon. Why could not Mr. Collins be more like her?

The party returned with a wagon heaped with evergreens. For the remainder of the day she tied bows around them and satisfied Mama with their placement throughout the house, a task made far easier by liberal amounts of Hill's hot cider.

Christmas Day began with a trip to the parish church for a rather lengthy morning service. It was almost as if knowing Mr. Collins was there prompted their own vicar to deeper, lengthier reflections.

About half the officers were in attendance, as were Colonel Forester and his young wife, Harriet, Lydia's particular friend. Somehow Lydia contrived to escape the family pew and sit between Harriet and Captain Carter. Beside them, Denny and Chamberlayne seemed as distracted by Lydia as she was by them.

On Elizabeth's right, Mr. Collins made little effort to conceal his disapproval over Lydia's antics. Jane and

Mama, though, were oblivious, occupied with the Bingleys and Hursts in the pew in front of them. They had stayed at Netherfield after Mr. Darcy's departure and were a constant and painful reminder of little Pemberley.

Elizabeth's eyes burned. How the little dear had snaked her long neck around Elizabeth's waist and looked so adoringly into her face. She blinked rapidly and ducked her head. The drakling had been with them less than a month. It was foolish that she should still feel so bereft at the hatchling's removal to Rosings and angry with Mr. Darcy for his agency in the matter.

But she did.

After church, the entire family paraded through town to stop at the baker's for their roast Christmas goose—the largest one amongst all his orders. Mama was oddly proud of the fact, remarking on it as she worked herself up into a complete twitterpation over the impending arrival of their dinner guests.

As they entered the house, Mama pulled her aside. "Lizzy dear, I need you to do something for me. I want you to make certain that all those … birds keep to their cages whilst we have guests. It is most unseemly to have them flying about loose in the house. I fear someone will get the wrong sort of impression of us. It is remarkable that Hill's cat has not eaten them by now—not that I would regard the loss to be sure, but I know the Gardiner children would be upset. It would be just my sort of luck if that very thing were to happen in the midst of my Christmas dinner."

"I will see to it, Mama. If you wish, I can keep them all in my room and stay with them to ensure that they do not venture out."

"Miss Christmas dinner for birds that can very well be kept caged? Do be serious, child! Just lock the cages, and it will be enough." Mama rolled her eyes as she swept past her and into the house.

"The children will be downstairs, and Mary will be downstairs. I do not understand why we should be expected to stay up here." Phoenix hunkered down on a delicately carved perch in April's cage-house, bright red feather-scales pouffed out in a decided pout.

"The officers have been invited and they are ... rather coarse. Particularly when indulging in the libations of the season. They are not known for being careful or gentle. All Mama's protests aside, I am honestly worried for your safety if you join us downstairs. You do not want to be stepped on." Elizabeth reached into the cage and stroked his fluffy head with a fingertip.

April zipped into the cage and sat on the perch beside him. "And that Collins man is going to be there as well. You were just complaining that you were tired of him. Do you wish to keep company with him again?" She preened his back.

"I do not like him, not at all." Phoenix fluttered his wings and huffed.

"Neither do I." Heather peered down from a higher perch, leaning farther and farther forward until she hung upside down on the perch, nearly eye-to-eye with April.

April snorted. "Must you act like a bat? The children may like it, but—"

"It makes my Mary laugh. She needs to laugh. She is too serious." Heather's tiny voice was still hard to hear, but was getting stronger each day.

And she was right. Mary was often too serious.

Perceptive little creature.

"You do not like Collins any better than the rest of us." April stretched to groom Heather's pale pink neck feathers.

"He cannot hear, so why bother with him?"

"He is difficult, almost impossible, to persuade." April lifted her beaky nose in her favorite authoritative attitude.

"Men might be persuaded in ways other than by dragon voices." Heather hung by one foot and scratched behind her ear. "Mary is very good at persuading."

Elizabeth's brow knotted. When had Mary done such a thing? No, Heather must be mistaken. She was so sweet, and believed that her Friend could do nearly anything.

"None of that has any bearing on dinner tonight. However, to make your confinement a little more pleasant, I have brought you these." She placed three small dishes in the cage.

Heather let go of the perch, flipped midair, and landed beside the dishes. The other two joined her, sniffing, eyes half-closed.

"Honey?" April cheeped, bobbing up and down.

"Strawberry jam!" Heather plunged her face into the dish. Luckily the jam matched her feather-scales. Otherwise, she would be stained for days.

Phoenix dipped his long tongue in the third dish. "Blood and treacle pudding?"

"With a little extra treacle as a treat."

He fluffed his wings and hopped a little closer.

"I trust this will make up for your lack of company this evening?" Elizabeth curtsied.

April flitted to her shoulder. "I still do not like you being amongst Collins and those officers without someone to watch over you."

"I do not blame you for not liking Collins, but not all the officers are objectionable. Mr. Wickham—"

"I know you like that Wickham man—far more than you should. But I do not. I wish you would not spend time with him at all."

She pinched her temples. "First Longbourn, now you? I do not believe I have asked either of you for your opinion on any of the men of my acquaintance."

"I liked Darcy. Walker is an excellent cockatrice. Even Rustle approves of him."

"I am not having this discussion again. You may like him, but I do not. Not that any of that matters." How could April like the arrogant man who separated her from Pemberley? She held her hand near April who climbed upon her finger. "Pray go back to your honey and enjoy it whilst I try to enjoy some pleasing company myself."

She returned April to the cage and latched the lock. It was only to make a statement, though. With the lock on the inside, they could open the door whenever they wanted.

Elizabeth joined the gathering in the drawing room, waiting for their guests to arrive. Long wax candles surrounded by mirrors bathed every corner with pleasing light. Papa would cringe at the expense, but they were necessary. One did not use tallow candles around good company, or so Mama insisted. Fresh evergreen and holly, tied with cheery red bows, filled the room with the season's fragrances that hung on the warm air from the fireplace.

The Gardiner children admired one garland, dashing across the room to admire the next. Joshua and Anna argued softly over who had tied the prettiest bows, their mother or Jane.

"Why do you not take a seat, Lizzy?" Aunt Gardiner patted the settee cushion beside her.

There was an excellent chance that she might not be able to sit still any better than the children, but it behooved her to try.

"How can they take so long?" Lydia peered out of the window, wrapping the curtain around her shoulders. "I cannot wait for the officers to get here."

"They are such agreeable company, so gallant and always in search of a spot of fun." Kitty bounced in her seat near the fireplace.

"Do sit still. It is unbecoming to twitch about like a hound waiting to be fed." Mary folded her hands in her lap and adjusted her posture to something entirely stiff and proper. "Do unwind yourself from the curtains before you tear them off the wall entirely."

"You need not be so disagreeable. It is not as if you are anticipating anyone special to arrive." Lydia sniffed and rolled her eyes.

"Lydia!" Aunt Gardiner slapped the arm of the settee.

"Well, it is true. None of the officers like her, for she is so very dull."

"Your opinions are not helpful, nor are they kind."

"But they are true." Lydia should really learn to recognize the danger in Aunt Gardiner's expression.

"Lydia!"

Lydia huffed and tossed her head.

Where was Jane? She had a way of distracting Lydia into at least the semblance of proper behavior.

She was upstairs, still dressing. How could she have forgotten? Mr. Bingley was to be in attendance along with the officers. He and his horrid sisters—for Mama could not possibly invite one without the others. Why could those harridans not have left when Mr. Darcy had?

The front door creaked, and voices drifted into the drawing room.

"Oh, oh, someone is here! I think I recognize Sanderson's voice." Kitty clapped softly.

Lydia and Kitty pinched their cheeks and checked their bodices, pulling them just a little lower.

"Mary, would you favor us with some music? A Christmas carol perhaps?" Aunt Gardiner asked, but it was more of a directive than a question.

Mary moved to the pianoforte, looking pleased to have her accomplishments recognized. Mama swept in with several officers in her wake.

"Wickham, Denny, and Sanderson!" Lydia and Kitty drew Denny and Sanderson away as Jane escorted Aunt and Uncle Philips in.

Mr. Wickham approached Elizabeth and Aunt Gardiner. He cut a dashing figure, even without his uniform.

But it was a mistake to pay too much attention to that. Noticing agreeable men, with excellent manners and good conversation only made Mr. Collins look worse by comparison.

Aunt Gardiner cocked her head and lifted her eyebrow at Elizabeth. "My niece tells me you are from Derbyshire, sir."

He pulled a chair close and sat with them. "Indeed, I am madam. Are you familiar with the county?"

"I spent my girlhood there, in the area of Lambton. I am quite convinced it is the most beautiful county in England."

Wickham's eyes brightened, his face softening with a compelling smile. "I lived on an estate very near there, Pemberley, if you know it."

"I do, indeed. One of the loveliest places I have ever seen. We were by no means in such a way to keep company with the family there, but we heard much of their good name whilst we lived there." Aunt Gardiner's face shifted into an odd expression, one she often used with the children when trying to work out one of the boys' stories.

"I was privileged to live at Pemberley. My father was steward there."

"Then you were well-favored indeed. Have you been there recently?"

"Very little since the death of old Mr. Darcy. While old Darcy was a very good and kind man, and very well disposed toward myself, I am afraid his son did not inherit his father's noble traits. I have no desire to burden you with such tales as would dampen your spirits on this very fine occasion. Let us talk of acquaintances we may share in common. Did you know the old apothecary there? Mr. Burris, I believe his name was."

"He was a great favorite of my father's."

"Of mine, as well."

Despite his long absence, Wickham still found it in his power to offer Aunt Gardiner fresher intelligence of her former friends than she had been in the way of procuring. It did not take too long for their recollections of shared society to turn to a discussion of old

Mr. Darcy's character, whom both liberally praised and that subject naturally progressed to the more relevant topic of the current Mr. Darcy and his deplorable treatment of Mr. Wickham.

Aunt Gardiner chewed her lip as she listened. "I grant you, that I recall the younger Mr. Darcy spoken of as a very proud, ill-natured boy, but the charges you lay at his feet are quite alarming, sir. With the strength of your claim against him, I am surprised that you have not been able to bring some kind of influence to bear against him."

She cast a sidelong look at Elizabeth, one eyebrow raised.

"Would that were possible, madam, I would probably be the better for it. In truth, though, I still hold his father in far too high a regard to be able to take action against his son."

"But surely you must consider how his own son's behavior would distress him. I know that to be the case if it were one of my own children charged with such heartlessness."

Her own children would never even consider such cruelty. They were raised much better than Mr. Darcy.

"You might be very right, but surely you can see I am not the one suited by station or inclination to bring correction to such a man. So, I shall continue on as I have been, grateful to such friends as I still have around me. I am truly blessed to have some very staunch supporters." He glanced over his shoulder toward the other officers.

Jane and Aunt Philips approached.

"Is not the company tonight delightful, sister?" Aunt Philips extended her hands toward Aunt Gardiner, but offered Elizabeth only a dark glance.

What joy, Mama had been talking—more probably complaining to her—likely about Elizabeth's reluctance toward Mr. Collins. If she was not crowing about Jane's imminent conquest of Mr. Bingley, Elizabeth's reticence was her favorite topic of conversation.

Aunt Gardiner took Aunt Philips' hands and kissed her cheeks. "Indeed, it is. But we always appreciate the hospitality at Longbourn. I should hardly expect anything else."

"Miss Lizzy, should you not be attending your duties as a hostess tonight?" Aunt Phillips' lip curled just the way Mama's did when she was angry.

"Whatever do you mean?" Aunt Gardiner's honey-eyed tone had been known to placate tired children and churlish adults alike. "Elizabeth is always a most attentive hostess."

"Then why is her cousin, Collins, left to stand in the corner alone?" She pointed her chin toward the far side of the room. "You should be far more attentive to him."

Elizabeth's face grew cold, but her cheeks burned.

Mama burst into the room. "Shall we all to dinner?"

"Might I escort you, Miss Elizabeth?" Mr. Wickham offered his arm.

Elizabeth muttered something, curtsied to her aunts, and took Mr. Wickham's arm.

"Thank you." The words barely slipped past her tight throat. "Pray excuse my Aunt. She is known to speak her mind without regard to the company present."

"There is nothing to excuse. Think of it no further. I have found when people resort to directness which some may consider disagreeable, it is most often attributable to indigestion."

Elizabeth snickered under her breath. Dragons must suffer a great deal of indigestion.

"Perhaps it would be wise to suggest she have a few words with her cook. A change in diet might be the very thing to relieve her discomfort and improve her general disposition. See there, how her husband is red in the face, and his hand is pressed so obviously to his belly? I would venture to say that he may be suffering from indigestion, too. Their cook, and no one else, is to blame."

It would seem Mr. Wickham did not, or chose not, to see Mama at Uncle Philips's side, speaking with great animation and casting sidelong glances toward Elizabeth.

"I shall suggest that to her." The words came easier now. She forced her lips into something resembling a smile.

"Ah, that is a far better expression for you, Miss Elizabeth. Unhappiness does not suit you at all."

"It is difficult to be unhappy in your presence, sir. Do you make it your business to drive away such specters wherever they might appear?"

"I certainly do. What better occupation in life than to bring happiness wherever I wander?"

How very true. And how very different to Mr. Darcy.

To maintain such a disposition, despite the very great unfairness and trials he had faced, Mr. Wickham was truly too good.

For all Mama's fussing and fluttering, she did set one of the finest tables in the county. Candlelight glittered off mirrors and crystal, filling every corner of the dining room with sparkling warmth. The table and sideboards groaned under the weight of the dishes heaped with fragrant offerings. The huge goose lay near Papa's place, waiting for him to carve it.

Elizabeth's mouth watered. Nothing tasted like a Christmas goose.

Wickham held the chair for her and sat beside her, politely ignoring Lydia's cross look. What did she have to be cross about though? With Denny on one side and Sanderson on the other, it was not as if she would be in want of company or conversation.

Aunt and Uncle Gardiner sat opposite each other at the center of the table, a child on either side of them. The children looked so adorable in their best clothes, so serious about being permitted to join the adults on this festive occasion. There was a very good chance that their behavior might well be better than Kitty's and Lydia's. Mr. Collins would probably still find fault though—he was not fond of children.

Mama rang a little silver bell. The door swung open, and Hill appeared, holding high a platter of roasted boar's head. Her arms quivered under the massive burden.

Denny and Sanderson jumped to their feet, nearly knocking their chairs to the floor, as they rushed to her aid. Together they made a lovely show of bringing the final dish to the table.

Was it gallantry? Or concern that the delicacy might not make it to the table? Either way, it was amusing to watch. Mama seemed very pleased at the officers' efforts and settled into her comfortable role, presiding over the table.

Wickham leaned toward her. "It has been quite some time since I have enjoyed such a Christmas feast."

"I hope then, that you will take every opportunity to enjoy this one."

He served her from the platter of roast potatoes nearby. "I will certainly do just that and secure it into my memory, a treasure against times which may be far less agreeable."

"I am sure it is difficult to spend Christmastide away from one's home and family. The militia requires a great deal from you."

"I find that it gives back as much as it demands. It is not at all disagreeable for one in my state. The hardships do not compare to those I suffered the first Christmastide of my banishment from Pemberley."

"Banishment?"

"Perhaps that is too strong a word, you are right. It does not serve to be so melodramatic." He bowed his head. "You must forgive me, for it is the subject of some trying remembrances. Christmastide at Pemberley was a most wondrous season, filled with warmth and generosity. My family was invited to dine there for Christmas dinner with the Master. A complete roast boar would be carried in by two footmen, with goose, venison, and roast beef besides. I am sure it was a month's worth of food for my little family at least, all brought to table at once." He closed his eyes and licked his lips.

"I can imagine that one might miss such extravagance."

"Pray, do not think I intended to belittle the wonderful hospitality that Longbourn offers. Not at all. It has reminded me of much happier days, and I am most grateful."

Mama's silver bell rang again and Hill, the maid, and two girls employed for just this evening hurried in to clear the first course.

Platters and used dishes disappeared along with the table cloth. The second course filled the empty table, and fresh china appeared before them. Mama announced the dishes, but the platter of minced pies needed no introduction.

Wickham placed a small pie on her plate, along with black butter and spiced apples. The first minced pie of Christmastide was always agreeable, but somehow it would be nothing to the ones that would later be made from the leavings of the Christmas feast. Even with all the extra company, many Twelfth Night pies would be made from the remains of tonight's first course alone.

Mama's bell rang again, and she slipped out of the dining room. Hill circled the room, snuffing candles until only one in each corner remained.

Although Mama repeated this ritual every year, somehow the flaming pudding entering on the silver platter, held high in Mama's arms, never lost its thrill. Blue brandy flames, glinting and multiplying in the mirrors and crystal, cast dancing shadows along the wall, turning the dining room, for those brief moments, into a magical fairyland.

Too soon, the flames died down. Hill and the maids scurried about relighting candles, and the normal world reappeared with Mama standing over a great cannon ball of plum pudding.

She broke into it and served generous slices. "Mind the charms!"

Elizabeth held her breath as the company partook of the pudding. Heavy, sweet, spicy and saturated with brandy, this was the taste of Christmas and family.

Pray let her not discover the ring in her pudding. The to-do Mama would make from that! She shuddered.

Uncle Gardiner laughed heartily. "What ho, what shall I do with this?" He held aloft a tiny thimble.

"Consider it for thrift, my dear." Aunt Gardiner winked at him. "It is far too late for you to be a spinster."

Thank Providence Mary was spared that omen!

Lydia squealed. "I have the coin! I shall come into a fortune."

Papa muttered something, but Elizabeth could not make it out. Probably best that way.

Wickham neatly pulled his slice apart with knife and fork. He dug in with his knife and lifted it to reveal a shining ring hanging on the blade.

"Now you've done it, Wickham!" Sanderson pointed at him, laughing.

"I would not go about showing that off, if I were you." Denny leaned back and held up open hands. "But whatever you do, keep it well away from me."

"So, you shall be married this year, Mr. Wickham." Mama glanced at Lydia, none too subtly.

Had there been any way to have achieved that end intentionally, Elizabeth would have thought Mama manufactured this result. But such a thing was not possible. Still, the smug way she settled into her seat and dug into her own pudding begged the question.

"You may threaten all you like." Wickham slid the ring off the knife and held it up in the candlelight. "But I have no fear of this innocent little ring."

Did he just wink? At her?

Heat crept over the crest of her cheeks, but Aunt Gardiner's brows drew a little lower over her eyes, and her forehead creased. No doubt Lydia would have made known to him her fate—consigned to Mr. Collins—so she would be safe to make the joke with, no? At least she had not found the ring.

She took a bite of pudding. Ouch!

"What did you find, Miss Elizabeth?" Mr. Wickham asked far more loudly than necessary.

The children began to giggle.

She removed the charm from her mouth … the wyvern?

"I have never seen a charm like that in a pudding." Mr. Wickham peered over her shoulder.

Papa cleared his throat. "It is a particular family tradition."

"How did you put that in the pudding?" Mama looked distinctly put out.

Daniel covered his mouth and turned away, snickering.

"You might be surprised at how much happens that you are unaware of." Papa's bushy eyebrows rose. "The heraldic wyvern charm is a family tradition—an omen of an opportunity to bring honor to one's family."

How had he managed to ensure it reached her plate? He was as shameless as Mama.

Little Joshua pointed to something high, near the ceiling.

Blast and botheration! Why could he not listen to her? Headstrong, stubborn little flufflebit!

Mama glanced toward the top of the curtains.

"There is nothing but a mite of dust here. You should not look at it, lest everyone notice your maids did not do their jobs," Phoenix whispered as he paced along the curtain rod.

Mama turned aside, but Aunt Gardiner flashed her a wide-eyed look. Elizabeth had promised the fairy dragons would be safely kept upstairs.

Elizabeth rose. "Come children, all of you." She glanced up at Phoenix, with her best draconic glare. "I can see that *all* of you have had enough polite company for one evening. We shall go to the parlor, roast apples, and have a lovely story."

With a nod from Aunt Gardiner, the children sprang to their feet and dashed to Elizabeth's side. Aunt Gardiner glowered at Phoenix and twitched her head toward Elizabeth. He flitted out ahead of them.

Hill had already seen to an ample fire. A basket of apples and a tray of bread to toast waited near the hob. Only a few tallow candles lit the room, making the room seem smaller with the shadows along the walls. It felt snug, though, and drew them toward the fireplace. Elizabeth assigned Daniel the roasting of the apples, while Joshua minded a rack of toast. Anna and Samuel sat on cushions on the floor and played with Phoenix until their treats were ready.

She gave each child their share.

"What about mine?" Phoenix squawked, flapping.

"You were disobedient. You do not deserve a treat. I asked you to stay upstairs. You even had a special bowl of blood and treacle pudding. Yet, you came to dinner anyway."

"I came to protect you."

"I am certain that Papa and Uncle Gardiner are quite capable of doing that." She folded her arms over her chest.

"I would not argue with her when she has that look." Daniel took a large bite of his apple.

"That is her cross face and nothing will make her satisfied when she wears it." Joshua brushed toast crumbs on the floor.

Phoenix pecked them up like a little songbird. Cheeky, defiant little fellows both of them.

Elizabeth scooped him up and held him eye to eye. "You may be a dragon, a very big dragon in your own mind, but you are a very small dragon and must understand that means you cannot always have your way."

"Who gave you the power to make such rules?" He pecked at her hand.

"April may have taught you that habit, but Aunt Gardiner will not tolerate it. I suggest you unlearn it very quickly." She tapped his beaky nose quite firmly with her index finger.

"And what will she do about it?" He cocked his little head, so much like Daniel that she nearly laughed.

"You are not a landed dragon. You do not have a claim on her home. She can—and she will—put you out if you do not behave with some propriety."

"But it is cold outside!" He fluffed his feather-scales until he was a poufy little crimson ball.

"Indeed, it is. Be grateful for the warmth you have inside. Show it by respecting the wishes of your Friends."

Samuel tugged her sleeve. "Surely Mama would not put him out. He is so little."

"I am sure the Blue Order would not permit it." Anna folded her arms in a vague imitation of Elizabeth and tried to glare. "And even if they did, he could just persuade Mama to do exactly as he wished."

No, no, she must not laugh.

"Perhaps, dear, you need to study the rules of the Order. A major dragon has a Keeper with whom he deigns to share his territory. A Keeper must meet the needs of the estate dragon—"

"What can a major dragon possibly need? They are so big and strong. Can they not just take what they want?" Daniel asked, inching closer to Elizabeth.

"Before the Pendragon Accords, they did, and that was the problem. They took whatever they wanted, from men and from each other, and there was constant war among the dragons and between dragons and men. The Accords established what dragons actually required and what they might demand, according to their size and strength. Each was assigned a territory—"

"Every major dragon is assigned a territory?" Daniel was always concerned with detail—just like his father.

"Dragons without a designated territory—rogue dragons they are called—are very dangerous. The Blue Order has done all they can to insure there are no more rogue dragons in England, so you do not need to worry about them. Now, as I was saying, each major dragon has a territory destined to be passed to their descendants and a Keeper to see to their needs of food, water, shelter, secrecy, and if the dragon is a hoarding type, a measure of the treasure they desire."

"Even gold?" Joshua whispered, hands cupped around his mouth.

"Only the firedrakes are apt to hoard gold. They know it is not easy to come by, though, so the Dragon Conclave closely restricts how much they can demand from their Keepers. Did you know that some dragons hoard things like books?"

"Dragons can read?" Anna's eyes bulged, and her jaw dropped.

"There are some who can. Certain wyrms in particular have a penchant for books and learning. Some of them are quite the know-it-all, you see. There are those who are even able to write! They are particularly annoying to deal with as they are certain they know everything.

"In any case, if the Keeper fails to provide what the dragon needs, the dragon may bring a complaint to the Conclave. If a Keeper is found negligent, then he may be replaced with another, of the dragon's choosing."

"A major dragon can throw a Keeper out of his home?" Joshua gasped and looked at Anna.

"If the Conclave agrees, then it is possible. It has not happened in centuries, though. Dragons and Keepers are strongly encouraged to manage their differences before the Conclave must step in."

"What happens when a Keeper dies and the estate is inherited by the eldest son?" Of course, Daniel would ask that.

"It can be a little complicated. Usually dragon hearing is an inheritance passed down in a family, and the heir is able to hear like his father. He will have grown up with the estate dragon and all proceeds very peacefully."

"But there is not always a son." Anna looked up at her, blinking her huge dark eyes.

"Then it can get complicated, my dears. But that is not for you to worry about. What you should be more concerned about is that everything is different for Friends to smaller, minor dragons." She tapped Phoenix's beak. "You cannot provide land or treasure to your Keeper. All you have is your wit and charm to recommend you. Your Friend is not obligated by the Conclave to provide all things you need. It must be a bond agreeable to all of you."

"Like Mrs. Hill and Rumblkins?" Samuel cast about the room as though looking for his favorite tatzelwurm.

"They are very good friends indeed. That is the bond of a Dragon Friend."

"Even if she does not know he is a dragon?" Samuel asked.

"Even if she thinks he is a large cat. They are Friends, and they treat each other with great respect." She tapped Phoenix's beak again.

He huffed and hung his head.

She turned back to Anna. "And as to persuasion, you must remember that the relationship between dragons and the men who hear them is based on trust. If a dragon were to attempt to persuade a hearer, it would be a violation of the worst sort. That is why it is utterly forbidden by the Accords."

Anna gasped and pressed her hands to her mouth.

"Now you have all had your story for the evening. It is off to bed with you. You have stayed up far past your bedtime."

Daniel drew a breath, probably to complain, but stopped midway. "Mr. Wickham!" He jumped up and rushed to the doorway.

Mr. Collins and Mr. Wickham stood just inside the room, concealed in the shadows. How long had they been there? Her face grew cold and tingled. How much had they heard? It should have sounded like a fairy story, but—

"You do not think we have to go to bed now, do you? We have only had one story, and it is Christmas after all." Daniel glanced from Mr. Wickham to Mr. Collins. "I hear music. Is that cousin Mary playing? Are people gathering to dance?"

"You heard Miss Elizabeth. You must obey her." Mr. Collins grumbled and clasped his hands behind his back.

Mr. Wickham leaned down close to Daniel. "I never wanted to go to bed when I was a boy, either. But you must be a good example to your siblings and be grateful that you were allowed to join the Christmas feast. Show us what a big boy you are and lead them all upstairs as Miss Elizabeth said."

Daniel sighed, but tromped back to gather Samuel and Anna by the hands. Phoenix hopped to Joshua's shoulder and they trudged out the door past Mr. Collins and Mr. Wickham.

"There is nothing on the boy's shoulder. Miss Elizabeth is far more interesting to look at. She likes to dance," Phoenix whispered as they passed.

"I should go upstairs and help them." Elizabeth tried to slip between the men.

"There is no need. Their mother is waiting for them in the nursery." Collins' brows knit into a heavy line. "Your mother expects you in the drawing room."

"Your sisters have begun to exhibit, and you are much wanted as a dance partner. Might I have the honor of the next dance?" Mr. Wickham bowed.

"And I the next." Mr. Collins bowed as well, nearly elbowing Mr. Wickham out of the way.

"I—thank you both. I would be honored." She glanced from one man to the other. One was glaring and grumpy, the other all good humor and ease. Too bad she could not accept only one offer to dance.

This might prove a long evening indeed.

The four and twenty families that regularly dined at Mama's table kept Elizabeth's social calendar full every day of the Christmastide season. Teas and card parties, a home theatrical and several dinners. She barely had time to think. In the odd moments she did, her thoughts turned, not to Mr. Wickham, as she supposed they should have, but to little Pemberley and how she fared under the taciturn Mr. Darcy's care.

How she missed that little dragon.

The highlight of the season, the Bennets' Twelfth Night Ball, threw the house into a frenzy that would likely take Papa a fortnight complete to recover from. Mama martialed all the women of the house into a demonstration of hospitality intended to be talked about for a full year to come.

The night of the ball, Elizabeth was almost too tired to attend. But the promise of agreeable partners—meaning of course Mr. Wickham and his fellow officers—roused her from her exhaustion to take her place in the drawing room.

She enjoyed two dances with Mr. Wickham prior to taking to the floor with Mr. Collins. Not only did he tread upon her toes and hem, but he caused her to twist her ankle when he went right and the rest of the dancers went left. Since she had already danced all she could with the only partner she cared to engage with, she indulged the excuse to sit out from the rest of the dancing.

Mr. Wickham was everything that Mr. Collins was not: engaging, charming, thoughtful, considerate. Mr. Collins could not think beyond how things might appear to his superiors and how they might relate to him as a result. Every thought, every concern, every conversation, absolutely everything, was all about him.

Whenever she was in his presence, her ears rang with his opinions, his reputation, the condescension he enjoyed. Had there ever been a more self-centered man?

He was such a man, and yet, neither Mama nor Papa ignored a single opportunity to throw them together as if that would inure her to his flaws.

"You seem to have enjoyed Mr. Wickham's company a great deal tonight." Aunt Gardiner brought her a stool on which to prop her foot and sat in the far corner with her.

"He is an excellent dancer." Elizabeth shrugged and glanced at Lydia and Mr. Wickham as they skipped down the line of dancers.

"I grant you that. And that, of course, is a sure sign of a man's character and his fitness as a friend." Aunt cocked her head the way she did at her children.

Elizabeth squirmed. No doubt her aunt's intended effect. "You do not find his company pleasing?"

"Of course, I did, and that is what concerns me the most. The more I have considered the tale he told us at Christmas dinner, the more uncomfortable I have become. No honest man is quite so pleasing, or tells quite so carefully crafted a tale. Honestly, it sounds more like some novel's account of a much-abused hero than a genuine experience. No true story is so ... perfect."

"That sounds alarmingly cynical, something I believe you have warned me of more than once."

"Not cynical, but cautious, my dear. You must grant that I have a great deal more experience from which to draw. Something about him just does not ring true to me."

"And the only faults you can find in him are that he is too handsome and his trials too lamentable?"

Elizabeth's head fell back against the edge of the settee. She stared at the crack in the ceiling plaster.

"Mr. Collins is not the only man with faults." Aunt pointed her chin toward the fireplace where he held Uncle and Colonel Forster hostage to his long-windedness. "And he is not without his admirable qualities."

Elizabeth's jaw dropped. "You are not suggesting—"

"By no means! I am merely offering that your views of Mr. Wickham might be unduly colored by comparison to others."

"It matters little what I think of either one. Papa is unmoved by my opinions and insists on having his way." Her throat clamped down over her words, so tightly that they barely escaped.

"I know, my dear. Your uncle and I are pleading your case to him. But even as we do that, I must ask you to be careful in bestowing your affections too freely. It is not helping our cause with your father for you to be seen expressing so much interest in Mr. Wickham."

Her interest was unacceptable? Hers? Not Kitty's who followed him around like a lost puppy or Lydia's who laughed and cavorted so loudly that half the town was talking about it? No, their behavior was beyond reproach, but hers, no, that was the problem.

But Papa was not trying to marry them off to please the estate dragon.

Blast and botheration.

Why did Aunt have to be so sensible … and so right?

And it was not as though there were any possible future with Mr. Wickham, given how Mr. Darcy—horrid man—had impoverished him. Was a passing flirtation too much to give up for the hope that Papa would take her dislike of Mr. Collins seriously?

If only Mr. Wickham were a more eligible man.

Why did it seem Mr. Darcy was once again at the source of her misery?

The next day Elizabeth urged Mr. Collins to keep Papa company in his bookroom whilst the ladies managed the task of returning the house to its normal state.

How surprising that Papa did not find the experience as pleasant as the rest of the family did. But did he really have to lock his study door after dinner? Watching Mr. Collins as he stood outside, knocking and trying the door, was painful at best. She chose to retire early rather than risk being drawn into that scene.

"If your father was unhappy with Collins' company, it serves him quite right, pushing you toward that ninny," April chittered in her ear the following morning as she pinned her hair into place. "Maybe that will help him to rethink this horrible plan."

"Do not ruffle your feathers over him. You know that attitude always makes Longbourn angry."

"Well, he is a selfish ninny as well." April stroked Elizabeth's ear with her cheek.

"You are very sweet. I can think of no better defender than you."

April chirruped a bit of a laugh. "Phoenix would be ready to try, though. I have never seen a fairy dragon so convinced that he was capable of taking on anything that comes, even a major dragon."

"As I understand, that is a trait all male fairy dragons share. It is possibly why males always seem in short supply."

April snorted and preened her tail.

Come spring, Elizabeth might be forced to do something about the shortage of male fairy dragons in Hertfordshire. April was coming to an age at which finding a proper mate would become an issue.

Lovely, one more business she would have to find a way to explain to Mr. Collins. Or avoid explaining to him.

She squeezed her temples. One problem at a time, just one at a time. And today's problem was chaperoning her sisters on their walk to Meryton.

"Will you come on our walk with us?" She picked up her green cloak and gloves.

"Of course. It is not nearly cold enough to keep me inside, though I would suggest that Heather remain inside. Her feathers are not nearly filled out enough to withstand the chill."

Elizabeth chuckled. How maternal April had become since the hatching.

She headed downstairs.

Papa met her at the bottom of the stairs and beckoned her into his study. "So, Lizzy, bent on pleasure again?"

"Mama has asked me to accompany Kitty and Lydia to Meryton." That it was not the same thing as a pleasure trip did not bear mentioning.

"Mr. Collins will accompany you when you go."

Her eyes bulged, and she clenched her teeth. *One, two, three* ... best get to at least ten before responding.

He peered at her through narrowed eyes. "I said, Mr. Collins shall accompany you."

"There is no need to raise your voice. I heard you quite well."

"I expect a response when I speak to you."

"You do? I had no idea any response I could give you would matter."

"Lizzy! I will not have you take that tone with me."

"Yes, sir. Pray excuse me." She ducked away from his gaze and wove through the tightly packed room toward the window.

"He spent the entire day with me, here, yesterday. He talked constantly, and I do mean constantly. I have never met a man who could talk so much about so little."

"I am well aware of his propensity." She leaned her face out of the open window, the cool air soothing the heat in her cheeks.

"You are much better equipped to deal with him than I."

"I am? That is quite a compliment you offer me. I do not know what I have done to deserve it."

His solid footsteps approached. "You need not be sarcastic with me. You know very well that you have a singular talent for listening to and engaging in—"

She turned to face him. "Meaningless conversation? Yes, we females are quite excellent at the little nothings that are so entertaining among society."

He pinched the bridge of his nose and exhaled a long breath. "Why, Elizabeth?"

"If you do not know, then there is nothing I can do to explain."

"We have been over this before. It is out of my hands. You well know that the decision is Longbourn's." He crossed his arms and gave her a look as though that should settle matters.

Perhaps once it would have, but today ... today it just sounded like the easiest solution to a problem he did not want to deal with.

"Have you chosen to ignore the changes that Uncle Gardiner—"

"Nothing has been decided. Dragons are known for taking a long time to make changes. What is being discussed now may not take effect until your own children are getting ready to marry."

"And then again, the papers may be signed tomorrow."

"Your uncle sees that because he wishes it to be so. The Gardiners are exceedingly fond of you—a fact that has always endeared them to me. And pray remember that I am as well. But I fear that fondness has blinded him to the reality of the situation."

"What of the letters he brings from the Secretary? Have you even read them?"

"Enough to know that I am right."

She clutched her temples. "You have not even read them? Why are you so utterly committed—"

"To seeing Longbourn's desires fulfilled? Because that is the role of a Dragon Keeper, as it has always been and how it always shall be. I have told you so all your life; you have always known it would be this way. Why have you become so petulant now?" He braced his hand against the window frame, leaning his head in the crook of his arm. "I should not have permitted you to read so many novels or to study so much philosophy. You have got far too many modern notions in your mind. All this rubbish about love and romance— utterly distracting to a Dragon Keeper."

There were good reasons why he believed that, but none of them would be appropriate to mention now. Possibly not ever.

"Go now, Collins and your sisters are waiting for you. And you will be pleasant to both your sisters and Collins. Your mother insists that your sisters should seek out the officers in town and is quite tired of your contradicting her."

"Do you not see the very great danger of the approach she suggests?"

"You seem pleased enough by Mr. Wickham's company." Did he have to employ that withering glare on her?

April popped her head out of Elizabeth's cloak. "That is the only sensible thing you have said so far."

"You have taught your Dragon Friend some very inappropriate habits. It is no wonder that Collins does not like her." He leaned in and glowered directly at April.

April squawked and crouched, ready to launch.

Elizabeth covered her with her hand. "That will not help," she whispered.

April popped her head up through Elizabeth's fingers. "It is not my fault. You are, of course, aware that Collins does not like Heather either, and she is as sweet as treacle and as bland as milquetoast."

"You would do well to recognize your situation and to work to be more agreeable. Your position is not nearly as assured as Longbourn's." Papa shook a pointing finger at them.

"There is no call to threaten her! Nothing and no one will induce me to eject her from my home. I would thank you not to intimate that it is even a possibility." She spun on her heel and stomped out.

Only the greatest level of self-control kept her from slamming the door behind her.

Truly that was beyond the pale, threatening April in such a way. No matter how impatient he might be with her, the Papa she knew would never threaten a dragon with homelessness.

What had got into him? Why was he so entirely unreasonable? Did Longbourn have something to do with it?

2
Chapter

DARCY SETTLED INTO the morning room as far away from Aunt Catherine's customary seat as possible. The room accommodated not only a table large enough to serve breakfast for ten, but also several reasonably comfortable chairs near the east facing windows, so the distance was not difficult to achieve.

By her standards, the decorations were "simple"—which still meant it was far too ostentatious for his taste. Were ormolu dragons necessary on nearly every surface? Yes, she was a Dragon Keeper, and yes, she was Friend to a rare and very fine cockatrix. But did she have to remind her guests—at least the ones who understood—of it at every turn?

The framed fan of cockatrix wing feathers—glossy jet-black alternating with deep blues and a few rich purples that must have come from the base of her ruff—was really taking things too far. How had she managed to convince Cait to give those up? As many as there were, it must have taken years. Walker avoided the room because of that ornament alone.

Too bad he could not do the same.

Why Aunt Catherine insisted on a "morning audience" was beyond him, especially when she was usually the last one in attendance. At least Anne did not usually bother with breakfast. One de Bourgh woman in the morning was enough for any man to cope with.

Arriving just before the start of the Christmastide season had offered him a welcome reprieve from many of her usual, intrusive audiences. The social calendar was so full with events to be hosted at Rosings and events in the village that she, at least in her own mind, had to oversee given the absence of her parson, that she had not a moment to spare for her nephew.

Not that he particularly wanted one, either. The help offered by the resident dragons was not only more welcome, but quite possibly more useful. For the most part.

He poured himself a cup of coffee and retrieved Fitzwilliam's letter from his pocket. Hopefully it would be good news.

Settling into a soft-but-lumpy chair near the window, he held the letter in a sunbeam. Fitzwilliam's hand was difficult to read on the best of days.

Georgiana had not recovered her spirits yet, but she was improving and had agreed to travel. That was a good sign. Before Darcy had left for Meryton, she would not even leave her chambers.

Fitzwilliam and Georgiana would arrive in a fortnight. Good. Good. He would have someone to share both the necessary work at Rosings Park and the tending of baby Pemberley. He leaned his head into the chair and closed his eyes.

Miss Elizabeth had made caring for the drakling look effortless, absolutely effortless. She always understood Pemberley's moods, her wants and needs, and addressed them almost before she cried. But without Miss Elizabeth, it was not nearly as simple. Between himself, Rosings, Walker, and Cait, they could barely keep up with Pemberley's demands.

A sunbeam warmed his face, almost soporific in its effects. He would not trade the privilege of keeping Pemberley for anything, but he could easily have done without the perpetual exhaustion. Too bad one could not hire a wet nurse or a nursery maid for a juvenile dragon.

Oh, the look Miss Elizabeth would give him for even having such a thought!

"Wake up, Darcy!"

He jumped out of his chair, nearly upsetting his coffee and dropping his letter. "Aunt Catherine. I did not hear you enter."

"Of course, you did not, you were sleeping! Where have your manners gone?"

He maneuvered around the over-furnished room and pulled her chair out from the table.

"Forgive me. Pemberley has been exceedingly demanding of late."

She sat and arranged her skirts. "Mark my words Darcy. You will spoil that creature if you are not careful. Rosings—"

"Rosings has said no such thing."

"A brood mother is always too partial to her offspring." She flicked her hand, the corner of her lips wrinkling in a half-frown. "Cait is in agreement with me." She flipped open a napkin and laid it in her lap.

"Speaking of Cait—"

"I will not have that discussion with you again, Darcy." She rang the little silver bell for the maid. "Not another word."

He slipped into the chair beside her. "Yes, Aunt, many more words. Walker is tired of her aggressive displays and demands. You must encourage Cait to more demure behavior if she has any desire—"

"Of course, he will sire her next brood, just as he has the last two. It is his duty. It unites our two houses, just as your marriage—"

"That is another matter we have yet to discuss, but one problem at a time."

"There is nothing to discuss. You will both do as you are told." She slapped the table, rattling the glasses.

"Cockatrices do not mate for life. Walker is under no obligation to choose your cockatrix this time." He folded his arms over his chest, settling in for what would, no doubt, be a long conversation.

"Their brood from ten years ago produced such superior specimens that he cannot pass up the opportunity—"

"Yes, he can, and he will. She is driving him away, and I will not have it. I need his help here with me. Pemberley needs him as well. You will call Cait off or—"

"Or what, Nephew? With what will you threaten me?" She canted her head to the left, eyes narrowing in an expression she surely learned from Rosings.

"Or I will do it myself."

That got her attention.

She sat up very straight, eyes wide. "You will do nothing of the kind. I will not have a broody cockatrix upset by your impulsive behavior. Do you have any idea what kind of damage she could wreak if unsettled?"

He raised an eyebrow and stared at her.

She huffed a breath through puffed cheeks. "I do not understand what has made you so disagreeable, Darcy! You barely attended any of the Christmastide affairs. You have hardly shown your face outside your room at all."

"I have had a dragon to attend. My time has been spent, not in my chambers, but in hers."

"So you complain, rather constantly. How did you manage when Pemberley was newly-hatched?"

"I had help from Miss Elizabeth Bennet, daughter of the Blue Order's historian. She is well versed—"

"Bennet, Bennet. That name is ... ah yes, I have it now. That estate, Longbourn, is entailed upon my vicar, Collins."

"Indeed, it is, despite the fact that Collins is entirely dragon-deaf and immune to persuasion." He rolled his eyes although it was probably a bad idea in her presence.

She grunted her disapproval. "Very unfortunate, that, especially when he is rather a gudgeon. Rarely have I met a man who holds his own opinions so loosely, particularly in response to a female voice. Do you happen to know if he has made an offer of marriage yet?"

"I do not think so." His brow knotted tight enough to ache.

"That fool had better get on with the process before the Blue Order finalizes those ridiculous liberal mandates. Really, what can they be thinking, permitting a Keeper to marry outside of a dragon's consent?"

"As I understood it, those new rulings also require that an alternate Keeper be present so that the dragon would not be without."

"Foolishness. Perhaps a young thing like Pemberley might be willing to do so, knowing no better, but an old dragon—bah! Dragons must be allowed to choose their own Keeper. There can be no other way." She waved her hand, nearly knocking over her tea cup. "Rosings determined that I should marry Sir Lewis, and it did us no harm."

It had not done them any favors, either.

"You young people are far too selfish, not submitting to your superiors as you should. You should take a lesson from Collins. I told him that he should choose a wife from among the daughters of the estate, trusting of course that Bennet would steer him toward the correct one, as it were, to satisfy the dragon with the entail. Thus, everyone's problems are solved. Not only that, but I have discharged any inconvenient debt you might owe the man for his assistance in returning Pemberley to you."

He dragged his hand down his face. Aunt Catherine did so love to be helpful.

"Now about Pemberley. It is high time I meet her. I insist. I will set things to right."

She was half right. It was time she met her youngest guest, but there was little chance anything would be set to rights.

Of course, Aunt Catherine required a change of garments before leaving for the dragon's lair. A walking dress, he was informed, was the proper attire for one to call upon dragons.

Thankfully Miss Elizabeth had no such notions when rushing out from the ball to rescue Pemberley. He really ought to replace that gown for her. It was the least he could do.

Rosings' cavern lay along an overgrown path, deep in the woods along the west side of the estate, well away from the grazing pastures, small farms, and tenant houses. Although Rosings would never violate the Accords and harm an accidental trespasser, she was grouchy by nature, and no one wanted to make her grouchier.

Cait flew out to greet them whilst they were still a hundred yards off. She was a spectacular example of a cockatrix in her prime, covered in glossy black feathers, punctuated with deep purple along her head ruff and deep blue under her wings. Her head ruff was so full and fluffy that it was hard to make out her face. Only the tip of her razor-honed beak stood out. She boasted tail feathers so long that they often dragged on the ground when she perched. If one considered looks alone, it was hard to understand Walker's adverse reaction to her, especially since she had chosen him.

"You have deigned to grace us with your presence." Cait landed in front of them and bent her head toward the ground, but her wings were still spread.

Cockatrix sarcasm at its finest.

"Do not take that tone with me. You well know I have been occupied. I should have thought that the two of you could manage a baby between you.

Especially considering that you have raised two broods already." Aunt Catherine flipped her skirts at Cait.

"Mine did not have teeth, and, I assure you, feather scales are not nearly so arduous to grow as teeth are." Cait flapped her wings and took off, trailing her tail feathers over their shoulders.

She must be tired and worn, too, stooping to such obvious insults.

Aunt Catherine gathered her skirts and stormed into the hillside cavern.

At some point long ago, small cracks had opened up in the ceiling, just enough to let some light through, but still overgrown enough to keep out the rain. He paused a moment for his eyes to adjust. At last, he could make out a broad expanse, swept clear by a dragon's tail. Along the nearest wall, a pile of soft leaves and underbrush formed Pemberley's nest where she lay fitful, whining softly. Several yards away, Rosings stretched out across the ground, forelegs thrown over her ears.

"Cowntess," Aunt Catherine called.

How she loved those reminders of rank, her own and her dragon's.

Rosings rose to her feet and shook. Starting at her head, it progressed down her shoulders, her wings, to the tip of her tail. A small cloud of dust stirred. Darcy sneezed into his handkerchief.

The firedrake cowntess, was an exemplar of her kind. Like Pemberley, she was various shades of red, from pale red at her underbelly to deep red, nearly purple, along her spine. As sharp as Cait's beak, her talons reflected the meager light. Her smooth scales, dusty now, shone when freshly cleaned. Nose to the base of her tail, she must have been fifteen feet long with another eight feet of tail behind her. Fully extended, her wings probably spanned over twenty feet. She only flew on moonless nights, so no one alive now had actually seen her in flight. She was a very private creature.

"Lady." Rosings bobbed her head, and Aunt Catherine curtsied.

How very different this meeting was from the warm, almost intimate greetings that Miss Elizabeth shared with her Dragon Friends. At first, Elizabeth's manner had seemed so odd, so improper to him, but now Aunt Catherine's words and actions seemed too stiff and formal.

"Will you introduce me to your guest?"

Rosings rolled her eyes. "If she will see you."

"Pemberley is much taxed by teething right now." Darcy hurried to her side.

"I shall determine that for myself." In a swish of skirts, Aunt Catherine stormed toward the nest, Rosings barely half a step ahead.

"You should rise and greet your guest." Rosings nosed Pemberley.

Pemberley lifted her head blinking. "She is not her. I want her."

"What is the drakling blithering about?"

"Nothing to be concerned with. She spent a great deal of time with Miss Bennet—"

"Yes, her!"

"And is having some difficulty adjusting to her removal," Rosings muttered.

Aunt Catherine snorted. "That is why nursery maids should be changed out often. It is always a problem when youngsters get attached."

"May I present my aunt, Lady Catherine de Bourgh?" Darcy gestured toward her.

"She is not her." Pemberley looked away.

"You will not be rude to my Keeper." Rosings slapped the tip of her tail on the ground.

"Yes, Cowntess." Pemberley clambered to her feet, eyes down. "Greetings, Lady."

"That is better." Aunt Catherine nodded, still scowling. "Now, I have heard your teeth are troublesome."

"I no have teeth." Pemberley turned her face away.

"Yes, but you will soon. Now open your mouth and let me see."

"No."

"I insist. Do as you are told."

"No."

Darcy edged closer. "Now, Pemberley. If she—ah 'her'—asked you, would you do so?"

"Yes."

"Then please do so now. Lady only wants to see."

Pemberley opened her mouth.

Hopefully she would not bite.

Aunt peered into Pemberley's mouth, but stopped short of putting her hand inside. She did have baby fangs after all.

Aunt Catherine turned her back on Pemberley. "There is no doubt the trouble is teething. But that is very good because now we have a solution."

"We do?"

"Of course. All she needs is to have her gums lanced to reveal the teeth, just like any infant. I shall make arrangements for it immediately. Perhaps Cait can do it. Her talons might do very nicely." In a swish of skirts, she bustled from the cavern.

"What she mean, 'lance?'" Pemberley tucked her head under Darcy's arm.

"It is a surgery to free your teeth from your gums. It is often done for babies as I understand—teething is very dangerous, you know." At least it was for humans, but who knew if it was for dragons?

Miss Elizabeth probably would.

"No, it not dangerous. It itches. It hurts. Make it stop. I no want Cait talons in my mouth. I will bite her." She rustled her wings.

That usually signaled the beginning of a tantrum.

Lovely.

"You must not bite. You know that."

"Rosings say I can if someone hurt me."

Technically she was right.

"Cait is your friend."

"No, she not. She thinks I am vex … vexanamous … vexatious. I not know what means vexatious, but it not sound good."

"She thinks Walker is vexatious too, and she likes him a great deal." He scratched under her chin.

She took his wrist in her mouth and gummed it, whining. "Make better."

He took her face in his hands and pressed his forehead to her. "I will find some way to make it better soon."

Pray he would be able to keep that promise. If only Miss Elizabeth were near.

"Cousin Elizabeth." Collins' voice slithered down the back of her neck, raising the tiny hairs in an itchy prickle. "Are you ready to join your sisters and me?"

"Yes, we should leave directly." She brushed past, not waiting for him to follow.

Kitty and Lydia raced on ahead. What was a three-mile journey when officers were waiting on the other side?

Their brisk pace offered a delightful boon. Who would have thought Mr. Collins unable to walk vigorously and talk at the same time? He huffed and puffed, unable to string together more than a pair of words at a time.

Under such pleasant circumstances, the distance passed quickly, and the buildings of Meryton's main street rose up before them.

"Oh, look! Officers!" Lydia pointed at a cluster of red coats standing near the haberdasher's window.

Kitty took off at a run, kicking up a faint trail of dust in the cool, clear air.

Elizabeth drew a breath, but what point in trying to curb them? They would not listen, and it would only look bad to any who observed her shouting at them.

"You should check your sisters." Mr. Collins huffed and panted, sweat glistening on his forehead and cheeks. "Their unrestrained behavior does not look well upon you or your family. It will lead to ruin, I am afraid. There are those among the community who already speak unfavorably about them."

"I wonder that you would take so seriously the word of one who would speak to you in such a familiar and inappropriate way." She shrugged and hurried ahead.

Who had he been listening to? Probably Lady Lucas who considered Charlotte an excellent prospect for Mr. Collins. But to stoop to such untoward means? Perhaps Lady Lucas was not the sort of friend that Mama thought her to be.

He muttered something she could not make out. No loss, it was not likely to be very sensible.

Lydia looked over her shoulder, squinting in the bright sun, and waved at Elizabeth to join them. She hastened her steps, not so much to run, but enough to ensure that Mr. Collins would not easily catch up to her.

"See whom we have found—almost the entire company." Lydia looped her arm through Denny's on the right and Carter's on the left.

Kitty hung off Chamberlayne's arm. Wickham stepped a little closer to Elizabeth and cocked his head.

"Walk with us—we are off to the vintner's, the butcher's, and the chandler's." Lydia pulled her escorts down the street.

Elizabeth and Wickham fell into step behind them.

Heads turned, probably at the sight of so many red coats. Still, it was disconcerting to be noticed by so many.

"Your sisters are quite energetic." Wickham chuckled under his breath, lacing his hands behind him.

"That would be one word for it, perhaps not the one I would choose, but it is an apt description."

"What word would you choose to describe them?"

"Oh, no, sir, you will not trick me into displaying those things which I do not wish to reveal—at least not so easily."

"Ah, Miss Bennet, you ascribe to me motives and subtlety that are far outside my purview. I am but a humble soldier, madam, not a clever-tongued gentleman." Did he just wink?

She laughed. April nipped her ear.

Why? She had only laughed at his joke. And his smile. And the twinkle in his eye.

"I see you have your pet with you. Do you bring her with you everywhere?"

"Not everywhere, to be sure. The cold temperatures do not agree with her any more than they do any small … bird. Too much time in the house bores her, I fear. It is dangerous for one so small to go out alone, so we satisfy her curiosity by walking out together."

"You do not fear she will simply fly away, never to be seen again?" Wickham peered into her hood.

April ducked into a deep fold.

"She is my friend, not my prisoner. If she wants to leave, she is free to do so. I would not hold her against her will any more than I would turn her out."

"I have never heard anyone talk so about a pet."

"She is my friend, not my pet."

"A significant distinction, I am sure." He dipped his head.

April snorted in her ear. "I still do not like him. You should not speak with him about me."

Wickham stared at April, but gave no sign of having understood her words.

That should not be disappointing, but it was. Even him hearing dragons would not change anything.

"Your little bird does not seem to be the only one excessively fond of you. Your little cousins seem utterly entranced by the story you told them. Quite imaginative, that: dragons and the Blue Order?" He winked again and smiled.

Something about the way his eyes crinkled at the sides … he could not hear dragons, but what did he know?

Her heart thundered hard enough to threaten her ability to speak. April tensed against her ear.

Calm. Remain calm.

"I have told them those tales since the eldest was old enough for bedtime stories. I have had to weave quite the intricate web to keep them all interested, but I confess, I enjoy the stories as well."

"You might consider writing them one day. As I understand, it is an acceptable diversion for genteel young ladies. Some are even interested in publishing such things. I know I should enjoy hearing more of your dragon adventures." He looked straight ahead, his face serene and serious.

And curious.

Uncomfortably, maybe dangerously, curious.

"That is a very peculiar interest for a gentleman and a soldier. I should think the affairs of the world would be of far greater import to someone in your position." It was difficult to keep her voice light when the conversation had turned so dark.

"Whilst that might be true, I have always found that making allowances for a liberal amount of fiction in one's life is necessary to maintaining equanimity. How else does one escape, even for a short time, from the drudgery that everyday life affords?"

Lydia and Kitty paused at the chandler's window. They stopped several steps behind them.

He turned and caught her gaze. "I was not joking. I have been fascinated with dragons all my life, and I am, can I say, thrilled, to find someone who shares my interests. You know the story of the Lambton Wyrm? I grew up just miles from that town. I spent much of my boyhood searching for any trace of that beast. Though the mythos says it was kilt, I have never been convinced of its demise. Surely something as sturdy as a dragon could not be so easily undone."

April growled in her ear.

Elizabeth edged back. "Dragons are for fairy stories and children—and perhaps artists who render them on signs and prints. Do be sensible, sir."

Wickham's gaze drifted to April. Her hackles rose, and she growled again.

"Perhaps you are right, Miss Bennet. But faced with the losses I have suffered, can you truly blame me for lingering upon memories of happier, childhood times?"

"No, no, of course not. Pray excuse me, though. I must go inside." She sidled past him, through her sisters, and into the chandler's shop.

Tables and displays littered the confined space, but with only one other shopper inside, it felt open and cavernous. She drew in a deep breath, filled with scents of tallow, tea, soap, and a hint of bacon.

April sneezed and pawed at her beak. Tea leaves often made her sneeze. "Mr. Darcy does not like him. Your Aunt Gardiner does not like him, either. You should heed them and avoid him. I fear he is a Deaf-Speaker. You know how dangerous they are."

Darcy's dislike proved nothing about Wickham, only about Darcy's hateful character.

"You know Deaf-Speakers are very few and far between. I am sure if you, Heather, Phoenix and Rumblkins, perhaps Rustle as well, band together, you will be able to persuade him that his interests are just a passing childhood thing."

"We have tried to persuade him."

She turned to stare at April, a chill settling over her shoulders. "When?"

"Several times. At first, I simply thought it was my high, thin voice. So, I asked Rumblkins with his low, purry speech. He could not persuade that man to even pet him. Rustle has the easiest voice to hear. He has tried on multiple occasions, but to no effect, either. The man is completely dragon-deaf just like Collins. I do not like it, not at all."

She stroked April's ruffled feathers smooth. "It will be well, do not worry."

Somehow it would. Wickham's interests must just be an odd coincidence, a misunderstanding. It had to be. After all he had suffered at Darcy's hand, it was not so far-fetched that Wickham would enjoy fantastical fairy stories—was it?

"No, no, I am not sure it will. I am afraid." April huddled close to Elizabeth's neck.

"I promise, I will not let either of them harm you."

"How delightful! You have your pretty bird with you today." The chandler, short, round and rosy-cheeked, waddled toward her, wiping his hands on his stained apron. "It is always such a delight to see such a bright little bauble in the crispy brown times of winter. Might she like a spoonful of sugar-flower water?"

"I think it would lift her spirits tremendously." Elizabeth encouraged April to perch on her finger whilst the chandler brought a large spoon, more like a ladle, filled with sugar water, with several rose petals floating on top.

April flitted to the edge of the ladle and sipped the treat, warbling happily, if a mite forced.

"Might I touch her?" He extended a fat, stubby finger toward April.

April looked at him, head cocked. "Gently."

"I think she will allow it, but you must be very gentle, like touching a flower so as not to ruin the petals. Just under her chin, she likes that a great deal."

He ran his fingertip under her chin. She stretched up to guide him to the itchy spots and trilled as he found them.

"She has such a sweet song. Makes one go all soft inside, like warm tallow, I say. A right ray of sunshine she is, Miss Bennet. I suppose I should be getting your order though, no?" He disappeared into the back of the store.

"I like him." April plunged her beak into the ladle.

"Of course, you do. He feeds you sweets, and pets you and tells you what a pretty little thing you are. What is there not to like?"

April hopped back to Elizabeth's shoulder. "He is not easily persuaded, but he is still kind and thoughtful, not frightening at all."

The door clattered open and heavy footfalls, familiar ones, clattered in.

Collins.

The back of her neck twitched.

At least he might be pressed into service, carrying Mama's order.

"Cousin Elizabeth," he gasped and panted, "I am glad to have finally found you. Your sisters are gone ahead, to the vintner I believe. We should hurry to catch up to them before … before …"

"I am quite certain no calamity will befall them before the chandler brings Mama's order out." She turned her shoulder and stepped toward the counter at the back wall of the shop.

He followed too closely. "I did not realize you were waiting on the shopkeeper."

What else did he think she was doing here? Playing buffy gruffy among the candlesticks?

She bit her lip. The man did not understand sarcasm, so any clever remark would be wasted upon him.

"We should hurry." Mr. Collins straightened his back and dusted off the edge of his coat.

"With so many officers to guard them, I hardly think Kitty and Lydia will come to any harm." She laughed as he edged close enough for their elbows to touch.

"That was not my concern."

She sidled away. "If you have something to say, sir, perhaps you should come out and speak more—"

"Here we are, Miss Bennet, exactly as your mother requested." The chandler trundled out, several packages in his arms. He handed them to Mr. Collins. "I trust you will find it all to your, and her, satisfaction."

"I am sure we will. Good day."

"Good day to you and to your little pretty as well." He waved fingertips at April who cheeped daintily.

Mr. Collins shuffled after her, tucking the packages awkwardly under his arm as they hurried toward the vintner. "About your sisters, Cousin Elizabeth, their behavior is positively wild."

"I wonder that you should speak to me about it. Are they not my parents' responsibility?" She stared resolutely ahead. If she caught his gaze, there would be no controlling her expression.

"Indeed, they are. That is true."

"And is it not my duty as a daughter to honor my parents?"

"Yes, of course. It is to your credit that you should see it so."

"And would it not dishonor them to take their place in correcting my sisters in their actions and attitudes, usurping, as it were, their authority?"

Mr. Collins' jaw dropped, and bobbed open and shut rather like a large trout on a hook.

"So, you must agree, that what you suggest, whilst you might find it pleasing and expedient, I can in no way do what you ask without compromising the values you and I hold dear."

His eyes bulged to complete his convincing impressing of a gaping fish.

April snorted in her ear. Elizabeth increased her pace. Hopefully that would relieve Mr. Collins of any excess breath for speaking.

Lydia and Kitty burst out of the vintner's shop, their packages carried by Denny and Carter. The merry little party laughed and carried on far too loudly.

Across the street, a party of matrons stopped and stared, whispering amongst themselves.

Why did Mr. Collins have to be right? He would certainly never hear that admission from her, though.

The trip to the butcher was mercifully quick. The officers announced their intention of escorting the ladies home. Elizabeth tried to stay close to Kitty, but Mr. Collins lingered behind the group and signaled Elizabeth to walk with him.

"Just ignore him. It is easy enough to pretend you did not see," April whispered from the depths of her hood.

"He will express his displeasure to Mama and Papa if I do not comply. They will in turn express it to me. I do not have the wherewithal to experience that again, at least not right now." Elizabeth slowed until Mr. Collins caught up with her.

"I believe you are correct, Cousin. I thank you for drawing it to my attentions. I should address your parents. It does you credit to suggest it. I acknowledge your wisdom and will do as you recommend immediately upon our return to Longbourn."

She squeezed her eyes shut. There was no way that would turn out well. Oh, what joy would be hers.

"Lady Catherine will surely be pleased to learn of your insight and your deference to your elders. Exactly the kind of behavior she most approves of in those in her domain."

Was he describing a woman or a dragon?

Probably both.

A shudder snaked down her spine. If she married him, would she have to spend time at Rosings and face the demands of another peevish dragon? From his description of its Keeper, Rosings sounded every bit as petulant as Longbourn.

She swallowed hard and forced her lips into a small smile, as befitted the compliment Mr. Collins intended to offer.

"There is though, a wee matter of concern that I would speak to you about." He held up thumb and forefinger.

Which whim of Lady Catherine did he expect her to cater … no, something in his eyes suggested it was nothing so simple or straightforward. She stumbled over a small stone.

He reached for her elbow to steady her, but she pulled away before he could touch her. April flapped her wings for balance and hissed at Collins as he passed too close to her.

He swatted at April.

Elizabeth ducked and dodged his flailing, but slipped on the gravel and bounced hard on her shoulder.

"Cousin Elizabeth!" Collins dropped to his knees beside her, reaching for her hand.

Elizabeth scrabbled back. "Pray leave me be!"

Collins jumped back, his hands in the air.

"Are you all right?" She searched over her shoulder for April.

April peeked out of her hood. "I am well. Please get me away from him." She trembled against Elizabeth.

She scooped up the tiny dragon and clutched her against her chest. "I would thank you to keep a distance. You could have injured both of us."

"Pray forgive my clumsiness, but no harm has been done. You are uninjured, are you not?"

"My shoulder will be worse for the wear, no doubt. But it is April—"

"That is precisely what I have wished to talk to you about. That creature of yours."

"That creature, as you call her, has been my companion since I was ten years old. I would thank you to treat her with a little more respect." She pushed to her feet and dusted sharp bits of gravel from her skirt.

Oh, that shoulder would need a hot compress tonight!

"It is not natural to be so attached to an animal. It is not right, even with one so unnaturally long-lived. I can see you are fond of the little thing, but do you not think it is time to pursue more … grown-up concerns?"

Every muscle tensed and trembled. "I have not the pleasure of knowing to what you refer, sir. Companion animals are quite common in society. How many have dogs or cats, even parrots and other birds? How is April any different? I cannot help but imagine that even Lady Catherine might keep such a creature."

His face shifted just slightly. "She does not permit it to ride upon her person, nor does it follow her everywhere she goes. The creature has a proper—containment—outside where such creatures belong. She does not talk to the bird as though it were a person—she hardly visits it at all."

"What kind of bird does she keep?"

"Some sort of fancy feathered chicken, I suppose. It boasts a feathered headdress many women admire and tail feathers an arm's length long." He waved his hand around his head suggesting many long fluffy feathers. "I have never seen the likes of one before—very rare I am told. It is a mark of her superior rank that she has it at all. The cage sits on the road to the main house, and all who drive past may see the exotic livestock she possesses."

A cockatrix?

The woman had a cockatrix for a Dragon Friend? The most difficult and arrogant of the minor dragons! Cockatrix were said to be well aware of their rarity and proud of it—at one time almost driving the cockatrice species into extinction because of their reluctance to accept any but the most superior males.

She pressed her forehead. Of course. Of course, it had to be.

"The relevant point here is that she treats it as an animal, not a person."

No, the relevant point was that Lady Catherine was excellent at hiding the true nature of her friend and their relationship. No cockatrix would tolerate the treatment Collins implied.

Heavens, a harridan, a cockatrix, and a firedrake—what kind of place must Rosings Park be?

"Cousin, are you listening to me?" He leaned far too close to her face.

"Of course, I am. I was carefully considering your words."

"Then you will do as I ask and relegate that bird to her cage."

She jumped back. "Absolutely not. As long as fine ladies carry about their pugs, then I shall keep April with me."

Collins' face screwed into tight knots as he ground his teeth. "That was not a request."

"You have no claim over me to be making such requests."

"I insist you hear me out. You do not understand what detriment that creature and all your talk of dragons is doing."

The blood drained from her face. Oh, for something she could lean upon until the dizziness passed. "What are you talking about?"

"That story you told your young cousins at Christmas. Dragons, the Blue Order and whatever other nonsense you were filling their heads with."

"That story was for the children and the children alone."

"You have no business plying them with silliness and hoping they will grow into sensible beings. Already they are confused and deluded. One of the boys and the girl were calling their ridiculous little bird a tiny dragon. They even called the housekeeper's cat a dragon. What nonsense!" He threw a hand in the air.

Did he do that for emphasis when he preached, too? Vicars who did that were so distracting and annoying. He probably did.

"And they have told you this?"

"No, I do not talk to children. But they are allowed to roam the house freely enough. It is difficult not to hear their—"

"Their play, Mr. Collins. That is what it is called, play and imagination. Something that is utterly normal and even considered good and appropriate by some."

"Perhaps by liberal philosophers, but not by me. They should be taught sense and reality, not this frivolous fancy. I am sure their father will agree with me. I will seek him out if necessary."

"Necessary?"

"To make you stop with all this fanciful dragon nonsense and to stop the horrible example you set with that bird. They are starting to permit their creature the same indulgences yours is allowed. Disgraceful!"

"So, that is what I am to you, disgraceful? It is a wonder then that you are even speaking with me. Do you not fear that you will taint your reputation with Lady Catherine? That she might not approve of the company you are keeping in me?"

"That is not at all what I meant. Not at all. Perhaps I should have taken time to first compliment your many perfections. I am told young females appreciate such things. Then allow me to begin again. Your person, your intelligence, your manners are all very agreeable—most agreeable." His eyes raked her up and down.

She wrapped her cloak tightly around herself.

"The only faults I can find in you are the ones I just related to you. Not faults of character or breeding; easily remedied I would say. You are all but a perfect—"

She lifted her free hand and stepped back. "I have heard entirely enough, Mr. Collins. Pray importune me no further."

His eyes bulged, and he drew a very deep breath that would no doubt fuel many, many irate words.

She spun and ran toward Longbourn Woods.

Chapter 3

APRIL'S SCRATCHY TOES pierced her bodice and rasped against her skin as she pounded away. Little matter, if it meant she was away from Collins faster.

Dreadful, dreadful man, thinking he could simply order her to give up dragons. The audacity! The pomposity! It was not as though he were her husband and had that authority in the first place.

The woods embraced her with open arms, closing around behind her. Lungs burning and legs protesting, she leaned against a sympathetic tree and gulped deep, heaving breaths.

April peeked above her hand. "Is he gone?"

"We are, my dear, which is nearly as good."

April hopped to her shoulder, fluttering until every feather-scale was back in place. "You should tell Longbourn what has just happened." April poked Elizabeth's ear with her sharp beak.

Had she any idea of what a very, very bad idea that was? As much as Longbourn wanted her to marry Collins, if the wyvern thought him any real threat … She shuddered.

A loud squawk resounded among the trees as wings crashed through the branches and stirred up dead leaves. Rustle flipped his wings to his back and bobbed his head. "We saw you running into the woods. Your father sent me."

She dragged her hand down her face. "I suppose I am directed to return to the house straight away?"

"I am not a messenger bird. You have heard no such thing from me." Rustle waddled toward her, head cocked.

He stretched out his neck. No doubt he was itchy.

She crouched and obliged his request. He cawed and pulled away, rattling his feather-scales in draconic contentment. Little made a dragon happier than a good scratch. Were it only that men were so easily pleased—and distracted.

She leaned her head against the tree trunk.

"I saw Collins with you. What did he do?" Rustle extended his wings, dry leaves kicking up in their wake.

Such a sweet, protective gesture. No doubt he would put Collins' eyes out if she asked.

April swooped down and hovered in front of Rustle. "He wants to see me banished to a cage and for her to give up all things draconic."

Rustle squawked—not a conversational squawk, but the one that preceded a hunt. Often the last sound his prey would ever hear.

"Mrow!"

That was a cry of pain!

Rumblkins crashed through the bushes, nearly landing on Rustle. He hissed, beating his wings, rising a hand span off the ground. Rumblkins' fur stood on end, and his serpentine tail swelled and lashed the ground.

Elizabeth jumped between them, raising her cloak to block their sight of one another until they regained their senses enough to recognize their keep mates. "Step back, both of you. I will drop my cloak, and you will greet each other properly, as friends. Do you understand?"

"Mrow!"

"Caw, caw."

Elizabeth lowered the edges of her cloak.

Rumblkins crouched low and touched his forehead to the ground. "Forgive me, Rustle. I did not look before I leapt."

Rustle squawked and plucked a hair from the back of Rumblkins' neck. "I receive your apology."

She crouched beside Rumblkins. "What sent you running blindly into the woods?"

He turned his side toward her and licked his serpentine scales. A dark bruise spread over his ribs. "Collins. I crossed his path. His boots are very hard."

She held her hand out to him. "Pray, let me see. How badly are you hurt? Might there be something broken?"

He grumbled as she ran her hands over his side. It was swollen, but the bones seemed sound and the swelling was not the kind that implied bleeding within.

April buzzed and circled over them. "This is bad, this is very, very bad. Violence against a dragon, even an unrecognized one, is a very serious act."

Unfortunately, she was right. Accidents were one thing, but this was certainly no accident.

Rumblkins licked his side, so cat-like. A cat with a forked tongue and scales. "Mrs. Hill saw him do it. She swung her rolling pin at him. Said he had no business kicking her friend and she had half a mind to kick him herself." He looked so satisfied as he licked his thumbed paw.

"Good. I hope she hit him." April zipped between them.

"I hardly think that a good thing. Papa would have to dismiss her. She might even be jailed for the assault, and then where would we be? I should like to put a poultice on this when we return to the house, and I will make you some special tea as well. It should be better in just a few days."

Rumblkins pressed his head into her hand.

"The fluffle-bit is right." Rustle hopped nearer. "This is a very serious business."

Serious and complicated. Very, very complicated.

She squeezed her eyes shut and clutched her temples. "He does not know your true nature, so it was not an intended act against dragonkind. A fit of temper, absolutely, but nothing more."

Now she was defending Collins? This was too much.

"That might be a mitigating consideration; however, it was against a creature with whom he was familiar, with whom he knew the family was affectionate. If he had kicked a random creature in his path, it would be different, but this—no, it is abhorrent." Rustle rocked from side to side, wings slightly extended. "A Keep Conclave is warranted."

She pinched the bridge of her nose. Now was not the time for a burgeoning headache. No, not at all. "Whilst I understand why you say that, pray let us not go to that extreme now. I can manage this without involving Longbourn."

"Why?" April hovered before her face. "After all Collins has said, and all he has done today, I think it exactly the right time to escalate this to the local Laird."

"Longbourn has been much agitated as of late. Bringing more to him right now cannot end well."

"You have not been able to manage either Collins or Longbourn very well so far." Rustle scratched at the ground.

Dragon directness and dragon stubbornness. What a truly delightful combination.

A dull thud reverberated in her feet. No! Of all times—now?

Dry leaves crunched, and branches snapped. Longbourn's enormous head poked through the trees. "What should you tell me?"

His voice rumbled in her bones.

"Nothing for you to concern yourself with." She hurried to his side and scratched under his chin.

"Ah, yes, right there." Longbourn cocked his head and exposed his ear. "You have been away too long. That is good!" His heavy tail swished through the underbrush.

"Turn a bit, you itchy creature, and let me reach the other side." She pushed his shoulder.

He shuffled sideways and contorted himself to give her access to his other ear. A solid, two-handed scratch elicited more happy groans and decidedly canine foot thumping.

"He most certainly should concern himself." April pecked Longbourn's nose.

"Pray do not bother him with trivial issues. All is quite well." Bulging her eyes did nothing for her headache, nothing at all.

April squawked and landed on Longbourn's muzzle. His eyes crossed as he tried to focus on her. She paced up and down his snout. He flicked his ears and grumbled.

"All is not well, ask Rumblkins." April pointed with her wing.

Rumblkins approached. How did he manage to limp through his funny tatzelwurm spring-and-hop?

Longbourn sniffed at Rumblkins' bruised side. April hopped over the wrinkles that formed on his snout. His huge, bulgy eyes turned on Elizabeth. "You are able to help him?"

His hot, acrid breath raised sweat on her cheeks. "I will take him back to the house and tend him there. He will be fine. Perhaps I should take him with me now. I can carry him—"

"Laird Longbourn."

No, not Rustle, too!

"Do you not wish to know why we would trouble you with something like this?" Rustle extended his wings and touched his forehead to the ground.

Elizabeth glared from Rustle to April. "We did not come to trouble you at all. You were the one who came upon us, remember? Perhaps for a nice scratch? Here let me—"

Longbourn shook his head and sent April flying. "No scratching until I hear this out."

Nose to nose with her, he snorted in her face. "Those of my Keep have presented a complaint. I will hear the full account. What happened to the fuzzy, hopping one?" He pulled up to his full height and towered over her.

What was it about dragons and men that they employed that same tactic when they were trying to intimidate her? It was not endearing in either incarnation.

"Can you not trust me when I tell you it is nothing for you to be concerned about?" She crossed her arms and tapped her foot.

Calm. Remain calm.

He sniffed her, from the top of her head to her feet and up again. "I smell ... fear! That is fear! Who has made you afraid?" Longbourn stomped. The branches rattled. "You all smell afraid. What made you afraid?"

Rustle and Rumblkins jumped over his whipping tail.

"Pray calm yourself before you hurt someone! That is what I most fear right now. The other is nothing I cannot handle on my own. You do not need—"

"I will make that decision, not you. I have asked you a question. I expect an answer." He reared up and beat his wings, roaring.

It was a soft roar, for a dragon roar, but it reduced her innards to jelly. She squinted against the dust kicked up in his wing-wind. He was not angry with her. Surely, he would not try to grab her again, as he did before. Surely not.

April landed directly between his eyes and pecked his snout. "It was Collins. He kicked Rumblkins for no reason. He grabbed at me and knocked Elizabeth to the ground, hurting her shoulder and nearly landing on me. He wants me locked in my cage and tried to forbid Elizabeth from talking to the children about dragons and the Blue Order. He is hostile to dragons and all things related to us."

Elizabeth grabbed Longbourn's face and pulled it toward her. "Do not bother yourself with these matters. It is nothing I cannot handle."

"Why are you defending him? You detest the man. He made you afraid of him today! You cannot handle him." April zipped back and forth between him and Elizabeth.

"What did he do to make you afraid?" Longbourn extended his wings again. He exposed his fangs, a tinge of ocher formed at their tips.

Apparently, he was the only one allowed to make her afraid.

"She ran from him into the woods." How kind of Rustle to make mention of that.

She covered her ears against another dragon bellow.

"Why did you run?"

"It was a simple misunderstanding. Entirely my fault. I will talk to him about it, and it will all come to naught."

"When he could not shout at her, he kicked Rumblkins." Rustle sounded like little Daniel tattling on his siblings.

"We are all afraid of him and afraid for her. He has already hurt one of us. It is only a small step from that to hurting her." April landed on her shoulder and touched her cheek with a wing.

"You are aware that when she marries him, the laws of man permit him that." Rustle said.

Longbourn growled and scratched the dirt, tearing deep trenches with his talons. "Then I will simply tell him to behave. The little man will not dare disobey me."

Elizabeth clutched her throbbing temples.

Longbourn flipped his wings neatly to his back and stared at her, like a school master who had just proven his point.

"I understand your desire is to protect me, to protect all of us. But it cannot be handled that way. He is completely dragon-deaf. He does not even respond to the fairy dragons' songs."

"What has that to do with anything?"

"If he is to be made a Deaf-Speaker, we must handle the transition very carefully. You know how dangerous such men can be. The Blue Order must approve it before anything can be done. The process cannot be hurried or all of us could be at very great risk."

"You cannot keep him in order, so I must step in and manage him for you." Longbourn thumped the nearest tree with his tail.

Dead leaves rained down upon them. She fanned them away from her face.

"This cannot be handled by dragon force. His transition must be subtle and careful—"

Both things that dragons were not.

Longbourn's fiery eyes narrowed. "Why must you constantly argue with me? Is this another means by which you are trying to escape your marriage to him?"

"No. If I am to marry him, then I must be allowed to manage him myself, without your interference."

"I am tired of you trying to shirk your duties."

"Are you even listening to me? Stay out of this. I will cope with it." She rose to tiptoes and stared in his face.

Longbourn turned to the minor dragons. "Have you forgotten that I am your Laird? You are here in my

Keep by my will alone. I will not have you conspiring against me with her. I may very well—"

Stubborn, ridiculous creature!

"You will not threaten our friends! I will not have it." She stomped so hard her heel stung. "Have you forgotten, the Keeper has as much say in the Keep as the Dragon? Perhaps you need to refresh your understanding of the Pendragon Accords. If you ever threaten them again—"

"You will what?" Longbourn roared in her face.

"Whatever I need to do to protect them—that is my oath as a Dragon Mate."

"And if I do not accept them?"

Enough of the pompous posturing. He was as bad as Collins.

She pushed his muzzle away with both hands. "Do not force me, Longbourn. You may not like the results."

He jerked his head back. "You would jeopardize your standing as a Keeper?"

"You would turn your back on your duties as Laird to his Keep?"

Longbourn huffed and stomped. "You wish to find fault with me?"

"No, actually I do not. What I would like most is to be able to oil your flakey hide and brush it properly. I would like to polish your teeth and sweeten your breath, and simply spend time with you again as we used to." Her throat ached.

"There is nothing stopping you."

"Then you do not understand anything at all. Pray excuse me." She curtsied and turned away.

"Come back. This conversation is not over." The ground rumbled beneath her feet.

"I have nothing more to say." She did not stop walking.

"I want you, Keeper. Here. Now." He stomped.

She jumped. "Then make me want to return." Her walk became a run.

Longbourn roared and thundered after her, cutting her off. "You are my Keeper. You must do as I say."

"There is nothing, absolutely nothing in the annals of the Blue Order which say such a thing. A Dragon and his Keeper are partners, equal partners. We should need each other, not consider one master and the other servant."

Or worse, slave.

"Exactly! I need you." He blinked at her with baleful eyes.

"I do not need to be ordered about by a brute that does not care about me."

"I do care about you. I would do anything to protect you."

"Except learn what I truly need." She pressed the back of her hand to her mouth. Why could she not manage to control her tongue?

"I understand perfectly. You do not—" There it was, that perfectly petulant draconic look. If she never saw it again, it would be a very good—if very un-likely—thing.

"Stop, I will not have that conversation again. Pray, leave Collins to me. I shall manage him—somehow."

Longbourn grumbled deep in his throat. "Very well." He nudged her with his snout.

No doubt he wanted scratches and to be told what a lovely fellow he was. Rumblkins appeared at her feet, looking very worn. She picked him up and held him to her chest. Oh, he was a heavy little fellow.

"Excuse me, now. I must return to the house and deal with Rumblkins' injuries." And the one who caused them.

He snorted and muttered, but did not follow.

Just beyond the woods, Elizabeth paused near a fallen tree and sat down, settling Rumblkins in her lap.

"He is a preposterous, grouchy old lizard. How could he think revealing our true nature to Collins would do any good at all?" April settled into Elizabeth's hood and pulled a fold over herself.

"That, dearling, is why I did not want you interfering. I know you were trying to be helpful, but pray, do not be so helpful again."

Rustle squawked overhead. "There was no reason to think Longbourn would resort to such drastic action."

"You do not know Longbourn as I do. He is apt to be rash and unthinking. He prefers to do things in the easiest way possible, not necessarily the wisest. Usually I can dissuade him from his most reckless ideas, but he can be stubborn. The situation is so dangerous right now, I cannot afford—we all cannot afford—to incite his stubbornness. Pray leave him to me." She massaged her temples.

"I was given to believe that major dragons were, by their nature, sensible creatures." Rustle scratched the side of his head with his talons.

"They would have you believe so, but they are not any more sensible than most men. Some are very wise and trustworthy, and some ... some are not."

April tucked her head behind Elizabeth's ear and cuddled. "I am sorry. I did not mean to make things worse."

Elizabeth petted Rumblkins with one hand and patted April with the other. "I know. You were afraid, and that does not leave anyone thinking clearly. It will all be well. Somehow. I know it will be." She stroked Rumblkins furry-tufted ears. "How do you feel?"

"Tired and sore and hungry. Longbourn might have a good idea, though. Collins could suffer an apoplexy on seeing him, and die. I would not complain about that." He pressed his head against Elizabeth's hand and purred.

"While the idea may have some appeal, I doubt it could work out so very simply. The next heir would have to be found. He might well be even worse."

"The estate would not go to you on his death?"

"No, that is not the way the laws of men work."

April and Rustle squawked an offended note.

"They are stupid." Rumblkins' long, scaly tail lashed back and forth, then wrapped tight, around her waist.

"I have had the same thought often enough." She rose and lifted Rumblkins to her shoulder. "I need to get you home."

Hill met them in the garden, swinging between delight that Elizabeth had found Rumblkins and outrage over Collins. With Hill's help, Elizabeth prepared the promised poultice for Rumblkins' bruises, and a tea to speed his healing.

He complained that it tasted funny, but with some coaxing and some dried cod from Hill, he drank it down and settled into his fireplace basket. A few minutes later, he purred very happily.

"Do you think it wise for me to bring his basket to my room tonight, Miss? I know Collins won't be going in there at all."

Rumblkins mrowed and flicked the tip of his tail, almost as though he suggested the idea himself.

"I think he would like that very much."

Hill was spoiling the tatzelwurm awfully, but it made them both so very happy—and the house and garden so very free of rats—that it was difficult to find fault.

"Very good, then. Come along, and we shall keep you away from that horrid man." Hill grunted as she lifted the basket and trundled out.

That horrid man. The sentiment summed it up very well.

At least Rumblkins would recover soon. Hill would probably carry a grudge though, and given that the house would be Collins' someday, that could be a problem.

But a problem for the future. There were enough to contend with now.

Elizabeth scrubbed her face with her hands. It would be dinner time soon. Her stomach churned. She asked Cook to inform Mama that she was unwell and would not be coming down for dinner.

Sleep. That would clear her head. In the morning, she would think of something.

Several days later, Darcy's morning ride took him past Cait's folly. The sun sat low in the sky, warming the morning to brisk and refreshing. Exactly as one should begin a day.

The carved limestone folly resembled a round Grecian temple topped with a wrought iron birdcage. The iron work was of the finest quality, and the swoops and swirls brought to mind images of wind and clouds. But it still resembled an elaborate bird cage.

According to Aunt Catherine, Collins had said as much in Cait's hearing once, and she nearly took out his eyes. Comparisons to birds and cages tended to bring out the worst in her temper.

Over the last few days, Cait's mood had become progressively worse, and the entire household blamed him. Technically it was Pemberley, and not him, who threatened to drive not just Cait, but every dragon and Dragon Friend to distraction, but no one was going to blame a vicontes when a human of no rank could be blamed instead.

In truth, it could not all be attributed to her, either. Rosings should never have explained what lancing meant. Truly, who would tell a youngster such a thing?

Now, Pemberley was nearly hysterical anytime someone unfamiliar visited the lair. What was more, she kept the old dog that had traveled in the dog cart with her to protect her. Thankfully, no one reminded her that the dog was nearly blind and deaf.

Darcy clutched his temples. There was no telling how long that dog would live. He probably needed to find a puppy to raise with Pemberley so she would not be without a companion when the old one died. Where exactly did one find a dog that would tolerate dragons? Perhaps Wellsbey, the minor drake who helped with the sheep, could assist.

Yes, that was a very good thought. Best be sure to remember that one. Good thoughts seemed in very short supply recently.

Cait swooped across the horse's path. It shied and nearly reared.

She perched on one of the iron curlicues near his eye level.

"You have been around horses enough to know better than to startle one!" Yes, scolding a cockatrix was a bad idea, but this habit was more than annoying. It was dangerous.

"I have far bigger concerns than horses right now." She picked at her shoulder feathers.

"If you had caused me to be thrown from this one, you certainly would! Can you imagine the disruption to the estate, and to Pemberley—and to Walker for that matter—should I have been seriously injured or killed? I know you care little enough for me, but think of your own convenience!"

"I wish you had never come." She stared at him and hissed.

"Believe me, I should much rather have stayed in Meryton with someone who knows something useful about baby dragons!"

"Then why did you not?"

Walker swooped down, chittering and scolding. He landed on a nearby tree limb. Heaven forbid he perch on Cait's folly.

"Because, you feather-pated ninny, he was told to leave by the estate wyvern who was playing host to Pemberley."

"A wyvern threw you out? Was he utterly insensible of the honor given him by the presence of a vicontes in his lair?" She extended a wing, showing off the vibrant blue feathers on the underside. "Is that not the estate the bumbling vicar is to inherit?"

"Unfortunately," Darcy muttered.

"The wyvern should just eat the man and be done with it. Surely they can dredge up a better heir even from the bottom of the Thames."

Darcy patted the horse's neck. "Whilst that might be true, that would be against the Accords, which are in the process of amendment right now. I think that is making the wyvern rather desperate and foolish in his attempts to horde what he considers his treasure."

Walker cast him a very odd look. Perhaps it was a bit dramatic to liken Miss Elizabeth to a treasure, but in some ways—many ways, in fact—her way with dragons was.

"Well it is a bloody shame—"

"Cait! That is not ladylike language."

"Which is not a problem considering I am a cockatrix." She preened her wing.

Walker snickered.

"You will not use that sort of language around my sister when she arrives."

"He is right. She is already shy enough around dragon-kind. It would be quite damaging for you to scare her off by threatening her delicacy with your vocabulary." Walker bobbed his head.

Cait ruffled her wings, making them large and fluffy.

Lovely, just what he needed, another fight between those two. Why did they not simply leave one another alone if they could not manage to get along?

She flipped her wings over her back. "Very well, I will restrain myself in her presence. But there is a price attached to that promise."

Of course, there was. Darcy dragged his hand over his face. "What do you demand?"

"You will tell Lady that I will not be the one to lance Pemberley's gums. She has got this addlepated notion that my talons are the perfect tool for the task. What kind of fool does she take me for, asking me to put my limbs into a cranky dragon's mouth?"

No one in their right mind would take on such a task. Of course, no one in their right mind would insist upon it either.

Darcy chuckled into his fist. "That I will do."

"It is too bad that Meryton Keeper did not have some sort of solution for all this muddle."

Walker squawked and flapped. "Darcy, you are an idiot!"

"That is ever so helpful, thank—" Darcy's jaw dropped. "I completely forgot!"

"Forgot what?"

"That Miss Elizabeth sent you with pages and pages of advice on baby dragons. Surely there must be something there on teething." Considering his tone, if Walker could have slapped his forehead, he would.

"You could have saved us all this inconvenience?"

"I do not know, but I am going to find out." Darcy pressed his heels to the horse's side, and they took off for the house at a trot.

Behind him, Cait and Walker chittered back and forth in dragon tongue, probably mocking him.

But they were right. Miss Elizabeth had given him ample notes of dragon lore, and somehow, in the strain of getting Pemberley settled in at Rosings, he had entirely forgotten about them.

He was an idiot.

At the house, he ran for the stairs, but Aunt Catherine cut him off. How did she know that he had just arrived? There must have been a dragon set to watch for him. The butler's puck, most likely. He was good at that sort of thing, especially if promised a shiny button—his favorite trinket—in return. When one visited Rosings, one always brought an ample supply of buttons.

"I have good news, Nephew." She positioned herself between him and the stairs.

"I do not have time for neighborhood gossip, Aunt." She must have used that maneuver often, for she knew exactly how to place herself to make it impossible to skirt past her.

"Gossip? How dare you accuse me of such a base activity? This has nothing to do with the neighborhood, and everything to do with you." She poked his chest.

"Pray then, tell me quickly. I am on an urgent errand."

"I have found a Blue Order surgeon who will come and lance Pemberley's gums."

He clutched his forehead. "Has he ever done such a surgery on a dragon?"

"He does babies all the time."

"Does he know he is to operate on a dragon?"

"Of course, what do you take me for?"

"Does he know the dragon is an infant firedrake?"

"I do not recall that I mentioned her species." She twitched her head and shrugged.

How kind of her to leave off a little detail that might make the surgeon think better of the assignment.

"Call him off. I believe I have another solution."

"And what might that be?"

"I do not know, yet. I have to do some reading." He brushed past her and bounded up the great stairs.

She muttered something behind him, but little matter. He would deal with her temper later.

Where had he put those pages? They were surely in his room somewhere.

He tore through the closet, his trunks, the desk. Nothing!

He was not in the habit of mislaying things. How could this have …

The bed curtains rustled.

"Quincy!" He stormed toward the bed.

A loud squeak, followed by a scratching of taloned toes on the wood floor.

Darcy dropped to the floor and stuck his head and shoulders under the bed.

"Good day." Quincy, the butler's puck, sat on his haunches and cocked his head, wearing a toothy dragon rendition of a smile.

"Out, now."

"As you wish." Quincy scuttled into a sunbeam.

He was a short, four-legged, long-tailed dragon, resembling a lizard that came halfway to his knees. His smooth shiny scales started at his nose in a pale green, blending to darker green and nearly black by the time they reached his tail. Subtle dark stripes covered the length of his body. A short fin ran along his spine between two little nubs on his shoulders, vestigial wings according to dragon lore. His hood was folded back along his neck right now, but when he became angry, as he soon would, it would flare out behind his head, making him look much bigger than he was.

"You know you are not allowed in my room." He tapped his heel hard enough to jar the floorboard Quincy sat upon.

"The maids let me in."

"No, they did not. I ordered them not to do so."

Quincy smiled and flicked his tail, like a dog wagging. Some thought him cute.

They were wrong.

"You have taken my papers."

Quincy chewed at a spot behind his wing nub.

Darcy pinched the bridge of his nose. "I do not have the time or the patience to play this game with you. If you do not immediately return them to me, I will tell Cait that you have taken them and now she must lance Pemberley's gums because they are missing. Pemberley will not appreciate it either."

Quincy's hood flipped out around his head. His body puffed, and he hissed.

"That display will hardly impress either of them. You know Cait's temper."

Quincy chewed the talons of his front paws. "Wait here. I will be back." He scurried through a small hole in the bottom of the servant's door.

That would have to be fixed immediately, even if he took hammer and nails to it himself.

A quarter of an hour later, sheets and sheets of paper were shoved, one at a time, under his door.

Cowardly little lizard.

He retrieved a button from his locked trunk and tossed it through the hole in the servant's door. That should mollify the puck's dignity.

Miss Elizabeth's hand was incredibly neat and easy to read. He traced his fingers down the pages, skimming.

There! Teething!

It was hardly surprising that she had never encountered a teething firedrake before, but she had comforted a teething drake. That should be similar enough. It had to be.

A bone instead of a teething coral, something he could acquire readily enough. Oil of clove, and oil of peppermint? A little lavender oil as well. Surely the local apothecary had those.

It was simple. Almost too simple to bother with. Perhaps it was a fool's errand.

But the alternative was to allow a strange surgeon access to Pemberley with a lancet. Pemberley might never forgive him, and then where would he be? At least, if he tried these methods, he could say he had tried "her" advice. Perhaps she might forgive him then.

And he had to do something. His dragon was suffering and could be in serious danger. No Keeper could stand idly by under such circumstances.

The trip to Hunsford proved successful, but annoying. Why did shopkeepers always ask the same things? Why had he not sent a servant for these items? Would he not be interested in better wares? Perhaps something more?

Gah! It took far too long to get what he needed and leave. At least the beef bones fit in the floor of the gig well enough. The horse did not like the smell, but horses and dragons were often in conflict, so that was neither new nor remarkable.

He parked the gig a quarter of a mile from the lair and gathered his parcels. Pray let this work, even a little, just enough that he could call off his aunt's efforts.

He paused at the opening, allowing his eyes to adjust. The old dog woofed. Probably more because of the smell than anything else.

"Rosings, may I approach?"

Her huge head poked out of the deeper darkness. "Do you bring … help … for the young one?"

"Yes, I have consulted an expert and had a different, much more appealing suggestion."

Rosings pressed her head behind his shoulders and pushed him, stumbling, toward Pemberley's nest.

"Keeper?" Pemberley whined and pawed at her jaws.

"'Her' has written to me and told me what to do."

"Her?" Her huge green eyes widened.

"Yes, 'her.'"

"She knows everything. She help." Her voice sounded so much like Georgiana's when she wept! "What she say? Not cut me?"

"No, she does not recommend that."

Pemberley laid her head on his shoulder and flicked his ear with her tongue. He wrapped his arms around her neck and held her a moment. Could a dragon cry for happiness?

The old dog snuffled at the parcels.

He crouched and removed a meaty bone from paper wrapping. "See, I have a treat for your companion. I have not forgotten him."

"Her would like that."

Miss Elizabeth probably would.

He removed a large beef bone and held it up to Pemberley. "Her says to rub this with a little oil of clove, of peppermint and of lavender. Then you are to chew it until you feel better."

"I … I like chew."

He anointed the bone and handed it to her. Pungent herbal aromas filled the cave. How odd. The scents mixed very well with dragon musk. Somehow that was very reassuring.

Pemberley flicked her tongue over the bone, brows wrinkling at the unfamiliar taste.

"Her says it will make you feel better."

She took the bone and laid down beside the dog. They gummed their prizes in tandem.

Several minutes later, Rosings tapped his shoulder with her chin and whispered, "I think it is working, look at her tail."

Pemberley and her dog were both wagging the tips of their tails in a happy rhythm.

"I will see you have fresh bones whenever you have need." He rubbed the typically-itchy spot right between Pemberley's wings.

"I like bones! Her knows everything!"

Perhaps not everything, but he certainly would not allow those notes out of his possession again. Once Georgiana arrived, perhaps she would be willing to write to Miss Elizabeth for further advice on Pemberley.

That would be almost as good as having her nearby.

Chapter 4

RUMBLKINS RECOVERED FROM his encounter with Collins, but gave the man a wide berth, staying very close to Hill whenever he could. Hill was quite content with both the arrangement and the excuse to avoid Collins. Mr. Collins hardly seemed to notice, keeping company with Papa far more than usual.

After several days of relative calm, an early morning rap at her door hardly seemed surprising.

"You are up. Good. Get dressed and come to my study, I would see you immediately." Papa shut the door firmly.

Lovely, such a mood he was in.

"That does not sound like an invitation to tea." April stared at the door.

Elizabeth retrieved a morning dress from the closet and shrugged it over her shoulders. "I cannot image what has him upset now. There are so many choices:

Rumblkins, Mr. Collins, Longbourn. I think though, it might be best if you were to stay here for now, Mr. Collins might well be with him."

April returned to her filigree cage and locked the door from the inside.

Elizabeth counted the stairs as she went, making sure their number had not changed since the last time she had traversed them. Given how arsey-varsey everything else had become, it seemed reasonable to check.

The study door stood open. How odd, that used to leave her feeling warm and welcome.

Papa waved her in. "Shut the door behind you."

He stood in front of the fireplace, hands clasped behind his back. His shoulders were hunched and his posture uneven. The cold must have settled into his joints, considering the two nearly empty cups of willow bark tea on the small table near his chair.

She minced inside and stood beside his favorite chair. "Yes, Papa?"

He stared at the fire. "It has been a most interesting evening. I have not yet been to bed."

She gulped. "Shall I call the apothecary for you?"

"Perhaps later, but that is not the reason for my sleeplessness. I had a visitor last night."

"Longbourn?" She covered her mouth with her hands, knees melting. Somehow, she made it into the chair next to his.

"He demanded an audience in the cellar. It was fortuitous that Hill was kept occupied by her much-recovered Friend."

Something about the way he said the word. "You do not believe Rumblkins was genuinely hurt? I saw the bruises myself—"

"You know tatzelwurms are not known for being reliable. That he was bruised, I am sure. That it was as serious as he suggests, I highly doubt."

She clenched her jaws. It would not do to argue with him right now.

"The tale Rumblkins told made quite an impression upon Longbourn, though. Quite an impression." He turned and glared, eyes so much like Longbourn's she shrank back.

Had the wyvern taught him to breathe poison as well?

"I did not take Rumblkins or any of the others to see Longbourn. He came upon us in the woods whilst I was telling all of them to allow me to handle matters myself." She clutched fistfuls of her skirt so tightly it might tear.

"So that was what you were telling them." He lifted a hand for silence and paced slowly. "You do realize what you orchestrated amounted to a Keep Conclave, without the senior Keeper, do you not?"

"I orchestrated nothing! It was a chance meeting in the woods, not a Conclave of any flavor." She rose, gripping the back of the chair for support.

"That was hardly Longbourn's opinion. Ironically, he rather approved of it all, seeing it as you moving into your role as Keeper and Mistress of the estate. The complaints had quite the impact on him." He snorted and rolled his eyes.

She pinched the bridge of her nose and exhaled a slow, measured breath. "I spoke with him at length and was certain I had calmed him down."

"Hardly. He paced the cellar half the night, demanding that I bring Collins down to meet him immediately."

She screwed her eyes shut.

Shuffling footfalls. Harsh, raspy breaths. His presence loomed near. "You did not demand it of him? That was his claim, you know. Longbourn said you were inconsolable at Collins' attitudes toward dragons, that you would not have him whilst he remained unaware of them."

"Longbourn is selfish, manipulative, and controlling, entirely insensitive to the feelings and rights of others, and apparently a liar as well." She dragged her hand down her face. "Despite Mr. Collins directly expressing his distaste for all things dragon-related, at no time did I say nor did I imply Mr. Collins should be forcibly initiated. I begged the little ones not to bother Longbourn with their most understandable dread of Mr. Collins—which is a matter that we yet must discuss. They chose to take their grievance to the Laird of their Keep, as is their right as per to the Accords."

"Do you have any idea what would happen if dragons were revealed to Collins in a single moment?"

"I insisted to Longbourn that it not be done. If the shock did not kill the man, then there is every reason to expect he would go far and wide with his discovery—which would be far worse than him simply dropping over dead of apoplexy." She spun on her heel and stormed toward the windows. "Longbourn is far too accustomed to getting his own way and is willing to do whatever is necessary to make it happen."

"It is his right as territorial dragon."

She raised her foot to stomp—no that would not help matters—and set it down gently. "No, it is not. We are not slave to him because of his strength any more than our Dragon Friends are slaves to us."

"A Keeper's task is to serve a dragon's needs."

"His needs, not his wants and whims. They are not the same thing." She leaned against the window frame and pressed her forehead to the glass. "Do you know what Mr. Collins said to me? He told me April belongs locked in her cage, like an animal in a circus. He wants to see her banished from company and denied her freedom. She is terrified of what he might try to do to her, and honestly, I do not blame her. He all but forbade me from telling stories to the Gardiner children. He accused me of polluting their young minds with nonsense!"

"Perhaps he has a point on both counts."

She stiffened, blood draining from her face. "You must be joking!"

"April has far too much freedom, more than any other fairy dragon I have known. It would be far safer for her to stay out of sight."

How satisfying it would be to turn a draconic glare on him. But it would probably work against her. Best just stare out the window. "She will not tolerate such terms."

"Then she is free to make other choices."

"You would turn her out?"

"I never said such a thing, only that if she does not like Longbourn, she has other choices."

"And what of Mr. Collins' attack on Rumblkins?"

"That was an unfortunate accident."

"That is not what I was told." She turned, slowly, deliberately, fists clenched.

"You provoked Collins to anger. He was merely taking it out on what he considered a dumb animal." He shrugged; his expression so mild it had to be an affectation.

"What other kind of stupid creature do you think he will take his anger out on next? Perhaps the children—he considers them stupid; I am sure—what might he do if he finds them playing at dragons again?"

"You have filled their heads with too many stories."

"Those stories are the best way to teach them of the legacy they have inherited. It is how you taught me."

He rubbed his palms together before his chest. "All in good time. You cannot teach them everything at once. In any case, their parents should take over the task. It is time for them to return home, to London. I shall make mention of that immediately."

"You are sending them away? You cannot be serious." She staggered back against the window frame. "You cannot put out your family!"

Heavens above, he probably would not hesitate in making any of the minor dragons homeless either. What kind of man had he become?

"I have more significant concerns right now. He needs to manage his family, and I need to manage mine."

"You mean you need to manage me."

He raked his hair. "We cannot have Longbourn becoming so agitated. It is dangerous to everyone. Who knows what kind of rash behavior he might commit? I calmed him down and assured him that Collins would be dealt with, but I cannot be certain the next time will be so easy. It is your responsibility to keep both of them, Collins and Longbourn, content and away from one another until such time as we can devise a gentle means of introduction."

One. Two. Three. She gritted her teeth and walked toward a chair. *Four. Five. Six. Seven.* One hand on the arm of the wingback, she sat down with all the grace and elegance Mama had taught her. *Eight. Nine. Ten. Much better.* "I have given that some thought. If the Order could assist us in finding a willing parrot-like cockatrix—"

"That will not work. Another dragon is only going to further agitate Longbourn. You know he barely tolerates the minor dragons of the Keep. Pemberley almost drove him to distraction."

Pemberley. Her eyes burned and she blinked furiously. Her dear, sweet baby. Of course, such a creature would have driven Longbourn mad. And according to Papa, it was entirely Pemberley's fault. Sometimes he was just as bad as Mr. Darcy.

"You are up to the task. I know you are. Yes, it is unpleasant, but that is the nature of life. We will find a way to make it tolerable for you. I promise you that." He patted her shoulder.

"Have you given any thought as to how that may be accomplished?"

"I will find a way, Lizzy. Trust me. Go now and have some breakfast. I am sure the Gardiners will be in need of your help with packing."

She curtsied and ran from the room. If he thought his promises were meaningful, he was sorely mistaken.

In the morning room, Mr. Collins sat between Mama and Mary, prattling on about some point no one could be interested in. Still Mary nodded, smiling as though she cared, and poured him a fresh cup of tea.

How could she be so easy, waiting on him?

Elizabeth sat beside Jane, a knot settling into her stomach. Was that what her life was to become: placating Mr. Collins with tea and genteel conversation at meals and appeasing Longbourn with oils for his itchy hide and mutton for his empty belly?

Mama laughed at Mr. Collins' remark. In truth that was very close to what Mama did daily, satisfying Papa's demands for comfort and solitude. Granted, she did not manage Longbourn, but she did see to all the minor dragons' needs, under the guise of tending the family pets.

Heavens! Perhaps Papa was right: their demands were normal and reasonable, but she really was being selfish and headstrong.

That thought was enough to ruin whatever appetite she might have had left.

A quarter of an hour later, Papa's study door slammed and heavy footfalls tromped up the stairs, the final punctuation of his conversation with Uncle Gardiner, no doubt.

At least it was a good excuse to leave the morning room.

She hurried upstairs behind him and tapped at the Gardiners' door.

"Come in, Lizzy." Aunt closed the door behind her.

"I trust you are aware of what has just transpired." Uncle tapped his large boot in an angry staccato beat. "Your father has always been a staunch traditionalist when it comes to dragon matters. He was taught by his grandfather, another Historian, who opposed every single change that came to the Order. I am not surprised by his demand."

"Pray let me help you prepare. Perhaps I might take the children for a walk, tell them one more story before you leave?"

"Only if you are well away from Collins." Uncle glanced up at Aunt who laid her hand on his shoulder.

Elizabeth covered her eyes with her hand. "I am so sorry."

Uncle took her by the shoulders. "Look at me, Lizzy. You are not responsible for either man's behavior—or for any of the dragons' for that matter. No matter what they might do, nothing will ever change our affection for you. Pray tell me you understand that."

She swallowed hard and nodded.

"Very good then." He kissed her forehead.

"If you will take the children for us, we will prepare to take our leave." Aunt slipped her arm around Elizabeth's shoulder. "Perhaps you might take them to Hill's office to visit Rumblkins. Mr. Collins is very unlikely to find you there."

After a quick consultation with Hill, Elizabeth did just that. The children gathered around Rumblkins' basket and nibbled on buttered hot rolls, while Hill looked on in grandmotherly contentment from her rocking chair. The children adored the purry tatzelwurm, and Hill approved of anyone who esteemed her Friend.

Elizabeth settled on a stool beside the basket and stroked Rumblkins' silky ears. "Of course, cats cannot speak." She glanced at the children, eyebrows raised.

"No, of course they cannot." Anna giggled, sending a wave of titters through her brothers.

"But if they could, just pretending of course, what do you think this one might say?" Elizabeth tapped

Rumblkins' nose. Now was not the time for him to be a cheeky little fellow.

He lifted his head, turned toward the children and mrowed. "I would say that I am very content here."

"He likes Longbourn very much, I think." Samuel glanced shyly at Elizabeth.

She nodded at him, smiling.

"I think he likes his basket," Anna added.

"I do, and I like dried fish even more." Rumblkins licked his thumbed paw and ran it over his face.

Joshua rose and walked around the little group, hands clasped behind his back. He looked so serious and so like his father when he did that. He was destined to become a solicitor. "Rumblkins has grown fat since we have come. I think he would say he likes dried cod a great deal, and Mrs. Hill is very liberal with it."

Hill laughed heartily. "Well, he has earned it. I have never seen a creature so adept at catching rats. I have hardly had a loaf of bread nibbled since he came to stay."

Daniel leaned forward and scratched Rumblkins' chin. "He is very proud of himself, I think."

"I am indeed." He rubbed his cheek against Daniel's hand. "I may not be a large dragon who can fly and spew poison, but I can do some things very well, indeed. I am proud to earn my place in the Keep."

Elizabeth pressed her lips tight. It might be a matter of debate within the Order whether minor dragons had to earn a place in a Keep. She had her own opinions on the matter.

The children continued their game of speaking for the dragon. Rumblkins played his part as well, even as the children's "translations" became increasingly outlandish. Who knew a tatzelwurm could make sounds so much like a laugh?

Fun though it was, the little game had a purpose. What better way to help train the children to cover any slips they might make if they discussed their Dragon Friends when non-Hearers were present? Papa and Collins might not approve, but it was a final instruction she could give them before they departed.

Aunt came to gather the children, letting them know that they would be returning to London immediately.

Anna grabbed her mother's hand. "Will Phoenix come with us?"

"Yes, of course, my dear. He is part of the family. He will ride in the carriage with us."

Anna dashed to Elizabeth. "Will you come too?"

"I am afraid not. I am needed here. Maybe someday, though."

Samuel and Joshua grabbed Aunt's hands. "Can she come to visit, please?"

Elizabeth crouched down in front of them and took their hands. "I fear it may be quite some time before I am no longer needed about Longbourn."

She swallowed back a painful lump in her throat. First Darcy had torn her from Pemberley, and now Papa was taking the children away. Who would be next? April? She dragged the back of her hand over her eyes.

"But when you are able, you are always welcome in Cheapside." Aunt slid her arms over the boys' shoulders. "Now it is time for us to go. Come along. Lizzy will help you into the carriage."

Taking Anna and Daniel by the hands, Elizabeth trudged outside. Mama and her sisters were already there waiting to say goodbye. Papa was not.

Given Uncle's expression, it was probably just as well.

Elizabeth handed the children into the carriage. Phoenix waved at her from the nesting basket of his dainty little cage. The cage door was unlocked—as it should be.

Mary came alongside her as they waved goodbye, until the coach disappeared around a bend in the road. Rustle flew circles over the carriage, cawing farewells that trailed away on the wind.

Heather flitted to Elizabeth's shoulder. "Why is Phoenix going? Why are the children going? I do not want them to leave. Everyone is so upset! I do not understand."

Elizabeth leaned her cheek against Heather's fluffy pink feather-scales. "Neither do I."

"Shall we take a walk? Jane will be having tea at Netherfield today, so Mama and Lydia will be much engaged in her toilette. We shall not be missed."

Elizabeth shrugged and looked over her shoulder.

"Oh, Lizzy." Mary patted her arm. "Mr. Collins went to call upon the vicar. He will not be available to join us."

"In that case, a walk sounds like a pleasant idea."

They turned toward the wilderness alongside the house. How forlorn it looked this time of year, all bare, and brown and crunchy.

"I suppose Rustle told you what happened and why the Gardiners have left so suddenly?" Elizabeth could still make him out on the horizon, a black speck, circling low.

"That is the advantage of having several dragons in the house now. I am much better informed than I have ever been." Mary chuckled and shrugged.

"There are fewer secrets kept with dragons than with servants. More than one aristocratic household has learned that the hard way." Elizabeth tapped Heather's beak with a fingertip. "So, take heed, little one, and do not be a carrier of tales. It is not a welcome trait."

Heather sneezed, and all her feather scales pouffed, turning her into a little pink dandelion.

Mary glanced at Heather. "What a silly little thing you are. Do you remember what you wanted to tell Elizabeth?"

Heather sniffed and sneezed again. "You had best tell her."

Mary huffed a little. "I am not sure what you have heard, but Mr. Collins was quite remorseful over what happened with Rumblkins."

Elizabeth turned aside and rolled her eyes. "I was under the impression he had little concern for dumb creatures."

"I am sure he said such a thing to Hill. But that is hardly surprising when she came after him with a rolling pin."

Heather squeaked a little laugh.

"It was rather like a scene from a pantomime, all told. I think Lydia enjoyed it a great deal, Mama not so much though."

"I can well imagine. I am sure that scene won Mrs. Hill no favors with Mr. Collins."

"No indeed, but I think I was able to calm him." Mary kicked a pile of leaves that crunched and skittered against her skirts.

"How did you manage such a thing?"

"I merely suggested to him that Mrs. Hill found Rumblkins excessively useful to her. She feared losing that aid in ridding the house of vermin. Her response was understandable especially considering Mr. Collins shares her dread of rats."

"I am surprised he has such a sensible opinion of them."

Mary frowned just like Mama. "That is not gracious, Elizabeth. He is not a stupid man."

"Perhaps he is not, but he does not make it easy to tell." She folded her arms across her chest.

"You are awfully prejudiced. If you were not always so hard on him—"

"Forgive me, but I do not think I am hard on him at all. Consider what he did and has threatened to do to the minor dragons! You think that tolerable? What is more, he forbade me from telling dragon stories to the children! The audacity!"

"I concede, he is apt to overstep himself, and he does indulge in a high level of what I can only call the ridiculous. But in all fairness, your stubbornness is of no help, either."

"My stubbornness! You know I am right. Should I just concede to him because he declares a thing so?" Elizabeth threw her hands in the air.

"If you would be a little more flexible, you might find him easier to manage. Instead of arguing, you could have explained the higher principles contained in your stories, ones he might appreciate. He would have supported you then."

"He has no right—" Elizabeth dragged her foot into the dirt. When had she picked up Longbourn's habit?

"As heir to the estate, some would argue he does have the right. Certainly, Papa does not see him as overstepping."

Elizabeth clutched her temples. When had Mary taken their side?

"What would it take away from you to help him to see things in a different and more favorable way, instead of always arguing?"

"It is an insult to be questioned by one who does not know what he is talking about."

"How is he supposed to know what he is talking about when dragons are a grand secret to which he has not been privy?" Mary cocked her head and raised an eyebrow. "Forgive me for being so bold, but is it possible that at least part of the problem is that you are very proud yourself?"

Elizabeth's head snapped up, briefly unbalancing Heather from her perch. "Proud? Me? Perhaps you have confused me with Mr. Darcy. If there has been anyone in the neighborhood who has suffered from pride, it is he."

"He was prone to pride as well, but he is far from the only one. Consider, you are Papa's favorite and are accustomed to being treated as such."

"That sounds unfavorably like jealousy." Who would have thought that Mary's vice?

"You are also the favorite of every dragon at Longbourn, at Gracechurch Street, and a few you have met on your journeys with Papa as I understand it. Do you deny it?"

"What has that to do with anything?" Elizabeth adjusted the buttons on her spencer.

"The dragons treat you with great deference. Papa makes no bones about treating you as his favorite. Of course, it is difficult for you when someone does not show you favor the way you want it. It hurts one's pride—"

"So, the reason I do not like Mr. Collins is that I am not his favorite?"

Mary threw her hand in the air and waved it near Elizabeth's face. "Not at all—can you not see; you are his favorite. He has singled you out, you know. He likes you very much indeed. But you have set yourself so against him that you will not see that."

"How can you say that when he is so ill-disposed to all things draconic?"

"He is not nearly so ill-disposed, as you call it, if one is not so dead-set on having things exactly her way. If you would just compromise a little, you would find that he is quite malleable and amenable to nearly everything that is important to you." She poked Elizabeth's shoulder hard enough to set her back a step.

"You would keep Heather in a cage because he insisted?"

Heather squawked and flapped her little wings.

"He made that suggestion to me. We merely demonstrated to him how very well-trained she was, and that she was able and willing to follow all my commands. That was exactly what he wanted to know. She did a few tricks, sang whilst perched on his finger, and retreated to an inconspicuous spot on the shelf when asked. All his objections were answered, and he is feeling quite indifferent to her presence now." Mary held out her hand for Heather.

"She performed for him like a learned pig?"

Heather lit on Mary's finger, snorted and shook her head.

"Hardly. She saw the advantage in convincing Mr. Collins of her agreeable nature and was happy to do so."

"Indeed, I was." Heather blinked her huge eyes. "He is little bother to me now. I do not understand why April is so troubled by him. He even scratched under my chin."

Elizabeth's eye's bulged. Collins, scratching a dragon? "April would never tolerate him touching her. She has not your easy-going temperament."

"While that is true, perhaps if you explained to her the need for it, she might be willing to be a little more … settled?"

Elizabeth scoured her face with her palms.

Mary sighed and pressed her hand to her mouth. "I just want to offer you some possible means by which your ends might be accomplished without you being reduced to a shell of yourself."

"I shall give what you have said a great deal of thought."

"And you will try to do it?"

"I will try."

Mary squeezed her hand. She and Heather returned to the house.

Elizabeth ran her hands along her upper arms and exhaled heavily. It was good that April had not been around to hear Mary's comments. She would have readily taken offense and was not one to easily forgive.

She kicked a twig, but its thorns tangled in the hem of her petticoat instead of skittering out of her way.

"Dragon's blood!"

Good thing no one was around to hear that oath—Papa would be horrified to hear her cursing like a common—well, an uncommon—sailor.

She tossed the offending branch aside and continued on.

Papa had not been pleased to learn that Longbourn had taught her all manner of coarse language. But even then, he had not been able to bring himself to curb the wyvern.

Longbourn had always been such a good friend to her ... until now. Until she argued with him, and refused to accommodate his wishes. If only he would try to be more understanding.

Great heavens! That is exactly what Mary was asking of her.

She grabbed the nearest tree trunk and clung to it. No, certainly not. Mary could not be implying that her own behavior was anything like Longbourn's.

She staggered to an unobtrusive bench tucked between the trees and pulled her knees up under her chin.

Her behavior was nothing like the wyvern's. She had not threatened to eat anyone.

She was Papa's favorite, though. But it was because of her dragon affinity. He was the Historian of the Blue Order, so of course he would favor any child who loved dragons as much as he. That was only to be expected.

He did treat her differently than her sisters, indulging her interests, her whims. He had taken her traveling on Blue Order business, to London, Bath, Manchester, Brighton, and more. None of her sisters or Mama had ever traveled with him. Even when he could have easily arranged for their entertainment in Brighton, he chose to bring only her. How must that have looked to her sisters?

She pressed her forehead to her knees.

Mama favored Jane and Lydia, doting on them. They could do no wrong in her eyes. Jane was so sweet and good, that it made no difference in her disposition. But Lydia? Even Charlotte Lucas had begun remarking upon Lydia's wild behavior.

Had she, in her own way, become as indecorous as Lydia? As proud and insensitive as Mr. Darcy? She dragged her sleeve across blurry eyes. Pray, no, it could not be so.

Could it?

Was it really so wrong that she had always wanted to marry for love? There was every indication that Jane would have the opportunity. Why should she not?

Because a Dragon Keeper had greater responsibilities.

And she needed to act like it.

Mary was right. It was time for her to rise above being a spoiled little girl. If Mary and Heather could manage Mr. Collins, surely she and April could do the same.

It required two days of coaxing and cajoling for April to agree to Elizabeth's plan and venture out into Mr. Collins' company again. She kept close to Elizabeth and followed commands like a show animal. Mr. Collins approved, most heartily, but April's resultant temper could only be quelled afterwards with copious amounts of honey. Hopefully, she would become accustomed to performing for Collins soon, or the poor dear would soon grow too fat to fly.

Elizabeth forced herself to remain in the parlor while Collins read to them. Silently reciting verb conjugations from a tome of dragon script she had found tucked in an odd corner of Papa's study did a great deal to make Mr. Collins' readings more tolerable.

Together with her sisters, they played spillikins in the afternoons. His short, pudgy fingers were not well adept for the game, but following Mary's lead, Elizabeth encouraged him and made suggestions that improved his play. His long legs gave him a slight advantage when they went outside to play battledore and shuttlecock. He was able to get to the shuttlecock rapidly enough, but hitting it was another story altogether. Even Mary complimented her on how patiently she had borne it when he accidentally struck her in the face with his battledore.

April, though, required a substantial dose of chamomile tea and honey afterwards to not claw his eyes out. At least no one objected to Elizabeth retiring to her chambers for the rest of the day after that incident.

All told, though, perhaps Mary was right. With a little flexibility and creativity, Mr. Collins might just be managed enough to be tolerable.

5
Chapter

FITZWILLIAM ARRIVED WITH Georgiana exactly on the date and time he said he would. One might think the military would have influenced him toward such precision, but he had been that way all his life. Nearly drove his family to distraction with his punctuality. Perhaps that was why he did it.

Aunt Catherine showed her new guests all the proper attentions and then some. Darcy's company had lost some of its shine. She was ready for guests who might better fit her needs as an excessively attentive hostess.

Darcy excused himself from the post-dinner drawing room entertainments as early as he could without drawing the ire of either of the de Bourgh women. Fitzwilliam was quick to take advantage of the opportunity, pinching the brandy decanter and a pair of snifters on the way out.

He pulled the door of Darcy's chambers closed behind him and leaned against the door as though barring it from the enemy. He balanced the snifters in one hand and poured brandy with the other. "That was a rather spectacular retreat. I see you have not lost your touch."

Darcy took a snifter. "It seems a necessary survival skill."

They dropped into a pair of wingback chairs near the fireplace. A gentle breeze brought in the scents of the night as they sat in blessed silence for several minutes. Why could the de Bourgh women not appreciate the value of quiet companionship?

"Where is Walker?" Fitzwilliam peered at the bed curtains and other high perches in the room.

"I expect he will be along as soon as he catches wind of the brandy. He appreciates it as much as you do." He pointed to a small glass on the table.

Fitzwilliam chuckled and filled the glass. "Forgive me, but I still find it odd to see your dragon drink. At least he holds his liquor better than most men."

"I will let him know you said that." Darcy raised his glass toward him. "Dare I ask how the journey went?"

Fitzwilliam took a deep draw from his glass. "If you are asking if Georgiana still suffers from sickness in the carriage, yes, most definitely. I have never seen anyone with such a delicate constitution. As if fretting over all of the dragon encounters that she would have at Rosings and her impending introduction to Pemberley were not enough to drive her to distraction."

Darcy leaned into the chair and stared at the ceiling. "I suppose it was too much to hope she had begun to grow out of her shyness towards dragons."

"She dreads dragons and is little happier about most people. The dear girl is nearly as bad as you in that regard. Some things, it seems, will never change."

"Perhaps a Dragon Friend of her own might help cure her of this rubbish?" Darcy bounced steepled hands off his chin.

"What possible Dragon Friend would not drive her to distraction? Even Walker who is more civilized than most men keeps her utterly tongue-tied."

"So, she has not changed." Walker landed on the table and harrumphed. He sampled the brandy. "Very nice."

"Whilst in Meryton, we met several fairy dragons."

Fitzwilliam snorted. "Those senseless flutter-tufts?"

"They are not all senseless bits." Walker grumbled.

Fitzwilliam's eyes grew very wide. "You are the last one I would expect to say such a thing."

Walker fluttered his wings in something that resembled a shrug.

"It is true. There was fairy dragon in Meryton with the venom to stand up to Walker. It was something, seeing her going beak to beak with him." Darcy covered his mouth and chuckled.

"April is a rare example of her kind and an excellent influence on the hatchlings. I confess she has forced me to rethink my opinion of her kind." Walker paced the table as he lectured, wings folded tightly over his back. He could have taught classes at Cambridge with that posture.

"Speaking of hatchlings," Fitzwilliam leaned forward, elbows on knees. "Do you think you can convince Cait to allow me to try to befriend one of your next clutch?"

Walker took a deep draw from his brandy and tucked his head under his wing.

"That is rather a sore point right now." Darcy sipped his brandy.

"But I thought—"

"Well then perhaps you should sire her clutch." Walker snarled. He picked up his brandy glass and up-ended it, downing the remaining liquid in a single gulp.

Darcy covered his eyes with his hands as Fitzwilliam laughed raucously. Unfortunately, a few of Rowlandson's more exotic prints flashed through his mind. Probably exactly what Fitzwilliam was thinking of as well. It would be days before he could shake those images from his mind.

"So, Georgiana is not the only one who has not changed." Fitzwilliam wiped his eyes on his sleeve.

"Hardly." Walker paced along the table.

"I am not sure who Cait favors more, Aunt Catherine or Anne." Darcy refilled Walker's glass.

"When she is not broody, definitely the Lady, but currently, she favors the young one."

It was not usually a compliment when a dragon refused to refer to one by name.

Except Pemberley's references to Miss Elizabeth as "Her"—that title was spoken with near reverence.

"Speaking of Anne—" Fitzwilliam reached for his glass.

"I would rather not."

"One more thing that has not changed." Fitzwilliam chuckled, then forced his features into a more proper expression.

Not that he succeeded, but at least he made the effort.

"Seriously though, Darce, we really must speak of Anne."

"I swear, if you tell me I should purchase a special license or even an ordinary one, I shall pitch you out of the window and blame the deed on Walker."

"I will help. But blame Quincy—he is a much more believable culprit."

Fitzwilliam threw up his hands as though in surrender. "Far be it from me to do such a thing." He reached into his jacket and removed a letter affixed with the blue wax seal of the Blue Order. "Father sends you his official greetings."

"How kind of him. I expect this missive contains his instructions to have the marriage settlements prepared and sent to him for his approval?" Darcy refilled his own glass.

"Though it is tempting to allow you to stew in your own venom, I would not have Walker consider me cruel. That letter does not condemn you. It contains your pardon."

Darcy sat bolt upright. "My what?"

"You heard me. Pardon, reprieve—if you wish to be dramatic, salvation. It is not merely a letter from your Uncle Matlock, but rather an official notice from the Chancellor of the Blue Order. The marriage clauses have been amended to reflect—how did they put it— 'the societal changes and customs of men.' The dragons have made the concession. As long as a proper Keeper is ensured, and the Keeper's desired marriage does not present a danger of exposure of dragon kind, then an estate dragon cannot enforce or prevent a marriage."

Darcy cracked the seal and read the letter. All the formal language aside, that was exactly what the letter said.

By Jove! He dragged in breath like a half-drowned man and sprang to his feet. Free—he was indeed free! He paced along the windows.

Fitzwilliam and Walker laughed heartily.

"You should see yourself, Darce—you look nothing so much as a man who has escaped Tyburn's tree."

"You would feel quite the same if you faced a marriage that would give you responsibility for two estates and two dragons!"

"You would complain of such wealth?"

"Have you any idea of how much work a major dragon is? Hardly the kind of work one can turn over to servants."

"Which is exactly why you would invite me to live at Rosings and manage it for you." Fitzwilliam leaned back and balanced one foot on top of the other.

Darcy rubbed his eyes with thumb and forefinger. "Better you should marry Anne and be the proper Keeper here."

"It is a nice idea to be sure, but as eldest son, you are a much more attractive match."

"Well, perhaps your fortunes have changed. Once Anne recovers from her disappointment, perhaps your father can press your suit for you."

"I suppose then I should be on my very best behavior." Fitzwilliam drained his snifter. "Perhaps if Cait will allow me to befriend—"

"If Darcy does not need to mate at a dragon discretion, then I do not do so at a man's." Walker growled and flew out of the window.

"Touchy fellow. I say, the resemblance between you two is utterly uncanny." Fitzwilliam smirked.

"You know mine is not the only betrothal connected to Rosings Park that will be affected by these changes."

Fitzwilliam rubbed his hands together. He enjoyed gossip as much as Aunt Catherine. "Indeed, I had no idea. Do tell."

"The Hunsford vicar, Collins—a dragon-deaf buffoon—has a dragon estate entailed upon him—the estate of the Order's Historian, Longbourn."

"The one who assisted you with Pemberley's recovery?"

"Bennet's second daughter has a particular gift with dragons. It was she who stayed my hand and insisted that Pemberley could still properly imprint. And she was right. Without her …" Darcy swallowed hard and dragged his fist across his chin.

"And she is her father's sacrificial lamb to the vicar?"

"The dragon is enamored of her just like Pemberley is, and Walker and every dragon she meets. Longbourn does not wish to let her go. He will be most distressed to learn she is no longer obligated to bow to his demands."

Fitzwilliam peered at him more closely. "It sounds as though you feel a debt toward her? Perhaps you should wheedle an invitation to Rosings Park for her—and get her away from that dragon of hers."

"Have you forgotten that the man she does not want to marry is vicar here? I can hardly think it would be an agreeable escape for her."

"That is a shame. It sounds as though she might be very helpful to Georgiana."

Darcy stroked his chin. "You have given me an idea."

Several hours later, Darcy gathered up several papers and tiptoed to Georgiana's room. He tapped at the door. A soft voice responded.

Georgiana was curled up in a large chair, near the fire, a large blanket wrapped over her—her way of recovering from too much company.

"I am glad you are come." He pulled a chair close and sat near her.

She peeked above the blanket, eyes in a narrow glare. "I had little choice. You insisted I come."

"You sound as though I am an ogre."

"I have heard they are as fond of dragons as you are." She tucked her head back into the blanket.

He patted the blanket where her shoulder should have been. "I know Old Pemberley frightened you with his tempers, and that he was crotchety in his dotage. But they are not all so difficult."

"Walker does not like me either."

"Walker is not particularly personable with anyone."

She pulled the blankets aside. "Quincy has already been through my trunks and has tried to steal buttons off my gowns! I do not even know the kitchen dragon's name, but she runs when she sees me—"

"Blanche runs from nearly everyone. She is shy. And as to Quincy, pucks are hoarders. He does that to everyone. I have brought buttons for him. I will give you some. If you offer them to him for good behavior, he will leave your things alone."

She shrugged.

"Little Pemberley is a very affectionate creature."

"She is a firedrake! How can you call a fire-breathing, fanged, winged monster affectionate?" Georgiana hugged her shoulders and shuddered.

"She is just a baby! Like that puppy you adored."

"I am sure she would be offended if you compared her to a puppy."

"She has her own pet dog. I think she would be pleased."

"She has a dog?" Georgiana's tone softened.

"An old hound. They are inseparable. They like to chew bones together. She is teething, you know."

"But is that not a very dangerous time for a baby?" A glimmer of interest—or perhaps sympathy lit her eyes.

"That is what I understand as well. I have some very helpful advice, written for me by the daughter of the Blue Order's Historian. You might find it helpful to read the observations of a young woman like yourself. She feels very differently about dragons and perhaps if you can see them through her eyes, it would be helpful." He offered the pages Miss Elizabeth had written.

She took them, suspicion in her eyes.

"I have not told you the full story yet, but Pemberley did not hatch as we expected. Miss Elizabeth was there with her when she hatched. I think Pemberley might not have lived if she had not been there."

"Do you like her?"

Why did Georgiana have to ask that?

"I think she would be a good friend to you. She said she would be happy to receive letters from you."

A little frown appeared, and she raised an eyebrow. "And you are not concerned that would be her way to get close to you? You have always been suspicious of young women."

"I am quite certain she does not think that well of me. One might believe that she preferred dragon company to that of men."

Georgiana giggled. "Exactly opposite to me."

"I suppose in a way. Still, will you read what she has written? I have read it and if nothing else, you will enjoy her rather unique sense of humor."

"It cannot hurt, I imagine."

Not quite the reaction he was hoping for, but it was better than an outright refusal. Why did young women have to be so utterly perplexing? He excused himself and returned to his own chambers.

It was a shame that Miss Elizabeth could not come to Rosings Park. Pemberley would enjoy her company. He would, too. If anyone could help Georgiana get over her reticence with dragonkind, it was her.

Anne de Bourgh's voice was just like her mother's—loud and unmistakable. Particularly early in the day. Especially when she screeched.

Especially then.

Anne's second outburst, which sounded vaguely like "Uncle Matlock cannot do that to me!" sent Darcy running first for his coat and then for Georgiana's chambers.

She sat wide-eyed in the window seat, like a mouse waiting for a cat to pounce.

"Gather your pelisse and bonnet and come with me." He waved her to her feet.

She scrambled for the items and followed him toward the servants' door.

"I know it is irregular, but if you wish to avoid Anne—" He opened the door and ushered her inside.

Georgiana had probably never seen a servants' corridor. She was far too meek and obedient to stray into forbidden territory. How scandalized would she be to realize that he knew his way around Rosings by them? That damage would be far easier to repair than what Anne or Aunt Catherine might leave in their wake.

They burst into the bustling kitchen. Cooks and scullery maids stopped and stared. The housekeeper's zaltys, Blanche, lived up to her name and turned nearly white—more a light grey to match the hearthstones. She coiled and hissed at them.

"Mr. Darcy! Miss Darcy! What ... how ..." Cook stammered.

"Pack us some bread and cheese, perhaps some apples and cold meat as well." Darcy nodded sharply.

Best pretend all this was as normal and natural as possible. No doubt the servants had heard the commotion upstairs and could easily figure out his intentions.

"Good day, Blanche." Darcy tipped his head toward the little snake-type dragon whose color was slowly returning.

She flicked her tongue at them, her bright black eyes scolding. "You should not startle me so."

"Pray forgive us for surprising you. That was hardly our intention. Georgiana, have you been introduced to Blanche?"

Georgiana colored as one of the undercooks stared at her.

She was far too concerned with what servants thought of her.

"Go back to your businessss. It is dear that he is ssso attentive to the cook'sss cat." Blanche spoke with the same odd lispy voice most snake-type dragons shared.

The undercook, smiled slightly, shrugged, and returned to chopping carrots.

Georgiana giggled.

"I am pleased to meet you." Blanche reached her head toward Georgiana.

Georgiana backed away slightly.

Blanche flicked her tail, decidedly irritated.

Darcy extended his hand, holding it open until Blanche rubbed it with her cheek. "She means no offense. She is still learning."

"She is ssstill rude."

Unfortunately, Blanche was right. But reminding her of it would do nothing to help Georgiana's confidence, either.

Cook trundled up with a generous basket and sent them on their way.

A quarter of an hour later, they were climbing into a smart little curricle. How fortunate that the weather was so agreeable for a ride out and about the estate.

"Where are we going, Brother?" Georgiana glanced over her shoulder as though she thought someone might be following them.

"Anywhere away from the manor, and until nightfall if we can manage it. Fitzwilliam brought news from the Order that Anne does not like."

"Does this mean you will not be marrying Anne?"

The horse shook its head and hesitated. A shiver ran down his spine.

"What is that awful sound?" She pressed her hands to her ears.

Cockatrice screeches did that.

A dark, sleek shape swooped down from the trees, a larger one in its wake.

The horse shied.

Blasted fool creatures!

Georgiana clapped her hands to her mouth. At least she had the sense to know a scream could agitate the horse as much as those flying nuisances.

He brought the horse under control and helped her out. If the damned creature was going to run away, it was not going to be with his sister in the curricle.

"I have neither asked for nor do I require your advice in hunting. I am neither hungry, nor do I prefer to eat muntjac," Walker screeched as he landed clumsily in a nearby tree.

"Of course, you do not ask my advice. Males never do, you are all so concerned with your appearances." Cait perched on a branch near him.

Lovely! A perfect balm to salve Georgiana's dragon reticence.

"I do not care what you think of me." Walker extended his wings.

"Yes, you do."

He flew to another tree. "No, I do not. Nor do I care how you hunt. I have managed quite nicely on my own."

"But wouldn't it be so much nicer to have a mate to do that with you?" Her voice turned syrupy.

Darcy had heard more than one young woman of the *ton* use that tone on him. His stomach roiled.

"With those ridiculous tail feathers and foolish ruff, you are entirely ill-equipped to hunt anything."

She extended her wings and spread her tail feathers. "I had not thought you noticed."

"You are the vainest creature—"

"Pride is entirely acceptable when there is true superiority involved." Cait fanned her ruff just a little bit fuller.

"Only in your own mind."

"Apparently on more than one occasion, you have quite agreed with me." She fluffed her ruff until it obscured her face entirely.

"Do not remind me of my youthful folly."

"Your sense of humor has not changed." She glided to the tree where he was perched, landing on a branch just above him.

He looked up at her. "Arrogant hen."

"Stubborn cockerel."

He flew off, and she launched after him.

This was as bad as a ballroom during the London Season!

Darcy clutched his temples. They had been like this the last time they mated: utterly insufferable.

"Must everyone here be so disagreeable?" Georgiana covered her face with her hands.

"I am afraid they are rather like people. There are some who will just never get along. And yet they have this strange affinity for one another."

"You mean they like to bicker, just like Aunt and Uncle Matlock."

"I will ask them to stay away from you. There is no reason why you should have to endure their ill-tempers."

"I wish you could warn Aunt Catherine and Anne away as well."

He guffawed. "As do I. Perhaps, though, I might introduce someone I think you will find far more agreeable."

"You are thinking of Pemberley." Her shoulders slumped, and she pouted, an expression she really should have outgrown by now.

"Yes, I am. She is just a baby and not in possession of the bad habits of the older dragons you know."

"I do not like babies. They cry and are so messy, and one is never certain of what they want."

"I will grant you that, but baby dragons are somewhat different. She hatched able to talk, you see."

"She can talk? I did not realize. The notes you gave me did not mention that." Her tone softened.

"You have read them?"

"Yes. They were very interesting, and entertaining. Your Miss Bennet writes very well you know. Very personable, almost as though I know her."

His Miss Bennet?

"I am pleased you feel that way. Pemberley is very fond of Miss Elizabeth, and if you feel warmth toward her, then you already have one thing in common."

"I suppose that would make it easier. I have never had anything in common with a dragon before."

It might not be much, but it was the first positive thing she had ever said about meeting a dragon.

"Come then. I think it is safe to take the curricle again."

They climbed in and headed toward the lair.

He stopped the carriage a quarter of a mile from the cavern. The horse would not tolerate getting closer than that to the major dragons. Who could blame it? Pemberley's first meal was horsemeat.

Dragon musk hung on the breeze. Georgiana hesitated.

He tucked her hand into the crook of his arm. "It will be well. I promise you."

She allowed him to lead her to the cavern.

"Rosings! We approach. I bring Georgiana. May we enter?"

"You brought her!" Pemberley bounded out to greet them. Her baby legs and wings still uncoordinated and clumsy, she tripped and landed at Georgiana's feet.

Georgina giggled.

"I brought my sister to meet you." Darcy helped Pemberley to her feet. "May I present Georgiana."

Pemberley cocked her head and squinted, sniffing Georgiana. "Georg ... gor ... Gigi?"

Georgiana held out her hand, a hint of a smile playing on her lips. "You may call me Gigi if that is easier for you."

"You not her." Pemberley slumped, her head hanging nearly to the ground.

"Miss Bennet," Darcy whispered.

Georgiana glared at him and mouthed *I know*. She knelt beside Pemberley.

Darcy edged back. Her reaction was unmannerly, but at the same time, very sympathetic to the drakling. Best not correct it now.

"I recently read something she wrote ... to my brother ... would you like me to tell you about it?"

"From her?"

"Yes, from her."

"Tell me." Pemberley laid her head in Georgiana's lap.

Darcy held his breath and tiptoed away. Somehow it just made sense that Miss Elizabeth would be at the center of such an auspicious beginning.

Rosings waited for him just inside the cavern. The creased brow and half-lidded eyes were not good signs.

"Cowntess, are you well?" He bowed.

"You well know that I am not." How did she manage an expression so like Aunt Catherine's? She snuffed hot, acrid breath in his face.

"I have nothing to do with the mandates of the Blue Order." He edged back a step.

"But you will use them to your ends."

"There is nothing untoward about that."

"Except that I must now deal with an angry Keeper. I do not appreciate it when you upset her." Rosings snorted. A blob of slime landed on his cheek.

He rubbed his handkerchief on his cheek before the slime burned his skin. That handkerchief would be ruined. Best not put it back in his pocket. "I am sure you can manage both of them."

Rosings glowered and bared her fangs. "Do not forget that I am doing you a favor. I expect—"

"Brother!"

"Pray excuse me." He dashed from the lair. Just as well, that conversation was not going to go well, regardless.

Georgiana waved him over. She sat beside Pemberley, one hand around her sinewy neck.

"What is wrong?" He knelt beside them.

"She is not her," Pemberley whined.

"No, I am not. We fully agree on the matter." She stroked Pemberley's head. "Look at the scales around her feet."

Darcy examined them. "They do seem a bit rough."

"Miss Bennet's pages describe something very like this that she calls 'scale mites.'"

"My feet itch."

"Dragons are always itchy." Darcy scratched Pemberley's chin.

"Not my chin, my feet!"

"She—that is 'her'—writes to say that the affected scales should first be scrubbed with vinegar, then anointed with sweet oil mixed with that hot seasoning Cook likes. We should put sachets of wormwood in her nest, too, to keep away the mites."

"I want do what her says. Please." Pemberley blinked up at him with huge baleful eyes.

"Of course, of course." He patted her head.

"May I take care of it? I can ask Cook for what we need. I am sure there is wormwood in the still room. The instructions seem very simple."

"By all means." Did she really think that he would object?

"And you tell her my feet itch?" Pemberley nudged Georgiana's elbow.

"I will write her a letter and tell her anything you wish."

"And I will take it to the post myself." Darcy nodded, smiling broadly.

"You will teach me read and make letter for her? Her said you would." Pemberley leaned into Georgiana hard enough to make her stumble.

She hugged the dragon's head close. "I will teach you whatever you like."

"You not her, but you nice. Want my bone now. Meet my dog?" Pemberley waddled off, presumably to find both, Georgiana following after.

What an astonishing transformation.

One more debt he owed a certain Miss Bennet.

Darcy tucked Georgiana's letter to Miss Elizabeth into his pocket and slipped out of her chambers. He sauntered down the long corridor towards his own chambers. A brief stop for his coat and he would be away to the post office before any would think to notice him gone. Except Georgiana, and she would probably be glad for his temporary absence.

Perhaps he should not have overseen her letter writing so closely. Given her expression, it was probably intrusive and controlling. But if she understood, she could hardly blame him. She might even agree.

It was utterly maddening to have so much to tell someone, so many questions to ask, and be utterly and completely unable to communicate in any way. Suggesting words, and phrases, and the occasional paragraph to Georgiana was the closest he could come to actually writing to Miss Elizabeth himself.

And he had so many things he needed to say.

Miss Elizabeth had brought such great comfort to little Pemberley with her suggestions on teething. Even Rosings was grateful, no longer subjected to the whining and tempers of the suffering drakling. And the treatment for the scale mites! Both dragons were benefiting from the thorough scrubbing and anointing that he and Georgiana had given them.

Of course, he was the one to scrub Rosings. Neither Aunt Catherine nor Anne would never stoop to such personal attentions to anyone, man or dragon.

That seemed to be what set Miss Elizabeth apart from every other Dragon Keeper he had encountered. There seemed to be no limits on what she would do for them, ignoble as it may be. Washing, scrubbing, scratching, petting, listening—no service was too humble for her to offer them. And they uniformly loved her for it. Even crusty Rosings seemed to be developing a soft spot for Miss Elizabeth solely on the basis of Pemberley's and Walker's recommendations.

"Darcy."

He jumped. Blast and botheration! Why was she not still asleep? It was at least an hour before she usually rose.

He turned slowly, gathering his composure, and bowed from his shoulders. "Good morning, Anne."

Light from the hall window silhouetted her, making it difficult to see her face. But the swirl of taffeta was unmistakable. No comfortable morning dress for her, no, she was dressed for the marriage mart.

He dragged his hand down his face.

"It is indeed a good morning, I think. Will you accompany me to breakfast?" She reached for his arm.

He edged just out of reach. "Forgive me, but I have already partaken. I am on my way to Hunsford."

"Hunsford? Whatever for? Surely you could send a servant for you." She cast about as if looking for one.

"I very much like a morning ride."

"Then take the gig, or the curricle, or the phaeton, and I shall come with you."

Darcy turned aside to roll his eyes. "I did not think you liked to be out in the morning air. I seem to recall it disagreeing with your constitution."

"I am feeling particularly well this morning. I am sure it will agree with me."

"I intend to visit the post office. You dislike the post master."

She balanced her hands on her hips. "Why, it sounds as if you do not wish me to accompany you this morning."

"I am rather accustomed to keeping to myself in the mornings."

"You will have to get used to my company at some point." She smiled and batted her eyes. "Do not offer me that stupid look. A married man has to spend some time with his wife."

"I am in no mood to have this discussion once again. I have entirely enough to manage with little Pemberley. I cannot possibly see to the needs of two dragons and two estates."

She flicked the idea away. "Hire stewards to attend the land. That is simple enough."

"What of the dragons? You hardly attend to Rosings' needs as it is. How do you think you will attend the needs of a drakling?"

"You are spoiling that creature entirely too much. Leave her to Rosings and it will all be well. You see, for our lifetimes, Pemberley will live here with her brood mother. Rosings will care for her, and all is settled."

"And in what book of dragon lore did you find such a ridiculous plan?" He clutched his temples.

"Book of lore? It is common sense, Darcy. Can you not see?"

"Most certainly not! It is a recipe for disaster—utter and complete disaster."

"What is more natural than a brood mother taking care of her young? You make this far too complicated. Any reasonably intelligent person—"

"Would realize that they had no idea of what they did not know, especially about a creature as rare, secretive, and dangerous as a firedrake!"

"There you go, prattling on again."

He took her shoulders in his hands. "Do you know how the firedrake population is kept in check?"

"They only lay eggs once every one hundred years."

"Even that is not enough. Like most top predators, they also are apt to kill off their young."

Her eyes bulged, and she gaped.

"Once Pemberley hits her first growth spurt and requires a substantial increase in her feedings, Rosings will see her as a threat. If I do not remove her to her own territory before then, Rosings will likely kill the competition for her prey."

"Surely you jest."

"Perhaps you should study your dragon lore and confirm my assertions before you try to call me out for deceit."

Her brow knit, and her eyes narrowed. A tantrum was imminent. He clenched his teeth.

"How dare you—" She stomped.

He answered in kind, nearly on her toes. "And how dare you think I would allow such an ignorant, selfish girl the care and management of a creature as rare as a baby firedrake."

She jumped back. "One whose egg you seem to have had stolen right out from under you."

"Enough!"

"You will have to do better than that. I have lived with Mother all my life." She turned on her heel and stormed away.

He stormed to the morning room where Aunt Catherine still held audience with Fitzwilliam.

Darcy pointed at him, then at the door.

Fitzwilliam jumped to his feet and dashed out. Smart, smart man.

Aunt Catherine planted her hands on the table and rose, eyes blazing. "What is the meaning of this, Darcy? How dare you …"

He stepped forward and glowered. Apparently, he had mastered his father's expression after all.

She returned to her seat and poured a cup of tea for him. "You look troubled. Why do you not sit down and tell me of it?"

He folded his arms over his chest. "I have had enough. I will tolerate no more."

"What precisely is that supposed to mean?"

"Georgiana and I, and Fitzwilliam if he chooses, will be leaving today."

Her head came up sharply. "You cannot leave. Pemberley is far too young to travel all the way to Derbyshire now."

"I am well aware of that."

"Then stop with your ridiculous bluffing. I do not appreciate your masculine posturing and bullying."

"We will take rooms at the Hunsford Inn or perhaps take a town house there."

She lost color in her face. "You cannot do that! Think of the talk. What will people say, you leaving my home but staying on in Hunsford?"

"Frankly, I do not care. It is not my problem."

"Gossip is always a problem! You must be concerned with your reputation."

"You mean your reputation, for which I do not give two shillings." He snorted.

"You would do this to me?"

"I am doing nothing to you. I am only acting in the best interest of myself and my sister. The situation here is intolerable, and I will have it no longer." He bounced his fist off the table.

"What is intolerable? You are talking nonsense."

"Anne still wanders about insisting that I will marry her—an illusion you are obviously supporting, despite the message Fitzwilliam brought from the Blue Order."

"That nonsense? They offer alternatives, not requirements. They do not stand in the way of your marriage to Anne." She rolled her eyes, but a light sheen appeared on her upper lip.

"Anne is the most ignorant excuse for a Keeper I have ever encountered. She knows nothing about firedrakes—she actually suggested that she and I take residence here and allow Rosings to raise Pemberley!"

She flicked the idea aside. "She is merely forgetful in her distress. I am sure you rattled the poor dear with all your shouting and stomping. You must remember her delicate constitution."

"Call off your daughter and your cockatrix. Give Walker and I some peace or I will set my man to packing immediately." He slapped the table.

Aunt Catherine covered her eyes with her hand and huffed. "I will speak to Cait. It is possible she has been … overzealous in her pursuit. Clearly that has not worked. I will suggest to her that it is time for a different tack."

"Walker will appreciate that, but what of Anne?"

"You and Anne have been promised since your infancy. It has been the dearest wish of your mother and me that you should unite our two great estates—"

He held up an open hand. "Pray stop. I know the litany. I have heard it since I was ten years old. That does not change my mind."

"Has Anne even met little Pemberley? You have complained that the drakling is pining for that Bennet girl. Introduce her to Anne. I have every confidence that she will immediately recognize Anne's superiority and quite forget about Miss Bennet. There has never been a dragon that has not taken to Anne."

"If they do not take to one another, then you shall instruct Anne to importune me no further on the matter of marriage."

She stared at him, jaw silently working. Clearly, she wanted another option, but none was forthcoming.

"Or shall I instruct my valet to pack my trunks?"

"Very well. You are as stubborn and unreasonable as your father."

"I shall take that as a compliment. Good day." He bowed from his shoulders and sauntered out.

He called for his horse and headed for Hunsford.

How could Aunt Catherine really think it possible that Pemberley would take to Anne as she had to Miss Elizabeth? Any fool could see that was utterly and completely impossible. Anne barely had the time of day for Quincy and flatly ignored Blanche—a creature that lived in the kitchen was far beneath her notice.

Had Miss Elizabeth the opportunity, she would be sitting on the floor in the middle of the small upstairs sitting room, listening to Quincy's stories of all the guests that had stayed at Rosings. She would insist upon knowing about the dragons, not caring at all about the peers and nobility that had graced the rooms of Rosings Park. She would probably tease out his passion for shiny buttons and find some way to make sure he had new ones to add to his horde. He would introduce her to Blanche, and they would sit together in the kitchen, sipping warm milk and honey while that fairy dragon of hers preened Blanche's head ridge.

What a mistress she would make to a Dragon Keeping estate. Her lack of fortune might make her seem unworthy, but everything else about her declared her exceptional.

Everything.

He fingered the letter in his pocket. It would not do to let Pemberley know how much he missed her, too.

Chapter 6

A WEEK LATER, the Bennet family, including Mr. Collins, was invited to dine at Netherfield Park. Mama received the invitation with great effusions. How successful Jane had been in catching Mr. Bingley's attentions. Certainly, she would be well-settled soon. How wonderful it would be to have one—or even more—daughters married.

Papa harrumphed and shut himself in his study. He was not just playing the curmudgeon, though. His legs and feet were in a particularly bad way, so much so, he could hardly tolerate an evening away from home. Heaven forbid he openly declare such limitations, though. Far better to be difficult and grumpy.

Jane insisted Elizabeth assist her in preparing for the evening. As Elizabeth arranged her hair, she carried on about the wonders of Mr. Bingley. He was everything a young man should be. Well-mannered, kind, generous, thoughtful, handsome. Everything Jane needed a man to be.

Oh, to be so in love.

Not that she would ever know such a thing.

Elizabeth had not been back to Netherfield since the ball … the night that Pemberley hatched.

No, tears would not be helpful now. Besides, it was silly and foolish to weep for a dragon who was well Kept. Maddening as Darcy was, he doted on the hatchling and would ensure she was given every advantage a drakling could have. He even showed himself capable of affection for the dragon, despite spitefully tearing her away from Hertfordshire just because he could. What more could the baby need?

Elizabeth dabbed her eyes with a handkerchief and set it aside. No, she ought to bring it just in case. She tucked it, and a spare, into her reticule and met her sisters in the vestibule.

Papa saw them off and shuffled back into the house, reminding her with a final glance to be attentive to Mr. Collins.

Mama and Lydia started their chatter as soon as they entered the coach and did not stop until the driver helped them out at Netherfield's front door. Sometimes, their nonstop prattle was a distinct advantage. Mr. Collins could not get a word in and kept silent the entire way. Moreover, with no response demanded from her, she could continue her mental recitations of the conjugations of the dragon word 'to aerosolize one's poison' in the future perfect tense.

Mr. Collins handed her out of the coach himself and offered her his arm to walk in. The forced smile hurt her face, just a little, but she would get used to it.

Self-satisfied fool. Not your equal. Too bad there is no choice.

She looked over her shoulder, but there was no one there. Botheration, she needed to get her thoughts under control.

"Is there something wrong, cousin?" Mr. Collins peered over her shoulder.

"No, it is nothing. I merely though I heard something." She shrugged and proceeded into the house.

The housekeeper greeted them and led them to the drawing room. Mama seemed honored by the formality, which only pleased Jane. Good for them both to be happy.

The Bingleys and the Hursts waited for them in the drawing room, rising to welcome them. If only she might slip away, perhaps back to the mapmaker's room for another glance at the dragon script written there. She had studied so much of that language recently; she might be able to make some of it out.

But alas, her absence would undoubtedly be noticed, and more importantly, the airborne venom would not yet have settled enough to make the sojourn safe. Perhaps Jane—and April, if necessary—could help her to secure an invitation in a few months.

Miss Bingley announced the dishes at the dining table. She set an excellent table, which Mama was good enough to remark upon for the first quarter hour of the meal. During said time, the footmen served an excellent carrot soup.

Across from her, Mr. Collins tucked his napkin into his collar and reached for the wrong spoon. Elizabeth cleared her throat, caught his eye and tapped the correct spoon. He quickly adjusted and continued on his way.

What was more remarkable, that he was so easily guided, a bit of a gudgeon really, or that he was so unperturbed about being led? While it was nice that he did not take offence, somehow it felt a little off-putting that he appeared to have no manly ego to injure.

Did Lady Catherine have someone at her table to offer him the same service, or did she perform it herself, with less subtlety of course? Perhaps his lack of ego served him well at that table.

"The mutton is excellent, Miss Bingley, just excellent. It puts me in mind of a favorite meal served at Rosings Park. Her Ladyship, Lady Catherine likes to serve it on Sundays, you see …"

Miss Bingley and Mrs. Hurst exchanged glances and rolled their eyes. It was rude, no doubt, but who could blame them? At the foot of the table, Bingley seemed unaware of any conversation besides his own with Jane.

The word 'besotted' might well be applied.

No, it would not suit to pursue those thoughts. Jealousy was unbecoming.

"With it she would instruct her cooks to serve a particular sauce, which originated in the south of France I am told. There is very little of French cuisine that she finds tolerable to be sure, but this particular dish …"

"Does she employ a French man-cook?" Mama asked, dabbing her lips with her napkin.

Mama had always held a not-too-secret ambition to hire such a man-cook.

"She did at one time, but found his dishes presumptuous, and he was dismissed. She says English cooking is far superior, and indeed she is correct." Collins sipped his wine.

Mrs. Hurst sniggered behind her hand.

"Preposterous!" Mr. Hurst brought his hand down hard enough to rattle nearby glasses.

Mr. Collins sputtered and drew a breath deep enough to support a great many words.

Mary nudged Elizabeth with her elbow, sending her an alarmed glance.

Elizabeth coughed and caught Mr. Collins' gaze, barely shaking her head. "It is fortunate that there are so many styles of food and wine available to us that everyone might claim a different favorite, is it not?"

Yes, it was a vacuous remark, but with it she set Mr. Collins on a different course of conversation. Who knew that he and Mr. Hurst would share a fascination with fine wine? At least it kept the conversation on safe ground for the remainder of the meal.

What relief, when Miss Bingley led the ladies away to the drawing room. Elizabeth lingered behind her sisters, savoring a few moments of peace. Keeping Mr. Collins under good regulation at the dinner table was far more exhausting than managing all four of the Gardiner children at once.

A painting she had not noticed on her prior stay at Netherfield caught her eye.

Something about it felt very familiar ... it must have been done by the mapmaker. Though a landscape, not a map, his style was too distinct. The strokes, the shading—and the dragon script in the bottom corner! Her head raced as she leaned close, mouthing the syllables as she read.

The words meant destination or meeting place. Or at least she thought they did. But what could that have to do with a bit of landscape that looked like nearly every coastline in England?

"Lizzy, do not dawdle! Miss Bingley is worried that you have not joined us!" Mama took her by the arm and dragged her to the drawing room.

Conversations swirled about her, but how could she pay attention to matters of lace and sleeve design when there was dragon script in that painting? Wait, what? That same style marked several paintings in this room as well. How had she never seen it?

With a muttered excuse, she wandered to the walls and studied the paintings. Two that hung side by side appeared to be different views of the same coastline portrayed in the corridor. Neither contained dragon script, but the shadows in one looked suspiciously like a wyvern, and wyrm tracks marked the sand in another.

Did anyone at Netherfield recognize these for what they were? What a fool she had been, so caught up in searching for maps, that she missed what was right in front of her!

She hurried to a larger canvas along the far wall. The floorboards below her squeaked loudly enough to stop Mama's praise of dinner, but for only a moment.

Elizabeth released a tightly held breath and focused on the painting. Shadows, tracks of not just wyrms, but of a basilisk, and an amphithere feather, there in the tree! It had a title plaque that read "The English Coast," but faint scratches in dragon script below the lettering read 'Uther's Sanctuary.'

And there, concealed among a grassy bit, more wispy script.

Dragon fire! What was she seeing? If she could just commit those figures to memory, she might be able to look them up when she got home.

"Are you well, Cousin?"

Why did the gentlemen have to repair to the drawing room now?

"Are these landscapes not fascinating? I have not noticed them before." Her voice was high and tight. Hopefully he was not good at discerning falsehoods.

He shrugged. "I am sure they are good enough as such things go. Lady Catherine believes portraiture a much higher form of art. Rosings Park is filled with the most exquisite portraits …"

As long as he kept talking, she could continue memorizing the dragon script. Who would have thought his prattle might serve her so well. She murmured monosyllabic questions and encouragements to keep him going as long as possible.

"Come, I see some portraits on the other side of the room. I am sure it will be far more satisfying to examine those." He all but dragged her away from the landscape. "See here, we might examine the painter's evocation of emotion through the remarkable expression of the eyes."

He was wrong. The eyes were flat and dull, like the rest of the portrait. If asked, which of course she was not, she would have said that the portrait was a journeyman's effort, like some of the maps upstairs, done to learn the skills which were later applied to the landscapes across the room.

Were there more like those in the house? She took several steps across squeaky boards toward the wall of landscapes.

Ignore the landscapes. They are unimportant.

What? She rubbed at her itching ear.

Collins glanced at her. Impertinent man! He was becoming far too intrusive, whispering such things in her ear.

"Come, we should join the rest of the party. They are setting up card tables, and it would not do to leave them for want of players." He trundled away, clearly expecting her to follow.

Mama turned their way and waved.

Now she had little choice. Pray her memory was good enough to retain those figures until she returned to her commonplace book.

Two equally unpleasant alternatives stood before her: conversation with the ladies and Mr. Bingley, or cards. She joined Mary, Mr. Collins, and Mr. Hurst at quadrille. Thank heavens it was a favorite of Lady Catherine, forcing Mr. Collins to become proficient—or at least proficient enough that she did not have to guide his every move.

Several of those painted symbols looked familiar. One resembled 'escape' or 'flee.' It was not a word commonly used among major dragons. The words connoted a dire circumstance, one serious enough it should be somewhere in the dragon histories.

Perhaps that beach had been a place that dragons had been slain before the Accords, and Uther had declared it a sanctuary? But would not such a place have been clearly marked in the Annals of the Blue Order? They were a sentimental lot overall. It seemed odd that they would not indulge in the opportunity for reverence and celebration of such a place.

What other beaches were relevant in dragon history? Perhaps, Papa knew more. Maybe what had happened there was so horrible that it became a shrine of sorts, where only the highest members of the Order meditated? But then the painter would have had to be a highly-ranked member of the Order to have seen it. Papa hardly made mention of Netherfield's past resident, so that was unlikely, too.

How maddening! None of this made sense!

"Lizzy!" Mary kicked her under the table. "Do take your turn to play."

She hastily played a card, much to the chagrin of her tablemates. Clearly it had been the wrong choice. Thankfully the game ended a few moments later, with Mr. Hurst declaring gleeful victory. The man relished winning a little too much.

Mr. Collins insisted the loss of a few pennies playing was entirely agreeable in this company. Better still, Lady Catherine would not find fault with it at all.

How comforting.

Miss Bingley moved toward the pianoforte.

"An excellent thought, Caroline. Dancing is definitely in order." Mr. Bingley beckoned to Mr. Hurst and Mr. Collins for help in moving bits and bobs of furniture. In short order, the floor was clear, and he extended his hand to Jane.

"Shall we, Cousin Elizabeth?"

Elizabeth bit her tongue and accepted Mr. Collins' arm.

Hurst was still sober enough to dance, so he invited Mary to the center of the room. Mama insisted that Lydia stand up with Kitty, giving them a tidy, four-couple set.

Miss Bingley's fingers danced over the keys, in a lively country dance. She really was a superior musician. It would be difficult for the rest of them to follow her in playing for the party. Such a gracious hostess.

Elizabeth craned her neck. Perhaps if she stood in the right spot whilst dancing, she might study the paintings a little more.

They lined up, paintings just in view. But Mr. Collins' dancing! Had there ever been such a man, with absolutely no sense of rhythm? Could he not simply count to eight? Just eight, it should not have been so difficult. He had plenty of fingers to assist in the process if he needed.

The only saving grace was that he was as easy to lead as Mary claimed. A tap to her own shoulder to indicate the next direction, an extended hand to cue his own, and he managed to keep up with the rest of the dancers well enough.

How exhausting, thinking for both of them and anticipating what instruction he would need next. All of the easy grace and the fun of the dance floor was lost in the work of shepherding him through the steps without mishap. Not to mention she had not a speck of attention left to devote to the paintings.

After the first set, Mrs. Hurst took Miss Bingley's place at the pianoforte. Mr. Hurst invited Kitty to dance and Mary relieved her as Mr. Collins' partner. Since Mr. Bingley was not about to give up Jane's companionship, Elizabeth danced the set with Lydia. Though she was silly and flirty, Lydia was an excellent dancer, and freed Elizabeth's mind to consider landscapes and dragons.

Gracious! Had anyone noticed that the feet of the pianoforte were dragon's feet, talons wrapped around large balls—no, they were globes! Dragon wings graced the backs of chairs and several small pillows were embroidered with brilliant amphithere feathers. The entire room was decorated with dragons! She had been so preoccupied with searching for maps that she had been blind to what was plainly before her!

Lydia grabbed her hands and spun her in a rapid turn, laughing heartily. The music ended, and Elizabeth staggered, dizzy and breathless.

Mr. Bingley kept hold of Jane's hand and waited until all eyes were on them. "I, we that is, have happy news to share! Miss Bennet has consented to be my wife!"

Mama shrieked and jumped up, nearly bowling Mr. Collins over in her haste to reach Jane.

"Oh, my dearest girl! I am so proud of you. I knew you could not be so beautiful for nothing. I am sure your father will approve."

Mr. Bingley smiled and chuckled in a self-satisfied sort of way. "I have already received his approbation, madam."

Another ear-splitting shriek. "I knew he would. I simply knew he would!"

Miss Bingley winced and grimaced. Mrs. Hurst mirrored the expression. Was it only Mama of whom they disapproved, or of Jane as well? Something about the way they narrowed their eyes made one wonder.

Lydia and Kitty clapped and bounced like little girls, each clutching at one of Jane's hands.

"I am very happy for you both. I cannot imagine a happier match." Elizabeth stepped slightly closer and smiled.

At least she would have one sister settled close to Longbourn. That was a good thing, indeed.

"What a very fine thing," Mr. Collins said at her shoulder.

Why did he always have to stand so close?

"It is always a desirable thing when the eldest daughter marries first." Something about his smile was entirely smug.

And nauseating.

If a man's thoughts could be writ upon his face, Mr. Collins' were inscribed with broad brushstrokes of paint.

Mary squeezed her hand and nodded. She had much greater faith in Elizabeth's fortitude than she did.

They stayed at Netherfield until the wee hours. Mama's effusions continued until nearly dawn as she indulged her considerations of what wedding clothes might be required and whether or not Mr. Bingley would commission a new carriage for the occasion.

The next morning, Jane came to her room to convey Papa's desire that Elizabeth join them for breakfast. Everyone was so happy this morning. It was only right that Elizabeth share in it, too. It was a testament to Jane's character that she could believe that, and only that, was Papa's intent.

Elizabeth turned to April. "You should stay here. I cannot imagine there would be any advantage—"

April zipped around the room. "Will this not affect me as much as it will you? I insist—I insist. You must allow me to know for myself what transpires. Wear your shawl, the blue one that the Gardiners gave you. I can hide in the folds of that and neither of them" — she meant Papa and Mr. Collins— "will notice I am there."

"Only if you promise me that you will not flit about as you are now if you get upset. If you cannot stay still, promise me you will come straight back here, to your cage, and lock yourself inside. Can you promise me that?"

"You do not have to treat me like one of the children." April landed on her shoulder and worked her way into the folds of the shawl. "I am quite capable of conducting myself with decorum."

Elizabeth stood before the looking glass and adjusted the folds in her shawl, rendering April quite invisible.

As much as she might like it, she dare not delay the inevitable any further. Dragon Keeping required sacrifices from all parties. The dragons resigned many freedoms as much as the Keepers did. She would be able to fulfill her responsibilities. Mary had shown her that she could. It would be well. It would be.

The entire family was gathered in the breakfast room. Sunbeams danced from the facets on the crystal glasses to the mirrors behind the candle sconces. The fragrance of fresh baked goods and warm jam invited her to indulge.

Mama, Kitty, and Lydia huddled close to Jane, giggling and whispering.

"Come join me, Lizzy." Papa pointed at the empty chair between him and Mary. Mr. Collins sat on his other side.

She sat, avoiding eye contact with him and Mr. Collins.

"So, what do you think of this business of Jane's?" Papa's large mug of willow bark tea was nearly empty and a second one steeped nearby. Any good humor he demonstrated was probably an affectation for Jane's and Mama's sakes.

"I know she is very happy. As is Mama." She kept her face turned toward Jane.

"I am pleased that he did not dither about as some young men are wont to do and that she did not decide to play those games of modesty that seem so in vogue among delicate young ladies. I approve very much." He glanced back at Mr. Collins.

Mr. Collins blinked several times; his eyes widened, and he looked Elizabeth's way. He cleared his throat. The room went silent and all eyes turned on him. "May I hope, sir, the honor of a private audience with your fair daughter Elizabeth in the course of this morning?"

Mama jumped to attention and fluttered her hands in front of her face. "Oh dear! Yes, certainly. I am sure Lizzy will be very happy! I am sure she can have no objection."

Elizabeth bit her lip, her temples pounding in time with her heart. Good thing that she had not yet eaten. It might be months before she was able to again.

Mary gripped her hand under the table. "This is a good thing, for everyone. You will be very satisfied, I am sure. Longbourn will have an excellent mistress."

"Might I make use of your study, sir?" Collins bowed and gestured toward the door.

Papa grunted and stared—no, glared—at her. "That is an excellent notion. In fact, Lizzy, I insist upon you going to my study and hearing Mr. Collins out."

Best get the business over as soon and as quietly as possible. Is that what the condemned thought on the way to Tyburn?

She followed Mr. Collins to Papa's study. April launched from her shawl just before Mr. Collins shut the door. The typical piles of books and papers had been neatly tucked away, leaving the room as tidy as the rest of the house. Almost as though he antici-pated—or actively planned—Collins' request.

April alighted on the heirloom dragon perch, look-ing a bit silly, a tiny little thing on furniture designed for a cockatrice. What did she think she was doing, insisting she have her share in the conversation?

It might be better to shoo her out of the window, but she settled so sweetly and gave such a happy cheep, Mr. Collins looked upon her and smiled. If he tolerated April's presence now when Elizabeth needed the support, why contradict him?

She sat near the perch and stared out the window. "The weather is very pleasant today, is it not?"

He centered himself in front of the fireplace and straightened his coat. "It is. But that is not the point of this interview. Surely you can have no doubt regarding what I wish to discuss."

She stammered random syllables, her face flushing hot. "Pray sir, there is no need, I am sure I am not—"

His expressions hovered between ingratiating and lascivious. Mr. Bingley never looked at Jane that way.

"Believe me, my dear Miss Elizabeth, your modesty, so far from doing you any disservice, rather adds to your other perfections. You would have been less amiable in my eyes had there not been this little unwillingness, but allow me to assure you that I have your respected father's permission for this address. Only just last night we talked on this very matter. However much your natural delicacy may lead you to dissemble, my attentions have been too marked to be mistaken. Almost as soon as I entered the house, I singled you out as the companion of my future life."

Did he really think his gawking at Jane or his disappointment to learn that another had claim on the first object of his interest went unnoticed?

"But before I am run away with by my feelings on this subject, perhaps it will be advisable for me to state my reasons for marrying—and moreover for coming into Hertfordshire with the design of selecting a wife, as I did."

The idea of Mr. Collins, with all his solemn composure, being run away with his feelings—it would be laughable if he were not so very sincere. Even if he were run away with his feelings, they were only feelings of self-interest and self-congratulation, nothing noble or laudable in any of it.

He dusted the front of his coat and pulled his shoulders back. "My reasons for marrying are, first, that I think it a right thing for every clergyman in easy circumstances like myself to set the example of matrimony in his parish. Secondly, that I am convinced it will add very greatly to my happiness." He licked his lips.

Oh, there was that horrid skin crawling expression again!

"And thirdly—which perhaps I ought to have mentioned earlier, that it is the particular advice and recommendation of the very noble lady whom I have the honor of calling patroness. Twice has she condescended to give me her opinion, unasked too, on this subject. It was but the very Saturday night before I left Hunsford—between our pools at quadrille, while Mrs. Jenkinson was arranging Miss de Bourgh's footstool—"

Would it kill him to come to his point? Would that she could be so lucky!

"—that she said, 'Mr. Collins, you must marry. A clergyman like you must marry. Choose properly, choose a gentlewoman for my sake; and for your own, let her be an active, useful sort of person, not brought up high, but able to make a small income go a good way. This is my advice. Find such a woman as soon as you can, bring her to Hunsford, and I will visit her.' Allow me, by the way, to observe, my fair cousin that I do not reckon the notice and kindness of Lady Catherine de Bourgh as among the least of the advantages in my power to offer. You will find her manners beyond anything I can describe. Your wit and vivacity I think must be acceptable to her, especially when tempered with the silence and respect which her rank will inevitably excite."

Silence and respect were what he expected from her? Charming.

You should accept him. Put him and you out of your misery and just accept him.

She probably should, it was not likely to get any better.

At least the knowledge that Lady Catherine was a Dragon Keeper and Dragon Friend made the prospect of Rosings Park less dreadful. Any place with dragons had to have its appeals.

"This much for my general intention in favor of matrimony. It remains to be told why my views were directed to Longbourn instead of my own neighborhood, where I assure you there are many amiable young women."

The reason for his interest is obvious. Must we have a recitation?

April squawked a soft warning sound. She cocked her head and squinted—the expression she used when she was listening intently.

Elizabeth bit her tongue. It would be best that neither one of them respond to the obvious insult, especially when Mr. Collins seemed entirely unaware of having offered it.

"But the fact is, that being, as I am, to inherit this estate after the death of your honored father, who, however, may live many years longer, I could not satisfy myself without resolving to choose a wife from among his daughters, that the loss to them might be as little as possible, when the melancholy event takes place—which, however, as I have already said, may not be for several years. This has been my motive, my fair cousin, and I flatter myself it will not sink me in your esteem."

It really is gracious of him. Staying at your home, forever, knowing none of your sisters or mother need to fear is a good thing.

"Indeed, it is most kind and gracious of you," she stammered and squeezed her temples. She had prepared herself for this moment. Why were her thoughts running away with her?

April cheeped and flapped her wings. "Do you hear it, too?"

Elizabeth's eyes widened, and she fell back into her chair as though slapped by an icy hand, its chill flowing across her face and neck in waves.

April heard a voice? A dragon voice?

Those words, they were not her own thoughts. Someone was attempting to persuade her!

But who?

Mr. Collins clasped his hands behind his back and paced in front of the fireplace. "And now nothing remains for me but to assure you in the most animated language of the violence of my affection."

He likes you. That is sufficient for now. Just give him your answer. Why draw out the unpleasantry?

It was a voice! Subtle and soft, but there could be no doubt now. She clutched her hands tight against the desire to brush away the trespass.

It was one thing for a dragon to persuade one who could not hear them. But to try persuasion on a Hearer—the very notion was indecent! Immoral. Illegal.

"To fortune I am perfectly indifferent, and shall make no demand of that nature on your father. I am well aware that it could not be complied with, and that one thousand pounds in the four per cents, which will not be yours till after your mother's decease, is all that you may ever be entitled to. On that head, therefore, I shall be uniformly silent, and you may assure yourself that no ungenerous reproach shall ever pass my lips when we are married." Mr. Collins pressed his fingers to his lips.

See how reasonable he is being? An excellent sign of a truly agreeable match.

She clutched the arms of her chair.

Make him an answer. What more do you need to hear?

"Stop!" She clapped her hands to her ears.

Mr. Collins staggered back, eyes bulging, jaw gaping.

She sprang to her feet and ducked behind the dragon perch, sucking in gulps of air against the drowning sensation. "Forgive me, sir, I am overwhelmed by your declarations."

He pulled his shoulders back and adjusted his lapels, eyes and jaw settling into their naturally smug attitudes.

If only she could catch her breath to speak. "Accept my thanks for the compliment you are paying me, I am very sensible of the honor of your proposals, but it is impossible for me to make you an answer right now."

"I understand," Mr. Collins, waved his hand in a formal flourish, "that it is usual with young ladies to reject the addresses of the man whom they secretly mean to accept, when he first applies for their favor, and that sometimes the refusal is repeated a second or even a third time. I am therefore by no means discouraged by what you have just said, and shall hope to lead you to the altar ere long."

She stammered something even she did not understand.

"When I do myself the honor of speaking to you next on this subject, I shall hope to receive a more favorable answer than you have now given me. I am far from accusing you of cruelty at present, because I know it to be the established custom of your sex to reject a man on the first application, and perhaps you have even now said as much to encourage my suit as would be consistent with the true delicacy of the female character."

Do not be a fool! Accept him now!

Where was the voice coming from?

She edged toward the door. "Is it not a demonstration of conceit that you presuppose my response?"

"You must give me leave to flatter myself, my dear cousin that your hesitancy toward my addresses is merely words. My reasons for believing it are briefly these: it does not appear to me that my hand is unworthy of your acceptance, or that the establishment I can offer would be any other than highly desirable. My situation in life, my connections with the family of de Bourgh, and my relationship to your own, are circumstances highly in its favor. You should take it into further consideration that in spite of your manifold attractions, it is by no means certain that another offer of marriage may ever be made you. Your portion is unhappily so small that it will in all likelihood undo the effects of your loveliness and amiable qualifications. As I must therefore conclude that you are not serious in your rejection of me, I shall choose to attribute it to your wish of increasing my love by suspense, according to the usual practice of elegant females."

He is correct. No other man is ever going to want you.

She gasped. Was it not enough that voice would try to persuade her? Now insults as well? Utterly intolerable.

The voice was coming from beneath them.

"Pray, understand me, sir, I have no pretension whatever to that kind of elegance which consists in tormenting a respectable man. I would rather be paid the compliment of being believed sincere in whatever I express. I thank you again and again for the honor you have done me in your proposal, but you must now excuse me. I am far too overwhelmed to think." She fled from the room, April flying in her wake.

7
Chapter

Foolish girl! Do not run off. You will lose this opportunity.

"Enough!" She stomped and ran for the cellar door. It flung open with a grouchy creak. The dark, narrow steps warranted caution, but she was long past any kind of restraint. Only the hand of Providence stayed her from breaking her neck on the way down.

Scrapes and slithers, deep down and far away into the dragon tunnels, taunted her. Cold, damp air enveloped her in teasing silence as dangling cobwebs tickled her face. But the musty, dusty smell of dragon was unmistakable. A dragon in the cellars had been trying to influence her response to Collins.

Coward. Longbourn was a big, scaly coward.

April landed on her shoulder. "Will you go after him?"

"Not through the tunnels. Longbourn might not object to slithering in the dirt, but I do. I will see him in the woods." She gathered up her skirts and traipsed back up the uneven stairs.

Where was the family? Voices came from the morning room, so best head in the opposite direction.

Once clear of the house, she sprinted towards the woods. Hidden in the cover of the trees, she paused in the dappled sunlight, panting hard. At least the air was not so cold that it hurt to gulp it down. She needed breath to speak, a great deal of it for all the things that she had to say!

April launched from her shoulder and zipped around the stand of small trees. "I do not know. I do not know."

"What do you not know?"

"The voice. I did not recognize it." If she kept buzzing about like that, she would whip herself into a senseless frenzy.

"Of course, you did not. It was a persuasive whisper. We have not heard it from him before because it is unethical for him to speak so to us."

"Still, I am not certain." April landed on a narrow branch, just above Elizabeth's head, panting.

"Who else could it be? There was a dragon in the cellar. You do not imagine for a moment that Longbourn would tolerate a strange dragon in his territory, much less in our house! He barely tolerates the minor dragons of his Keep."

"No, no, he would not. But the voice, it did not sound at all like him."

"I know you are afraid of him now. Perhaps you should not be here. Return to the house. I will handle this." She folded her arms over her chest and scanned the woods for signs of the wyvern.

"No, I will not leave you. I would see how he defends himself for such behavior." She huddled close to Elizabeth's neck.

She pulled her shawl over April and cupped her hands around her mouth. "Longbourn! Where are you? Longbourn! I would speak to you immediately." She stomped.

A black bird cawed in the distance.

"Stop this right now. You cannot avoid me. If you do not come out, I will come to you. Decide where we will converse, for it will happen one way or another. Longbourn, come out!" She grabbed a large branch and slammed it against the nearest tree trunk in a deep resounding tattoo.

A thunderous thump answered.

At least he was listening.

The ground trembled beneath her feet. Trees shook and limbs rattled, raining dry leaves upon them. Longbourn crashed through a curtain of saplings. "So, is it done?"

She batted leaves from her face. "Is it done? Is it done? That is all you have to say after your shameless behavior?"

He pulled back and blinked, squeezing his eyes shut tight several times.

If he tried to play dumb, she might just swat his nose. "It was not enough that you provoked Papa into ordering Collins to propose to me. You had to try to manipulate me, too."

"What are you talking about?"

She clenched her fists until they shook. "Do not insult me by pretending not to know. I may be a woman, but that hardly makes me a fool. I would thank you not to treat me as one."

"I will treat you that way when you are acting like one. I have no idea what you are talking about." He lashed his tail across the ground, clearing a wide swath.

"You were eavesdropping in the cellar whilst Collins offered the most ridiculous proposal I have ever heard."

"How would you know it was ridiculous? You have never heard a proposal. You have not had an offer of marriage before."

"That is hardly the point here."

"How can you fault a proposal as ridiculous if you have nothing else to compare it to?" He sat back lightly on his haunches.

"Do not play that game with me! The material issue is that you were listening in on a conversation to which you were not invited."

"I was not."

"There was a dragon in the cellar, one that ran away from me when I went down to see." She tucked her elbows under her shawl and balanced her hands on her hips. She would never be as big as the wyvern, but whatever size she could muster to her advantage would be helpful.

"And you assume that was me? It sounds like a trick of that sneaky tatzelwurm who now lives with you." He cocked his head, the very picture of innocence.

"There is no way Rumblkins could have made those noises. They came from a major dragon."

"But you admit he might have tried?"

"Hardly! He detests Collins and would not have tried to persuade me to marry him. He would sooner see you eat Collins."

"It was agreed you would marry him. Why would you need to be persuaded?"

"Why indeed?" She threw her arms in the air, very near his face. "I am at a loss, but I expect you will have a rather good explanation for the dragon voice from the cellar, trying to persuade me to marry Collins."

"I did no such thing." He slapped the ground with his tail.

Now he was trying to intimidate, the bully.

"You would entertain another major dragon in your territory and permit it to meddle in the affairs of your Keepers?"

"It was not me." He stomped hard enough to shake the trees.

"Stop lying to me." Now he had done it—provoked her to shout. Few could boast that accomplishment. "Why would you violate our relationship that way? A Dragon does not try to persuade his Keeper. It is not a done thing."

"I did not!"

"Just like you did not scoop me up like a bit of prey, rendering me unconscious, breathing venom in my face."

"I would not have hurt you. The venom was an accident. You made me so angry." At least he had the grace to sound remorseful.

"No, you lost control. That is no fault of mine. You may not have liked what I said, but you violated my trust. And your stunt today did nothing to earn it back."

They stared eye to eye until he turned away, grumbling.

"You promised to marry Collins."

"No, I did not. I said I would see. And perhaps you do not believe it, but I have been diligently working to adjust to the idea of a husband I can hardly tolerate and who certainly does not respect me. I have been trying to learn how to manage him and see that I might have some sort of a decent life with him."

"Then that is good, and it is all settled." He sat back, mouth widening in an eerie wyvern smile.

"Hardly. I did so in good faith that we would all be working toward an amenable future. But you have stooped to trying to manipulate me to get your way, not even treating me like a Keeper, just some inconvenient warm-blood. I will not have it. I cannot live without respect, and you have shown me no more than Mr. Collins does."

"You are not being fair. I told you I did nothing, and I meant it."

"Declaring it so does not make it so. I came here hoping that you might own to what you did and we could come to some resolution, but I see that was a pointless hope. If you will not be honest with me, there is nothing more I can do."

"What does that mean?" The smile disappeared, replaced by deep, worried lines.

"I will not live like this." She wrapped her shawl tight around her and stormed away.

Arrogant, maddening, cold-blooded—

"What if he was telling the truth?" April whispered in her ear.

"Give me one reason to believe he might be, just one tiny bit of evidence to hold on to, and I will consider it. I promise you, I will." It would be so much easier if she could.

"It is such a serious offense, and he has never shown any sign of violating the Accords before. Do you really think that he would do such a thing to you?"

"I would not have thought so until today ... until I heard it myself." She clutched her forehead.

April cuddled against her cheek. "What will you do now?"

"Return to the house and have a very long talk with Papa. He certainly cannot condone such behavior."

She slipped in the back door. Rumblkins met her several steps inside.

"We have been so worried since you ran off into the woods." He rubbed his long body around her ankles.

"Do you know anything about a dragon in the cellar this morning?" She crouched to fondle his silky ear tufts.

"There is often a dragon in the cellar. I saw no cause to worry."

"You see, April." She pressed her temples. "This is intolerable."

"What is?" Rumblkins reared up and reached his paws up as high as he could.

She scooped him up and rested him on her unoccupied shoulder. "Nothing for you to worry about. Keep Mrs. Hill happy. That is all you need concern yourself with."

He rubbed his face against hers, purring.

"But now I must talk with Papa." She set him down, straightened her skirts, and slipped out of the kitchen.

Halfway down the hall to Papa's study, the voices became clear.

No! She needed to talk to him now, before the fury subsided and she surrendered to the temptation to excuse Longbourn's transgressions.

Mr. Collins' voice filtered through the closed door, almost as clearly as if he was standing with her. "I cannot say that she refused, more that she did not give me an answer of any kind. It is entirely likely that my eloquent offer of marriage left her quite speechless. Indeed, I am apt to believe this the case as she fled my presence, color high and unable to speak. I trust it was the natural outflowing of her bashful modesty and genuine delicacy of character."

She had been speechless as it were. How shocked he would be to learn the cause.

"But depend upon it, Mr. Collins," Mama's shrill voice pierced the air like a hat pin, "that Lizzy shall be brought to reason. I will speak to her about it myself directly. She is a very headstrong foolish girl, and does not know her own interest; but I will make her know it."

"Pardon me for interrupting you, Madam, but if she is really headstrong and foolish, I know not whether she would altogether be a very desirable wife to a man in my situation who naturally looks for happiness in the marriage state. If therefore she actually means to reject my suit, perhaps it were better not to force her into accepting me because if she is liable to such defects of temper, she could not contribute much to my felicity."

Naturally, his felicity was his only concern. Was it a surprise, though? He had never once asked after her desires or preferences. Selfish buffoon. What a disaster he would be as master of a dragon estate.

"Oh, Mr. Collins!" Mama shrieked, her hands probably waving to and fro. "Lizzy is only headstrong in a very few matters. In everything else she is as good natured a girl as ever lived. Mr. Bennet shall very soon settle it with her, I am sure. Will you not, sir? You must make Lizzy marry Mr. Collins, for she vows she will not have him, and if you do not make haste, he will change his mind and not have her."

"Calm yourself, Mrs. Bennet. You have invented things which have not yet occurred. As I understand, Lizzy has not actually refused Mr. Collins, nor has he threatened not to have her." Several loud thumps must have been Papa rapping on his desk with his knuckles. It hurt his hands so that he only did that when entirely provoked.

"No indeed, sir, she did not. She only said that she could not yet offer an answer and that she needed time to think."

"You see there, Mrs. Bennet. She has not refused, so we are hardly in a position of forcing her to accept."

"But what is there to think about in such a matter? With such a desirable offer before her, what has a young woman to think about?" Mama's voice rose and fell as though she was pacing across the room. "Truly, this must be your fault for insisting that she begin thinking in the first place. That is not the province of a woman, you know. We are made for sensibility and men for sense. You should not have taught her otherwise."

"Enough! You are doing our daughter no favor in the eyes of her suitor." Papa slapped the desk.

Elizabeth winced. No doubt he would be paying for his rash acts tonight.

"She is a very good girl. You must believe that, Mr. Collins. She will be an excellent manager who will run your household very well. Have no doubts on that point."

"I am sure, with a little persuasion, she will easily be made to understand her own mind."

There, he had said it. Papa had said it—all but admitting he and Longbourn had colluded together. Neither trusted her enough to uphold her duties. They would stoop to the most disgusting, unethical means they could to control her.

Her stomach lurched; bitter acid burned the back of her tongue.

It was one thing to consider a life spent managing Mr. Collins by legitimate, honest means, but to face a life being played like a marionette on a stage—

No! That was beyond the pale.

She gathered her skirts and pelted upstairs to her room.

The plain oak door was solid and strong behind her, bearing her up as her knees trembled.

Remember to breathe ... deep breaths. One cannot think if one does not breathe.

"I heard what he said! I heard it! This is very, very bad! What are you going to do?" April peeked out from the folds of her shawl. "What are we going to do?"

"I am leaving. I cannot stay when they will take such means against me. If even the dragon of my Keep does not respect me, then what have I?"

"Lizzy?" Mary slipped into her room, quietly shutting the door behind her. "I heard Mama shrieking downstairs. What happened? I thought that you were going to accept Mr. Collins."

"I was, until Longbourn decided he needed to try and persuade me to do so." She brushed past Mary on the way to the closet.

She grabbed a large carpet bag, the one she used when she and Papa traveled together. How long had it been—

No time to reminisce now. Later. There would always be later.

"Mary, in my drawer, I need body linen, a night dress, a dressing gown, and handkerchiefs."

"What are you talking about? Where are you going?"

"I cannot stay whilst they would lower themselves to unscrupulous means to manage me." She grabbed several day dresses from the closet and roughly folded them into the bag.

"Are you sure that is what happened?" Mary handed her a pile of folded linens.

"I am certain." She shoved the linens in alongside the dresses.

Mary sighed, her eyes pleading. "I cannot believe they would have so little faith in you that they would—"

"I thought the same, but I know what I heard. Hand me my commonplace book. All three volumes are in the drawer there."

"Three? I have only seen one and have only begun to comprehend that." Mary wrestled the sticky drawer open and rummaged through it.

"The others are very early, hardly so useful. But when we are reunited, I will let you peruse them all you wish."

Shoes, she needed shoes, from the closet.

"Where will you go?" Mary handed the books over.

"I cannot tell you." She slid the shoes down to the bottom of the bag.

"You do not know where you are going? That does not sound at all like you."

"I know it very well, but you cannot."

"You do not trust me?"

Elizabeth paused and caught Mary's gaze. "I do not want to be a blot on your conscience. No doubt someone will ask you if you know where I have gone. I would not have you lie for me."

"I do not like it. Someone should know where you are going."

"You could look our father in the eye and deny him an answer, or worse, lie to him?"

Mary's head dropped, and she dragged her foot on the carpet. "I suppose not."

"Then let me have my secret and keep you from feeling guilty." She returned to packing—stockings, gloves, shawl and spencer.

Papa often gave her little notice when they were to travel. How odd to be grateful for the experience of panicked packing now.

"Will you wait just a moment? I have something for you." Mary headed toward the door.

"All right, but hurry, I must leave as soon as I have finished packing."

Mary tiptoed out.

She unwound her shawl and tucked it into the bag. Her hairbrush, some hairpins, her reticule—what else did she still need?

"Here." Mary handed her a small purse. "I have saved some pocket money. I know you have your own, but I will feel much better knowing you have a little more."

"I know you too well to refuse. Thank you. Take care of Rumblkins ... and Longbourn for me. But beware of his tricks. I do not want you—"

She grasped Elizabeth's arm. "I understand. It will be difficult without you. Write to me and let me know you are safe, please?"

"Not under my own name, for Mama is too apt to read our post. I will write to you under the name of Heather Rose. Heather may persuade Mama that it is the name of an old friend of yours. Now pray go and tell me if I may make my escape unnoticed."

Mary hugged her briefly and slipped out, returning a moment later. "The way is clear, but you must be quick."

Elizabeth tied on her bonnet, flung her green cloak over her shoulders, and grabbed her bag. With April on her shoulder, she picked her way downstairs and out of the side door, where there were fewer windows to reveal her escape.

After nearly half a mile, Elizabeth finally slowed her pace, struggling to catch her breath. She sounded like Mr. Collins. Heavens, what a horrible thought that she had anything in common with him.

Think on such things later. There were more important things to consider. The sun was already past its zenith. How was she to get to London and would the Gardiners take her in when she got there? Surely, they would. They had promised such, had they not?

London was only twenty miles, she could walk.

What was she thinking? Maybe as a very last resort, but a woman alone on the road, even with a dragon—it was a very bad idea. Not to mention it would be dark before she could get there.

Stop and breathe, take a moment to think clearly. Their lives might depend on it.

First to London—all her hopes hinged on that.

The Phillipses would be no help, so the public coach was the best alternative. If she was able to take the next coach, she could still arrive during daylight and make her way to Gracechurch Street.

But the public coach? She swallowed hard. She had never ridden a public coach by herself. Usually they had traveled in Papa's carriage. The few times she had been in a public conveyance, she had been safely tucked between Papa and Uncle Gardiner, both wearing such severe expressions that none of the other passengers dared speak to any of them.

A respectable young lady did not ride in a public coach alone. That was a given. Her reputation would be damaged, no doubt—someone she knew would certainly see her, and they would talk. She might lose her respectability.

But respectable dragons did not persuade their Keepers. And respectable fathers did not encourage dragons to do so. The entire situation was well past respectable. She would do what she had to and manage the consequences as they came.

The buildings of Meryton rose up before her, painting the street in stripes of shadows and light. Her object, the coaching station, was on the corner, two streets beyond the house that Colonel Forster had taken.

Pray let her not encounter the officers. They would ask questions, and worse, bear stories back to her sisters. They could keep secrets no better than Lydia.

No sign of red coats on the street. Excellent.

Now, if only she could slip through the crowd and into the coaching station—

"Miss Bennet?"

She stopped, a chill sliding down her spine. Turning, she forced her face into a smile. "Mr. Wickham, good day."

"Good day indeed. I am surprised to see you without your usual company." He bowed, eyes fixed on her shoulder, as if waiting for April to peek out.

"It is still early for them to be out and about, I think. We were up late last night celebrating some very good news."

"Concerning your eldest sister and Mr. Bingley? Miss Lydia might have mentioned her expectations at some point. I probably should not confess this to you, but there was something of a bet going on amongst the officers about when the happy event would finally take place."

Elizabeth licked her lips. What exactly did one say to such a thing? She forced a smile.

"You might be pleased to know that I am the winner, having the greatest faith in the constancy of Mr. Bingley's affections." He winked.

"I am sure Jane will be gratified to know." She looked over his shoulder. At least no other officers seemed to be in his company.

He chuckled deeply. "I see that I have scandalized you, Miss Bennet. Pray forgive me. I did not mean to make you uncomfortable."

"Consider it forgotten, sir, but pray excuse me, I must be about my business." She tried to step around him.

With a backward step, he cut her off. "Forgive my forwardness, but what business might you have at a coaching station, alone no less." His smile faded slightly and warm concern filled his eyes.

"Pray do not think me rude, but I have no intention of speaking of it." If only she could get past him—

"You have rather a large bag with you. It looks very much like you are intending a trip."

April peeked out of the hood and squawked a warning at him. Several people nearby turned to look at them.

No! More attention was the last thing they needed!

A grin which could only be called self-satisfied broke out over his face. "And you have your friend with you. I am sure you would never leave her behind if you were to sojourn from Longbourn."

"Please sir, I beg you to importune me no further." She gathered her skirts and tried to sidle past him, but he cut her off again.

"Forgive me, but I am concerned. It is most unusual for a woman in your circumstances to travel alone. I fear there may be something wrong."

April growled in her ear.

"The matter is nothing of your concern."

"It might be of interest to you to know that today I am charged with the task of accompanying Mrs. Forster's maid to London where she is to stay with her sick sister. I am then charged with bringing her replacement back to Meryton." He cocked his head and raised an eyebrow.

"Indeed, sir. And why might that be of interest to me?"

"There is room, quite comfortably, for another in the colonel's carriage. If your business carries you to London, you might find the company far more agreeable if you travel with us."

The maid was to stay in London. If she left Mr. Wickham's company before the new maid joined him, there would be none but him to bring tales back to Longbourn. And the maid's presence would preserve her reputation—

"I do not like the idea of traveling with him," April muttered.

"I just heard the coaching agent say there was no room available on the next two coaches." He cocked his head and shrugged.

"How do you know he is telling the truth?" April hissed.

Elizabeth bit her lips. If she could not travel to-day—no, that was unthinkable. She squeezed her eyes shut.

April might not like it, but neither would she like the conditions of a public coach, if they could even get on one. And staying the night in a public house was even worse.

"It seems you have discerned my intentions, sir. I will accept your offer, but I must impose two conditions. First, ask me no further questions of my motives. And second, say nothing of this to any of my family."

"You ask me to keep secrets for you?"

"You are right, that is too much to ask. Pray excuse me." She curtsied and dodged around him.

He blocked her way just before she made it to the coaching station door. "I never said it was too much. What you hear is the concern of a friend. I can only surmise something very serious has happened that would have you striving to keep secrets from your dear family."

She turned her face away.

"For the privilege of your company, I shall ask nothing more of you, and I shall say nothing of our sojourn together." He bowed from his shoulders.

April flapped her wings and chittered. "I do not like this."

Elizabeth pressed April against her neck and cuddled her cheek against the downy feather-scales. "Thank you for your understanding, sir."

"It is my privilege to help friends in distress." He offered to take her bag.

He was right. She was in distress, and his offer was generous. What did he stand to gain from it? She blinked furiously to clear her blurring vision. Perhaps she had been too quick to judge, too suspicious. It seemed Providence had just provided her the very friend she needed.

Mr. Wickham escorted her to the Forsters' house, where she paid a quarter of an hour's call on Mrs. Forster. Then, he ushered her out the back door, and into the mews where the carriage, sans driver, awaited. He handed her into the carriage where her bag waited.

It was newer and better maintained than Papa's. Probably refitted in honor of Colonel Forster's wedding. The leather still smelt fresh and new, and the side glass was sparkling clean.

Had Mr. Wickham arranged for this, for there to be no witnesses to her escape? He was a far better friend to her than Mr. Collins would ever be, able to see the distress of another soul and work to do something to alleviate it. What more noble act could there be?

The coach rocked as the driver and a groomsman climbed aboard. Mr. Wickham opened the door and handed a very groggy maid inside. She staggered to her seat, half sitting on Elizabeth in the process.

"Pray forgive me, Miss. I get powerful sick in a coach. The mistress give me a cordial to help." She giggled and settled into her seat. "I feel so very boosey and flustered."

Mr. Wickham pulled the door closed behind them and took the opposite seat. "A strong cordial will have that effect. There is no need for concern. You might sleep as we drive, and you will feel better when we arrive in London."

The girl yawned and leaned into the corner. She was softly snoring before they reached the outskirts of Meryton.

"She truly cannot tolerate the carriage. It is best for her to sleep." Mr. Wickham leaned back and extended his legs just a little. "I have done as I promised, perhaps even a wee bit more. So now I shall make a demand upon you. But just a small one." He winked.

April chittered and hunkered down in her grumpiest posture.

"And what might that be?" She drew her cloak over her chest.

"It is three hours to London. I require some form of entertainment. I know you to be a fine storyteller. Why do you not tell me your favorite myth? But not one from a far-off place. I wish to hear a myth from our own fair countryside." He leaned into the squabs.

"I fear that Hertfordshire does not have many stories attached to it."

"Then what of your favorite myth of England? Surely there is something for you to choose from in all our shores."

From the way he looked at April, surely he was asking for a children's teaching story about dragons. But April would not tolerate it. Best not to agitate her.

Still though, there were stories that would reveal nothing about the current state of dragons or the Blue Order.

"That seems little enough to ask. Have you ever heard of the Laidly Wyrm of Spindleston Heugh?"

April harrumphed, but did not twitter.

A broad smile lit his face. "No, I have not, but I look forward to doing so now." He balanced one boot atop the other and laid his hands over his stomach. "In the words of your young cousins, tell me a story Miss Elizabeth."

She smoothed her skirt over her lap. "Many centuries ago, in the Kingdom of Northumbria, Northumberland to us now, of course, the good king who lived in Bamburgh Castle lost his beloved wife to a most tragic death. She left behind a son, the prince Childe Wynd, and a daughter, the princess Margaret. Childe Wynd was his father's son with a brave heart and a lust for adventure that drove him to rove farther and farther from home. After his mother's death, his jaunts became journeys, and the journeys became longer and longer until he crossed the sea. In fear that he would never see his son again, the king took comfort from his daughter. Margaret was the image of her mother, beautiful as no other woman in Northumbria and gentle and kind in equal measure to her beauty."

"A handsome prince, a beautiful princess, what more does a fairy story need?" Mr. Wickham laced his hands behind his head.

"Dragons. It seems he wants to hear of nothing but us," April grumbled against her neck.

Elizabeth stroked her ruffled feather-scales smooth. "An evil witch sir. What kind of story would there be without one?"

"So then tell me of this witch."

"After years without his wife, the castle was cold and lonely. The king's judgement had been addled by too much wine. He called for eligible women to be brought to him. A beautiful, but cruel witch caught his eye and soon became his wife. Poor Margaret, she was bereft. She saw the witch for what she was, but the King would not believe her."

Mr. Wickham leaned forward a bit. "Ah, now it gets interesting."

"The witch cast an enchantment over the poor princess." Elizabeth hunched over her lap and worried her hands together, cackling. "I weird ye to be a Laidly wyrm, and borrowed shall ye never be, until Childe Wynd, the King's own son come to the Heugh and thrice kiss thee. Until the world comes to an end, borrowed shall ye never be."

"The princess became a dragon?"

"Indeed, she did. By the witch's spell, she became a dragon."

"What kind?"

"The myth calls it a wyrm, but I think she must still have been beautiful even in the transformation. I have always considered she became an amphithere. They are more beautiful than even the loveliest of wyrms."

Though some might not agree, there were some very pretty wyrms.

"What do they look like?"

"Of course, they are not real, but according to myth, they are not wyrms, but enormous snakes the color of jade. Unlike any serpent, they have great feathered wings with iridescent feathers, glistening in every color. Their wings are powerful enough for flight, although they only do so under great duress. Sometimes they are depicted with powerful forepaws as well. Their heads are as serpents, but well-feathered, and their eyes, penetrating."

"Frightful or fascinating?"

"Both, I would imagine. It is said they are creatures of exquisite beauty."

"So then, very fitting for a lovely princess."

"Indeed. I suppose in that, the witch was merciful."

"Or limited, perhaps. Her magic might not have been strong enough to completely transform a woman of such beauty." His brows flashed up in a playful challenge.

"That is indeed an interesting interpretation. It sounds as though you have spent a great deal of time considering fairy tales, sir."

"It had been a pleasant pastime during some of my darker times. I have always found the character of a prince removed from his inheritance rather compelling."

April shook her head and snorted. Perhaps she was right. That was a bit much.

Wickham chuckled. Perhaps he did not take himself as seriously as April did. "Do not leave me hanging. You must finish your story."

"Of course. The Laidly Wyrm, the princess, left the castle, banished to be a rogue dragon, without a territory to call her own, facing death if she trespassed on the territory of another, scourge to man and beast alike, stealing what she could to preserve life and limb. Finally, she made her way to Spindleston Heugh on the Great Whin Sill escarpment. It is said that the stone can still be found in the parish of Easington, Northumberland, you know."

"I should very much like to see it one day."

Should she mention that Papa had taken her there? April probably would not approve. She probably should not have mentioned the specific location at all.

Botheration, it was very easy to talk to him.

"Perhaps I would see the Laidly wyrm there, if I were very lucky." He stroked his chin.

"Even if you were very lucky, the Laidly Wyrm is naught but myth. Even if she were not, you would not find her, for you have not heard the end of her tale."

"Do not keep me in suspense! I do not see how you ever get children to sleep if you constantly keep a story so provoking."

"You are being quite vexing yourself. Naughty children who interrupt do not get to hear the end of a story."

"Pray tell me what must I do to hear the end?" He smiled beatifically.

April huffed and tucked her head under her wing.

"I suppose that will do. In any case, after ten years the prince returned. He expected to find his sister a grown woman, maybe even married. But instead, her chambers were empty. The witch told him that his sister had been eaten by the Laidly Wyrm and if he wanted to honor her memory, he would avenge her life and bring back the head and wings of the wyrm."

"A witch in all ways. Horrid woman."

"Indeed, she was. She even gave the prince a dragon-slayer sword with which to perform the deed."

April shuddered. She had seen the one Mr. Darcy had carried and it had given her nightmares for weeks.

"Childe Wynd rode off in search of the Laidly Wyrm. When he reached the spindlestone, he called out a challenge to the dragon."

"In the fashion of heroes everywhere, I imagine."

"They are rather a predictable lot, are they not? Princess Margaret recognized his voice and hurried down to see him. Naturally he did not recognize her in dragon form and brandished the sword at her."

"I should say he is lucky that he did not get himself immediately crisped by fiery breath."

"Do not be silly. Amphitheres do not breathe fire. That is a myth about the myth." She laughed.

There, April should be satisfied that he really did not know anything about real dragons. No feathered dragons breathed fire.

"Princess Margaret restrained her draconic instincts. She extended her wings and hovered over Childe Wynd's head, singing a song they had made up as children, one none other knew. Her voice was sweet and high, unmistakable in his ears. 'Margaret?' he cried. She told him of the witch's curse and that her only hope was her brother's kiss."

"And of course, he simply believed her, never once considering it was the sort of trap a clever dragon might set for him? That is the way soldiers get killed." He snorted and folded his arms over his chest.

"I suppose you are correct, taking an unfamiliar dragon at its word is not a mark of wisdom, but this is a fairy story, remember. And in this story, he embraces his sister and kisses her. She transforms before his eyes, all scales and feathers falling away. Once again, she is a young woman, even more beautiful for her trials than she had been before."

"And they lived happily ever after." He rolled his eyes.

What had he been hoping for, bloodshed and tragedy?

"Not yet. They gathered the scales for Margaret's dowry, enough to fill several chests, and secreted them in a crag under the spindlestone. The feathers they bundled up to bring to the witch, proof the dragon was no more."

He sat up a little straighter.

"Treasure would catch his attention," April muttered.

"The feathers carried a powerful enchantment upon them, the same form that the witch had cast upon the princess. When Childe Wynd presented them to the witch, she picked one up and was immediately transformed herself."

"Into a dragon?"

"No, each feather contained only a small measure of transformation magic, not enough to accomplish so large a transformation. She was instead turned into a toad."

Wickham snorted. "A toad? A fitting fate, I should say."

"Childe Wynd became king and assisted his sister in marrying a very suitable man. And now we have come to our happy ending."

Mr. Wickham yawned. "Just in time I suppose. Your voice is quite soothing."

"I am glad you approve, sir."

"You should not have told him that tale." April nipped her ear.

Nothing would please her. Poor little dear was so unsettled. Who could blame her?

But still, the story was quite safe. Who could believe that a princess might be turned into a dragon? That was impossible. The truth—that Margaret was turned out by a cruel stepmother and taken in to live among a mated pair of amphitheres who were incubating a clutch—was hardly like the story at all.

Still, the real Lady Margaret had always been her heroine. She had been instrumental in bringing an understanding of the amphitheres to the Blue Order. For her efforts, she had been made the first woman to hold office in the Order.

Perhaps, if the Gardiners did not take her in, she could find help among some sympathetic dragons.

The outskirts of London rose up on the horizon. It would not be long now before she would know if she would have to resort to that.

.

8
Chapter

DARCY HURRIED DOWN to the sheep barn. Warm sunbeams caressed his face, hinting to what might be an unusually warm afternoon to come. Wellsbey, the shepherding drake had sent him word to come immediately. Perhaps he had a solution to Pemberley's—and Darcy's—latest crisis.

Her old dog had wandered off and not returned. Nearly blind and deaf, it was not hard to believe it had got lost. The creature had been missing for three days now, and the poor drakling was nearly sick with worry about her pet.

Why had Wellsbey sent the message via tatzelwurm? Any other dragon could have brought him a complete message, more than just "Come now." But not a tatzelwurm. No, every last one was positively flighty—all the spring-hopping about must addle their brains. What a bizarre mode of locomotion.

Wellsbey met him at the open barn door. Standing on all fours, he stood waist high to Darcy, lean and lanky in leg and tail. His hide was dirt brown, making it difficult to tell where the scales ended and the dust and bits of hay began. Behind his head, he sported a hood that, when folded, hung down behind his head like a hound's long ears. Once one got accustomed to seeing him among the sheep dogs, his canine qualities became very apparent. Not the least of which was his personality, easy going and desiring to please—in a draconic sort of way, of course.

"Have you found the old hound?" Darcy paused to allow his eyes to adjust to the dim barn. There was something very pleasing about the scent of a barn filled with clean hay.

"Not yet, but there is some good news in that regard." His voice was low and raspy, like a hound's bark. "One of the barn wyrms heard a pair of wild fairy dragons chittering something about a loose hound. I have him looking in that direction now."

Darcy groaned and dragged his hand down his face.

"Do not despair. It was one of the older wyrms, a dependable one."

"Hardly a word applied to tatzelwurms or fairy dragons."

Wellsbey's laugh was more yip than anything else. "Indeed, that is true. But there are a few here and there who are less addlepated than the rest. Still, I also asked Walker to make a search of the area."

If the creature was to be found, Walker would be the one to do it. A little of the tension left his shoulders.

Wellsbey beckoned him to a pen in the corner. A dozen mewling puppies, splotched with white, black, and brown, and their mothers occupied the pen heaped with hay.

"You asked for a puppy. I think I have found the right one." Wellsbey scrambled over the edge of the pen and crouched in the corner. "Not weaned yet, but you can pick them out early. See."

Fully half the pups skirted away. That was to be expected. Most dogs instinctively avoided dragons. The bitches having grown up with Wellsbey, ignored him. The remaining pups did the same, continuing to tumble with one another across the hay. One though, a nearly white pup with a half brown, half white face bounced up to him.

He extended a paw to the pup which licked it and bounded closer. It pressed in close to Wellsbey and allowed the drake to pick it up in his mouth by the scruff. Wellsbey dropped it in Darcy's waiting hands.

"What a handsome little fellow." The puppy licked Darcy's face, wriggling and squirming.

"And a very calm one, with no aversions to dragons." Wellsbey climbed out of the pen. "That temperament seems well-suited for your needs."

And if Pemberley did not take to it, Georgiana certainly would.

One of the bitches ambled to the edge of the pen and jumped up on her back legs to peer at them. She whined softly.

Darcy returned the puppy to her, and she carried it back to the rest, wagging her tail. "How long until it can be introduced to Pemberley?"

"I should think within a fortnight. In a month complete, mayhap a bit less, it should be able to go live with her."

"I am grateful—"

The barn door flew open and slammed against the wall, amidst loud cawing and flapping of wings.

Darcy jumped to his feet. Wellsbey's hood extended and his body puffed up.

"You are needed immediately, Darcy! Immediately!" Cait landed on the floor near his feet, her wings beating up a small storm of hay.

He bit the sarcasm off the end of his tongue. She had landed on the barn floor. She never landed on the floor and risked damage to her spectacular tail feathers.

"What happened?"

"Georgiana insists you come. Pemberley is inconsolable!" Cait launched and sped out of the barn.

"Pray excuse me." He bowed towards Wellsbey and dashed out.

What could possibly have happened? Georgiana had gone to Pemberley with the intention of helping her write yet another letter to Miss Elizabeth. Both were becoming frustrated that none of their letters had been answered.

Was that the problem? Miss Elizabeth had not written yet?

It was so utterly unlike her, though. Was it possible she carried some grudge against him? Even if she did, she surely would not take it out against Pemberley. Perhaps something was wrong. Perhaps the letters had not gotten to her. Perhaps she was sick or injured. Perhaps Longbourn had …

What was that commotion? Cait's shrill scolding tones and the grumble could only be Rosings. Pemberley could not yet achieve that depth of tone. Two female voices as well. One was Georgiana's, the other … bloody hell and damnation!

He sprinted the last hundred yards to the cavern.

"Brother!" Georgiana met him at the opening panting, her face tear-streaked.

He held her arms until she caught her breath.

"Please, please, stop them. You must. No one is listening to me. I do not know what to do."

He steadied her on her feet and ran into the lair.

Anne stood near Pemberley's nest, hands on hips, a posture so much like her mother, Darcy almost mistook her for Aunt Catherine. But Aunt Catherine would never use such uncontrolled tones. Even when she lost her temper, she was still elegant and ladylike about it.

Just behind her, Rosings shuffled from one side of the cavern to the other, pacing as it were, though the fluttering of wings and a lashing of tail gave it quite a different character all together.

"You see, I told you. Your foolishness would bring him here, and now you may see how you have displeased your Keeper." Anne wagged an angry finger toward Pemberley.

"Anne!" Darcy ran past her to Pemberley.

She ducked her head into her nest and covered it with her wings. Her color was off—an odd grey-red, and she trembled.

He climbed into the nest with her. "What has she told you? What is wrong?" He glared at Anne over the edge of the nest.

Pemberley's hide sported pale and flakey patches—how could she have changed so much in just three days?

"Nothing is wrong except that you have spoiled her, and I mean to put an end to it. You will both thank me for it." Anne crossed her arms and nodded sharply.

Darcy wrapped his arms around Pemberley and pulled her a little closer. "And Rosings, you have condoned this behavior?"

The elder firedrake shook her head in great sweeping swoops of her long neck. "Do not implicate me in any of this … this … madness! The young one came sweeping in like the Lady herself, but without nearly so much sense—"

Anne whirled on Rosings.

Darcy gasped and covered Pemberley's eyes.

Rosings barely constrained her pouncing instinct. She pulled herself up short just feet from Anne.

The fool truly knew nothing about dragons. Had she been in the presence of an unfamiliar one, she might well be dead.

"Did you just call me senseless? How dare you? Have you forgotten to whom you are speaking?" Anne shrieked.

"Do not be afraid. I am not upset with you," Darcy whispered in Pemberley's ear. "I will remove her and then we may talk." He jumped out of the nest and stormed towards Anne.

"You see, Darcy will defend me!"

"Hardly." He passed Anne to stand between her and Rosings. "It is you who has forgotten to whom you are speaking. You do realize that Rosings could have killed you—"

"She is a civilized beast. She would never harm me."

"Not purposefully, I am sure. But if you provoke her prey instincts, she cannot be held responsible for her behavior. Or have you forgotten that clause in the Accords?"

Anne rolled her eyes. "Pish-posh! You insult her to suggest she is so base as to be controlled by instinct."

"What are you doing here anyway? You have not been out of your room for days. A sick headache, I have been told."

"I thought I would surprise you by coming here and resolving this little problem with your dragon." She smiled beatifically.

He gripped his hands behind his back lest he shake her. "What have you done?"

"What should have been done from the beginning. You know nothing about raising young things. I sent off that ridiculous, unhygienic dog. No one keeps a dog with a baby! Really! And I have begun instructing Pemberley in proper decorum."

"Pemberley has not eaten in three days," Rosings muttered.

"You sent her dog away? How dare you!" He turned to Rosings. "Why did you not tell me she had been coming here for three days?"

"It is her right as junior Keeper." Rosings lip curled back and revealed her fangs.

Darcy stomped toward Anne, stopping toe to toe, nose to nose with her. "Allow me to make one thing utterly and completely clear to you. There is absolutely no way I would allow you to become Friend to even a fairy dragon, much less Keeper to Pemberley."

She patted Darcy's shoulder. "Mama assured me once you saw how much good I could do for Pemberley, all your objections to our marriage would be over."

"She sent you here?" He clenched his fists until they shook.

"Not precisely. It seemed the obvious thing to do." How dare she try batting her eyes at him now!

"Get out. Get out! You are not welcome near Pemberley ever again. I give her leave to consider you a threat should you ever approach her in the future. Do not be surprised if she bites you."

"You cannot be serious!"

Rosings turned her back and muttered, "I'd like to bite her, too."

Anne stalked toward Rosings. "What did you just say?"

That shriek might work with the servants, but Rosings ignored her and lay full length on the stone floor, covering her ears with her forepaws.

Darcy grabbed Anne by the elbow and propelled her out of the cavern. "Return to the house, and tell your mother everything that has just transpired. She will know what to tell you." His father's glare proved sufficient to send Anne scampering away.

Georgiana rushed to his side, and they hurried back to Pemberley.

Her head was propped up on the edge of the nest. She whined like an injured hound.

"Tell me what is wrong." He sat on the edge of the nest and pulled her head into his lap.

"Want dog. Miss dog. She not like her. She terrible. She say she will be my Keeper—"

"I promise you; she will never be your Keeper. Never." He stroked Pemberley's head.

How dry and rough her scales had become. Her color was even more faded along the crest of her head.

"Why her not write? I want her." She thumped her tail.

Georgiana stroked her neck. "Shall we write another letter?"

"Why? Her not answer."

"Sometimes letters take time to be delivered. Perhaps she is busy with Dragon Keeping?" Georgiana shrugged and looked at him as though he might have an answer.

"Longbourn no like me. He not let her write?"

"I do not know. I had not considered the possibility." Darcy stroked his chin. "I am sure you will have a letter from her soon."

"No! She not like me anymore."

He patted her neck. "You are tired and hungry. You must eat something, then we will talk."

"No want." She slid her head off his lap and tucked it under her wing. She whipped her tail across the nest.

"Brother look!" Georgiana gasped.

Dark streaks lined the nest. Blood!

"Please, still your tail. Let me see." He lifted her tail and squinted in the meager light.

The underside of her tail was lined with blisters, many broken and bleeding.

Georgiana leaned into his ear. "Miss Elizabeth wrote of those too. She said dragons are apt to injure their tails when they are upset. They lash their tails and cause the blisters. She recommends a salve for it. Shall I make some?"

"Yes, yes, do. I will stay with her."

Georgiana hurried off.

Walker swooped in and beckoned Darcy to him.

"I will be right back." He jogged toward the cavern entrance and hunkered down near Walker.

"I have good news. I found the hound and two of the tatzelwurms are bringing it to the barn. I do not think it has eaten for days. I believe some food and water and perhaps some rest shall set it to rights."

"I can hardly imagine more welcome news."

"You do realize, it would still be far better if Lady Elizabeth were here."

"I hardly see how that can happen." He rubbed his eyes with thumb and forefinger. It was not as though the thought had not already occurred to him.

"Either you are being facetious or stupid. With you it can be difficult to tell."

Darcy grumbled under his breath.

"You know she would do anything for Pemberley. If you were to write asking for her to come—"

"I know you cannot appreciate the human conventions that prevent me from doing so. If she would simply answer Georgiana's letters, then we might extend an invitation. But until then, propriety requires—"

"Propriety be hanged. You have a drakling that has made herself sick missing Lady Elizabeth. She has not eaten in days because of Anne's ill-conceived interventions, and now she has torn her tail into a bloody mess because of it all. Just how much worse are you going to permit this to get before you relinquish your pride and seek out the help you know you need?"

Darcy sat back on his haunches. "How am I to do that?"

Walker smiled a slightly eerie cockatrice smile. "That is all I needed to hear. I will go to Meryton myself and talk with her. No letters necessary. Rosings and I have talked, and she has extended an invitation herself. We both know Miss Elizabeth is unlikely to ignore a draconic invitation. With any good luck, I shall have her here in a se'nnight."

Darcy swallowed hard. A se'nnight. That was too long and yet not long at all. She would be there with him again, and everything would be returned to rights.

For Pemberley.

And maybe for him, too.

"Have I your approval?"

"Yes, go. Pray though, take a moment and give Cait a take-leave before you fly off. She has complied with Aunt Catherine's requests and deserves your courtesy."

Walker chittered something under his breath in dragon tongue. "Fine."

He flew off, and Darcy returned to cradle Pemberley's head in his lap. "It will be well very soon, little one. It will be well."

"I want her."

"So do I."

The Forster's carriage paused to allow traffic to pass.

"You never told me your ultimate destination. Perhaps it is time to instruct the driver?" Mr. Wickham asked.

April flapped and stomped on Elizabeth's shoulder. "Do not tell him. I do not trust him."

"After the service he has offered us, so willingly—why do you persist in your distrust?" She whispered and laid her hand on April's back.

"Because I am not charmed by an easy smile and attractive features." She nipped Elizabeth's ear, lightly, but enough to sting. "You did not tell Mary where you were going. Why should you tell him?"

She did have an excellent point. Mary would be heartbroken if she trusted Wickham with what she did not trust her own sister. And April was likely to make sure Mary knew.

"I would like to go to the place where St. Mary Hill Road and Tower Street meet." Halfway between the

Gardiners' home and the offices of the Blue Order, she could reach either by an easy walk.

"What is there for you?" Mr. Wickham did look vaguely hungry for more information, but then who would not?

"Pray allow me my privacy, sir. I do not wish to discuss the matter." Or rather her dragon did not.

"I am wounded that you do not trust me. Have I not been a good friend to you?"

April pecked at her ear. That one probably drew blood.

"Indeed, you have, sir, and I am deeply indebted to you for your assistance. However, I must insist, press me no further on the matter."

His expression shifted several times, but his easy smile returned. "Of course, I would never intrude upon a lady's privacy. Forgive me. Consider it a mark of my regard that I am concerned for your safety."

"His regard you can do without." April snorted. "As for your safety, I still question that."

"You are very good, sir, and I deeply appreciate all you have done on my behalf. I pray you, though, make no mention of my travel to anyone."

He pressed his hand to his chest, and his shoulders sagged a little. "You have had my promise on that matter. I am wounded that you would even think it necessary to say more."

"Forgive me, sir. I have no wish to cause you pain when you have been so very good to me." She bit her lip.

April growled.

"Pray do not worry for my feelings. I merely feel responsible for your well-being. It would be a constant weight on my mind if I were not certain you were safely delivered to your destination."

"Can you not see he is trying to persuade you as surely as that voice from the cellars was? If he does not stop, I will scratch his eyes out!"

She scooped April up and cupped her hands over her. "Be assured, I know this part of London quite well, and there is nothing to be concerned for. I fear my little friend is becoming much agitated by the carriage. It would be best for us to depart as soon as possible."

He sighed and rapped the roof. The carriage slowed, and Mr. Wickham gave the driver instructions. "The driver says we should be there in less than a quarter of an hour."

"None too soon." April picked her way back up Elizabeth's shoulder and ducked into the folds of her hood.

The familiar edifices along Lyme Street as they turned on to Fenchurch Street seemed to soothe some of April's agitation. It was nice to be surrounded by the familiar once again. The coach slowed and stopped.

"Are you certain I cannot take you farther?" Mr. Wickham opened the door and stepped out.

"I thank you for everything. I shall be very well from here." She picked up her carpet bag.

He handed her out and climbed back into the coach.

"Walk in the wrong direction until he is out of sight." April pressed tight against Elizabeth's neck.

If that would quell the fairy dragon's fears, then so be it. It could hardly hurt her to stretch her legs a bit before setting out for the Gardiners'.

The streets were crowded, as London nearly always was, but the air had a cool, crisp note, bracing and re-freshing after the confines of the coach. Dodging hurried pedestrians not looking where they were going was almost fun.

April tapped the back of her head twice. "They are gone now. You can go on to Gracechurch Street."

"I think I know how a carriage driver feels now." Elizabeth sidestepped a mother and children and turned to go back in the direction she had come.

"You would rather have me fly on my own? I am happy to do so, you know." She flapped her wings.

"This is hardly a safe place for you to fly, and you know it. There are enough birds of prey here to whom you look like a tasty blue snack. Best keep covered until we reach the safety of the house."

April chirruped and pulled the green hood over her until only the tip of her beaky snout remained visible. One mention of birds of prey was usually enough to quell all arguments. She dreaded them like nothing else, even cats.

Elizabeth shifted her carpet bag to the other hand, gathered her skirts, and picked her way across the dirty street. Even if there had been a street sweeper available, she could have hardly justified paying him. Best reserve her limited funds for what was truly essential. And who knew what that would be?

Her stomach lurched as she dodged a group of children dancing around a peddler's cart. She had never walked alone beyond the borders of Longbourn. Even in Meryton, she always had one of her sisters or a maid with her. But now, she was alone, completely alone.

Worse still, she knew no dragons to call upon here. How strange and insecure it felt to be without their constant and reassuring presence. Certainly, there were dragons in London, but she did not know them. They were not her friends. Not yet. Perhaps if she stayed long enough, though, she would come to know them. She had met many dragons, major and minor, traveling with Papa and became friendly with most of them. These could not be too different, could they?

She turned the corner to Gracechurch Street. The Gardiner house was at the center of the street, the finest, most prominent one. A bright blue door, distinctive iron railings with swirls in the vague shape of dragon scales, and the steps freshly swept. How many times had she visited there? Always it had been a warm, welcoming place.

Would it be so now?

There would be no way to know until she asked. She drew a deep breath and pulled her shoulders back. If she could not feel confident, at least she could look the part.

She marched up the stairs and rapped the brass, dragon claw knocker against the freshly painted door.

The door opened to reveal the Gardiners' housekeeper. Tall and positively gaunt, her sharp nose and chin always gave her a severe expression even when she smiled. She jumped back half a step and blinked rapidly. "Miss Elizabeth? I was not told you were expected."

"Good day, Mrs. Hart. Indeed, I am not expected."

Mrs. Hart gaped a moment, then seemed to regain her senses. "Do come in. I am certain the mistress will be very happy to see you."

The door closed behind her, and April poked her head from her hood.

"And the little blue one, too! We have a little red one what looks just like her now, you know." Mrs. Hart smiled. She extended a finger to ask permission to scratch April under the chin.

Though she looked perpetually irate, the housekeeper and the fairy dragon had a long and cordial relationship. April favored anyone who would ply her with honey, and Mrs. Hart delighted in the fairy dragon's soporific song.

Ladylike footsteps descended the broad marble stairs. "Lizzy?"

"She just came to the door, madam. I was on my way to get you."

"Of course, of course. Lizzy, where is your father?" Aunt Gardiner caught her hands, and Phoenix launched from her shoulder to join April in her hood.

She swallowed hard and turned away from Aunt's seeking gaze. "He is not here."

"Is he off to the Order's offices? Should we expect him for dinner?"

"He is not in London."

"Then your sisters, perhaps? Is your carriage pulling around to the mews? Shall I notify the grooms?"

"No, I have come on my own."

Aunt gasped and caught her by the elbow. "Come, we must talk. Mrs. Hart, see that Lizzy's room is made up for her."

The housekeeper curtsied and scurried away. Aunt led her to her private sitting room and closed the door.

The small room at the back of the house looked out over the back garden. Flowered paper hangings covered the walls, a close match for the dainty pillows on the chairs around the low table. Neat, feminine, and functional—everything in the room reflected Aunt Gardiner.

Elizabeth sat near the window. "If Uncle is at home, you may want to bring him in as well. It might save repeating the entire story."

"I will be back in a moment."

Elizabeth unfastened her cloak. Phoenix and April flitted to a fairy dragon-sized perch—an elegant wrought iron affair painted white—on the tea table.

Phoenix fluffed his feathers, making himself as big as he could. Did he even realize that he was barely more than half April's size?

"Was Longbourn a bully again? I expect I need to have a conversation with him." He snorted and narrowed his eyes. It was probably meant to be a threatening expression, but he looked too much like little Samuel.

He would be offended if she laughed, so she held her breath and bit her lower lip.

"You will hear it all soon enough, my fiery little friend." She soothed the ruffled feathers along his back. "How do you find London?"

Rustle swooped in through the open window. "He would find it much more appealing if he were not required to always have my company whilst leaving the house without the Gardiners."

"You would fly in London alone?" April gasped.

Phoenix puffed out his chest. "Of course, there is nothing to fear."

"You had best learn that the skies here are not safe. You would cause the family great grief if you were made a snack by some marauder," April chittered.

"Perhaps he will listen to you. He ignores me." Rustle preened his wing.

"You had best listen to him." April hopped closer and pecked his needle-like beak.

Elizabeth coaxed him to her finger. "You are such a brave little thing. But you must remember that if something happens to you, you will not be here to protect the children or Mrs. Gardiner. It behooves you to listen to your elders. You may be big and strong, but you have not their experience and wisdom. Remember, listening to their wisdom is your best teacher. Is that not the prime tenet of the young dragon's code?"

He huffed a sound that she would have thought required fleshy lips to make. "I am no fool."

"I did not say you were. By listening to them, you may prove you are not."

Fairy dragons were decidedly cute when they glared whilst pouffed and fluffy. No wonder few Dragon Friends took them seriously or even tried.

The door flung open and banged against the wall.

Uncle Gardiner stormed in. "Lizzy! Maddie tells me you are here alone. Pray tell, what has happened?"

Aunt followed him in, and they sat on either side of her.

The tale should not have been so difficult to tell. It was just a set of facts—cold, hard facts. But those facts lodged in her throat, rasping and tearing as she struggled to divulge them.

"Of course, you may stay with us!" Aunt Gardiner covered her hands with hers.

"As long as may be necessary." Uncle laid a heavy hand on her shoulder.

Good news, even very welcome good news, should not make her cry. Nor should it leave her sobbing and gasping for breath.

But it did.

The fairy dragons flew to her shoulders, drying her tears in their fluff. Rustle perched on the back of her chair and extended his wings over her. Dear soul, every bit as protective as her aunt and uncle.

"I only wish you could have sent us word, let me come for you." Uncle worried his hands together. "I dread to think what could have happened alone on the road with that Wickham fellow. I can only imagine how desperate you must have been to have taken such a risk to come to us."

"He was everything gracious and gentlemanly. Truly."

Aunt clucked her tongue. "I am grateful for the service he rendered you to be sure, but neither of those words is an apt description of the man. Now is hardly the time for that discussion, though."

"We must visit the Blue Order as soon as possible, tomorrow if I have my druthers. A formal complaint must be filed."

"Surely nothing about Longbourn can be important enough to bother the Order. He is only a country wyvern, without title or influence." Elizabeth studied her hands.

"But your father is Historian of the Order, and that alone makes all matters pertaining to Longbourn significant. Even if that were not the case though, it seems yours will be the first case to test the new laws, and thus precedence-setting. And that is very, very significant."

The next morning, Aunt Gardiner brought several dresses to Elizabeth's room, a snug, tidy little space on the same floor as the children's rooms. Though she was hardly the only one who stayed there, Aunt included touches that were just for her: a looking glass, a nesting basket for April, a favorite coverlet, embroidered in lavender flowers. It felt almost like home.

"I cannot imagine you were able to pack very much in just your carpet bag. Hopefully some or even all of these will fit you. It is so much easier to face people when one feels herself dressed adequate to the occasion."

Elizabeth picked out a deep blue gown and held it against her chest. Each was well made and fashionable but not presumptuous, just like Aunt.

"I have not been able to wear that gown since Samuel was born. Let me help you put it on."

Elizabeth twirled in front of the mirror. Though a few small alterations would be necessary to perfect the fit, she could certainly wear it as it was.

"I had thought to have it remade, but it fits you so well, you must have it. These others should fit you as well. I insist on you having them. You should wear the blue one today."

It was a lovely gown, far nicer than anything than she had packed with her and more fitting for an audience with the Secretary of the Order.

"Are you nervous, dear?" Aunt helped her pin up her hair.

"I like to think my courage rises to meet the occasion, but this, this is entirely different. I know you and Uncle are convinced that this is the right and necessary step to take, but I am still uncertain."

Aunt sat on the edge of the bed and patted the coverlet. Elizabeth sat beside her. "I understand. You have never faced such a thing before, and it could well be as life-changing as … a marriage would be."

Elizabeth dug her nails into her palm. "No matter what, there is no pleasing outcome. I hate the thought of Papa facing censure by the Order. I admit I am a little less concerned about Longbourn. He is unlikely to feel anything deeply. What if Papa is asked to step down as Historian? The humiliation might kill him."

And if that happened, Collins would surely throw Mama and her sisters into the hedgerows. Longbourn would not be properly tended, and he would no doubt take that out on Collins by decimating the herds, which could lead to the shepherds discovering the dragon—

Aunt patted her hand. "I can assure you; he will not be asked to step down. If for no other reason than there is no one waiting in the wings to take over the office. It takes a special disposition and set of skills to manage that responsibility, and few seek it. Very few. And if he is reprimanded, he will by no means be the first to whom it has happened, nor would he be the last. He might be disgruntled, but hardly more, though he would be apt to try and ply you with guilt. It is an excellent way to gain your capitulation."

No doubt he would look at her, his blue eyes wide with hurt and shame, and ask her why she would bring such ignominy upon her father and her dragon. She pressed the back of her hand to her mouth and sniffled. "Is there truly no other way?"

"To convince your father and Longbourn that you are not obligated to marry Collins? No. Come now, no sense in delaying any further. Your uncle is waiting downstairs."

She wrapped her cloak over her shoulders, and April took her spot in the hood.

Uncle offered her his arm as they stepped out into the crisp morning air. How odd, the one day where the typical London fog would have been fitting, even comforting, it was bright and clear. Fickle, perverse weather.

"We have two appointments at the Order, the first with Baron Chudleigh, Secretary of the Order. I shall present the complaint on your behalf. According to the rules, you could present it yourself, but Lord Chudleigh is brusque and ..."

"I am not sure my courage is sufficient to this either."

"There is no shame is allowing a bigger dragon to fight a battle for you." April nodded her approval.

"I am honored to be considered among dragon-kind." Uncle chuckled, bowing slightly from his shoulders toward April.

Elizabeth stroked April's head. "Tell me about Lord Chudleigh's dragon. I expect I will entertain her whilst you speak with him. She is an amphithere, is she not?"

"Barwines Chudleigh, and her reputation precedes her. Rustle calls her 'Bustle and Wind Chudleigh.'"

April snickered.

"That is why he has not joined us today?"

"The nickname got back to the Barwines. She has threatened to see his wings clipped for the insult." Uncle winked at April.

"Well, that is a bit cranky. But amphitheres are known for their vanity. They do not accept insults graciously."

"No, they do not. But Barwines Chudleigh has progressed from cranky to thoroughly grouchy. Many have been avoiding her recently. Still though, the story of Pemberley's hatching has intrigued her, and she wants to meet you."

"An invitation I will gladly accept. I will take a cranky dragon over the Secretary of the Order at any time."

He patted her hand. "You are a unique young woman, my dear. I know of no one else who would say such a thing. In any case, you will enjoy our second appointment much more. I will present you to Sir Edward Dressler, the Lord Physician of Dragons. He has expressed a great interest in your commonplace books and, of course, in Pemberley's hatching. Though a man of science, his disposition is far more open and pleasing than Lord Chudleigh's."

"And his dragon?"

"That is what you would ask." Uncle Gardiner laughed. "He is Keeper to a rather impressive blue pa snake, Castordale. An even-keeled fellow if ever I have met one. I rather like him."

"Then I shall look forward to that introduction very much."

Uncle smiled, but the edges of his eyes did not crinkle. He knew she was saying the right things simply because they were the right things. Sometimes being known so well was truly a mixed blessing.

But what else was there to do? Nothing would change the creeping dread that shadowed her as Longbourn's wings had … She shuddered.

"Lizzy?"

"Just a bit of a chill. There is a nip in the breeze now." She hated to lie.

No more of those unhelpful thoughts. None of these dragons would be so ill-mannered as to treat her that way. Certainly not on a first meeting, with their Keepers in sight.

Longbourn's petulance might have stolen a great deal from her, but it would not steal her equanimity around dragons. That was under her control, and he would not have it from her. Today she would prove that. She drew a deep breath and squared her shoulders.

The Hall of the Blue Order rose up before them, a relatively nondescript white building of five stories, with fine iron railings, many windows, and double doors painted the Order's signature blue. It blended into the surroundings and was easy to ignore. What made it truly impressive was the labyrinth of tunnels underneath the building.

The cellars, multiple levels of them, had been dug out particularly with dragons in mind. The building extended farther underground than it did above. A myriad of tunnels that ran under the whole of London, connecting many of the great structures and houses, joined at the Hall of the Blue Order, at the Great Court, on the deepest subterranean level.

The Great Court hosted all manner of Order events, both social and judicial. It was the one place where major dragons and Keepers could come together in large numbers with the dragon-deaf populace left none the wiser.

It had been nearly five years since she had been there last. The year she turned sixteen, Papa had brought her for the Keepers' Cotillion where the dragon-hearing daughters of the Order made their come out into Dragon Keeping society. It had been so difficult not to tell her sisters of the event. It was the sort of affair Lydia would have adored. The most spectacular ball she had ever—or probably would ever—attend.

Even then though, Papa had made it clear to all the young men who asked her to dance, that she was expected to marry the heir of the estate. None asked her to dance a second time. It was almost as humiliating as Darcy's remarks at the Meryton Assembly.

Her cheeks burned. Those were not helpful thoughts either.

Uncle Gardiner rapped at the door. A somber, blue-coated butler opened the door. His shoulders seemed to fill the entire doorway, so formidable no undesirables would be admitted. Uncle presented his signet ring and she the one on her chatelaine, and they were ushered inside.

White marble lined the floor and the grand, sweeping staircase. The oak railing was carved in the form of large wyrms. A minor dragon graced each spindle. The carving of the fairy dragons was so realistic that April left Elizabeth's hood to investigate.

A blue-liveried footman greeted them.

"Lord Chudleigh is expecting us: Mr. Gardiner, Miss Bennet, and April." Uncle Gardiner handed him a blue bordered card.

Uncle was carrying Blue Order cards now? Why had Papa not told her that Uncle had been given "Honored Friend" status? That was something worth celebrating.

"When?" she whispered.

He leaned to her ear. "After I found a way to supply a favorite treat amongst the wyrm-type dragons. They are incredibly fond of a certain beetle from India. One can go far catering to dragon bellies. Phoenix is quite fond of them, too."

"This way, please." The footman led them to a locked door that opened on another staircase, equally grand, sweeping down into the cellars.

They stopped one level down. Narrow window slits, covered in frosted glass, lined the edges of the broad corridor. A row of polished brass mirrors below magnified the light. Just above street level, they let in enough light during the day that candles were not needed in the hall. How much polishing was required to keep those mirrors bright?

Their steps echoed in the tiled hall. A minor drake wearing a livery badge scurried past, a satchel strapped to his back.

They stopped at an imposing door, carved with the signet of the Secretary of the Order. Carefully carved agates were inlaid in the dragon's eyes, giving them an eerie, lifelike quality.

The footman announced them, and they stepped inside, pausing a moment for their eyes to adjust to the dim light.

Half a dozen mirrored wall sconces lined the perimeter of the office, with several more candelabras around the desk. Dragon musk mixed with the bacony smell of burning tallow hung in the air. At the back of the room, a roughhewn tunnel entrance seemed to suck away a great deal of the light. Of course, it was just an illusion, but still, the slight breeze coming from the tunnel exacerbated the sense. Shelves of official-looking tomes and several globes lined two walls whilst a carved mural bearing the title plaque: *Dragons of the World* stretched across the remaining wall.

Some of those dragons Elizabeth had never heard of, let alone seen. Perhaps he would allow her to examine it further.

"Gardiner." Lord Chudleigh rose.

His name sounded like it should belong to someone short and stout; he was anything but. Tall, and slender, almost willowy in his movements, he approached, official blue robes fluttering in the breeze behind him. On his watch fob he wore a trio of amphithere feathers, tips dipped in gold.

"May I present my niece, Miss Bennet, Keeper to Laird Longbourn and Friend to April." Uncle gestured toward her.

She curtsied deep enough to touch her knee to the cold stone floor.

"I am pleased to make your acquaintance, Miss Bennet." Lord Chudleigh's voice was softer that she had expected, not the voice of authority one usually expected with such a role.

"Thank you, sir. I am honored to be recognized by one an amphithere holds in such regard."

He touched his watch fob. "They do not part easily with their feathers, do they?"

"No, we do not." A large dragon slithered from the shadows, scales rasping against the stone.

The amphithere rose up on her serpentine tail, head just above Lord Chudleigh's. Her body was long and slender—elegant was the best word—covered in striking jade green scales. With a rustle of feathers, she unfolded her wings—her show of dominance. They extended three quarters the width of the room, covered with iridescent, multicolored feathers. The feathers continued along her shoulders and up her head, giving the impression of a woman's elaborate headdress. Bright, intelligent blue eyes sparkled in the candlelight, examining, judging them.

"I would be introduced to that one." Her voice was almost a hiss. She pointed a wingtip at Elizabeth.

"Barwines Chudleigh, may I present my niece, Miss Elizabeth Bennet."

Elizabeth gripped the edges of her cloak and brought them up to cover her as she curtsied deep and dipped her head toward the floor. Beside her, April covered herself with her wings and touched her head to the floor.

The amphithere slithered toward her and tapped the back of her head with the end of her tail. Had she been displeased—and not bound by the Pendragon Accords—it could have been a killing blow.

"This one will do. She understandsss how to properly presssent herself. The tiny one, too." She touched April with the tip of her forked tongue.

"I am honored by your recognition." Elizabeth rose slowly, keeping her head down.

"I have heard much about you. Bedford holds you in high regard ssstill."

"I am grateful to have been able to serve him."

"Come with me. Let the men sssort out their affairsss. I would sssee to you myself. I wish to hear more about this wild hatchling that managed to imprint." She pointed with her wing to a cavern beyond the office.

Uncle nodded, and Elizabeth followed the amphithere into the cavern.

Along the walls, hollows contained candles and mirrors, just enough light to permit her to see the graceful swish and sway of the dragon's lithe body. The tunnel opened up into a smallish cavity on the right.

A large pile of silk pillows littered with downy dragon under-feathers lined one wall. Chudleigh—the name hardly fit the dragon any better than it did the man—curled up on the pillows and reclined against the wall. She looked every bit like a grand lady taking an audience in her dressing room. She tasted the air with her long, forked tongue, revealing the tips of her fangs.

Amphithere venom was known for its healing qualities. She probably did not offer it up easily.

"Ssso, Miss Bennet, impresss me."

"Pray excuse me, Barwines. I do not have the pleasure of understanding you."

"You are the daughter of the Order's Hissstorian and have seen a wild-hatched dragon imprint. Impresss me with your dragon prowesss."

"She means to trick you," April whispered.

"Hold your peace, tiny one. I will not hesitate to dismisss you from my presence. Your kind is more nuisance than anything else."

"I cannot imagine there is anything about me that you would find impressive. You are far more interesting. I imagine that your responsibilities to your Keep and to the Order would be most demanding, perhaps even overwhelming at times."

Chudleigh sighed, flicking the tip of her tail and laying back into her pillows. "You would be sssurprised at how few warm-bloods understand that sssimply being a dragon does not make life easy. There are so many demands." She extended a wing to shove a thick pillow toward Elizabeth and gestured her to sit.

"Particularly when your kind is so few and far between among the dragons of England. Are not most of your kind found in the north, Northumberland and beyond?"

"Many of my kin make their homes in Ssscotland, and even on the continent—though dragons there are not nearly ssso well favored as we are here." Her wings slumped a little.

"Your wing feathers seem ruffled. Might I smooth them?"

Chudleigh extended a wing and Elizabeth, with April's help, stroked and smoothed the elegant feathers into place.

"Have you kin that you wish to see? Or perhaps someone a bit more interesting?"

Chudleigh straightened, her head feathers nearly brushing the ceiling. "There, you have noticed; it should not be ssso difficult to undersssstand!"

Her tail-tip beat a sharp tattoo against the stone. April dove into Elizabeth's hood.

"Your Keeper does not wish you to make the journey to visit … him?"

Chudleigh's chin fell, and she closed her eyes. "He sssays it is too dangerous, that I am being flighty and frivolousss—"

"And there is a less distant amphithere he would see you matched with?" Elizabeth bit her lip. She was only guessing now. A wrong assumption could cost her dearly. Some dragons did not appreciate interference in their private affairs.

Chudleigh sighed and sagged to the ground, her head resting on the stones at Elizabeth's feet.

The poor dear. She must be very distressed and lonely to be so vulnerable to a veritable stranger.

Elizabeth stroked her head feathers while April ventured out to preen them. "Your Keeper does not understand that amphitheres mate for life, even if you only live together for those brief times?"

The great feathered head traced an arc on the floor.

"He does not know you ever mated, does he?"

Chudleigh squeaked.

Elizabeth drew her head into her lap and hugged around her neck. "You poor sweet creature. I am so sorry, dear one."

When a young amphithere was able to hunt on its own it would leave its mother. At their parting, it would give her neck a small bite that would result in a small patch of scarlet feathers, a mark of their permanent bond. Chudleigh's neck had no scarlet.

Their tears mingled into a tiny pool that glinted in the candlelight.

Chudleigh rested her head on Elizabeth's shoulder. She tried not to sneeze at the feathers tickling her nose. "It is not the sort of thing that is easy to talk about. Shall I explain it to your Keeper for you? I cannot promise that he will listen to me, but he might."

"She is good at explaining things." April rubbed her fluffy head along Chudleigh's nostril.

"You think you can make him undersssstand?" Her long tongue tickled Elizabeth's ear as she spoke.

"I will certainly do my best. Keepers can be surprisingly understanding when things are put to them simply. Have you a dust bath nearby? You might find that very soothing whilst I speak with Lord Chudleigh."

"That does sssound pleasant. Would you like to join me, tiny one?" She crossed her eyes to focus on April perched on her nose.

"That is an excellent thought." While Elizabeth might be good at explaining things, April was not.

Chudleigh slithered off, April balanced on the top of her head.

Elizabeth made her way back to the office where Uncle and Lord Chudleigh were finished with their discussion and reminiscing over a glass of brandy.

Lord Chudleigh rose and brought another chair near theirs. "Has my dragon dismissed you too, Miss

Bennet? Do not despair. She is not tolerant of many these days."

"Actually, no, sir. I come bearing something of a message from her."

Lord Chudleigh's eyes bulged. He reached for his brandy snifter. "A message, from my dragon? Why would she send a message through you when she can talk directly to me?"

Uncle Gardiner shot her a look half way between amused and concerned.

She folded her hands in her lap and adopted her most authoritative voice. "Perhaps she has hidden it from you, but her nest is full of feathers she has plucked from her own breast. She is sorely taxed and does not know how to explain her grief to you."

He took a gulp from his brandy. "Grief? What could possibly grieve my dragon?"

"The loss of her hatchling, decades ago, possibly even before you were born."

"Hatchling? She has never mated."

"Yes, sir she has, and something happened to the snakeling. It is nearing time for her to mate again. She wants to return to her mate in the north, but you have opposed her journey."

"She has feather mites, nothing more." He flicked his hand and looked aside.

"There are no mites. My fairy dragon checked."

Lord Chudleigh grumbled deep in his throat. Why did men do that, especially when they were wrong?

"Why would she keep a secret like that from me?"

"Dragons are loath to reveal weakness, even to their Keepers."

"But she told you, whom she has never met until an hour ago?" He gripped the arms of his chair.

Uncle arranged his features to hide a smile. What was he enjoying so much?

"She told me nothing. I told her what I knew and gave her the opportunity to speak."

"And you should know my dragon better than I?"

"It is the province of a woman to understand some things that men find difficult. There is a reason that women are Keepers, too."

That was too much for Uncle. He tried to hide his chuckle in his hand, but utterly failed.

Lord Chudleigh huffed and laughed a bit half-heartedly. "I heard the rumors that you had a special bond with dragons, but did not believe them. I will go to her."

"You will find her in her dust bath."

He rose, rolling his eyes. "Sir Edward is waiting to see you. Go on to him. But expect a summons from my office. I expect there will be a great deal I will wish to discuss with you, young woman."

That night, Elizabeth lay in bed, staring at the ceiling. Normally the familiar little guestroom was restful and comforting, but tonight the street noises and unfamiliar shadows urged her to remain wakeful and vigilant. Not that she would have been likely to have slept even if she had been back in her own bed at Longbourn. It was all so strange, the events of the day, the Blue Order, the people and dragons she had met there.

It felt more like a dream than reality. Was there really such a place, such a life, where keeping the secret of dragons was not the overarching preoccupation? What would it be like to live among them: Chudleigh and the Secretary, Baron Chudleigh, Castordale, the blue pa snake Kept by the Lord Physician, Sir Edward, and Bylock the drake Kept by the Chief Scribe, Lady Astrid?

What a force that Lady was! Like none Elizabeth had ever met. Sharp-nosed, with penetrating blue eyes that seemed to see right through anyone she looked at, the Lady was treated with the same deference and respect with which any of the male Officers were treated. Her presence, her knowledge, her very being, commanded deference, and it was offered without question or hesitation. No other woman she had known received such reverence. Somehow, that made the Blue Order seem more otherworldly than the dragons did.

More startling was Lady Astrid's response when Sir Edward introduced her, and spoke of her commonplace book. He described it as a significant contribution to dragon lore, not the silly scribblings of a young girl as Papa seemed to regard it. And those were not idle words. When, on Uncle Gardiner's request, she showed it to Sir Edward, he perused it for half an hour, silent and a little slack-jawed. Then, the questions began—not to challenge what she had written, but to learn more and encourage her to add to what she had recorded.

Now she was requested—no, to be honest, it was something between begged and ordered—to return daily for appointments with Sir Edward and Lady Astrid. Both insisted on reviewing her commonplace book with her—all three volumes of it. Even when she tried to explain away the earliest entries as mere childish babblings, they would not hear of it—in fact, they sharply corrected her. Though perhaps somewhat immature, there were new insights to be found even in those pages.

To have her writings considered with the accepted dragon lore. How could that be possible? Papa would never believe it.

How ironic, considering it was his proudest achievement when the volume he had written on minor dragon hatchings had been accepted and added to dragon lore canon. It would have been pleasing if he were proud of what she had done, not embarrassed by it.

She chewed her knuckle.

Would they find her wanting in her understanding? Would they examine her books and deem them childish and irrelevant? Uncle Gardiner assured her they would not. But still ...

A few hours before dawn, she finally fell asleep.

9
Chapter

THE NEXT FORTNIGHT passed in a whirlwind. Her days were spent at the Blue Order, divided between the Royal Physician and the Chief Scribe, the vast library of the Order—lost in research, mostly related to ancient forms of dragon script—and a variety of tea and nuncheon invitations, offered by Dragon Friend and dragon alike.

Never had she felt so at home. If she was not sharing her own draconic observations, she was sitting at the feet of an elder—human and dragon—learning from theirs. Almost the entire library was open to her, with experts ready to assist her study. And when her eyes were too tired to read, there was always a dragon at the ready to keep her company. Tea with dragons, several times a week! Who would have thought?

And the welcome they gave April! Like a new heiress among the *ton*. Who would have thought the little dear was so social?

In the evenings, she returned to the Gardiners' home to keep company with the children, plying them with as many dragon stories as they would hear. On occasion, a minor dragon—and sometimes even their Dragon Friend—would come back and join them for dinner or tea, expanding their acquaintance and giving the children and Phoenix valuable experiences in socializing with other dragons.

That was probably a very good thing for all of them, Phoenix in particular. Good manners did not seem to come to him naturally. But being a hatchling, and the novelty of a male fairy dragon, was enough to earn him a great deal of leniency—as well as several volunteer dragon-tutors. Several female fairy dragons were already expressing interest. He was well on his way to attracting his harem.

That topic Aunt Gardiner could explain to the children herself.

At night, she fell asleep whilst battling her own musings. Was it right to be so happy when she had run away from her home and abandoned her duties to her family and dragon?

One morning, Elizabeth rose particularly early and carried her newest dragon script reference and commonplace book down to the morning room. Lady Astrid had given her special leave to take it from the library. There was a particularly useful table she wanted to copy.

With it there was every chance she could finally make some headway into understanding the Netherfield paintings.

April cheeped from her cage and tucked her head back under her wing. Poor little dear was still exhausted from Barnwines Chudleigh's salon the prior afternoon. A fairy dragon invited to a salon? What a sight!

The Gardiners' morning room was plainer than Mama's—a testament to the fact that the children often joined their parents there. The paper hangings—yellow with blue flowers—were a mite faded and dated, but they captured the feelings of spring skies and sunshine, making the room warm and cheery on even the dreariest winter morning.

Aunt Gardiner was already at her place at the morning room table, sipping her tea and reading what looked like yesterday's afternoon post.

"After the late hours you kept last night, I am surprised to see you awake so early." Aunt chuckled and poured her a cup of tea.

She held up her precious book. "I do not wish to wear out my welcome at the library, as it were. I should like to return this tome as soon as possible."

"You have your eye on another, I assume?" Aunt cocked her head and lifted an eyebrow.

Elizabeth chuckled and opened her books.

"You might want to wait a moment on that. I received a letter from Mary that I am certain was intended as much for you as it was for me." She handed the letter to Elizabeth. "She mentions a friend called Heather that she believes might be a mutual acquaintance. I can only assume she is referring to you."

She rubbed her forehead. "I told her I would write to her under that name."

"But you have not, I imagine. The Order has kept you quite busy?"

"Do you think me quite horrible for not writing yet?"

"No. I am glad someone from Longbourn cares enough to write to us, though. I would have thought your mother or Jane would have told us—"

"I expect there is some persuasion going on. Mary—and Papa of course—are probably the only ones currently aware that I fled." Somehow that thought left a little pang in her belly.

She unfolded the missive. Mary's hand was neat and regular, like a teaching page to copy. Her letters never deviated from the correct form, not even once. Every 'e' looked exactly like every other one. None of Elizabeth's hurried scratching or the fancy swoops and curls she added when she was delighted with what she wrote. No, Mary was eminently legible and proper.

My dear Aunt,

So much has happened that I hardly know where to begin.

Jane and Mr. Bingley are engaged. Uncle Phillips has just finished the settlement papers. Mama, Jane and Lydia, and even Kitty on occasion, have spent a great deal of time at the dressmaker's, ordering Jane's wedding clothes. Mama should have liked to go to London to visit Uncle's warehouses there, but Papa has forbidden it. He cites time and budgets as his reasons, but I am certain there is something else on his mind.

Although I think he is happy with Jane's situation, he has been wholly cross these recent weeks, and I fear it will not improve soon. I am sure you will not be surprised to learn that Mr. Collins has made Lizzy an offer of marriage. Rather than accepting it as we all expected, she has fled Longbourn, and none of us know where she has gone.

Rumblkins, Heather, and I have Mama, my sisters, and Mr. Collins convinced that she was suddenly called away to tend a sick relation—an old, wealthy and well-connected aunt. The kind of relation that Lady Catherine would heartily approve of her waiting upon.

I know what you are thinking now. Mr. Collins still does not respond to Heather's persuasions, but he listens to me well enough. For the moment, they are all placated and asking very few questions.

Papa and Longbourn know the truth of Lizzy's absence, though. She believes them to have been in league, trying to exercise draconic persuasion upon her. But they both insist they are innocent. I fear it will be a rather hopeless business. They will not be moved to apologize because they believe they have done no wrong. She is not likely to return unless they do.

I hope she is happy and safe wherever she is. Heather and Rumblkins are well and have become fast friends in the absence of Elizabeth and April. I am not sure Rumblkins is the best of influences upon her. He has taught her some mischief that I am working hard to train her out of. Luckily Mr. Collins finds it amusing to see a cat and a bird at play.

I believe Mr. Collins is content, for the moment, to await Lizzy's return, but he will soon be required back at Lady Catherine's side. I do not know for how long he will continue to wait, though. The future of Longbourn estate hangs in the balance. I know Papa is deeply concerned.

I am, too. Longbourn deserves a proper Keeper, which we all know Mr. Collins cannot be.

Jane's wedding is planned for a fortnight hence. They will be taking a honeymoon trip to the Peaks—a full six weeks I am told. In an odd turn of events, Kitty, and not Lydia, is going to go with them. Since Miss Bingley will be moving back to London immediately after the wedding, taking the Hursts with her, the house will be left without a mistress for some time. Lydia has taken it into her mind that she will oversee the house whilst Jane and Bingley are away. Odder still, Mama and Jane both agree. I do not know what to make of it.

Elizabeth set the letter aside. "What do you make of this business with Lydia?"

"It seems a very odd thing, does it not? It is not as if the housekeeper cannot manage to keep things running in the absence of a mistress for a few weeks."

"I hardly think any of them believe this to be a learning opportunity for Lydia. Perhaps she sees it as an opportunity to get away from Papa's temper?" How bad had things become in her absence?

"He can be unpleasant when cross." Aunt Gardiner nodded but looked unconvinced.

"And do not doubt he is that. Mary says the fate of Longbourn is hanging in the balance." She propped her forehead on her hands and swallowed the acid at the back of her tongue.

"Perhaps she has bought into the same rhetoric that your father and Longbourn proclaim." Aunt grumbled under her breath.

"But what if—"

Aunt rapped the table with her knuckles. "You have been torturing yourself with that idea long enough. I want you to go to the Order today and ask that question of Lady Astrid, ask her to introduce you to Minister of the Keeps and Minister of the Blue Court to get their opinions as well. In fact, if you tell Lady Astrid your concerns, I think she would arrange a tea for all of you to discuss the matter."

"I ... I could not. It would be presumptuous. I dare not ask so much."

"My dear, she drafted much of the language in the amendments to the marriage clauses. I am certain she would welcome any opportunity to discuss it."

"She was permitted to—"

"To compose the legislation, yes, she was. You can imagine it might be very satisfying for her to talk with another woman about such things."

Elizabeth rubbed her forehead. "It is still difficult to believe such things can happen."

Aunt hid a chuckle behind her hand. "Where do you think the Bluestockings derived their name?"

Elizabeth's eyes bulged. "Surely not!"

Aunt shrugged, lips curved in a tiny smile.

The housekeeper scurried in with the morning post on a silver salver.

"Another letter from Mary? Here, this is definitely for you." Aunt passed a thick missive to her.

She opened the seal and a pile of sealed letters tumbled out.

These came for Lizzy some time ago, but Papa has kept them hidden away in his desk. I believe his intent has been to burn them. I think that unfair. She deserves to have letters directed to her. Would you please keep them safe until such time as we find her?

Elizabeth's face went cold. Three, no four letters with the return direction listed as Pemberley, Rosings Park, Kent. Though they were written in a young woman's hand, they were no doubt from little Pemberley.

The poor dear, she must be thinking terrible things because her letters had not been returned! Hopefully it was not already too late to remedy—

"Are you ready to go, Lizzy?" Uncle stuck his head into the morning room, shrugging on his coat.

Elizabeth tucked the letters inside her common-place book and gathered her books. "As soon as I get April and my pelisse."

Uncle escorted her to the Order and promised to return for her that afternoon. Everything she had planned for the day would wait until she read her letters in the library and penned her response. Perhaps she might even press one of the messenger dragons into service to deliver them immediately.

Just inside the door, Drew, a minor drake she frequently saw in the library, nearly ran her over.

April squawked and scolded, hovering close to Drew's long green nose. "Open your eyes! Get your nose out of your book, and watch where you are going!"

Elizabeth picked his book off the floor and handed it back to him. "You read dragon script?"

"Read, write and tutor it." He bowed, bending his front knees to drop his head and shoulders below hers.

Why of all times did she have to run into the very scholar she needed now?

"I have never met a dragon who could write before."

Drew puffed up a bit. "It is not a common accomplishment among dragon kind. It requires a certain disposition—"

"And thumbs." April snorted and flittered back to Elizabeth's shoulder.

"Opposable digits are helpful, but be assured, it requires more than just that to be a true dragon scribe. I have yet to meet the tatzelwurm who can write." He raised his head just a little higher than Elizabeth's, glaring at April.

"Perhaps I might ask your assistance. I have been studying dragon script, but I am in a terrible muddle sorting the vowel markings from the accent marks."

The crest on the back of his head lifted. Oh, he was a proud fellow.

"I would be honored to be of assistance. It can be a difficult point to decipher, especially if the script was not written neatly in the first place."

"Perhaps we might find a worktable in the library. I can show you the sample I am struggling with?"

Hopefully this would not take very long. He did not seem the long-winded type.

Drew followed her to the library where they found a large table, brightly lit by a sunbeam.

She laid out her commonplace book and the two books she had been consulting on the matter. "Here is the sample I have been trying to decipher." She pointed to a segment she had copied from memory from one of the Netherfield paintings and another similar one from the map room. "It seems like this book from the library and this one from Papa's collection are at odds with one another. This one says I should read this character as a vowel, the other says it is an accent mark, but it cannot be both—"

Drew squinted at her commonplace book. "Forgive my boldness, but it can be both."

"I have never heard such a thing."

"The way you formed this character, is it an exact copy of the original?" He tapped a word with his neatly trimmed talon.

"I wrote this from memory, but yes, I think it is accurate."

Drew gazed at the characters, turning this way and that, until his head was nearly upside down. "This is very, very interesting. May I copy it?" He fumbled in his satchel for a journal and a pencil.

"Of course."

His pencil was unusual, clearly made for a dragon's paw. Thick and knobby, it conformed to his boney toes. "I have rarely seen characters such as these. It is a sample of very old script, but more than that, it does not seem to have originated in Britain."

"What are you saying—"

A large man laden with a stack of books backed into her.

She jumped. He stumbled, dropping most of the books.

"Pray forgive me ..."

"Mr. Darcy!"

He dropped the final book and bowed. "Miss Elizabeth ... that is, Miss Bennet. I ... I had no idea of finding you here. Is your father with you?"

"No, he is not. My trip was rather unexpected."

"So, I have heard." Walker landed on the table near the open books, ruffling the pages as he folded his wings to his back. "I went to Meryton and was most distressed to hear of your departure from there. We need you very much. Our trek here was our last resort to find answers."

April landed on the table next to him. He bowed to her, and she to him.

Drew's forehead creased, and his lips retreated to bare his teeth. An expression of surprise, not aggression—at least not yet.

She fumbled with her commonplace book and withdrew the letters from Pemberley. "My sister sent these to my aunt for safekeeping. They arrived just an hour ago. I assume these might explain Walker's trip to Meryton?"

"Yes, indeed." He stooped to pick up the dropped books. "I came to the library in search of answers for Pemberley's woes, but it does not seem there is a single useful one in all these pages."

"I cannot imagine I have anything to offer that you cannot find here." She gestured to the many shelves. "I am sure Lady Astrid—"

"Has been of no help. Nor has Sir Edward. Infant firedrakes are so rare, the situation is outside of their experience—"

"He needs your help with Pemberley." Walker gently wrapped his foot around her wrist.

She grabbed the table and fell into the nearest chair. "Is she ill? Is she hurt? What has happened?"

How could he be so negligent in so short a time? With Rosings and Lady Catherine to turn to for help no less! What kind of Dragon Keeper was he?

"Nothing, everything." Darcy raked his hair. "I have no idea." He sank into the chair beside her.

"Tell me exactly what is going on. Everything. No detail is too small." She pressed her fist to her lips.

"I took her to Rosings, her brood mother, and at first all seemed well. Rosings bonded with her, and she seemed to respond to Rosings. Only a few days later though, Pemberley started teething—"

She clenched her fists and pressed them against the table. "But I told you exactly how to handle that, wrote it out in careful detail."

Pray let him not be so arrogant that he did not even read what she had given him.

"And it was immensely helpful. My sister and I have both read your notes so often they have nearly been committed to memory. We followed your recommendations to the letter, and they brought her such relief."

Walker caught her eye and nodded just a bit. Mr. Darcy was not exaggerating.

"I do not understand. What was the problem?"

"My aunt began to step in, suggesting that Pemberley's gums needed to be lanced—"

"Tell me you did not do anything so barbaric—and dangerous!"

He raised open palms. "No, no, I forbade it. But the threat frightened her, so I introduced Georgiana, my sister to her. She helped Pemberley write to you—"

She clutched her forehead, squeezing her eyes shut. "And she is upset I have not written back."

He nodded. "Then my cousin Anne heard of the amendments in the marriage clauses and determined to show me that she was the Keeper that Pemberley needed."

"You are betrothed to a cousin?"

"Only in Anne's and my aunt's minds." He threw up his hands.

He was in the same situation as she?

"Anne made things dramatically worse. She nearly lost Pemberley's dog and convinced her that you did not care for her anymore."

Elizabeth gasped and pressed the back of her hand to her mouth. "No! I will right that immediately."

"I assured her of that." Walker bobbed his head and shoulders. "But with everything else—"

"What else happened?"

Darcy groaned and scrubbed his face with his palms. "As near as I can put together, Lady Catherine's cockatrix made some mention of Mr. Collins' soon-coming wife. Pemberley took that to mean you would be coming to visit her directly. But then Collins wrote saying that he would not be returning with a wife at all."

Walker grumbled under his breath.

Darcy rested steepled hands against his forehead. "Since then, Pemberley has refused her food, even taken to hiding from me and Georgiana. She ignores Rosings and has lost interest in the new puppy we brought her. The only creature able to reach her seems to be the old hound. I have no idea how long that will last. I have done everything I know to bring her around, but I am at a loss."

"Has she lost weight?"

"I fear so."

"And her color?"

"She is more pink than red now. Lady Catherine called upon Pemberley and ordered her to eat properly, but it made little impression on her."

"What kind of Dragon Keeper does such a thing? One does not order a distressed dragon to do much of anything. Especially a baby." Elizabeth rose and paced along the table.

Walker huffed. "Just get to the point, Darcy. The little thing sleeps and sulks in Rosings' cave most of the time. She just lies on her nest and cries for you." He poked Elizabeth with his wingtip.

"Me? You must be joking. Certainly, there is some misunderstanding. Is Rosings—"

Walker leaned up and squawked in her face. "Contrary to what you might think from descriptions of her Keeper, Rosings could not be a better mentor or care-taker, far better than a typical brood mother. The problem is not her care or her Keeper. The problem is your absence." He poked her again.

"No, that cannot possibly be—"

"It sounds like something called 'attachment sickness.' Minor drakes can suffer from it, but I have never heard of it in a major dragon. Who would think ..." Drew said softly. "It is very serious. There is a book—" He scurried off.

"I have never heard of such a thing." Darcy scoured his forehead with his handkerchief.

"I have never heard of a name for it, but it sounds like something that affects some fairy dragons, too." April hopped toward Darcy and jumped up on his proffered finger.

He held her up as Elizabeth sat beside him.

"When hatchlings make particularly strong attachments, like Heather to Mary, separating them from their Dragon Friend too early can leave them pining at the loss. Some never recover. Perhaps it is the same for minor drakes. They are known for being very affectionate, too."

"Here." Drew dropped an open book between them with a dusty thud.

Shoulder to shoulder, they peered at the handwritten text.

... pallor, loss of appetite, leading to loss of strength. In extreme cases, death follows.

If the hatchling cannot be made to eat meat, bone broth and calves' foot jellies may be offered. But the best remedy is reunion with the missing Dragon Friend. If the separation has been caused by the death of that Friend, sometimes a close family member may be substituted.

"My heavens! That sounds like what you described in fairy dragons." She chewed her knuckle.

April landed on the page and examined the text closely as though she could actually read it. "I am glad to have a name for it: Attachment Sickness. You must write to Mary immediately and warn her!"

"I will, tonight. Do not worry."

"I know it is a great deal to ask of you, Miss Elizabeth, Pray, is there any way you could come to Rosings Park and see Pemberley, and perhaps stay with her until she recovers?"

"The text suggests it is her best chance for recovery." Drew pointed at the page.

"Yes, yes of course. I am staying with the Gardiners. We must speak with them, but I am sure they will supportive. He is solicitous after Pemberley's welfare. He became quite fond of her on the journey to Kent. Drew, are there other books that might be useful to consult before we leave?"

"Possibly." He led Darcy away to the shelves

She opened her commonplace book to a fresh page and pulled her pencil from her reticule. The receipt for bone broth was one she had not seen before, and if there was a chance it would help Pemberley, she could not risk forgetting it.

Darcy glanced over his shoulder at the luggage wagon, squinting in the nearly noonday sun. Her trunk was still there, nestled between his two larger ones. He had not been dreaming.

The weather was nearly perfect for travel, just a hint of crispness in the air and a bit of a breeze to keep everything fresh. The roads were clean and easy to traverse. All together a nearly ideal situation.

A little too perfect. His stomach tightened again. Too many things had gone right recently. She had appeared like some Grecian oracle among the library shelves, ready and willing to come to his aid. Uncle Matlock always said it was a double-edged sword when Providence smiled too broadly upon one. There would always be a dear price to be paid for the favor.

But to save Pemberley's life, no price would be too high. If only it were not already too late.

"Have a care, Darcy!" Walker cawed overhead. "That horse you are riding is going to wander off the road for a graze if you do not pay attention."

Darcy shook his head and steered his horse back toward the road.

Walker was right, of course. He ought to pay better attention. For as little sleep as he had recently, he probably should have ridden in the coach with Miss Bennet and her Uncle, but somehow doing so felt like intruding on their privacy.

No, that was not entirely true.

Unless they were discussing Pemberley or dragons, she seemed perpetually annoyed with him. Taxing her patience when she was doing him such a favor seemed ungrateful.

Walker landed on the luggage cart and beckoned Darcy to ride nearer. "I spoke with Rustle whilst you were dining with the Gardiners last night. There are things you should know." His voice was low as he looked over his shoulder at the carriage.

Darcy pinched the bridge of his nose. "And you could not tell me any of this last night?"

"With you in a flurry of packing and planning? I hardly think you would have remembered anything I said, if you had even listened at all."

Starting well after midnight to pack for a journey at dawn probably was not the best of plans, but there had been little choice.

He yawned. Probably best not dwell on just how tired he was right now. "What is so important for me to know?"

"Do you wonder why she fled her father's house?"

"I assume it has something to do with Collins. Since he is not returning to Kent married, she probably refused him and is escaping her father's temper."

"According to Rustle, Longbourn attempted to persuade her to accept while Collins was making an offer of marriage. He says also they believe her father complicit in the entire affair."

"Bloody hell! I would never have thought they would stoop so low."

Surely the Blue Order would not tolerate their Historian so flagrantly violating the Accords. If they knew. But did they?

Considering her character, probably not.

"It is utterly despicable on both their parts." Walker flapped sharply. "Who could blame her for running? But now that she has spent so much time at the Blue Order offices, there are enough who know her whereabouts that word could make it back to her family. It would take little to trace her to Rosings from there. She might have very little time in which to help Pemberley."

"I cannot imagine her being willing to leave before Pemberley is safe once again."

Walker squawked, loud enough to make him wince. "Are you truly so thick?"

He clutched his forehead. "Apparently with so little sleep, I am. Just come out with it."

Walker flapped his wings, shouting without volume. "You owe her a tremendous debt whether or not she is able to help Pemberley. If her family comes for her, you cannot turn her over to them. You must have some plan to keep her and her reputation safe."

He should have thought of that himself.

If Bennet knew she was at Rosings, he would probably send Collins for her and with Lady Catherine to support the match, it would be exceedingly difficult for Elizabeth to deny him again, especially if Aunt Catherine promised her free access to Pemberley and the rest of the dragons at Rosings Park.

"That is not the only thing you must protect her from. You must insure she does not fall under the influence of Wickham."

"Wickham?" The name sliced like a knife through his ribs. "What has he to do with any of this?"

"How do you think she got to London? The minor drake that lives in the mews behind Colonel Forster's house saw it all. He said that Wickham arranged for her to accompany him and Mrs. Forster's maid to London, in the Forsters' coach."

"Why would he continue to bother with her when she had no further connection to Pemberley and nothing of material value?"

And why did it bother him so much to think of Wickham's lascivious stare on her for hours on the road? It was probably just natural, considering what he had done to Georgiana, that any thought of him would be repugnant.

"He heard her telling the Gardiner children dragon stories at Christmas and has deduced she is a Keeper. I am told that Wickham has also been seen in Meryton with her and April, trying to address April himself. Of course, she will have nothing to do with him—she is far more clever than the average fairy dragon. Even she can see Wickham is not finished meddling in the affairs of dragons."

Darcy dragged his hand down his face. That simply was not possible. His duties in the regiment should be keeping him too busy to have time or energy for any further mischief. They certainly would after he wrote several letters.

"You should have told her the truth about Wickham long ago."

"And reveal Georgiana's secrets? No, I promised her that no one would know she had nearly eloped with him." Darcy drew a long breath and exhaled slowly. "I will see she is safe without exposing Georgiana. Besides, he is in Hertfordshire, and we are for Kent. I do not see how he could affect Miss Bennet from there."

"He has poisoned her against you, you know." Walker picked at something between his toes.

The insult was not lost.

"The truth will be out, eventually."

"Eventually is usually too late." Walker muttered something insulting under his breath and took to his wings again.

Apparently, Walker's his informant drake did not tell him what Clarington's last letter had informed Darcy, that the militia would soon be leaving Meryton. At that point any remaining threat to the Bennets would be over.

The bigger problem would be protecting Miss Bennet from her own family. Walker was right. He did owe her that. But how? He would find a way, somehow.

That could wait, though. The more immediate problem was less than a mile in the offing and probably contributed more to Walker's ill temper than either Wickham or Longbourn's despicable behavior.

Cait's folly.

Cockatrix, unlike their stodgy male counterparts, were by their very nature vain, prideful, and difficult. They considered most humans and dragons below their notice and did not hesitate to make that opinion clear. Cait would not appreciate another female, especially one that Walker respected, entering her territory, even if she was merely human.

Perhaps it was best Walker had flown off.

Darcy pulled up to the side of the coach. Gardiner slid open the side glass.

"Before we go on to the manor, I must introduce you to Lady Catherine's cockatrix. Her lair is just ahead." He gestured toward the folly whose edge they could just make out around the bend in the road.

"Walker has told me of her." Miss Elizabeth peeked through the window.

"He has told you?" Walker never spoke of Cait to anyone but him.

A shriek from the folly pierced the air and a large black mass of feathers flapped toward them.

Cait was a glorious creature in the air. Iridescent black feathers streaked with deep blue and purple caught the sunlight. Her wingspan was as large as Walker's but looked larger for the length of her feathers. Long, slightly curling tail feathers trailed behind her, at least a yard long. She usually perched above ground to show them to their best advantage. But her true glory was the massive ruff of head feathers. Streaked with purple throughout, they stood straight out from her head, like a fluffy turban, often obscuring her eyes and all but the razor-sharp tip of her beak. When one could see her eyes, they were shining onyx beads, following every movement in her surroundings. For all her stunning, showy looks, she was still a vicious predator, not to be taken lightly.

"Who do you bring into my domain?" Cait perched along the edge of the carriage's roof.

Technically, the domain belonged to Rosings, who tolerated Cait under most circumstances. But it never went well to mention that to Cait.

Darcy dismounted and tied his horse to the luggage wagon.

He approached Cait and bowed. "I bring help for Pemberley, the one she has been crying for."

"That heartless woman comes here? I will not tolerate her—abandoning a baby—"

The coach door flew open, and a Grecian fury jumped out. Surely there were flames in her wake.

Miss Elizabeth's bonnet was gone, her hair, unpinned and flowing loose behind her in cascading curls that reached below her waist. She held the edges of her cloak in either hand. "How dare you! She was taken from me. I did not abandon her."

Darcy swallowed hard.

Cait extended her wings and swooped to the ground.

Elizabeth extended the edges of her cloak and bent slightly forward, matching Cait's posture. They circled, gazes locked on each other.

Cait screamed, sending chills down Darcy's spine. Somehow Elizabeth matched the sound.

He shuddered.

Beside him, Gardiner lunged forward. "No."

Darcy stayed him. Coming between two females vying for dominance would only escalate the conflict. For all her pomp and show, Cait could be deadly. They would all be fortunate if no blood was spilt.

Cait pecked at the ground near Elizabeth's feet. Any rational creature would have jumped aside. Elizabeth stomped near Cait's tail feathers.

Walker circled overhead. "Elizabeth, no!"

Cait squawked and took to her wings. She cawed at Walker and dove at Elizabeth.

Elizabeth dodged, catching one of Cait's tail feathers as she did.

Cait seemed to halt midair, screaming.

No one, human or dragon, touched Cait's tail feathers.

Elizabeth pulled her down with just enough force to ground her, but not pull the feathers out.

Cait pulled up to her full height and rotated slowly, displaying her full glory in a sunbeam.

Elizabeth raised the edges of her cloak and spun, her hair and cloak whirling behind her in a display equally glorious.

A bead of sweat tricked down Darcy's temple. He ran a finger under his collar. Such a woman! She would probably be embarrassed to know he had been watching. But then again, maybe not. Where dragons were concerned, she had shown little self-consciousness.

Cait launched and folded her tail back. She was about to dive.

Elizabeth ran three steps toward her and leapt at Cait, screaming and cloak-wings flapping. How had she perfectly mastered a cockatrix shriek?

Cait faltered and back-winged, retreating. Elizabeth held her eyes a moment longer, then dropped the edges of her cloak and stepped back. Cait landed at Elizabeth's feet, wings wrapped around her body, and touched the ground with her beak. Elizabeth brushed the top of her head ruff with her cloak, a gracious and gentle acknowledgement of her victory. By all rights, she could have decimated her rival's feathers, marking her as the inferior female for all to see.

Rosings would approve, and Pemberley would only adore her more for her kindness.

Elizabeth's face glowed with the flush of dominance and a sheen of sweat. She turned to him, hair and eyes still wild. "Pray sir, would you introduce us properly?"

Darcy jumped. "Of course. Miss Bennet, may I present Cait, Dragon Friend of Lady Catherine de Bourgh?"

Cait bobbed her head. Would she hate him now for witnessing her defeat?

"I am pleased to make your acquaintance. May I present April," Elizabeth looked toward the coach and beckoned her forth, "my Dragon Friend?"

Thankfully, the little flutterbob had kept out of the dominance display. She landed near Elizabeth's feet, well away from Cait, and bobbed her head.

Cait nodded an acknowledgement, honoring Elizabeth by recognizing something so inconsequential as a fairy dragon.

"I will make Rosings aware of your arrival." Cait flew off in a flutter of feathers.

Several ruff feathers floated to the ground.

Mr. Gardiner rushed to Elizabeth's side. "That was an incredibly foolhardy, dangerous thing to do."

Walker landed on the front corner of the coach squawking and scolding. "Have you any idea of what she could have done to you?"

She scooped up the loose feathers. "Yes, I do. But I am not willing to live in the shadow of a dominant cockatrix, even briefly. I am surprised you tolerate it."

Walker snorted something that sounded very much like a laugh. He would never have tolerated such a remark from anyone else.

"Is this the kind of greeting we are to expect when we reach the house?" Gardiner handed her a small reticule and she retrieved a set of hair pins which she held in her teeth. She began smoothing and twisting her hair.

Darcy gulped. Somehow this seemed far too intimate a moment for so public a setting.

Walker looked at him and smirked. "The Lady is far more conventional in her displays. But she does prefer to be the superior female in the room."

"That is good to know. At least I do not need to fear having my eyes scratched out when I meet her. That is something." She tucked the final hairpin into place.

"Elizabeth!" Gardiner gasped. "Please remember we are entering refined company. Moreover, I am bringing her the goods she ordered. I have no doubt she will welcome—"

"A merchant? You will be lucky not to be ushered to the servants' entrance and housed with them." Walker snorted again. "Only those, like Collins, who believe she has something to offer them consider her refined."

Darcy clutched his temples. Yes, dragons were direct, but this was a step too far.

"Do not be embarrassed for Walker, sir. I quite understand how dragons talk about people. I know what they have said about my family. In that we are equal." She curtsied and returned to the coach.

His face flushed. Their families equal? Of course, they were not. But perhaps to the dragons they might be.

Gardiner followed and in short order, they set off toward the manor.

Darcy mounted and followed the luggage wagon where Walker perched. "She blames you for taking Pemberley away."

"I had gathered as much." He rubbed his eyes with finger and thumb.

"That does not bother you?"

Of course, it did—that she should be in the world, thinking ill of him.

"There is little I can do about it."

"You could tell her the truth." Ah, Walker's schoolmaster voice.

"I will not; it is not best for her."

"And you know what is best for her?" He flapped sharply, his serpentine tail lashing.

"In this case, it is obvious."

"You are so full of yourself, Darcy." Walker flew off.

Probably in search of Cait. How ironic, she would probably be much better company for the set down Elizabeth had delivered.

When her uncle handed her down from the carriage at the front of the manor, Elizabeth looked as tidy and put together as she had when they had left the Gardiner house that morning. How was that possible with no lady's maid or even a mirror? No other woman he knew could manage such a feat.

The butler showed them in to the small parlor Lady Catherine favored during the spring. Stuffed and over-decorated like the rest of the house, he was told it demonstrated good taste and refinement. He and Fitzwilliam secretly believed it demonstrated the ability to hire a good staff to keep the dust at bay. At least Elizabeth would probably enjoy the dragon images on nearly every surface.

"So, you have returned, have you Darcy?" Lady Catherine rose from her seat nearest the fireplace. The taffeta of her gown rustled. She was dressed to preserve the distinction of rank, from the cut and blue hue of her gown, to the grand dragon signet she wore, all who saw her should know exactly where they stood.

"I have, madam, and I have brought back—"

"The source of your problem in the first place." She slowly approached Elizabeth, eyes narrow, examining her.

Elizabeth lifted her chin and held Lady Catherine's gaze.

"If you consider me the source of the problem, then, madam, I shall take my leave. It is not my habit to stay where I am unwelcome." Elizabeth curtsied and turned away.

"Not so fast there, young woman." Lady Catherine stomped and stormed after her, cutting her off at the doorway.

Gardiner opened his mouth, but Darcy stayed him with an open hand.

"I pray you importune me no longer. There is just enough time for us to make it back to London before dark if we leave immediately." Elizabeth sidestepped.

"I have not dismissed you yet." She lifted and arm to block Elizabeth's way.

"I require neither your acknowledgement nor your dismissal. I come on Rosings' invitation. Cait has gone to announce my arrival."

"Cait? I hardly imagine—"

Elizabeth reached into her reticule, pulled out several of Cait's feathers, and allowed them to float down to Lady Catherine's feet. "I fear her dignity may be a bit bruised at the moment. She will probably not bear it well. You might consider offering her a special treat tonight. I know cockatrix are particularly fond of muntjac, if you have any on the estate. Giving her leave to hunt one, perhaps with Walker's company, might go a long way in soothing her temper."

"Impudent girl, presuming to tell me how to manage my cockatrix."

"One does not manage a cockatrix, madam. One negotiates with a cockatrix and finds peaceful ways to live with one. But manage, never."

Lady Catherine's jaw dropped, and she broke eye contact. Was it possible? Lady Catherine conceded?

"It says a great deal of you, Lady Catherine, that you have been able to coexist so amiably with one for so long. A cockatrix is a particular companion and as choosy in their Dragon Friends as they are their brood-mates." Elizabeth stooped to retrieve the feathers and handed them to Lady Catherine.

A small, slow smile bloomed over Lady Catherine's features.

Heaven's above, she was impressed—annoyed to be sure as well, but she was impressed.

"May I present Miss Elizabeth Bennet? You know her uncle, Mr. Gardiner." Darcy cut in.

"So, then, Miss Bennet. Assuming you choose to grace us with your presence, you will see to Pemberley's needs?"

"As much as I am able, madam. I am anxious to see her."

"I suppose that is a signal that I should see your things sent to your rooms and arrange for someone to show you the way to Rosings' lair."

"If you please, madam."

Something on Elizabeth's face hinted that she was about to suggest that Lady Catherine perform the service herself. Probably best that she had found the self-control not to say that. It might have been too much.

"I will take you myself as soon as you are ready." Darcy bowed from his shoulders.

10
Chapter

"I SEE NO reason to wait." Elizabeth peeked at April still tucked in her hood.

She nodded silently. Apparently, she was not prepared to face Lady Catherine on her own.

"Please, come this way." Darcy gestured toward the door. "I hope you do not mind if we leave through the kitchen. It is a much more direct route."

He led her to the back of the house through pretentious and over decorated corridors. Mama would have found it spectacular and overwhelming. Elizabeth found it difficult to breathe.

What relief to enter into a spacious kitchen, bustling with activity. A dainty little zaltys—with bright green scales, shiny black eyes, and long, lush eyelashes—curled in a basket on the generous hearth. The basket blanket had been embroidered with a dainty "B." Monogrammed blankets for the house dragons?

The zaltys lifted her head and stared at Elizabeth.

"I shall introduce you when we return. We are to see Pemberley now." Darcy spoke softly and bowed from his shoulders.

A kitchen maid glanced over her shoulder and smiled. Did the staff think him dear or daft? It was difficult to tell. Still, his attention to the little dragon was pleasing.

The zaltys flicked her tail amiably and lay back down.

Interesting. The little dragon liked Darcy.

So did April, and Rustle, and Rumblkins.

If he was such an irresponsible Keeper to Pemberley, why did they tolerate him?

From the back door, they took a western-leading path.

"Is there anything more you can tell me about Pemberley's condition?" She fought to keep her voice pleasant. That was the ladylike thing to do.

He kicked a small rock out of the path. It skittered into the undergrowth. "Her tail blisters have not healed. Georgiana made up the salve from your notes and has been applying it several times a day. But since Pemberley continues to lash her tail about, they have only got worse."

"How long has this been going on?"

"Better than a fortnight, I think. It began when Georgiana's letters were not answered …"

Had he intended that as a slap in the face? His expression did not suggest so.

"I wish I had known sooner." She chewed her knuckle as they hurried down the narrow, deeply shaded path. If only she had not run off, she might have received those letters when they arrived.

Surely Papa would not have prohibited her from responding. She could have advised them on Pemberley's care and even offered the little dragon words of encouragement in her own hand. The entire situation might have been averted had she not been foolish and impulsive.

They paused at the mouth of a large cavern, perhaps half again as large as the entrance to Longbourn's cave. Shuffling and rasping sounds filtered from within.

She edged a little closer and peered into the darkness, barely making out a nest to one side. The tip of a lashing tail poked just above the edge of the nest, along with the crest of Pemberley's head. But there was no acknowledgement, no reaction to their approach at all.

How utterly unlike the little drakling she knew. Her stomach twisted into a tight knot. What had she done!

"Cowntess Rosings," Darcy called.

Scrapings and heavy footsteps approached, and a flapping of feathers that surely must be Cait.

Cait landed on a rock jutting from the cavern entrance. A mature, red firedrake poked her head out of the cavern. Stately and ancient, she was a presence not to be taken lightly.

"Cowntess Rosings, may I present Miss Elizabeth Bennet." Darcy gestured toward her.

Elizabeth folded her cloak around her body and curtseyed deep, knee to floor, head bowed.

Rosings stepped closer and sniffed Elizabeth thoroughly. "You smell like wyvern."

And the firedrake smelled vaguely like sulfur.

Elizabeth slowly rose. "Our estate dragon is a wyvern, Cowntess. I expect everything at Longbourn smells like him."

The corner of Rosings' mouth lifted. Probably as close to a smile as the old dragon ever got. But at least it was a good sign.

"You are 'her?'"

"Her?"

Rosings pointed toward the nest with her chin. "The one the baby calls 'her.'"

"I am afraid I do not actually know what she calls me. May I and my Friend April enter?" April peeked out from her hood.

"A fairy dragon?" Rosings sneered.

"Indeed, Cowntess. Walker calls her Lairda April."

Rosings blinked and peered closely at April.

April hopped to Elizabeth's shoulder, covered herself with her wings and bowed.

"That is saying a great deal coming from Walker. You may both enter. Announce her, Cait."

Elizabeth stopped mid-step. That was a different protocol, but well within Rosings' right to regulate her territory as she saw fit. Not every dragon ignored protocol the way Longbourn did.

Cait glided to the edge of the nest, perched and peered inside. "Get up and look. 'Her' is here."

The tail tip and head ridge disappeared into the nest with a plaintive cry. Rosings pointed at the nest. Elizabeth ran toward it.

Pemberley huddled in a tight ball, whimpering and shaking.

"Dearling, it is well now. I am here, and everything will be all right." Elizabeth climbed into the nest and tried to embrace her.

Pemberley pulled away. "No! You no like me now."

"Of course, I do."

"You no write me. You no want talk me. You not like me."

April perched on the edge of the nest and trilled softly. Pemberley unfurled a little.

"That is better." She scratched under Pemberley's chin. "Something happened, and your letters were hidden from me. I only received them yesterday."

"How that be?" Pemberley lifted her head a little. Darcy had been right, her color was very bad, and her eyes dull. "Who did that?"

"It does not matter. I have read them all now and came myself to answer them. That is what matters."

"I want know who took my letters. Grouchy Longbourn?"

"I do not honestly know. I was in London when they arrived."

"What London?"

"A big place with a library of many books of dragons. I … I went to there to learn more about baby dragons."

"Like me?" She pressed her head into Elizabeth's side. "You not forget me?"

"Never. I could never do that."

"You still like me?"

She took Pemberley's face in her hands. "My darling, I love you very dearly and always will. I cannot tell you how I have missed you and longed for your company. I am so happy to be here with you now."

Pemberley squeaked an odd little sobby-sound and wrapped her neck around Elizabeth's waist. Elizabeth returned the embrace.

Cait and Rosings exchanged glances, simultaneously skeptical and somewhat pleased. Clearly neither of them had a great deal of patience for the cranky baby.

"There now, that is much better. Much, much better." She held Pemberley and rocked for several minutes. "I have heard you are teething."

"Keeper gave me and Dog bone. I like bone. I like chew." Pemberley sent an adoring look toward Darcy.

He colored and looked aside. Funny, he often wore the same uneasy expression in company in Meryton.

"May I touch your new teeth?"

Pemberley started. "You no cut me? Lady want lance—cut—me."

"Heaven forfend! I would never do such a thing. Do you not trust me anymore?"

Pemberley whimpered and opened her mouth.

It smelt of lavender, peppermint and clove. Thank heavens! Darcy had been following her instructions.

She massaged Pemberley's gums with the heel of her hand. Hard knobs poked from just below the surface.

"That feel good!" Pemberley muttered, Elizabeth's hand still in her mouth.

"Will you allow Keeper and I to do this for you until your teeth come in?"

Pemberley purred.

Draklings purred? She had never read or heard that before. One more thing to add to her commonplace book tonight.

Elizabeth beckoned Darcy nearer. "Now if we are to do this for you, you must promise never to bite, even if there is an accidental pinch. Sometimes there is one when a tooth pokes through. Remember, your baby fangs can do great damage if you bite."

"I not bite—not you or Keeper." Pemberley rubbed her head against Elizabeth's waist.

"All right, then open. I will show Keeper what to do."

Pemberley opened her mouth wide, a gaping maw equipped with sharp baby fangs in the front and red swollen gums behind.

"Take your hand like this." She curled her fingers tight and pressed the heel of her hand forward. "Rub the hardest part of your hand against her gums, going in parallel, not against them. It is even better to add a few drops of peppermint and clove oils, but it can be done without."

She demonstrated.

At least he did not hesitate when she urged him to try. His hands were big and a little clumsy, but Pemberley seemed to trust him implicitly. That was a good sign.

But it was in the nature of babies to trust. Darcy was lucky for that. An older dragon would not have tolerated an inattentive Keeper. Darcy's willingness suggested he was only ignorant, though, not willfully ignoring the little dragon's needs. Perhaps there was time to right the wrongs done here after all.

Pemberley purred again.

"Does that mean she is happy?" Darcy asked.

Elizabeth tried not to roll her eyes. "Are you happy, Pemberley?"

"I happy."

Darcy offered her a handkerchief to wipe her hands.

"I think you shall have your first set of teeth within a fortnight, a month at most." She wiped her hands and returned the handkerchief. A firedrake's saliva was viscous, sticky stuff, designed to protect when they exhaled flame.

"I still have bones, too?"

"Of course, you may."

"Dog, too? Dog like bones. Want meet Dog?"

Darcy bit his upper lip, probably trying not to chuckle. "We would certainly like to see Dog."

Pemberley clambered out of the nest and waddled off deeper into the cavern. He helped her climb from the nest, and they followed Pemberley.

"This Dog." Pemberley gently bumped an old hound with her nose.

He licked her face and wagged. Beside him a puppy yipped and wagged, climbing over Pemberley's neck.

"This Puppy. Have Dog and Puppy, now. I like Dog and Puppy." She nuzzled the puppy.

"A puppy, sir? What made you present her with one?"

Was his face coloring?

He shrugged. "It seemed a sound idea. To ensure she has a warm companion."

He was right—and she probably would have tried it herself had it occurred to her. But who had ever heard of a dragon keeping a pet dog? One more addition to her book.

"Rosings Park has a shepherding drake who helped me find one with the right disposition."

She knelt beside the dogs and played with them. "They are delightful creatures. Have you thanked Cowntess Rosings for allowing you to have them with you?"

Pemberley hung her head.

"Then you must do so now. Go on." Elizabeth pointed toward Rosings and Cait.

"Thank you."

Rosings nodded somberly. Cait snickered under her breath.

"Good manners are especially important when one is a vikontes. We must ask Cowntess Rosings to begin to teach you. Those things are easiest to learn when one is small." She stroked under Pemberley's chin.

"You teach?" Pemberley looked over Elizabeth's shoulder.

"Of course, I will. 'Her' is quite correct." Was Rosings laughing under her breath?

Cait swooped past and landed on ledge in the wall. "It is time for her to retire to her chambers in the manor now."

Pemberley wound her neck around Elizabeth in a choke hold. "Her not go!"

"Stop your complaining little one, and be a proper hostess." Cait squawked. "You can come with us—"

"Pray forgive me, Cait, but is that wise?" Darcy asked.

"Come." Cait's voice turned shrill. Pray let her not screech! Pemberley did not need to be frightened now!

Rosings grumbled under her breath. "The feathered one is correct. You should come." Rosings lumbered deeper into the cavern.

Elizabeth unwound Pemberley from her, but laid her arm over Pemberley's shoulders. They followed Rosings down a dark passage. Once her eyes adjusted, the trickles of light from cracks in the rock above were just enough to be able to see a step or two ahead.

The tunnel was just wide enough for Rosings to pass without scraping her wings against the rock, so she, Pemberley and Darcy were able to walk abreast comfortably. Cait flew behind them, gliding from one wall perch to the next.

"Where going?"

"I have no idea. I have never been in this tunnel." He turned to Elizabeth. "I thought Fitzwilliam, my cousin, and I had traversed every passage at Rosings Park when we were boys."

"So, there are yet some secrets kept from you, sir?"

"It appears so."

Why was he smiling at her like that? He was a well-looking man to be sure.

And one who took Pemberley away from her, only to the baby's detriment. That she could never forget. Or forgive.

The rocky corridor opened up ahead of them into what looked like household cellars.

"Are we beneath the manor?" Elizabeth asked.

"Indeed. Come." Rosings headed toward what looked like firelight coming through a very wide door-way on the far side of the cellar.

"Those are your chambers." Cait glided past and into the open door.

"I am to stay in the cellar?"

Darcy shook his head, gaping.

"I had supposed Walker to be exaggerating when he suggested that sort of welcome as likely."

"I cannot imagine that is what my aunt truly intends for you." Who would have thought him capable of such an expression? His sheer astonishment alone was worth spending a few nights in a cellar.

"Be quiet Darcy, that is precisely what Rosings intends," Cait called from inside the room.

Uncle would not be pleased when he learned of this. She bit her lip. If they had to, she and Uncle could take rooms at the inn in Hunsford.

Rosings nudged her into the room. Three steps in, she stopped and stared, slack jawed. Darcy halted beside her.

The chamber was twice as large as the elaborate parlor Lady Catherine had seen them in, and the ceiling at least twice as high. All the normal accoutrements of a bed chamber filled the room, fine elegant furniture, but not nearly as ornate as what she had seen at Rosings manor—far more to her taste, if truth be told. It seemed to all be pushed up near the walls, though, leaving large open areas throughout the room, like many of the rooms at the Blue Order.

Rosings ducked her head and shuffled into the room.

"These are quarters for my guests. I hope they are satisfactory." Rosings seemed to smirk.

Elizabeth curtseyed. "I am honored to be your guest."

"Do not sound so surprised. You did not expect you would have to stay in Pemberley's nest, did you?" Cait laughed.

"It would have been acceptable to me, to be able to stay near her."

Darcy gasped.

Rosings laughed hard enough to make the walls rumble. "Pemberley may stay here with you." She pointed toward a drakling-sized rug laden with clean hay.

Pemberley gave a happy squeal and waddled toward the hay. She leapt and landed in the middle of it, sending hay flying. Good that the fireplace was on the opposite side of the room.

"Be warned, the baby snores." Rosings snuffed.

"My father does too. I am accustomed to it."

"What will you do with her?"

"The first thing is to see that she starts eating again. Once her color is back, and her hide is in good condition, we will begin following the recommendations for dealing with attachment sickness."

"What is that? I have never heard of it." Rosings scowled.

Perhaps she did not like the reminder that she did not know everything. Her Keeper certainly would not. "It is something young drakes are susceptible to. We think that the peculiarities of her hatching have made her vulnerable to it. But there is every reason to believe we shall be able to remedy the problem."

"She will always want you."

"That may be so, but it does not have to make her ill."

"You should simply stay with her." Rosings punctuated her statement with a flick of her tail.

"That is not easily managed."

"I do not see why. She is a vikontes. Her needs outrank those of any wyvern."

"But she already has a Keeper, and I am Keeper to another dragon. One simply cannot order away a dragon's Keeper to another dragon."

Rosings snorted. "Foolish nonsense. For all we have to tolerate from you warm-bloods, we should at least have a choice of which warm-bloods we associate with."

Darcy shot her a warning glance.

Ah, Rosings was one of those who did not favor the changes in the Accords. All the oldest dragons probably felt similarly. Now was not going to be the best time to present the case from the "warm-blood" side of things. Considering that Lady Catherine was her Keeper there might never be such a time.

Rosings tossed her head. "If you require a human attendant, the bell on the mantel will alert her. Behind the red door is a stairway. Use it to reach the ground level of the house when Lady requires your presence. As far as I am concerned, you need never go there, though Lady may try to demand it. I leave that to you to settle. Darcy, see that Pemberley is not disturbed by Lady's demands."

Darcy briefly shut his eyes. Was that his attempt not to roll his eyes in Rosings' presence?

"I will leave you now to enjoy the quiet of my lair. Cait will attend you if you need anything further."

"I will what?" Cait dove past Rosings face as she swooped from one side of the room of the other. "I am not a servant."

"I am not the one who lost my feathers to her." Rosings shambled out.

Cait stared at her, feathers in full fluff.

"Rosings says that to taunt you." Elizabeth kept her voice soft and level.

"She says that because she is an arrogant firedrake, so full of herself—"

"That she will make sport with the finest creature on the estate, simply because she can."

Cait cocked her head sharply. "Precisely! You understand!"

"I do, and perhaps you might find that Walker would as well."

"You think so?" Cait flipped back her head feathers to reveal her eyes.

"Cockatrice dignity is something only another of your kind would truly understand. I think you would find him rather sympathetic. If, of course, you approach him properly."

Cait pretended to preen her wing. "And how might that be?"

"I have found cockatrices as a rule are rather no-nonsense fellows. Present your wounds of the day in simple terms, without swooping or shrieking, and in as few words as possible."

Beside her, Darcy's jaw dropped.

"He barely listens to me if I shriek. He would ignore me all together if I were quiet."

She shrugged with a little flourish of her cloak. "My quietest sister, Jane, consistently receives far more attention than Lydia who shrieks constantly."

"Truly?" Cait peered at Darcy, challenging.

Darcy edged backward. "Ah, yes, I am certain Miss Elizabeth's observations are quite correct."

"And you think it would please Walker?"

Darcy dragged his hand over his face. "I dare say it might."

"Nothing else has worked." Cait flew out.

"Walker may hate you for this." Darcy grumbled under his breath.

"More likely he will thank me. He is as ready for a broodmate as she. Have you not noticed all the signs in him?"

"There are signs?"

Elizabeth pressed her temples. "Males become as broody as the females."

"That is not included in any of the dragon lore I have studied."

"Truly, I wonder at how little scribes have seen fit to write about. Shall I write it all down for you?"

"I would be grateful."

How had he missed the sarcasm in her tone? Well it would serve him right when he was deathly embarrassed by all the detail she would have to include.

Pemberley waddled up to them. "You stay here now? With me?" She wrapped a wing around each of them.

"You, Keeper, and I shall have a nice long visit. Are you hungry?"

She bobbed her head from side to side. "I hungry."

"Would you care for sheep or—" Darcy asked.

"I like sheep. Bring Dog and Puppy here, too? I want them play her."

He patted Pemberley's head. "Of course. I will see to all of that. Pray excuse me."

"Keeper good." She pressed her head to Elizabeth's chest. "You like him?"

"I … I … he is your Keeper. What more needs to be said?" She cradled Pemberley's head.

Vexing, perplexing man. How could he be so different among those at Rosings from how he was everywhere else?

For the next three days, Pemberley tolerated no separation from Elizabeth, nearly panicking when Uncle Gardiner came to take his leave. It required half a day to reassure her that Elizabeth would not leave with Uncle Gardiner in a dog cart with a dog of her own.

Outside of that one instance, keeping constant company with the drakling proved no hardship. Darcy's constant presence, though, proved awkward at best and annoying the rest of the time. His very diligence and politeness made him most aggravating. He plied her with questions about Pemberley, Walker, Cait, and every other dragon he knew. And it seemed he knew quite a number.

Just how many dragons were there at Rosings Park? With Dragon Friends among the servants, not like Mrs. Hill who thought of Rumblkins as a cat and an ordinary pet, but genuine dragon-hearers recognized by the Blue Order, there seemed to be a dragon just about everywhere one turned. And if not an actual dragon, multitudes of dragon imagery filled every nook of the house. Who could have imagined such a place?

A steady stream of visits from the household and other estate dragons provided a welcome distraction, and many opportunities to teach Pemberley how to interact properly with minor dragons—a lesson Longbourn had never learnt.

Good to his word, Darcy brought Blanche, the little kitchen zaltys down for an introduction, along with her friend Quincy. That little puck was all mischief and good intentions; so much like the Gardiner children she felt a brief pang of homesickness for them. Wellsbey came by from the fields to check on the puppy, though it seemed a slim excuse to gain an introduction. He was a good, steady sort of drake and Darcy treated him with the same respect he showed every dragon. Darcy even welcomed a rather frenzied, pell-mell visit from a group of barn tatzelwurms that made Rumblkins seem calm and reliable.

How was it then that he could be so good to dragonkind and so horrid to mankind? It made no sense. Why would he tear Pemberley away from her only to insist on reuniting them? Why would he do everything he could to ruin Wickham, when he was so generous with the dragons?

Heavens above! The man even brought a special supply of buttons just to keep Quincy happy—and not cheap ones, either. Each was unique and chosen to match the dragon's tastes. Who did that while impoverishing a childhood friend?

The more time she spent in Darcy's company, the more vexing the dichotomy became.

On the fourth day, Lady Catherine sent Darcy with an invitation to compel her to take nuncheon with the rest of the company at Rosings Park.

"Pray forgive the rather forceful language of my aunt's invitation. She feels the loss of your company greatly." Darcy looked vaguely uncomfortable.

One could only imagine exactly what Lady Catherine had said.

"Not as much as Pemberley will."

"I have asked Wellsbey to take her and the dogs for a bit of a ramble. There is a small clearing in the woods near Rosings' lair that will give them a secluded spot to stretch their legs. It will also give Blanche an opportunity to come down with some of the other minor dragons to clean Pemberley's nest."

"I did not realize Blanche was a maid."

"She is not, but as the housekeeper's Friend, she takes pride in the house and wishes to see the same standards below stairs as above." He smiled, a kind smile that approved, not mocked, the concerns of the little dragon. "It is difficult to persuade the maids into making a proper dragon's nest. As you well know, some persuasions are far easier to achieve than others."

Did he know about what Longbourn had tried? Her cheeks flushed.

"I hope it will not be an imposition upon you, but I should very much like to introduce my sister and my cousin Fitzwilliam. They are very anxious to meet you. Pemberley has convinced Georgiana that you are some form of angel incarnate. Walker has Fitzwilliam believing you are some sort of cross between a sage and a saint."

"And you would have me come and disabuse them of their outlandish ideas?" She laughed.

April landed on her shoulder and chittered in her ear. "Mind your manners!"

Alas, she was probably right.

"Far be it from me to call my Dragon Friends liars." He cocked his head and raised an eyebrow. "Shall we?"

He held open the red door and ushered her up the steep stairs. At least the stairs were properly deep and regular, not a typical, cheaply made servant's staircase. It would be easier to face Lady Catherine, not having just risked life and limb picking her way up a dangerous staircase.

"Does Rosings often entertain guests of her own invitation?" she asked.

"I do not know for certain, but I do not think so— not recently in any case. I believe Sir Lewis' father was quite well connected in his day. Rosings was more apt to entertain then."

Elizabeth chewed her lip. Perhaps she had taken Rosings' invitation a bit too lightly.

Nuncheon was served in a large parlor on the west side of the house. The yellowy-gold paper hanging with the dragon scale pattern must have been especially printed for the room. Why did Lady Catherine seem to need to occupy every surface in the house with dragon imagery? Or was it simply the product of generations of proud Dragon Keepers, each one adding to the next?

Lady Catherine was in deep conversation with an overdressed young woman and a more plainly dressed older woman who seemed to be her companion. The famed Miss de Bourgh and Mrs. Jenkinson she had heard so much about from Mr. Collins? The younger woman looked like Lady Catherine, sharp in all her features, but lacking the classic beauty the vicar attributed to her. Little surprise he would overstate her virtues. Her genteel temper and gracious character were probably overstated as well.

Which might be why Pemberley took such a dislike to her.

From a settee in the opposite corner of the room—with feet in the shape of dragon paws clutching a sphere—a young woman, possibly not yet out, and a confident-looking young man beckoned. Both shared something of Darcy's profile.

Darcy strode toward them. "Miss Elizabeth, may I present my sister, Georgiana and my cousin, Colonel Fitzwilliam."

They rose, and Georgiana curtsied deeply. Fitzwilliam made a very smart bow.

"I am very pleased to meet you." She curtsied and sat in a chair near the settee.

Darcy brought another chair close and joined them.

"May I ask; how is Pemberley?" Georgiana ducked her head and bit her lip as she spoke.

Given the adoring way she looked at Darcy, it was more likely that she was shy than she feared speaking out in his presence.

"She has been eating well the last few days and her color has returned. I think she is very much improved."

Georgiana clapped softly. "I knew you would be able to help her. After reading all that you have written, I just knew."

The hero worship in Georgiana's eyes was sweet, but a bit much.

"Your friendship means a great deal to Pemberley. She misses you. I think it would be very appropriate for you to begin visiting her again."

"I would so enjoy that." Georgiana glanced at Darcy who nodded.

"Something I would never have thought to hear you say." Fitzwilliam chuckled, turning to Elizabeth. "You know, she was in mortal dread of dragons until she began reading your notes."

"Indeed, sir? You have just revealed your nature. You are either a flatterer or one prone to exaggerate. In either case, I shall have to weigh your words very carefully."

Georgiana gasped, eyes wide.

April nipped her ear.

Fitzwilliam threw his head back and laughed. "It seems your little Friend does not agree with you. I believe she thinks more highly of me than you do." He offered his hand for April to perch.

April flittered to his finger and offered her chin for a scratch.

Such a fluffle-bob to be moved so easily by a compliment.

"What is that you are saying, Fitzwilliam? What is it you are talking of? What are you telling Miss Bennet? Let me hear what it is." Lady Catherine half-rose in her seat and stared at them with narrowed eyes.

"We are speaking of music, Madam." Fitzwilliam flashed a warning gaze toward her. It shifted to mischievous as he turned it on Darcy and Georgiana.

April warbled a little tune, looking proud of herself indeed. Little show-off.

"Of music! Then pray speak aloud. It is of all subjects my delight. I must have my share in the conversation if you are speaking of music. There are few people in England, I suppose, who have more true enjoyment of music than myself, or a better natural taste. If I had ever learnt, I should have been a great proficient. And so would Anne, if her health had allowed her to apply."

The overdressed girl beside her dipped her head with a demure smile and straightening of her shoulders.

Gracious, did she think Lady Catherine's remark was praise?

"I am confident that she would have performed delightfully. How does Georgiana get on, Darcy?" Lady Catherine's eyes narrowed as she glanced at Elizabeth.

Darcy cleared his throat. "She does very well, thank you. Pray forgive me, sister, as I know you do not like praise, but her piano master believes her the most accomplished student he has ever taught."

She must be very accomplished to earn such praise from her brother. Georgiana turned aside, face coloring. Poor dear looked utterly horrified, exactly how Lydia never looked. If she could give Georgiana a touch of Lydia's boldness and Lydia a touch of Georgiana's reserve, both girls would probably benefit.

"I am very glad to hear such a good account of her, but her progress will not continue if she does not practice a great deal." Lady Catherine wagged her finger at them.

"I assure you, Madam, she practices constantly." Darcy's voice dropped in pitch—a warning tone if she had ever heard one.

"So much the better. It cannot be done too much. Do not neglect it on any account. I often tell young ladies that no excellence in music is to be acquired without constant practice." Lady Catherine turned her pointing finger on Elizabeth. "I have heard that you play, Miss Bennet. Of course, you will never play really well unless you practice. I have not heard you do so once since you are come to Rosings Park. You may play on the pianoforte in Mrs. Jenkinson's room. She would be in nobody's way, you know, in that part of the house. Play for us now, Miss Bennet. I insist. We are in need of diversion."

Colonel Fitzwilliam escorted her to the pianoforte and drew a chair near, as though he meant to turn the pages for her. April perched on the music stand. It was a very fine instrument; one she could not do justice to.

But what to play? Best keep to something light and simple that would not elicit too many comparisons with superior performers.

Colonel Fitzwilliam offered her a piece of music for her approval. A light country tune with no fiddly bits. That was true gentlemanly behavior!

Lady Catherine listened to half a song, and then resumed her conversation with her daughter—probably critiquing her performance. At least she would not want for issues to discuss.

Mr. Darcy and Georgiana joined them at the pianoforte.

She lifted her chin. "You mean to frighten me, Mr. Darcy, by coming to hear me? I will not be alarmed though your sister does play so well. There is a stubbornness about me that never can bear to be frightened at the will of others. My courage always rises with every attempt to intimidate me."

"I shall not say that you are mistaken because you could not really believe me to entertain any design of alarming you. I have had the pleasure of your acquaintance long enough to know that you find great enjoyment in occasionally professing opinions which in fact are not your own." The twinkle in his eye and the lift of his lips gave every impression he enjoyed this.

How very odd.

Elizabeth turned to Fitzwilliam, eyebrow raised. "Your cousin will give you a very pretty notion of me and teach you not to believe a word I say. I am particularly unlucky in meeting with a person so well able to expose my real character in a part of the world where I had hoped to pass myself off with some degree of credit. Indeed, Mr. Darcy, it is very ungenerous of you to mention all that you knew to my disadvantage in Hertfordshire—and, give me leave to say, very impolitic too—for it is provoking me to retaliate, and such things may come out, as will shock your relations to hear."

Fitzwilliam glanced at Georgiana and chuckled.

The poor girl looked shocked, again. At this rate, she might well not survive the afternoon.

"I am not afraid of you." Darcy's eyes crinkled at the sides.

"Pray let me hear of what you have to accuse him. I should like to know how he behaves among strangers." Fitzwilliam winked.

"You shall hear then—but prepare yourself for something very dreadful. The first time of my ever seeing him in Hertfordshire was at a ball—and at this ball, what do you think he did? He danced only four dances! I am sorry to pain you—but so it was. He danced only four dances, though gentlemen were scarce, and more than one young lady was sitting down in want of a partner."

"I had not, at that time, the honor of knowing any lady in the assembly beyond my own party."

"And, of course, nobody can ever be introduced in a ball room."

Darcy's eyes lost a little of their shine.

Perhaps she had gone too far.

She chewed her lower lip. "Well, Colonel Fitzwilliam, what do I play next? My fingers await your orders."

"Perhaps I should have judged better and sought an introduction, but I am ill-qualified to recommend myself to strangers." Darcy's tone was more shy confession than well-grounded defense.

"Why is a man of sense and education, who has lived in the world, ill-qualified to recommend himself to strangers?" The words slipped out before she could quell them.

Now she had definitely wandered out of the bounds of polite conversation. Why did he always bring out the worst in her?

"I can answer your question," Fitzwilliam said. "It is because he will not give himself the trouble."

"Do be fair!" Georgiana gasped and pressed her knuckle to her lips. "My brother is truly the best of men. How can you say such things of him?"

Darcy tipped his head. "I certainly have not the talent which some people possess of conversing easily with those I have never seen before. I cannot catch their tone of conversation, or appear interested in their concerns as I often see done."

"My fingers do not move over this instrument in the masterly manner which I am sure your sister's do. They have not the same force or rapidity and do not produce the same expression. But I have always supposed it to be my own fault because I would not take the trouble of practicing."

Darcy glanced away. "You are perfectly right. We neither of us perform to strangers."

The doors flew open, and the housekeeper led in three maids carrying an elaborate nuncheon. Two footmen followed and moved a low table into position. Somehow, Elizabeth found herself seated between Georgiana and Colonel Fitzwilliam, across from Darcy. Lady Catherine managed to keep her conversational partners close to her though it hardly seemed that they were able to get a word out, unless it was "yes" or "no."

"So how does Meryton since the departure of its most illustrious guest?" Fitzwilliam asked.

She dodged both men's gaze and scowled at the floor. He was not going to bait her into anymore ill-advised remarks.

"I … I am sure that Mr. Bingley misses him a great deal," Georgiana offered.

"Bingley? He is that fellow you take prodigious good care of, is he not?" Fitzwilliam reached for a plate of sandwiches.

"He asked my assistance in securing the lease on Netherfield Park," Darcy muttered, dodging Elizabeth's gaze.

"Was he pleased with the neighborhood?" Georgiana received a cup of tea from her aunt and handed one to Elizabeth.

"I believe the neighborhood has been very pleased with him. Perhaps you have not yet been made aware. Mr. Bingley is now engaged to my sister."

Darcy looked up. "Indeed, I was not aware."

Surprise highlighted his face, but not disapproval.

How unexpected.

"I am surprised he would not have sought your advice. He seemed reluctant to make decisions without you." Fitzwilliam took a bite of his sandwich, far too dainty a treat for his large hands.

"You underestimate Bingley's mettle." Darcy hid behind his teacup.

"Would you have approved, had he asked you?" Fitzwilliam laughed.

"You can hardly expect an honest answer to such a question. How could he tell you, in front of me, her sister, that he did not approve?"

"I have always found my cousin to be eminently forthright in all our conversation. I think he would tell me very directly." He turned an arched eyebrow on Darcy. "Would you not?"

"Indeed, you have sketched my character quite distinctly. You expect draconic candor from me." He bowed slightly from his shoulders. "It is probably for the best, then, that I can honestly say, I saw a genuine attachment between Mr. Bingley and Miss Bennet. Exactly what I would wish for my friend. I think they can be a successful match."

"And it shall ever be to your credit that Bingley met his angel during your watch, I am sure." Fitzwilliam clapped Darcy's shoulder.

"I take no credit as a match maker. It is a distinction I have never sought."

"And yet I may well apply to you for the service myself."

Georgiana gasped again. She did seem to have rather a limited repertoire of reactions. Or possibly, Fitzwilliam took great delight in seeing her shocked. That was quite likely, too.

"In fact, I already have." Fitzwilliam's cheek twitched. "I have asked his assistance in finding me a proper Dragon Friend."

"If you are interested in a fairy dragon, there is a very good chance I will know of a clutch later this year." Elizabeth glanced at April on her shoulder.

"All due respect to you, Miss Elizabeth and your fair companion, I do not think I am a fit companion for a fairy dragon. They are not known to hold their liquor well."

April fluttered her wings and huffed.

Elizabeth giggled. "That is very true, I will concede. Although my aunt's Dragon Friend, a bright red fairy dragon, would look quite smart with a red coat. A bit like a hat plume I would think. He is excessively fluffy."

"And does not like to be reminded of it." April nipped her ear.

Georgiana giggled.

"Pray forgive me if I am too forward, but should there be a clutch later this year, Mr. Darcy do you consider your sister ready for a Dragon Friend?"

What a very odd expression on Darcy's face— hopeful and trepidatious at the same time.

"What do you think, Georgiana?"

She colored and pressed her hands to her cheeks.

"My sister's fairy dragon hatchling looks very much like a pink dandelion and has a penchant for strawberry jam. She has a far sweeter disposition than my little friend." Elizabeth patted April's head. "She also likes to hang upside down like a bat on her perch."

"Truly?" Georgiana asked.

"Silly little feather-pate," April mumbled.

"I ... I ... it is all so different to think about now. Until Pemberley, I was not sure I wanted much to do with dragons. Now I am finding I rather like ... some of them."

"If you would like that, it will be necessary for you to be presented to the Blue Order first." Darcy's voice was very quiet as if trying not to frighten her.

"I ... I will think about it. Really I will."

"If you have finished your tea, Georgiana, perhaps you will favor us with some music."

How rude of Lady Catherine, calling across the room like that.

Georgiana curtsied and hurried to the pianoforte.

"I am astonished, Miss Elizabeth. You have worked wonders." Fitzwilliam shared a wide-eyed glance with Darcy.

Darcy nodded somberly, but his lips turned up a mite as he turned his attention to the pianoforte.

What a puzzlement he was. How could this be the same man she had met in Meryton? The same one of Wickham's tale of misery? The same one who allowed Pemberley's egg to be stolen with nearly catastrophic consequences? It seemed he could please when and where he chose, but woe to the one he chose against.

Vexing, confusing man.

11
Chapter

OVER THE NEXT several days, Georgiana regularly ventured below stairs to Rosings' guest room, astonished that such a place existed. Her girlish delight reminded Elizabeth of times spent with her sisters. Times that seemed so long ago.

Pemberley seemed so easy with Georgiana's company that Elizabeth took advantage of it for solitary rambles. Getting Pemberley accustomed to her absence was a good thing for them all. Or so the texts on attachment sickness suggested.

It would be hard to be separated from her again. But hopefully it would not be such an abrupt or complete separation as the first. And there would be correspondence between her and Georgiana and Pemberley. That would make it better.

Surely it would.

The morning was cool and comfortable. The breeze carried the distinct smell of rain on the horizon, but it was not imminent. Probably would not come before nightfall, more than enough time for all the walking she wanted.

More than once, Elizabeth had encountered Mr. Darcy on her walks. What perverse mischance that should bring him, and only him, into what should have been her private moments. Finally, she informed him that the particular path was a favorite haunt of hers. Yet he did not seem to take the hint.

On further reflection, though, it did not seem so surprising. He had said he was not well able to catch the unspoken meaning in a conversation. The next time she met him, she would have to be more direct.

But she did not have the chance. On their next meeting, he struck up a conversation—odd on several accounts. For the first, he rarely spoke whilst they walked. For the other, he asked some odd, uncon-nected questions—about her pleasure in being at Hunsford, her love of solitary walks, her opinion of Mr. Bingley and Jane's future happiness, and could a lady be settled too near her family for her liking? What was her opinion of the house and grounds of Rosings Park? Did she find the house to her liking? What did she think of so many dragons on a single estate?

To what could all these questions portend? Was it possible he was entering into the very venture he fores-wore—matchmaking? He could not have her in mind for Colonel Fitzwilliam, could he?

Overbearing, pretentious—

Colonel Fitzwilliam broke through the trees. "Miss Bennet! I had no idea that you ever walked this way. I have been making the tour of the Park as I generally do every year when Darcy and I visit. Are you going much farther?"

"I have only just left Pemberley in Georgiana's care."

He offered her his arm. "Then might I have the privilege of sharing your outing, or were you, like Darcy does, hoping for some time in the absence of all company?"

Darcy walked to avoid company?

She placed her hand in the crook of his arm. "As much as I enjoy Pemberley and the other dragons, a bit of human companionship is very welcome, too."

"Are Quincy and Blanche spending a great deal of time below stairs?"

"They and Wellsbey, and several of the barn tatzelwurms come by regularly as well."

"I was told you had a way with dragons. It seems it was not an exaggeration."

"I admit I do like them very much. It is always a pleasure to meet more of them." She glanced up into the trees. Was that a fairy dragon's twitter? "Do you find it common on great estates to have so many Dragon Friends and minor dragons?"

"I think it is largely up to the preference of the major dragon. Rosings seems to like having many minor dragons look up to her."

"Longbourn barely tolerated any minor dragons larger than fairy dragons. I wonder what Pemberley will prefer. She does seem to like the company."

"It is a good thing then, that Darcy tolerates draconic company with great equanimity." He sniggered, leaves crunching under his boots. "I think he may like them better than people."

"I think he would be hard pressed to deny Pemberley what she wants, considering how much he likes to have his way. I do not know anybody who seems more to enjoy the power of doing what he likes than Mr. Darcy."

"He likes to have his own way very well. But so we all do. It is only that he has better means of having it than many others because he is rich, and many others are poor." He tapped his chest. "A younger son, you know, must be inured to self-denial and dependence."

"In my opinion, the younger son of an earl can know very little of either. Now, seriously, when have you been prevented by want of money from going wherever you chose or procuring anything you had a fancy for?"

"I cannot say that I have experienced many hardships of that nature. But in matters of greater weight, I may suffer from the want of money. Younger sons cannot marry where they like."

"Unless they like women of fortune, which I think they very often do."

Fitzwilliam shrugged. "Our habits of expense make us too dependent, and there are not many in my rank of life who can afford to marry without some attention to money."

Was he referring to her lack of dowry? Had Darcy warned him against interest in her?

Her cheeks heated, but she forced her voice to remain lively. "And pray, what is the usual price of an Earl's younger son? Unless the elder brother is very sickly, I suppose you would not ask above fifty thousand pounds."

Fitzwilliam threw back his head and laughed heartily. "Perhaps I might be willing to settle for just thirty thousand."

"I wonder that Mr. Darcy does not marry. It seems it would be great convenience to him. But, perhaps his sister does as well for the present, as she is under his sole care—"

"No, that is an advantage which he must divide with me. I am joined with him in her guardianship."

"Are you, indeed? And pray what sort of guardians do you make? Does your charge give you much trouble? Young ladies of her age are sometimes a little difficult to manage, and if she has the true Darcy spirit, she may like to have her own way."

He looked at her, expression darkening.

Gracious!

She edged back several steps. "You need not be frightened. I never heard any harm of her. I dare say she is one of the most tractable creatures in the world. Pemberley adores her, and the minor dragons are becoming equally fond of her. I find dragons an excellent judge of character."

"Indeed, they are, Miss Bennet, indeed they are." He fell silent for the next dozen paces and kicked a clump of dirt. "Forgive me if I am too bold, but you do not seem to be a great admirer of my cousin."

"On that point, I fear, I should remain silent."

"But if you did not, you would agree with me?"

"Yes, she would!" Where had April come from? She was supposed to stay with Pemberley for her tea party with Georgiana and the minor dragons.

"Your little friend reveals an uncomfortable truth?" Fitzwilliam stopped and offered a finger for April to perch upon.

"You do not have leave to speak of my opinions." Elizabeth clenched her fist behind her back.

April flapped her wings. "Then I shall speak of mine. I think she is a fool for what she holds against him. I am certain there is a misunderstanding, and she does not know the truth of the matter."

"I know he can be offensive. It seems he offered you great affront at the ball you mentioned the other day. But those do not seem deep enough infractions to earn such great resentment." All amusement faded from his features.

"I like to credit her with better sense than that!" April said. "At least she has the wit to imagine substantial offenses, not addle-pated ones."

"I see your Dragon Friend thinks very highly you of. Pray tell me, what has my cousin done to offend?"

How honest an answer should she offer? Clearly, he would not permit her to avoid one altogether.

"He is a very perplexing man, Colonel, and I do not know what to think of him. Here, he is all charm and consideration. Mr. Bingley said that is true of his character. However, he is not that way universally. What am I to make of a man who can be two different men in different company?"

His eyebrows knit as he addressed April. "What did he do?"

Elizabeth stamped her foot, narrowly missing his. "If you insist upon knowing, sir, then you will at least have the courtesy to address me."

"Very well, madam, I put the same question to you. What did he do?"

"He has left a trail of harm in his wake, both to me and to one I consider a friend."

"Wickham is no friend!" April growled.

"Wickham? What do you know of him?"

"He is part of the militia stationed in Meryton and has become a friend of my family. He did me a tremendous favor—"

"Which was dangerous and foolhardy to accept." April flitted to her shoulder and nipped her ear.

Elizabeth covered her ear with her hand. "For which I am very grateful. Mr. Darcy has done him great harm."

"And that is what you hold against him? No, you said that Darcy had harmed you as well ..."

"Not just me, but Pemberley, too. Through his incompetence, he permitted her egg to be stolen away, endangering her. She hatched alone and could easily have failed to imprint! Then, he tore Pemberley away from me without consideration of her—or me." She pressed her fist to her mouth.

Fitzwilliam pinched the bridge of his nose. "I have warned him. Walker has warned him. He has been a fool to ignore us. There is a very great deal you do not understand about this entire situation. Darcy's pride has prevented him from sharing some very important information that I believe will entirely change your opinion of him and of the situations you describe."

"I do not see how that can be."

"Pray, come with me to Rosings' lair. April, would you gather Walker and Cait? I think you will be happier to hear the tale directly from the dragons. Whilst you might accuse me of favoritism toward my cousin, you know the dragons will be entirely forthright."

"Very well." But what could the dragons possibly tell her that would change her mind?

Walker and Cait were already perched just inside Rosings' lair when they arrived. Rosings sat nearby, a vague expression of annoyance on her face. The tip of her tail flicked slowly like Papa tapping his foot whilst he was angry.

"I have heard you are in possession of a number of very foolish notions." Rosings huffed a hot breath in her direction. Firedrakes' breath was always hotter than that of other dragons. "Ordinarily I care little for the ignorance of warm-bloods, but since in this case your foolishness could have a direct influence on Pemberley, I cannot sit idly by and allow you to continue to be stupid."

Elizabeth bit her lip. She did not appreciate being called stupid, but it was not wise to argue with a cowntess.

Rosings turned about twice and settled back down. "I have been told that there are two offenses of very different natures, and by no means of equal magnitude, you laid to Darcy's charge. The first, that he detached Pemberley from yourself, considering nothing for the welfare of either of you. The other, that he willfully and wantonly he threw off the companion of his youth, the acknowledged favorite of his father, a young man who had scarcely any other dependence than on the Darcy patronage, and who had been brought up to expect its exertion, ruining the immediate prosperity, and blasting the future prospects of Mr. Wickham. Am I correct in my understanding?"

"I am not sure I would have put it in those terms."

Considering Rosings expression, she did not actually expect an answer.

"Yes, you would." April peeked out from behind Walker.

"Dodging the truth." Rosings snorted. "Your human affectations of politeness do not impress me. I am known for my directness, and you shall find me to be no other way."

That was something she usually appreciated about dragons, but perhaps not so much just now.

"Darcy went to Hertfordshire in search of Pemberley's egg—"

"Which was placed in jeopardy due to his carelessness!" She probably should not have taken that tone.

"Another point upon which you are sorely deluded, but I will come back to that. You will refrain from further outbursts until I have finished speaking." Rosings breathed sulfurous fumes on her face.

Her eyes burned. "Yes, Cowntess."

"Upon his arrival in Meryton, Darcy consulted with your father who failed to extend appropriate courtesies and aid to him. There is some thought he was even working at cross purposes to him."

"What has my father to do with any of this?"

"Everything when one considers that it was because of his lazy Dragon Keeping that Longbourn was permitted to throw Pemberley off his estate."

"Pray excuse me?"

"That is precisely what happened." Walker glided to the cavern floor beside her. "Darcy would have stayed at least another month. Longbourn insisted that he remove Pemberley immediately because of you."

"Me?" Chills coursed down her neck and shoulders.

"He told Darcy that Pemberley was not good for you, was exhausting you."

"But that was not true."

"Darcy knew that. But he is smarter than to try and argue with a jealous wyvern."

April flew to her shoulder. "Longbourn cannot abide the notion of sharing you with anyone."

"Then why did he try to persuade me to marry Collins?"

"You despise the man! What better reason?" Cait squawked from her perch near Rosings' shoulder.

She braced her hands on her hips, more to hold herself up than for a show of bravado. "That is not usually considered a good reason for marriage."

"But if his desire is not to share your affections with another, it is an excellent one." Cait accentuated her point with wing flaps.

"Marrying Collins would keep you at Longbourn estate and lonely for company which Longbourn would be happy to provide." Walker paced in front of her.

The edges of her vision blurred. No, she would not falter, not in front of Rosings.

"Typical wyvern reasoning. They are a despicable lot. Selfish, lazy creatures." Rosings snorted.

Surely Rosings had to be mistaken. She swallowed hard. "How exactly did he reason I would be available to meet his demands if I had a self-centered boorish husband to attend?"

"Wyverns are also not very smart. I doubt he even considered it." The side of Rosings' lip curled back. "The material point is that it was not Darcy who separated you from your dear Pemberley. It was your own dragon."

Her knees wobbled like jelly. Fitzwilliam caught her elbow. Walker dragged an old log near for her to sit.

She covered her face with her hands and drew in ragged breaths. It had been Longbourn's doing the whole time? Bad enough that she had wrongly blamed Mr. Darcy, but that the dragon she Kept should have turned on her so? Bile burned the back of her throat. If he had already betrayed her so thoroughly, no wonder he was willing to try to persuade her as well.

Horrid, hateful creature!

"So you see, you did not know as much as you thought you did. If that bothers you, you will be horrified to discover how wrong you have been about Wickham." Now Rosings was just gloating.

She squeezed her eyes shut and rocked back and forth. "Pray, do not say. I fear I cannot bear it."

April trilled softly in her ear, just enough to ease some of her tension, but not enough to put her to sleep.

"Mr. Wickham, is the son of a respectable man who had for many years the management of all the Pemberley estates, and whose good conduct naturally inclined Darcy's father to be of service to him. George Wickham was named for Darcy Senior and was his godson, thus his kindness was liberally bestowed." Her tone suggested Rosings did not approve.

Elizabeth covered her mouth and bit her lips.

"Darcy Senior supported Wickham at school, and afterwards at Cambridge." Walker folded his wings behind him like a school master. "Though I warned him otherwise, Darcy Senior was not only fond of young Wickham's society—you have seen how engaging his manners can be—he also had the highest opinion of him and hoped the church would be his profession, intending to give him a family living when the time came."

Rosings lashed her tail, nearly knocking Walker off his feet. "But old Darcy died before he could see it done. He left a legacy of a thousand pounds upon young Wickham. Shortly thereafter, he received another three thousand from Darcy when he declared he had no desire to go into the clergy but would study the law instead. Of course, by this time, Darcy had begun to see through Wickham, his debts, his gambling, his—what you call—debaucheries. Darcy was glad to have all ties cut and intended to have nothing more to do with him. Good riddance, I said. Especially since Old Pemberley found him poking about near the lair, more than once."

"Are you suggesting—"

"That Old Darcy had permitted Wickham some knowledge of dragons? In his dotage, it is entirely possible."

"You see! You see!" April shrieked, "I told you he was dangerous. He was asking indirect questions about dragons, encouraging her to tell him myths and stories—"

Elizabeth covered her face with her hands, throat almost too tight to speak. "He is not a deaf-speaker is he?"

"We do not know certainly. He stole Pemberley's egg, but then had it stolen from him by someone unknown in Meryton." Walker said.

"That came after Darcy thwarted his attempt to elope with Georgiana when she was just fifteen," Cait cut in.

Fitzwilliam cleared his throat. "On that point, I must own my part of the blame. We both trusted Mrs.

Younge, her companion, and thought going to Rams-gate would be good for her. But her dowry of thirty thousand pounds proved sufficient inducement to Wickham to put him in collusion with Mrs. Younge. Darcy arrived just in time to prevent the scheme."

"On Earl Matlock's suggestion, Darcy packed Wickham off into the militia to keep him away from his sister and Pemberley." Walker snarled. "I should rather have pecked his eyes out."

"Any reasonable creature would have thought that enough to keep them both safe from the villain." Rosings thumped her tail.

Elizabeth jumped to her feet, shaking. "Wickham tried to steal Georgiana and succeeded in stealing Pemberley's egg? To what end?"

"It is hard to say." Walker dug his talons through the dirt. "He might have been trying to sell it not fully knowing what it was. There are those—on the conti-nent where the Accords have no bearing—who would pay handsomely for such a prize."

"It is also possible, if he is a deaf-speaker, he was going to try to befriend her himself and convince her that he was her Keeper," Rosings said.

"Without being able to hear her?"

"He might have made the ruse work when she was newly hatched. More importantly though, it is possible he would have tried to make a claim on the estate through Pemberley." Walker glanced back at Rosings who nodded.

"The Blue Order would never uphold such a claim."

"No, I grant you that. But they might have found something to placate him, a small estate somewhere—he has always tried to lead a gentleman's life. Even as a small boy, he wanted to leave the sphere to which he had been born." Walker shrugged his wings.

"The Duge Cornwall could have eaten him instead! Would he not suspect the risks whilst dealing with dragons?" She threw up her hands.

"He has always been willing to gamble with very high stakes. The four thousand pounds given him by the Darcys lasted him only a few years. How do you think the fortune was lost?"

She began to pace, nearly tripping over Rosings' tail. "This must be false! This cannot be!"

But dragons did not often lie. And they also confirmed April's suspicions. And Aunt Gardiner's.

What a fool she had been! An arrogant, prejudiced fool!

"Pray excuse me! I must consider all you have said." She dashed from the lair, barely able to breathe.

A sick headache kept her to bed all the next day. Only fear of causing Pemberley anxiety roused her for her typical walk the following morning. Naturally it was a cold, drizzly day, exactly designed to reflect her mood and remind her of what a buffle-headed, shallow-pate she was.

How could she have been so entirely mistaken? Perhaps one could forgive her blindness regarding Longbourn. A Keeper was supposed to be partial to their dragon, patient and forgiving, that was after all the foundation of dragon-human relations. Both species had to choose to endure the peculiarities of the other. It was only natural that she should fail to see

Longbourn's real flaws until his transgressions became very heavy, indeed.

But to be so wrong about Mr. Wickham?

The account of his connection with the Darcy family was exactly what he had related to her himself. The kindness of the late Mr. Darcy, though she had not before known its extent, agreed equally well with his own words. What Wickham had said of the living though— his gross duplicity! Resigning all pretensions to the living in lieu of so considerable a sum as three thousand pounds! More than Papa had in a year! And a thousand pounds at old Mr. Darcy's death beyond that!

That sort of money could have kept him comfortable for a lifetime. At least, a lifetime not marked by extravagance and general profligacy. How many families lived well enough on such a sum?

Yet Darcy had never laid such a charge at Wickham's feet. Why would he protect Wickham so? Respect for Wickham's father, or perhaps his own?

Aunt and April both suspected Wickham and tried to warn her that there was no actual evidence of some instance of goodness, some distinguished trait of integrity or benevolence. The only signs in his favor: the general approbation of the neighborhood, and the regard which his social powers had gained him.

Powers that Mr. Darcy lacked.

That first evening she had met Wickham at the Phillips'—the impropriety of such communications to a stranger! How had she missed it before? The indelicacy of putting himself forward as he had done and the inconsistency of his claims with his conduct. He had no scruples in sinking Mr. Darcy's character, though he had said that respect for the father would always prevent his exposing the son.

Precisely the opposite to Darcy.

It was all there had she only chosen to look. And Wickham's attentions toward her must have been like those to Georgiana—designs to acquire by force a draconic legacy which he had not been given by nature. No wonder the Order considered deaf-speakers the greatest danger to dragonkind.

And through it all, Darcy had refused to reveal anything that could harm his sister's reputation.

She wrapped her arms tight around her waist. How despicably she had acted! She prided herself on discernment and wit, valued her own abilities above Jane and Mary's warnings. Good reason to heed the warning that pride goeth before a fall.

Had she been in love, she could not have been more wretchedly blind. But vanity, not love, was her folly. So pleased with the preference of one, and so offended by the neglect of the other at the very beginning of both acquaintances, she courted ignorance, and drove reason away where either man was concerned.

To finally see herself now, without the trapping of conceit, it was not a pretty sight. How could she ever face—

"Miss Elizabeth?"

After encountering her on this path so many times before, why did Darcy still look surprised to do so?

She curtsied, pulling her cloak a little closer around her shoulders.

"Are you well?" He peered at her in a way she would have previously considered as looking for fault, but now just seemed concerned. "Has your headache improved?"

"I am as well as can be expected."

He matched her stride, and they walked on together in silence for a dozen paces.

"Forgive me if I am intrusive, but I understand from Walker that you had an audience with Rosings yesterday." How could he look at her that way—so kind and concerned—after he must know everything that had transpired?

"You might call it that." She would call it a thorough dressing-down.

"Dragons are by no means delicate, but I fear that Rosings is probably worse than most. Much like her Keeper."

"Do you find dragons often resemble their Dragon Mates?"

"It has been my experience that they do."

Her cheeks burned hot. After time solely in Darcy's care, Pemberley was sweet and affectionate.

"Or perhaps it is that the Mates begin to resemble their dragons. I have been finding myself in want of a new dog recently." He cocked his eyebrow.

She giggled. Had he always had such a charming sense of humor?

"Do you not keep a pack of hunting hounds at Pemberley estate?"

"True enough, but I was rather thinking of a house dog. What would you think of a pug perhaps?"

"Oh, they are temperamental little creatures. Lady Lucas keeps one that does unspeakable things to the pillows."

Darcy hid a laugh in a cough. "I believe I met that dog whilst in Meryton. Definitely then, no pugs."

Her caught her gaze, his eyes so deep and expressive they dismissed all words from her tongue. Had he always looked at her that way?

Unable to breathe, she broke eye contact.

"Forgive me, sir, but I must speak. Pray accept my deepest apologies for both my father and Longbourn. I have been given to understand they treated you and Pemberley most abominably. I am mortified that he failed to render you more aid on your urgent errand. He is fortunate that you do not report him to the Order for his negligence."

He clasped his hands behind his back and walked on. "Pemberley is well, and that is all that matters, is it not? One could argue that the additions that have been made to dragon lore regarding the imprinting of newly-hatched dragons are worth what we all experienced."

"The additions to lore have not been accepted, yet. As I understand, the Conclave still wishes to examine Pemberley themselves. Rosings is still willing to sponsor her before them, is she not?"

"Most definitely. She is convinced that Pemberley has imprinted properly, if not more strongly than usual."

She studied the dirt on the toes of her half boots. "I am grateful both for that and for your forbearance with my father. I know being old, ill, and set in one's ways is little excuse, but it is all I have to offer on his behalf."

"Few of us are perfect."

"I am afraid though, I have no such excuses for Longbourn. To have thrown you and Pemberley out is utterly inexcusable by all standards. Not only was she a baby in need, but her rank alone should have compelled him to offer far more hospitality than he did. It is all the worse for having caused Pemberley's current sufferings. Longbourn could have caused her serious harm, even her death. It is inexcusable."

Darcy dragged the toe of his boot through a clump of thick moss. "I confess, it will be difficult to see wyverns in a positive light after this, but I prefer to dwell on the fact that Pemberley is much improved and is forming a bond with my sister who is also much improved. For all the mischief wrought, there is some good to come out of it."

Perhaps he was right. It was best to remember the past as it gave one pleasure, not pain.

"Whatever left your sister in such dread of dragons?" Hopefully he would not find the question impertinent.

"When she was just ten years old, she ran away from her governess—a rather horrid woman, though she heard dragons. Apparently, she had been telling Georgiana horrible dragon histories. She had some wretched fascination with the period before the Pendragon Treaty and preferred stories of people being eaten by dragons. One can hardly blame Georgiana for running away. Unfortunately, she ran into Old Pemberley's lair. She had not yet been introduced to him, and he was in his decline and decidedly cranky. She surprised him, and he her—"

She pressed her hands to her cheeks. "Oh heavens! I can just imagine! One's first meeting with a major dragon can be shocking even when one is fully prepared. My sister Mary nearly fainted the first time she met Longbourn. I had prepared her for the sight, but the smell of his breath was too much for her."

"The venom does leave him with a ... rather remarkable odor." He wrinkled his nose.

"You are very gracious, sir."

"How long will you be staying on as Rosings' guest?"

Was that a hopeful note in his voice?

"I do not know. I have to suppose that it is better to go too slowly than too quickly, in weaning her away from my presence."

"I pray you will forgive my intrusion in the matter, but I have been giving this a great deal of thought. Rosings has begun teaching Pemberley to hunt. Her first great growth spurt is supposed to happen in perhaps six weeks or so. I think it would be best to have her away from Rosings in about a month."

She gasped. "I had not thought of that! You are right! We cannot risk two hunting dragons in the same territory!"

"I am relieved you agree. I did not want you to think I was trying to divide you from Pemberley again. Still though, there is no way to know if she might be able to separate from you without harm by then. To that end, I should like to offer an invitation to Pemberley, on behalf of my sister, of course. You might come as her particular friend and remain as long as you wish— as long as you feel it necessary—"

A clumsy, darkly-clad figure crashed through the trees. "Mr. Darcy! Cousin Elizabeth?"

Mr. Collins?

"I just called upon Lady Catherine and was told that you were staying at Rosings Park as her guest. Imagine my surprise! I had been under the impression that you were tending a sick relation. Should not your family know of your whereabouts?"

"I ... I ..."

"Miss Elizabeth has indeed been tending a sick relation, a good friend of my own who lives nearby." Mr. Darcy's voice shifted, subtly, into the more commanding tone that he used when in the presence of those below him—or was it with those who irritated him? It was difficult to tell.

"Indeed? Lady Catherine made no mention of a mutual acquaintance."

"Probably because my friend has no good opinion of Lady Catherine," Darcy said.

No, now was not the time to laugh, despite the mischievous look in Darcy's eyes.

"In such a case, cousin, I think it may behoove you to spend some time in consideration of the appropriateness of your solicitous care of this person. If she has no good opinion of Lady Catherine, I cannot imagine that is the sort of company you should be keeping."

"Perhaps her opinion is the result of her illness, sir. Is it not the case that when we are ill, our judgement can be suspect?" Elizabeth asked.

Darcy nodded, slow and somber. "I think it quite possible. Her infirmity has made it difficult for her to appreciate my aunt's most unique qualities."

Collins clasped his hands behind his back, bobbing his head, almost a caricature of a sober vicar. "You may be completely correct. In that case, I feel it my duty as a clergyman to help set her thoughts straight. Take me to visit her directly, and I shall offer her my assistance."

"That is gracious of you sir, but her companion, one of my aunt's choosing, is very, very protective. She is very cautious in who she allows to visit her charge."

"But I am vicar of this parish!"

"A point well taken. Perhaps we might be able to convince her of your suitability as a visitor, but she is quite old and set in her ways. Allow us to approach her and see if she might be convinced." How did Mr. Darcy manage to remain so serious?

"Is Lady Catherine aware of this person? I am certain she cannot approve—"

"I am certain that she would offer a great deal of forbearance in her condescension toward the ill and infirm." Darcy's brows knit, and Collins blanched. "Are you by chance on your way to the parsonage, sir?"

"Indeed I am. I have not yet been there, instead going directly to see her ladyship first."

"Excellent, perhaps I may accompany you then. I was on my way there, taking my yearly tour of the park, identifying those maintenance issues which should be addressed. You might show me the needs of your parsonage first hand?"

Collins' knees buckled just a little. "I am grateful for your notice, sir. How kind, how magnanimous, that you would wish to see it with your own eyes."

Darcy turned to Elizabeth and bowed. "Pray give my greetings to our mutual friend."

He walked off, Collins chattering gratitude with every step.

Why now of all times for him to return? How was she to manage Pemberley with Collins so close nearby?

She clutched her temples. Another headache was not what she needed right now.

Chapter 12

THE NEXT MORNING, Georgiana came to her chambers an hour before breakfast was usually served.

"Pray forgive the intrusion so early, but my aunt has sent me to fetch you immediately." Georgiana curtsied. "I do not think she will accept any delay."

"My, it is early for her to have worked herself up into high dudgeon is it not?" Elizabeth chuckled. Lady Catherine was more like her cockatrix than she would have liked to admit.

Pemberley came up behind her and peered over her shoulder.

"It does seem so. I cannot guess what is in her mind right now." Georgiana chewed her knuckle.

"I have just promised Pemberley a walk. Will you take her?"

Pemberley bumped Georgiana with her nose. "I want play tatzelwurms. The fur tickles my nose."

Georgiana scratched Pemberley under the chin. "You have become very fond of the barn wyrms, have you not?"

"Dog and Puppy seem to like them as well." Elizabeth laughed as the two hounds trotted up for their share of the scratches.

"I will be happy to take a walk with her." Georgiana hugged Pemberley's neck.

"I regret not being able to say the same about speaking with your aunt. April, perhaps you should go with Georgiana. I would not have you nipping at Lady Catherine's ears."

April chittered but landed on Pemberley's shoulder without further argument. Elizabeth saw them out and headed upstairs.

Quincy met her just outside the door at the top of the stairs. "I was sent to ensure you go directly to Lady." He sat back on his haunches and rubbed his forepaws together, his hood half raised.

"She is agitated this morning?"

"Most agitated, I am afraid. Please come." He led her to a small parlor, talons clicking on the marble tile. "Good luck. If there is anything you need, you have only to say the word and all the house dragons will be here for you."

She swallowed hard, eyes stinging. It was a very sweet sentiment, but what could Lady Catherine want that would require draconic intervention? Taking a deep breath, she bit her lip and strode into the parlor.

Lady Catherine sat in a large chair, bathed in shadow. Her silhouette looked vaguely like Rosings.

How fitting.

"Miss Bennet, close the door and come closer."

That tone of voice did not bode well. It was too cheerful and too commanding.

"Sit down. I have a matter to discuss with you."

She sat in a small, hard chair near Lady Catherine's. No doubt it had been placed there to reinforce the distinction of rank. So thoughtful.

"I have a solution to all our problems." Lady Catherine flipped her hand with a flourish as if nothing more need be said.

"Pray excuse me, madam, but I do not recall having a problem for you to solve."

She rapped the arm of her chair with her knuckles. "Impudent girl, but I am too pleased with the recent turn of events to take notice. Everything has fallen into place exactly as I would wish."

"I do not have the pleasure of understanding you."

Lady Catherine leaned forward and glowered. "Then be silent, and I shall explain."

How much like Rosings she sounded. Elizabeth bit her tongue.

"Yesterday, Mr. Collins returned to the parsonage. He is your cousin and the heir to your father's estate."

"I am well aware of all those facts."

Lady Catherine grumbled deep in her throat. Would she breathe sulfur fumes next? "I sent him to Longbourn to marry one of the dragon-hearing daughters there, thus getting him a wife, and solving the problem of Longbourn's next Dragon Keeper."

"I do not recall Papa ever applying for assistance in the matter, either to you or to the Blue Order."

"Silence. I am always solicitous of the needs of lesser Dragon Keepers. It is the duty of rank. I do not know why Collins did not offer you marriage whilst he was at Longbourn—probably some stubborn foolish male thing—"

Now she sounded like Cait.

"But it may be remedied now. I have it all planned out. You shall marry Collins and stay at the parsonage while Pemberley remains here under your attentions. You can be near the little dragon until she outgrows whatever attachment she has to you. With Pemberley well-cared for, Darcy might marry Anne as he should."

Elizabeth clenched her teeth. The notion was nearly as disturbing as her marrying Collins.

"Forgive me, Lady Catherine, but two major Dragon Keepers should not marry. Though not a law, it is the strong recommendation of the Blue Order. I know of no couple that has violated it. How can they possibly hope to manage the needs of two dragons on two separate estates, especially with one as young as Pemberley? She will need focused attention for at least a decade, if not more."

"Pemberley shall stay here. Rosings can assist in her care."

"Forgive me Lady Catherine, but you are sorely mistaken if you believe that Rosings will tolerate another dragon hunting in her territory."

"I have no doubt you can manage to convince the two to live together peacefully. You did after all succeed in getting a wild-hatched dragon to imprint properly on humans." Lady Catherine's eyes narrowed.

That was not a compliment. It was a threat.

Horrid woman!

"You would risk Pemberley's life on this marriage scheme of yours?"

Lady Catherine brushed aside her concern like a fly. "You will be handsomely rewarded for your efforts. I will see that your sons are all educated in the best way, properly connected and established in life. Your daughters will attend the finest seminaries and will be matched with gentlemen. They will want for nothing."

"Even with such an inducement, and it is a very great one, I cannot in good conscience engage in such an undertaking. It is far too dangerous."

"Miss Bennet, you ought to know that I am not to be trifled with. I will not play games, negotiating back and forth with you. I have made my offer, and it is the only one you can expect. My character has ever been celebrated for its sincerity and frankness, and I shall certainly not depart from it."

Had Rosings taught her that speech? If she closed her eyes it would be difficult to tell whether it was Lady or dragon speaking.

She leaned forward, face tightened into knots Elizabeth would not have supposed possible. "A report of a most alarming nature reached me that you, that Miss Elizabeth Bennet, would, in all likelihood, be soon united to my nephew, my own nephew, Mr. Darcy. Though I know it must be a scandalous falsehood, though I would not injure him so much as to suppose the truth of it possible, I resolved on making my sentiments known to you."

"If you believed it impossible, why would you give it credence by addressing me on the point? What could your ladyship propose by it?" Control, she must maintain control. It would not do to stoop to Lady Catherine's level.

"Can you declare that there is no foundation for it?"

"I do not pretend to possess equal frankness with your ladyship. You may ask questions which I shall not choose to answer."

"This is not to be borne. Miss Bennet, I insist on being satisfied. Has he, has my nephew, made you an offer of marriage?"

"Your ladyship has declared it to be impossible."

"It ought to be so. It must be so while he retains the use of his reason. But your arts and allurements may, in a moment of infatuation, have made him forget what he owes to himself and to all his family. You may have drawn him in."

Elizabeth balled her fists in her lap. "If I have, I shall be the last person to confess it."

"Miss Bennet, do you know who I am? I have not been accustomed to such language as this. I am almost the nearest relation he has in the world and am entitled to know all his dearest concerns." Lady Catherine waved a pointing finger.

"But you are not entitled to know mine; nor will such behavior as this ever induce me to be explicit." Elizabeth folded her arms over her chest, shoving fists under her arms.

"Let me be rightly understood. This match, to which you have the presumption to aspire, can never take place. Mr. Darcy is engaged to my daughter. Now what have you to say?" Lady Catherine slowly rose.

Was that supposed to be menacing? The gesture had far more impact coming from a dragon.

"Only this; that if he is so, you can have no reason to suppose he will make an offer to me."

Lady Catherine stopped her next rebuttal before it passed her lips. She closed her mouth, brow furrowed, and blinked. "The engagement between them is of a peculiar kind. From their infancy, they have been in-tended for each other. While in their cradles, we planned the union. And now, at the moment when the wishes of both sisters would be accomplished in their marriage, it is to be prevented by a young woman of inferior birth, of no importance in the world, and wholly unallied to the family! Are you lost to every feeling of propriety and delicacy?"

"What is that to me? If there is no other objection to my marrying your nephew, I shall certainly not be kept from it by knowing that his mother and aunt wished him to marry Miss de Bourgh. If Mr. Darcy is neither by honor nor inclination confined to his cousin, why is not he to make another choice? And if I am that choice, why may I not accept him?"

"Because honor, decorum, prudence, nay, interest, forbid it. Do not expect to be noticed by his family or friends if you willfully act against the inclinations of all. You will be censured, slighted, and despised by everyone connected with him. Your alliance will be a disgrace; your name will never even be mentioned by any of us." Lady Catherine turned her back.

Oh, what a flair for the dramatic. Had she not been born to fortune, she might have been an actress.

"These are heavy misfortunes, but the wife of Mr. Darcy must have such extraordinary sources of happiness necessarily attached to her situation that she could, upon the whole, have no cause to repine."

She whirled on Elizabeth. "Obstinate, headstrong girl! I am ashamed of you! I will not be dissuaded. I have not been used to submit to any person's whims. I have not been in the habit of brooking disappointment."

"That will make your ladyship's situation at present more pitiable, but it will have no effect on me."

"I will not be interrupted. Hear me in silence! My daughter and my nephew are formed for each other, and what is to divide them? The upstart pretensions of a young woman without family, connections, or fortune? Is this to be endured? But it must not, shall not be! If you were sensible of your own good, you would not wish to quit the sphere in which you have been brought up."

"In marrying your nephew, I should not consider myself as quitting that sphere. He is a gentleman; I am a gentleman's daughter; we are both Dragon Keepers of the Blue Order. So far we are equal."

"Tell me once for all, are you engaged to him?"

"I am not."

Lady Catherine heaved a labored sigh and dabbed her forehead with her handkerchief. "And will you promise me never to enter into such an engagement?"

"I will make no promise of the kind."

"Do not deceive yourself. I shall not go away till you have given me the assurance I require."

"And I certainly never shall give it. You have widely mistaken my character, if you think I can be worked on by such inducements as these. How far your nephew might approve of your interference in his affairs, I cannot tell. But you have certainly no right to concern yourself in mine. I must beg, therefore, to be importuned no farther on the subject."

"You are then resolved to have him?" Lady Catherine shook her fists at her side.

"I have said no such thing. I am only resolved to act in that manner which will, in my own opinion, constitute my happiness, without reference to you or to any person so wholly unconnected with me."

"And this is your final resolve! Very well. I shall now know how to act. Do not imagine, Miss Bennet, that your ambition will ever be gratified. I came to try you.

I hoped to find you reasonable, but depend upon it, I will carry my point."

They glared at each other for a moment. Elizabeth turned on her heel and fled the room.

She nearly tripped over Quincy who waited just outside the door.

He bounced on his toes, hood opening and closing. "Is it true then, that you will have Darcy? Oh, that is very good news. Very good. There is no one better suited to little Pemberley. And he is a very good Keeper, you know, very good to dragonkind. Such a spectacular match—"

She caught his face between her hands and held his gaze. "I have said no such thing, and would pray you to keep your thoughts to yourself on such matters. Do not spread gossip or speak about this anywhere."

"Of, course, of course. I would do nothing to displease you." He scurried away.

The little scamp must have been listening at the door. Anyone listening might have drawn the same conclusions. She pressed her hands to her face. To have heard it all, it did sound as though she were quite set on having Mr. Darcy.

Of course, it was not true. Not at all, she had only just come to understand he was not the man she had thought him to be. No longer despising him was hardly the same thing as having her cap set on him.

He was a good man and did not deserve to have an arranged marriage forced on him the way one was still being forced on her. That was why she spoke out as she did.

Of course, it was. She smoothed her skirt.

Still, though, there was little chance that Quincy would believe her or keep any sort of intelligence to himself. Soon every dragon on Rosings Park would think them engaged!

Pemberley must not hear such a rumor. The setbacks this could cause! Only Rosings herself could put an end to the notion.

Elizabeth rushed out through the kitchen.

Why did the path to the dragon's lair have to pass by the parsonage? Perhaps if she ran very quickly—

"Cousin Elizabeth, how delightful to see you this morning. I had hoped to call upon you at Rosings manor, but this is far more agreeable."

No, this definitely was not!

And what was that stench? Was he wearing some sort of cologne? And a silk cravat?

Deep breath. Panic would not serve her now.

"How is a rather muddy garden path more agreeable than a parlor at the manor? You have very strange tastes indeed."

He laughed and gave her a condescending look that he must have learned from Lady Catherine. "There are some conversations that one would like to have in a more ... private setting."

No, no, no! Not again. "Forgive me, sir, but I am in a great hurry—to see my sick relation, you see." She curtsied and stepped around him.

He turned and matched her stride for stride. "I can be silent no longer. In vain, I have struggled. It will not do. My feelings will not be repressed. You must allow me to tell you how ardently I admire and love you."

Such a vivid imagination for so early in the day!

"Mr. Collins! Please now is neither the time nor—"

"I think nothing of the obstacles, the degradation that the association might be, to myself or my esteemed patroness."

She stopped short. "Degradation?" Had not Lady Catherine tried to manufacture the connection herself?

He braced his hands on his thighs as he caught his breath. "As a vicar and a gentleman, I must consider my connections carefully. The situation of your mother's family—a merchant and a solicitor are no gentlemen, I must remind you. Though they are objectionable, it is hardly one's choice to whom they are related. I am sure those connections can be ignored. At the very least, there is nothing to be done for them."

"And you think this magnanimous?"

"But they are nothing in comparison of that total want of propriety so frequently betrayed by your mother, by your three younger sisters, and occasionally even by your father. Consider their behavior at nearly every social occasion in Meryton. How can you defend them? Even simply walking into the village, your sisters draw the stares and censure of nearly every proper citizen. I can hardly conscience my own ardent desire to be so tied to them as to call them my own sisters."

"You have said far too much, sir. I pray you desist immediately." She lifted open hands and edged away.

"I understand your displeasure at this representation of them, so let this praise give you consolation: you and your eldest sister have conducted yourselves so as to avoid any share of the censure."

Her jaw dropped. "I am at a loss how you can consider that praise—"

"It is a testimony to the warmth of my attachment that, in spite of all my endeavors, I have found it impossible to conquer. My thoughts wander to you. I dream of you. I find myself whispering your name in odd moments."

No doubt it was draconic persuasion that was at the root of his malady. Somehow, Longbourn must have found a tone of voice which the man could actually perceive.

That he should be subject to persuasion should be a good thing. It would make him easier to manage. She had a duty and now, with some proof that he was susceptible to persuasion she should—

"Despite the compromises I have made to my own character, I hope now to be rewarded by your acceptance of my hand." His eyes traveled down her body and he licked his lips.

Her stomach roiled.

"In such cases as this, it is, I believe, the established mode to express a sense of obligation for the sentiments avowed, however unequally they may be returned. If I could feel gratitude, I would now thank you. But I cannot."

He gasped and stammered, obviously trying to cut her off with more blathering of his own.

She waved him down. "I have never desired your good opinion, and you have certainly bestowed it most unwillingly. I am sorry to have occasioned pain to anyone. It has been most unconsciously done, however, and I hope will be of short duration. Pray excuse me now."

She only made it three steps.

He grabbed her arm and spun her toward him. "And this is all the reply which I am to have the honor of expecting? I might, perhaps, wish to be informed why, with so little endeavor at civility, I am thus rejected."

"I might as well enquire, why, with so evident a design of offending and insulting me, you chose to tell me that you liked me against your will, against your reason, and even against your character? Was not this some excuse for incivility, if I was uncivil?"

"You have been most uncivil, especially considering what your own behavior has been."

"You just said—"

"In Meryton, perhaps, but I have it on excellent authority that you have been shockingly inappropriate here at Rosings Park."

"Of what have I been accused?"

"Your behavior toward Mr. Darcy has been entirely inappropriate, so much so, the entire village expects an announcement of your betrothal to him."

Lady Catherine—and now Quincy—was the only one who believed that. She must have set him to this!

"You have absolutely no concern for the hopes of Miss de Bourgh which you have been treading upon like a swath of wildflowers in your way."

"I have done nothing to Miss de Bourgh."

"You know she is meant for Mr. Darcy."

"You take an eager interest in that lady's concerns."

"Anyone who knows what her misfortunes have been cannot help feeling an interest in her."

She stamped her foot. "Her misfortunes! Yes, her misfortunes have been great indeed. She is heiress to a great estate, not entailed away to a male heir. She can make any choice she pleases without consideration to the limitations of her future or that of her sisters. I would say those are great misfortunes indeed."

"You have come in and seduced away from her the only man she had been interested in. Stealing away her future, her children, all the advantages which she has been born for. You have done all this, and yet you can treat the mention of her misfortunes with contempt and ridicule. What kind of woman are you?"

"And this is your true opinion of me! This is the estimation in which you hold me despite your declaration of ardent love?"

"You suggest I should have concealed my struggles, and flattered you into the belief of my being impelled by unqualified, unalloyed inclination? I suppose you would have enjoyed the fabrication, but disguise of every sort is my abhorrence." He pressed a hand to his chest and tossed his head.

"Indeed, sir. That is good to know, particularly in that the sentiment is so strong that you will sacrifice every finer feeling and sentiment to it."

"Heartless, unfeeling creature! I am not ashamed of the feelings I related. They were natural and just. Could you expect me to rejoice in the inferiority of your connections? To congratulate myself on the hope of relations whose condition in life is so decidedly beneath my own? Or to ally myself with the behavior of young ladies so at odds with every moral teaching I conduct?"

"You are mistaken, Mr. Collins, if you suppose that the mode of your declaration affected me in any other way than to spare me the concern which I might have felt in refusing you had you behaved in a more gentleman-like manner. You could not have made me the offer of your hand in any possible way that would have tempted me to accept it."

His eyes grew wide, and he slipped half a step back.

At last a bit of room to breathe!

"From the first moment of my acquaintance with you, your manners impressed me with your arrogance, your conceit, and your selfish disdain of the feelings of others. I had not known you a month before I felt that you were the last man in the world whom I could ever be prevailed on to marry."

His expression mingled incredulity, mortification and something that resembled seething anger. "Your father wills that you marry me. Lady Catherine wills it. You cannot—"

"I can and I will most definitely make up my own mind considering the issue of marriage!"

He lunged for her. "Then you certainly will live to regret it when I put you out of the house as soon as your good father is—"

She pelted headlong down the path. Who knew what he could be capable of?

Darcy set the package of bones by the remains of Pemberley's old nest in Rosings' cavern. There was little left of it, save a few stray leaves and twigs. No doubt, sharing her lair with another major dragon, even a baby, had been a trial.

At least she had been more gracious than Longbourn.

Rosings nosed the package. Darcy opened it and handed her the largest bone, almost the length of his arm. Who would have thought she would have taken to gnawing the same big bones that Pemberley liked? He would have to tell Elizabeth.

"You should know Pemberley made her first kill yesterday. She caught a hare."

A little warm spot ignited in his chest. "Is that not a full fortnight sooner than you expected?"

"More like a month I would say." Rosings ripped a shred of meat from the bone, flipped it in the air, and caught it before it hit the ground.

"You do not say it like it is a good thing."

"It is not."

Something in her tone chilled his blood.

"I will not share my hunting grounds."

"Of course not." Hares? Rosings did not bother with such small game. She would begrudge Pemberley something she would not be bothered with?

"Lady insists I should."

"I have told her otherwise." Darcy pinched his temples. "It would be helpful if you would explain to Aunt Catherine and Anne your stand on the matter."

"I am a dragon and a cowntess. I do not need to explain myself to her or anyone."

"Of course not, still, it would be helpful—"

Rosings puffed a hot breath, smelling vaguely of sulfur, in his face.

Not a good sign.

"Brother! I did not know you would be here!" Georgiana skipped up to him.

Rosings snorted and turned aside to attend her bone, but the conversation was far from over.

"I just came from the butcher."

"Bones?" Pemberley and Wellsbey said together.

"Yes, I have bones—for all of you." He opened the package completely and handed out the treats to both dogs and dragons alike, setting all tails wagging.

"I like bones!" Pemberley settled down where her old nest had been and began chewing. Now that some of her teeth had broken though, she made vague crunching sounds as she gnawed. Dog and Puppy crowded close to her sides, wagging tails and slobbering.

Wellsbey set the bone at his feet. "Thank you very much, sir. She had an excellent walk. Chased down several hares. Her agility is quite remarkable. I think she could have caught them had she been hungry."

"You should have seen her!" Georgiana clapped.

"She was very impressive." April twittered, buzzing from Georgiana to Pemberley and back. "I showed her how to dive for prey, and she did very well."

Rosings grumbled and turned her back.

The idea that a fairy dragon could teach a firedrake anything probably offended the very fabric of her being.

"Have you any idea how long before she will move on to larger prey?"

Wellsbey's brow wrinkled, "If she were a minor drake, I would guess perhaps a week, no more than a fortnight. But for a firedrake, I really cannot say."

The tip of Rosings' tail thumped the floor.

Walker and Cait swooped in and perched above Pemberley, side by side. Cait cheeped and preened between Walker's wings. He nuzzled her cheek.

Darcy squeezed his eyes shut and rubbed them with thumb and forefinger. Elizabeth's advice seemed to have worked—but great heavens, this might just be worse than the two of them constantly bickering.

"Is it not lovely to see them getting on so well? I am sure this is a nearly perfect—Miss Elizabeth!" Georgiana jumped up and ran to the mouth of the cavern.

Elizabeth dashed inside, eyes wild, sweat trickling down the side of her face.

It was the look prey wore.

"What is wrong? What happened?" Walker glided down to her feet.

"I ... I ... Collins!" Elizabeth looked over her shoulder.

"Collins? I do not like a Collins. Where is a Collins?" Pemberley trotted up to Elizabeth.

Collins broke through the underbrush and into the cavern behind Elizabeth.

"By Jove! Cousin Elizabeth—those are ... are ... dragons! Get back, I will protect—"

Cait squawked and flapped from her perch. "From what, you useless, ill-begat—"

Elizabeth's jaw dropped. Cait's voice, it was not a dragon's voice. She sounded like a parrot!

"It speaks!" Collins staggered back.

Rosings turned to face Collins.

Collins lost all color in his face. Wellsbey edged closer to Pemberley and the women. Good guard dog—rather, dragon.

Pemberley jumped toward Collins, growling. "No like a Collins!" She spat a small puff of smoke into his face.

Collins wobbled and fainted dead away.

Elizabeth wrapped her arms around Pemberley. "You have done a very brave thing to defend me. But you must remember the teachings of the Accords. You cannot harm him just because you do not like him."

"You scared. He want hurt you. I can protect." Pemberley pulled herself up a little straighter. The top of her head reached Elizabeth's now.

When had she grown so big?

Elizabeth scratched her chin. "You are very dear and very brave to protect me, but truly, he would not have harmed—"

"Forgive me, Lady," Walker bobbed his head. "But she is right. We can smell the fear on you. What did he—"

"He renewed his offer of marriage." Elizabeth looked away. "I should not have come here."

"Marriage to that—"

"Pray, Cait, do not introduce Pemberley to that sort of language." Darcy glared.

"Foolish human conventions." Cait squawked and flapped. "You realize, he is very dangerous now, having seen us."

"I breathe fire him?" Pemberley cocked her head, mouth lifted in a draconic smile.

"No!" Elizabeth took Pemberley's face in her hands and stared directly into her eyes. "You cannot harm him. I will manage—"

And by manage, she probably meant marry.

No. Not while he could intervene.

Collins stirred, grunting softly.

"Pray forgive my intrusion, Miss Elizabeth, but this has become a matter for the Blue Order now. They must decide what kind of threat he represents to dragonkind and how to proceed from here." Darcy approached Collins.

"Threat to dragons?" Collins rolled to his side. "They are the threat to us! I do not understand why you have not been eaten—why we have all not been murdered in our beds!"

April flew, chittering, at his face. "You are the threat to us. You are the one who kicked Rumblkins and injured him! We have never hurt you!"

Collins swatted at April. "That noisy creature is a dragon too? Not a bird?"

Cait flew to a perch near Collins. "No, you addle-pate, she is not a bird. And she says you hurt one of Longbourn's dragons!"

Her parrot voice was decidedly odd, but Collins clearly understood it. Did Aunt Catherine know she was capable of that?

"There are dragons at Longbourn, too? Is the country overrun with the creatures?"

"Yes, it is." Cait leaned closer and sneered.

"I must tell Lady Catherine!" He scrambled back like a trapped animal.

"She has served me as Keeper for most of her life." Rosings grumbled. Cait translated.

"Preposterous! She cannot be a servant, she is—"

"A passable Keeper, but not worthy of airs higher than that." Cait flew to Rosings shoulder as she repeated for Collins.

"Lies and insults! Her Ladyship—"

"Enough!" Darcy adjusted his tone to that he used with querulous tenants and interposed himself between Rosings and Collins. "There is a very great deal of which you must be made aware. Walker, would you please bring Fitzwilliam?"

Walker chuckled. "I am sure he will enjoy this very much." He took off.

"Colonel Fitzwilliam is a part of this, too?" Collins ducked as Walker flew very low over his head.

"Pray, Miss Elizabeth, will you conduct Georgiana and Pemberley back to the house—"

"That ... that thing has been in the house?"

"I no thing! I Pemberley!" She flapped and growled.

To one who could not understand her baby-talk words, she really did look rather menacing.

Rosings snickered.

"She has her own guest chamber in the house. I would caution you not to refer to her as a 'thing'. She is a vikontes, and worthy of the same respect and reverence you offer my aunt."

Collins stumbled toward Darcy. "You have certainly been perversely affected by these—"

Cait shrieked her best terror-inducing tone. Georgiana clutched Elizabeth, pale as her white gown. Collins fainted again.

"Now might be the best time to make your escape." Darcy gestured toward the tunnel toward the house.

"Indeed. Thank you, sir. Since he is the heir to Longbourn, this could—"

"Fitzwilliam and I will do our best to ensure that this works out for the best. But ultimately, it is in the hands of the Blue Order. They will determine Collins' fate."

And in the course of that decision, hers as well.

And quite possibly his own.

"Of course, sir." She wrapped her arm over Georgiana's shoulder. "Come, let us return to our chambers, Pemberley. Perhaps we might arrange another tea party with the other house dragons."

"Dog and Puppy come?"

"Of course, what would a tea party be without them? Will you bring their bones along? I am sure they would prefer those to biscuits."

Pemberley waddled toward the dogs and bumped them with her nose. She picked up their bones and they followed her down the tunnel toward Rosings manor.

"My aunt may be quite unsettled by this turn of events. Might I suggest—"

"That I take a dinner tray in my room tonight? I would like nothing better." She smiled a little weakly.

"May I join her, too?" Georgiana whispered still ashen and trembling.

Pray that this did not ruin all the progress she had made in connecting to dragonkind.

"I shall make arrangements with the kitchen for all of you."

They curtseyed together and headed for the tunnel.

Once Walker returned, they would need him to summon Uncle Matlock as well. The longer this went without the attention of the Order, the more complicated, and dangerous this situation would become.

13
Chapter

DARCY ACHED DOWN to his bones. Between hunkering down on the cold stone floor, alternately subduing Collins from fleeing and picking him up off the floor when he swooned, it had been a very long evening. Finally, with Fitzwilliam's assistance and copious amounts of alcohol, they had Collins asleep in a pile of blankets. Between Rosings and Fitzwilliam keeping watch, Collins would be under control.

Darcy staggered from Rosings' lair, every joint screaming in the bright moonlight. Darcy laced his hands behind his head and stretched, neck and knuckles popping with the strain. Yes, a brisk walk was just the thing he needed. If only it was a simple walk he was taking.

Fitzwilliam had sent him to break the news to Lady Catherine, assuming one of the minor dragons had not already done so. The discovery of dragons by the dragon-deaf was no small event. It had been a long time since a true Deaf-Speaker was recognized, and he had been a far more acceptable man than Collins. What was Uncle Matlock going to do with the news when Walker delivered it?

"Caw!"

Walker? Bloody hell, how grave the news that he should return so very quickly?

He landed on Darcy's outstretched arm, hide pale and dusty, weary lines etched on his face. His wings drooped, and he huffed for breath.

"Are you well? What do you need? Water? Meat?"

"Yes, and brandy would be capital." Walker panted hard, unable to stand upright.

Walker leaned into Darcy's shoulder as they hurried to the manor by way of the kitchen.

In half an hour, they were settled comfortably in his chambers with a pan of raw meat, a dinner tray, and a bottle of brandy. For a quarter of an hour, they ate in silence, the soft nighttime breeze whistling through the window and the crackle of the fire the only sounds between them.

Darcy poured Walker's small glass and a snifter for himself. Oh, that was a welcome bit of civilization after a day and night that had been anything but.

Walker downed his glass and pointed to the bottle. Darcy obliged.

"Before you finish this one, perhaps it would be wise to share the news from Matlock with me first?"

Walker shuffled to turn his back on Darcy. "There is official word in the satchel."

"Which cannot possibly tell the entire story." Darcy released the satchel straps and scratched between Walker's wings.

He turned this way and that as Darcy tended to the many itchy spots the satchel straps left in their wake. "Lady Elizabeth has finally taught you something truly useful!"

"I am sure she will be grateful to know that."

"You should let her know of your regard toward her."

"And that is the urgent news from Matlock?"

"I think it is related."

"How is that possible?"

"Pemberley." Walker stuck his head in the brandy glass and gulped.

Cold prickles coursed down the back of his neck. "What has any of this to do with her? Matlock should be concerned with that bumbler Collins."

"That might have been your purpose, but it is not Matlock's only concern."

"Perhaps I should just read the missives." Darcy reached for the satchel.

"Matlock asked that I tell you myself first, to soften the blow."

Darcy jumped to his feet. "Soften what blow?"

"Finish your brandy, and I will tell you."

Darcy gulped the last of the fiery liquid and slammed the snifter on the small table. "Tell me."

"Despite Bennet's reports—which by the way he wrote strongly in your favor—there are those who still doubt that Pemberley can be properly imprinted upon humans."

"What more do they want than Bennet's word? Cowntess Rosings agrees. Anyone who has seen her pining for Miss Elizabeth can see—"

"That is rather the problem. They have not seen, and so they doubt. The possibility of a dragon that would readily harm humans is no small matter in the Order. There must be a consensus very soon."

There was something very ugly and ominous in Walker's voice. "Or?"

"Pemberley's life is in the balance. Duge Cornwall has declared that she must be ... dispatched if there is any question at all as to her imprinting. She has been called to appear before the Blue Order Court and defend herself."

Darcy fell into the nearest chair. "She is an infant! How can she possibly be expected to do so?"

"You will be permitted to be with her. Rosings will give her testimony as well. And I and Cait, every dragon who has been in contact with her—"

"Including that ghastly wyvern?"

"Longbourn has been summoned to appear as well, but his own matters will be his primary concern. And before you ask, it is not something I am authorized to tell you." Walker looked aside.

Darcy grumbled under his breath. "When?"

"The hearing is in five days."

"How am I to get an infant dragon to London in five days?"

"She will still fit in your carriage. If Miss Elizabeth rides with her, she will be fine."

"How can I ask her to do such a thing?" He squeezed his eyes shut and pinched his temples.

"Lady Elizabeth is as solicitous for Pemberley's well-being as you are."

"Perhaps, if Georgiana invites her to stay with us at Darcy House, then it will be a respectable visit."

"I am quite certain that after this afternoon, they will both be anxious to get away from the hub-bub at Rosings."

"I am sure of it. But will not Miss Elizabeth be necessary to inducting Collins to the world of dragons?"

"Earl Matlock has remanded the issue to the Blue Order. He does not want to bother designing a course of introductions if Collins is deemed a danger to dragon-kind."

"You cannot be suggesting—"

"I am suggesting nothing; it is a given. If Duge Cornwall deems him unworthy, he will not leave the court proceedings. Collins has been the source of significant concern for quite some time, having Longbourn entailed upon him. But that is not your concern. It is Lady Elizabeth's. Which returns us to the salient point: tell her how you feel about her."

"No, not now. It will sound insincere in the midst of asking so many favors from her." Not to mention he did not need a dragon meddling in his personal affairs.

"Why are you so stubborn?"

"When I want your advice in these matters, I will ask. Keep to the tasks at hand."

Walker ducked his head under his wing for a moment, his way of regaining his composure. "You should leave tomorrow as early as possible. Pemberley will need time to acclimatize to London before facing the Blue Order Court."

"The household has gone to bed. I cannot—"

"I will wake your sister and Lady Elizabeth. You can talk to all of them, including Pemberley in the cellar chamber." Walker took off before Darcy could protest.

He finished his brandy and let his head fall back against the chair. Dealing with the Collins calamity was bad enough. But this? A summons from the Blue Order to Court, to stand before the Dragon Conclave and defend his dragon and his reputation. He scrubbed his face with his hands.

At least he would not have to face it alone. With any luck, Miss Elizabeth would be by his side.

"Wait just a moment there, young woman." The words hung like dust motes on the morning light.

Why did her feet obey Lady Catherine's commands when her mind screamed *run*? The hairs on the back of Elizabeth's neck stood as Lady Catherine's distinct footfalls approached down the corridor of the guest wing.

"Where do you think you are going?"

"I cannot imagine that is actually your question, Lady Catherine, for I know you have had that answered several times."

Six times as a matter of fact, the first time at dawn that morning and nearly every quarter hour thereafter.

"Stop your impertinence at once! I have no patience for it now."

Perhaps, if that was what she wanted, Lady Catherine should stop asking stupid questions that incited it.

Elizabeth clenched her fists. "Then pray, detain me no further, your ladyship. Mr. Darcy is impatient to get underway."

"I will not have you in a carriage with my nephew!"

"He is not riding in the carriage. There is no room with a dragon, two dogs and two young ladies."

"You know what I mean. Do not pretend that you do not." Lady Catherine shook a pointing finger in her face.

"Madam, I must hurry, pray state what you require of me, and allow me to leave." It would have been so satisfying to stomp like a dragon, but it would have been decidedly unladylike.

"I require that you stay and marry Mr. Collins. I myself will procure a special license and engage a Blue Order Bishop to be here tonight. You may have the honor to be married from Rosings Park."

"Whilst your offer is no doubt generous, I have no intentions of marrying Mr. Collins."

"It is your fault he is now aware of dragons. Marrying him is the only way you may right the wrong that has been done ... that you have done."

"Lord Matlock's directive has expressly forbidden any such action be taken until the Order decides what is to be done with him."

"Have you no compassion for your own cousin? If they decide against him, it will be your fault. If he is safely married to you, they will be reluctant to make you a widow. Had you accepted him as you should have—"

"Aunt Catherine!" Darcy's booming voice filled the corridor.

She whirled to face him in an angry wind of swishing skirts. "You will not speak to me in that tone, Nephew."

"You will allow Miss Bennet to pass and you will cease haranguing her on this issue."

"Listen to you taking up for the little light skirt who has distracted you from your family duty."

Elizabeth's cheeks burned.

Darcy pulled himself up to tower over Lady Catherine. "You will not insult Miss Bennet, who is here doing a favor for Pemberley."

"She has done nothing as far as I can tell. You spoil your dragon terribly. Anne would have been able to manage the problem had you merely given her the chance."

He turned his back and ushered Elizabeth toward the grand stair. "Pray forgive her. I am appalled—"

"She is who and what she is, Mr. Darcy. Not unlike most dragons. There is no hope of changing them."

He paused on the steps and caught her gaze. "My aunt is entirely out of order. You have already done so much for us, and yet we have asked even more. I do not even know where to begin in expressing my appreciation …"

His eyes, they were so striking—especially when he looked at her like that—why had she never noticed?

"Of course," she looked aside and descended the stairs, her cheeks flushed for an entirely different reason.

The carriage waited near Rosings' lair. Pemberley chased the puppy around it—or was it the puppy chasing her? It was difficult to tell. April zipped back and forth between them as they went. Georgiana stood aside with Dog, her head whipping around to follow them all. With any luck, they would all be tired and ready to sleep on the journey.

"I believe Rosings expects a take leave." Darcy escorted Elizabeth to the lair. "May we enter, Cowntess?"

Rosings met them at the entrance. "I will see you at the Conclave. I will speak in support of Pemberley. You have convinced me, Miss Bennet, and I will stake my reputation on Pemberley's fitness to join the dragons of England."

Elizabeth curtsied deeply. "I am honored by your recognition, Cowntess."

"As you should be." The corner of Rosings' mouth rose. Perhaps she did have a sense of humor after all. "Cait will accompany you to London. You may send her to me should there be need to communicate with Rosings Park prior to the Conclave."

"You are most gracious, Cowntess. We will welcome her company whilst we travel." Darcy bowed from his shoulders.

"You are well-mannered, but not much of a liar. We all know she may not be the best of company, but she is loyal to me and to Pemberley. She asked to accompany you."

Now that was surprising.

"I imagine this is going to be a very memorable journey." Elizabeth laughed. "Thank you for your hospitality. You have been all things gracious and kind, to me and to Pemberley."

Rosings nodded and shuffled back into her cavern.

"I believe we have been dismissed." Darcy quirked an eyebrow. "I fear the coach may be a bit crowded. I hope it is not too uncomfortable for you."

"It shall be fine. I am accustomed to riding six ladies to a carriage, sir, I am certain this can hardly be more taxing."

Darcy handed her into the carriage to join Georgiana. It required both he and Fitzwilliam to assist Pemberley into the carriage. She had to wrap her tail tightly around her feet and tuck her wings back a mite awkwardly, but all told, it was more comfortable than squashing up between Kitty and Lydia.

April zipped in and perched on the frame of the side glass. Cait took one look inside and perched on top of the carriage, beside Walker, which was, of course, why she volunteered to join them on the journey. At least she and Walker were getting on well.

Finally, Dog and Puppy jumped in and Darcy shut the door with exaggerated care.

"You will like Darcy House very well, Miss Bennet. I know you will." Georgiana leaned into the side wall. "It is a lovely place, though I find I may not know it as well as I had thought. I never knew there were chambers in the cellars or dragon tunnels beneath."

"It is rather exciting to learn the entire city of London is connected by such tunnels. All the great houses and important buildings—even the Houses of Parliament are accessible to the dragons."

"Is your uncle's house part of the tunnel system?"

"He is an Honored Friend of the Order, but his house is not great enough to be part of the tunnels."

Pemberley lifted her head. "Uncle drove cart here?"

"Yes, he brought you here."

"You stay me? You stay me!" Pemberley thumped her tail against the side wall.

Elizabeth patted Pemberley's shoulder. "You will break the carriage, dearling, pray stop."

"But you stay me! No go!"

"I will. I will be at Darcy house with you, just as I was here. There is no reason to be so upset." She stroked Pemberley's neck.

"I ... I scared." Pemberley tucked her head under Elizabeth's arm.

"What are you afraid of?" And who had been telling her frightening tales?

"Big dragons live London?"

"Big dragons, small dragons, and many Dragon Mates. London teems with dragons."

"They not like me?" Pemberley forced her head behind Elizabeth's back.

"I feel that way often," Georgiana said softly. "Whenever I meet new people, I wonder if they will like me or not. It is very ... uncomfortable."

Pemberley pulled her head out so fast, she nearly knocked Elizabeth out of her seat. "Gigi scared, too?"

"Yes, I am scared, too. I do not want to go, either." Georgiana stared at her hands, wringing them hard enough to muss her gloves.

"We all feel afraid, sometimes," Elizabeth said. "It is natural to be afraid, but you cannot allow it to run away with you. So, Georgiana, pray come sit beside me, and Pemberley, put your head in my lap."

They obeyed. She slipped her arm over Georgiana's shoulder and cradled Pemberley's head in her hand. "There that is much better. We will be in London before you know, and I am sure it will be a very busy time, so I want you to close your eyes and rest while we can."

Georgiana and Pemberley were asleep before a quarter of an hour passed.

The Conclave was in just four days. Time enough for a visit to the Blue Order library. Surely there she could discover what the Conclave needed to see to be secure in Pemberley's imprinting and ensure the court would see it. They had been through far too much together. It would not end in the Blue Order Court.

It could not.

It simply could not.

The journey to London was as uneventful as any might be in a carriage carrying two dogs, two young women and a baby dragon. If they had to do this again—but pray they did not!—both Georgiana and Pemberley might benefit from a dose of the same cordial used by Mrs. Forster's maid before they next traveled by carriage.

In the mews behind Darcy House, a well-kept garden greeted them, hedges and a stone fence shielding the house from the view of the necessary out-buildings. But even those were clean and tidy.

The carriage pulled up directly to a wide stair leading to an area much like the front service area. Surrounded by a graceful wrought iron fence, wide steps led to a door far deeper than the typical service door. Darcy dismounted and handed his horse off to a waiting groom and unlocked the iron fence with a large key, the head of which vaguely resembled a dragon's head in profile.

He handed Elizabeth and a nearly green Georgiana out of the carriage. She hurried into the house. Hopefully the housekeeper would have some peppermint tea for her.

Pemberley nearly tumbled arsey-varsey onto the cobblestones. "No like carriage."

"Get her some water." Elizabeth looked for a pump.

Darcy dashed off and returned with a large bucket. Pemberley promptly stuck her head in and guzzled the entire bucketful.

"Was it a very difficult journey?" Darcy asked.

She tried to smile, but it was certainly a weak effort. "Two of my sisters do not ride comfortably, so it was not entirely unfamiliar."

He dragged his hand down his face. "At least we are here with time enough for her to recover before—"

"Yes, before that." She touched the edge of his sleeve. "It will be well. You must believe that whole-heartedly. If you have any doubt, the Order will see that. Dragons are incredibly perceptive to such things. It is part of their prey instinct, to find the one in the herd that is easiest to run down, the one most afraid, lacking confidence. Your certainty is as important as the testimony we offer."

He licked his lips and swallowed hard, a bead of sweat forming on his brow. "Of course, you are right."

She stayed her hand just before she wiped the sweat from his forehead.

Pemberley bounded up to them, splashing them with drips of water from her face. "Better now."

"Very good. Let us get you downstairs to your chambers. The servants have fitted it up just for you." Darcy ushered them toward the stairs, wide and deep enough to accommodate a rather large dragon.

"Have you Dragon Friends among your staff?" Elizabeth stepped down the first step, steadying Pemberley as she tried them.

Neither one of them had realized Pemberley had never traversed stairs before. This might be more difficult than expected, particularly with the two dogs underfoot.

"The housekeeper and butler have Dragon Friends. Not as exotic as Blanche and Quincy, they are rather mundane minor drakes. I think they will be pleased with my sister's newfound appreciation for dragons, though. I suspect they always resented having to keep themselves hidden from her." He opened the door at the base of the stairs. "The house has no chamber to accommodate both human and dragon together, so Miss Elizabeth will have to stay upstairs."

Pemberley gasped. "Her not stay? Her leave me?" She wound her neck around Elizabeth's waist.

"No, dearling, I am not going to leave you. I will simply be upstairs, which is very close to you. It is not at all the same thing as leaving you." She glanced at April in her hood. "Will you stay with Pemberley so she will not be alone?"

April wrinkled her snout a bit.

"The dragon chamber is very comfortable, and anything you request will be brought to you," Darcy said softly.

"I am sure the kitchen has some honey …"

"Indeed, it does."

"Very well." April flitted to land on the top of Pemberley's head crest. "I shall stay in the cellar."

She took Pemberley's face in her hands. "You know, I do not go anywhere without April. As long as she is with you, you can be certain I am nearby. If you need me, you can send April to find me, and I will come directly."

Pemberley hung her head and huffed. "But want you."

"We do not always get what we want. Sometimes even dragons must compromise."

"But I vikontes." She stamped a front foot.

"I will not have you behaving that way." She thumped Pemberley's nose.

Darcy drew in a sharp breath.

What was he thinking? That this sort of behavior should be coddled? Heavens, what kind of dragon would she grow up to be if they did that?

Pemberley whimpered. "You come visit me?"

"Of course, I will. Very often. You will hardly know I have been anywhere else."

Two knee-high minor drakes scurried up, a livery badge with what must be the Darcy crest slung around their necks. Male and female and, given the way they looked at each other, they must be a mated pair. Drakes without such a bond rarely lived together.

"Miss Elizabeth, Pemberley, may I present Amber and Slate, Dragon Friends to the housekeeper and butler."

The little dragons stepped forward and bent their front legs, touching their heads to the ground. They must have been named for their sparkling wide eyes which matched the corresponding stones.

"I am pleased to meet you." Elizabeth nudged Pemberley.

"Pleased, too. You live here?"

Slate, the larger and bolder of the two took half a step forward. "We do. Our Dragon Friends have suggested that, if Mr. Darcy so wishes, we might stay present in the cellar to attend to your needs."

"You play with me?" The tip of Pemberley's tail wagged.

"If ... if ... the Master desires." Amber glanced at Darcy, eyes wide.

She seemed nervous, but it was not the sort that came from ill treatment. The little drake gazed at him with a mix of respect and an almost canine desire to please. Only a very well-treated dragon looked at a man that way.

"That would be very pleasing." Darcy nodded and smiled at them.

Both drakes' tails flicked happily.

"May we take you to your chamber?" Slate asked.

Darcy gestured them on.

Soon they had Pemberley happily established in a clean, spacious dragon lair complete with a well-appointed nest for her and two baskets for her dogs. Amber even pointed out a lovely carved niche where a nesting basket for April might be placed. That mollified April's bruised pride.

Shortly thereafter, Pemberley instigated some sort of romping game that made sense only to the dragons. Darcy beckoned Elizabeth to another set of stairs and led her up.

After introducing the housekeeper and butler, a couple as bonded as their dragons, he took her on a brief tour of the house. Elegant understatement characterized every room, and though the evidence of dragons appeared throughout, it was subtle and tasteful, rather the exact opposite of Rosings Park. Finally, he showed her to her chambers.

"Your trunk should be waiting for you. The housekeeper has assigned a maid to assist you. She should be up shortly."

"Thank you. May I ask a small favor? Might I send word to the Gardiners that I am here? I am sure they will understand why I must stay here with Pemberley, but it would be thoughtless—"

"Of course. Would you like to pen them a note? I will have a servant ready to deliver it."

Several hours later, after a light meal, Darcy, Georgiana, and Elizabeth gathered in the parlor—not the formal drawing room, for none were up to anything so proper. The décor was like the rest of the house, quiet and elegant, but mostly comfortable. It was a room where one could relax and feel welcome. Exactly the sort of place she most needed right now.

Georgiana played the pianoforte while Darcy read and Elizabeth added observations to her commonplace book. Though maintaining a perfectly correct posture, his regular glances in her direction shouted his abiding curiosity about the contents of her book.

Perhaps she would offer to allow him to read some of it, only the most recent volume, though. Perhaps after she re-read it herself, just to be sure—

The butler bustled in and whispered a few words to Mr. Darcy who nodded. The butler returned a moment later, "Mr. Gardiner and Miss Mary Bennet."

Elizabeth jumped, dropping her pen and nearly knocking over her ink. She dashed toward them. "I am so pleased to see you! I had no idea you would come!"

Uncle caught her hands and kissed her cheeks. Mary was oddly more reserved, but Heather peeked out from under the edge of Mary's bonnet. Phoenix popped out from the other side.

"Georgiana, I have told you about Heather and Phoenix. May I introduce them now?" She held out her hands and they perched on her fingers.

"Perhaps you should introduce your sister first?" Uncle chuckled.

Elizabeth blushed. "Forgive me, Georgiana. This is my sister Mary."

Mary curtsied. "Pleased to meet you."

"What adorable little fairy dragons!" Georgiana stared with wide-eyed wonder.

Heather and Phoenix obliged with their cutest looks.

Darcy arranged chairs in a conversational knot and invited them all to sit as the housekeeper brought tea.

"Where is April?" Mary smoothed her skirt over her lap.

"She is downstairs keeping Pemberley company."

"Pemberley is here?" Uncle asked, his brow knotting in thought.

It probably would not take a great deal for him to work out why that might be.

"May I see April? It has been so long!" Heather hopped and flapped her wings. "And Pemberley too, of course. Is she much grown now?"

"Might I show them downstairs?" Georgiana asked.

"I think Pemberley would enjoy that a great deal." Elizabeth glanced at Darcy.

"Pray come, Miss Mary!" Georgiana rose with all the charm of a little girl hosting her first tea party.

Mary followed, wearing her tolerant older-sister mien, one she often donned for Kitty.

"I confess, your presence in London is a surprise, but a very welcome one. Might I surmise that it has something to do with the upcoming Dragon Conclave?" Uncle asked.

"We have been summoned here to plead Pemberley's case for imprinting to the Court."

Uncle nodded, chewing the side of his lip. "Multiple cases are usually addressed at the Conclave."

"Multiple cases?" Elizabeth's face turned cold.

"I have been charged with presenting you this." He reached into his coat pocket and handed her a letter sealed with a blue wax dragon seal. "It is a summons to appear before the court when they convene with the Conclave."

"The complaint against Longbourn?" Her hands trembled as she took the document.

"It is a bit more complicated than that. Longbourn has filed a counter complaint against you. You will be required to answer those charges as well."

She rose on quaking knees. "Charges? Against me?"

"He accuses you of neglecting your duty as his Keeper, refusing to marry Collins and running off entirely, thus abandoning your Keep."

"Abandoning my Keep?" Her voice rose barely above a squeak as she wandered toward the windows. Outside, traffic bustled and children ran past, most of them probably utterly oblivious to dragons and all the drama they caused.

"Pray, do not think I support these charges in any way. I am only the bearer of the summons. We did talk about the likelihood that this would happen."

"Yes, yes, I know we did. Pray excuse me a moment." She slipped from the room.

Where could she go? It was not as if she knew her way around the house very well. But she could get to the mews.

Quick steps took her through the back doors and into the little garden.

Uncle had warned her to expect this response from Longbourn. Had she been a fool to hope that Longbourn would have owned his transgressions and repented?

Probably.

Definitely.

Soft steps echoed from the stairs. Mary's. She had heard them too many times in the hall at home to mistake them. "Pemberley is very sweet, is she not?"

"She has grown a great deal since she left Hertfordshire." Mary stood just behind her shoulder.

"How is everyone at Longbourn?"

"I am sure I should not say so, but I wish you had not left. Papa has been unwell since that day and has only got worse. Mama has only been kept in tolerable order because of Jane's wedding—which you missed. Jane was very disappointed over that. And now it is over, Mama is diligently trying to see Kitty and Lydia married off to officers. And Longbourn! The creature is inconsolable in your absence. He does nothing but grump about, demanding to be placated in every possible way whilst complaining all the while that I am not you. Please come back."

Elizabeth held her breath and counted to ten—almost to ten—and slowly turned to face Mary. "I told you what Longbourn did."

"He has denied it most categorically. And I believe him."

"So, then what did I hear coming from the cellar?"

"Your own conscience reminding you of what you must do for the good of all."

"And you truly believe that?"

Mary pressed her fist to her lips. "I am sorry. It was not kind of me to say such a thing. I am just overwhelmed."

She took Mary's hands between hers. "What has happened?

"Everything. Or nothing. I really do not know. Everything is so different and confusing. And Lydia has been saying some very strange things of late."

"You know I have never been able to make her out. If she were a dragon—"

"How can you make jokes as such a time? Lizzy, I am truly frightened."

"I wish I had answers, Mary, but I am as much at a loss as you."

Mary covered her face with her hands, muffling a sob. Elizabeth pulled her into her shoulder and held her close.

Uncle approached and laid a hand on Mary's shoulder. "She has been beside herself with worry over the summons. She has invented all manner of disastrous outcomes."

"She is not far from right."

"Whatever do you mean?"

"Whilst in Kent, Mr. Collins discovered dragons. I am sure they are planning to try his fitness before the Conclave. They will not permit him to leave if he is found wanting."

Mary's sobs grew louder.

"Great heavens, I had no idea." Uncle slipped his arm over Mary's shoulders. "We shall make it through this. I am certain of it. I had best take her home, though."

He guided Mary to his carriage and a few minutes later, they were gone.

"Miss Elizabeth?"

Why did Darcy choose now to appear—and stand so very close?

"Forgive me, I could not help but overhear ..."

"The ability to hear dragons does make one apt to hear other things, too, does it not?"

"Whatever may happen with regard to Longbourn and Collins, I hope you know you have all the support my sister and I can offer."

How hopeful his expression, here in the moonlight.

He ran his fingers along the edge of her shawl. "It is chilly out here. Perhaps you should come inside. You would like some drinking chocolate, perhaps?"

No, she really did not. But the offer was so thought-ful and his eyes so warm, she could hardly say no.

14
Chapter

THE NEXT TWO days flew by in a frenzy of researching and preparation, which might have proved overwhelming had it not been for Darcy's unwavering presence and calm. How welcome it had been when he had placed himself between her and those who might distract her from her work. No one had ever left her feeling so protected.

Pemberley's case was not as clear cut as they had hoped, but with what they had learnt and Rosings' support their chances of success were good.

Elizabeth stared up at the ceiling. Plaster moldings—ivy with tiny fairy dragons playing amongst the leaves—stared back down at her. A moonbeam reached the little mantel clock. An hour before dawn. Just an hour and she could begin preparations to face a day that would forever change everything she knew. It did not seem right that a single day could make such a difference. Then again, Pemberley's hatching had changed everything in a single day, too.

How many other lives could change in a mere moment today?

Mr. Collins'.

Now that he had seen dragons, the only way the Court would accept him into the Order would be for him to have a full-time supervisor, one who would tutor him in all aspects of dragon-kind until he was fully initiated. Since it was her fault he made the discovery, it would probably fall to her to be his keeper.

She pressed her knuckle to her mouth. How much of this trouble was, at its heart, her fault?

To start, she had spoiled Longbourn. She could see that now after dealing with Pemberley and trying to train her up properly. So much of his petulance she had tolerated, even abetted by giving him precisely what he wanted.

If she had not allowed him to have been so selfish, he would not have sent Pemberley away. If she had not been so impulsive, she would not have run away, and Georgiana's letters would have reached her. If she had not been so stubborn, she would not have run from Collins; she would have accepted him and his life—and possibly the fate of her mother and sisters—would not hang in the balance at the Blue Order Court today. How many were suffering for her selfish, headstrong ways?

But those thoughts were not at all helpful. She dragged herself out of bed and donned Aunt Gardiner's blue gown. She had been right; a suitable gown did make it easier to face the demands of the day. Not very much, to be sure, but even very small bits helped.

Darcy handed her into the carriage and climbed up to sit beside the driver. Without a chaperone to accompany them, it was the only proper thing to do. Still, she would have welcomed the company.

April, Cait and Walker had already gone ahead with Pemberley and Rosings through the dragon tunnels. Minor dragons were not usually included in the Court proceedings and never attended a Conclave, but their testimony was essential to several of the matters of the day. So, they were permitted to attend under escort from a Ranking dragon.

Someday Pemberley would be able to perform that function. Was it too much to hope she might have the privilege of seeing that one day? It was unlikely, though. Longbourn usually did not attend Conclaves and probably would not begin to do so.

They walked into the Order. Colonel Fitzwilliam met them in the front hall. His silence echoed the tension that seemed to fill the building. Liveried servants, human and dragon, scurried about, footsteps soft, voices muffled. They might not know the precise issues facing the Conclave today, but they were obviously aware of their gravity.

A Court Bondsman, dressed in blue court robes with his hood nearly covering his face, escorted them deep into the bowels of the building to a witness box along the side of the court floor. He latched the wooden gate behind them. It was a little like being in a cage, symbolic more than functional, but the sense was still there.

They sat in the front of three rows. Would Lady Catherine arrive later to fill one of the empty chairs? Who might be called to the others?

The court room was the only room on this deepest level of the Order offices. The ceiling rose four, perhaps five stories above them, above a round stone floor as large as four substantial ballrooms put together. Flying dragons could easily soar within. Dragon tunnels entered the floor from nearly every direction with mirrored wall sconces mounted between each tunnel. Three levels of balconies circled the room, guarded by somber wooden rails. Between each section of railing, brass mirrors backed tall, eight-hour candles. Cockatrices flew around each level, lighting the candles, the room brightening as they went.

Three imposing stations graced the head of the round room. Three rows of elaborate chairs on raised platforms rose in the center: The Gallery where the Order officials would sit when the Court assembled. On either side were the judge's bench for the Minister of the Blue Court and the raised station and desk for the Chancellor of the Order, The Earl of Matlock, who would preside over the Conclave.

The levels above them gradually filled with Dragon Keepers, by rank, the highest ranking on the nearest levels. Major Dragons of every shape trickled onto the broad floor with what appeared to be dignity but was really more tension. Only the most important of matters could convince them all to gather so close together. Liveried attendants escorted them to their designated place in the court.

How much thought had to go into the placements of the arriving dragon peers? Like-types and ranks had to be separated. Certain types had to be kept apart—

and basilisks had to be separated from all, including each other. Perhaps that was what those partial walls near the far tunnels were for.

Distinctions of rank had to be preserved, placing the biggest dragons closest to the proceedings. Raised platforms circled behind that rank to lift the lower-ranking major dragons high enough to see, but not to have their heads above the highest dragons.

No wonder Longbourn did not attend Conclaves. Assignment to the rearmost rank would remind him of his insignificance, and that would not do.

It was sometimes easy to forget that the Pendragon Treaty was as much a peace treaty between dragons as it was between men and dragons.

The noise level rose as the chamber filled, a dull, deep roar that pounded at the base of her skull. How would they hear anything above that?

Fitzwilliam elbowed her. "There, Pemberley arrives."

She followed his pointing chin to a tunnel almost directly opposite them. The room's roar dulled as Rosings entered, her right wing sheltering little Pemberley.

No doubt that little demonstration of maternal affection was designed precisely to communicate to the Conclave. Walker, Cait and April flew in behind them. The roar increased even louder than it had been before, not unlike a ballroom when unexpected guests arrived. The party was escorted to a dragon-sized railed and gated box close to the Minister of the Court's bench.

Rosings looked calm and in her element. April landed on Pemberley's head and seemed to be singing. The tension in Pemberley's posture seemed to ease. There was nothing like a fairy dragon to calm one in a crisis.

"Collins arrives." Darcy whispered, not looking at her. His hands were clenched and shoulders tense.

Collins walked behind Lord Matlock, flanked by two very large, robed escorts. Probably footmen pressed into service as Bondsmen. Most likely they were there for Collins' safety should he try to bolt, able to stay him before a dragon's prey reflex was triggered. She shuddered. That was a sight she could happily live without ever seeing.

He was secured in a witness box between Matlock's station and the Officials' gallery. Interesting. The rails were higher, nearly shoulder height, and the gate locked behind him. The burly Bondsmen remained stationed outside either side of his enclosure.

A Bondsman approached with Uncle Gardiner and Mary, and another escorted Lady Catherine. Interesting, Anne was not there. Had she not been summoned or was her "health" keeping her away?

Uncle and Mary slipped in the row behind her. Lady Catherine took the chair beside Fitzwilliam.

Uncle laid a hand on her shoulder. "How are you?"

"Ask me again when the Conclave is dismissed. I will not know before then." Elizabeth glanced back.

Mary clutched her hands together, rocking slightly, face ghastly pale. Hopefully she would not swoon. Longbourn was the only major dragon she had really ever known. Seeing so many at once must be overwhelming to her. Had Papa not thought to prepare her better for this? Elizabeth reached back and found Mary's hand. Mary squeezed back, the edges of her lips lifted for just a moment.

Elizabeth scanned the room again. Where was Longbourn? If he missed the Court—

A loud gong cut through the room's roar, and an eerie hush fell over the room. The Minister of the Court led in the Blue Order officials, robed in blue, gold and ivory. They took their place in the gallery.

Lord Matlock, blue robes resplendent with heavy gold trim, mounted the steps to his station. He nodded at the Minister of the Court whose white wig identified him amongst all the other officials.

The Minister carried a heavy oaken staff toward his bench. Fully a foot taller than himself, gold—or possibly ormolu—vines wrapped the length. A firedrake, wings spread, holding a blue spherical gem in its mouth topped the staff. He rapped it on a large metal plate embedded in the floor just behind the judge's bench.

The tones reverberated in her skull. Across the room, Pemberley and April cringed at the sound. A lindwyrm in the back row snapped at the wyvern next to him. Two Bondsmen ran between them—brave souls—and hoisted a large black curtain strung on heavy poles to block their view of on another. Two more intervened, one for each dragon, talking them down from their defensive postures.

The minister mounted the steps to the bench and opened the proceedings by reading a summary of the Pendragon Treaty and the Accords. While it satisfied the peers' need for pomp and circumstance, it was also an obviously necessary reminder to all the dragons of the behavior required of them.

A softer, higher-pitched gong chimed three times. "The Court of the Blue Order and the Dragon Conclave of England are now in session."

A brief roar of assent, then silence.

"Secretary, Baron Chudleigh, read the first case."

Chudleigh rose from his place, front and center of the officials' gallery, and unfurled a scroll.

That bit of drama was probably unnecessary, but it was very showy.

"The case of The Blue Order versus William Collins."

A Bondsman urged Collins to rise and face the Conclave. He needed support on either side, his knees too weak to hold him. Given his pallor, he might faint at any moment. Not an excellent way of obtaining dragon respect.

Cait swooped past the Minister of the Court's bench and landed on the railings near Collins. He jumped back.

"I am to translate for you," she squawked in her parrot-voice that sounded nothing like her.

"Collins is the heir to Longbourn estate, an established dragon territory. Despite being totally dragon-deaf, he accidentally discovered dragonkind. The Conclave must decide whether to accept him as a deaf-speaker—or not." Chudleigh's voice boomed through the room.

Collins gulped and wobbled between the Bondsmen.

"Is he truly dragon-deaf and immune to persuasion?" Cownt Matlock grumbled from the front row. What a stunning blue-green firedrake, even larger than Rosings, with flaming orange eyes that missed nothing! What stories he would have to tell!

Instead of translating, Cait said, "April, please come and sing to him."

April zipped to the box and hovered in front of Collins' face, singing sweetly. The Bondsmen beside him yawned, and their eyes drooped. Matlock and the

Minister of the Court did the same, but Collins remained white-faced, eyes wide.

"Perhaps I should bite off his generative bits?" Cait
hopped toward him.

Both Bondsmen jumped back, hands shielding their
family jewels. Collins remained unmoving.

A wave of laughter cut through Conclave, human
and dragon alike. Fitzwilliam chuckled, though neither
Darcy nor Uncle Gardiner did. Mary was probably
blushing painfully. She never appreciated dragon
bluntness.

"The point is established. Collins is entirely dragon-
deaf." Matlock stretched and shook his head.

April looked a little too satisfied with herself.

Matlock went on to ask for the case in favor of Collins' provisional admission into the Blue Order. It
began with his standing as heir to a dragon estate and
ended with Lady Catherine and Mary testifying to his
tractability in the right hands, not that Collins appreciated the latter point very much, though.

He should have. It could very well be the thing that
saved his life.

Collins' treatment of Rumblkins, as told by Rustle
and April and tempered by Uncle Gardiner, was a mark
against him, as was his anti-dragon attitude. Collins
himself, though, managed to argue that it had changed
since coming to know that dragons existed. Now he
was actually quite fascinated by them.

Terrified by them was probably more accurate.

"And just how did you become aware of the exist-
ence of dragonsss?" Barwines Chudleigh slithered
forward, toward Collins.

Collins shuddered a bit. Snake-types in particular
unsettled those unaccustomed to them.

"I ... I ... that is to say, it was Miss Elizabeth Bennet's fault all told. I made her an offer of marriage, one sanctioned by her father and Lady Catherine and, as I understand, the dragon Longbourn himself. Yet, she refused me. Refused me and ran off into the woods. I chased after her and came, unknowing, into a lair full of dragons."

A roar resounded from a tunnel at the back of the room. "She should have accepted the offer. She promised to do so!" Longbourn stormed in.

Bondsmen with curtains dashed to his side, raising the black cloths to shield him from the view of the nearby dragons.

The Minister of the Court struck the floor gong. "Order! Come to Order."

Matlock rose. "Since these cases are inextricably intertwined, Lord Secretary, I recommend we pause in the case of Collins and hear the case of Miss Elizabeth Bennet versus Longbourn."

The Conclave roared their assent.

The Bondsmen escorted Longbourn to the final empty box near the center front of the court. Collins stared at Longbourn, blinking hard. No doubt, the first time he had seen was had been lurking in the Longbourn estate cellars.

Elizabeth and Uncle Gardiner rose. Her mouth went dry. She licked her lips, but it did not help.

Chudleigh lifted his scroll. "Miss Elizabeth Bennet, junior Keeper to Laird Longbourn, has filed a complaint charging first that Longbourn insists she marry against her will, an act now forbidden by the recent changes to the marriage clauses of the Accords. Secondly, he threatened her, treating her as prey—"

That drew gasps from the gallery above. A cold wave trailed from her face down to her toes. She would never forget that moment.

"—using his venom until she fainted and could have suffered substantial harm. And finally, that Laird Longbourn attempted to use draconic persuasion upon her when Collins first offered her marriage."

The dragons hissed at that. Longbourn cringed and roared.

"In his rebuttal, Laird Longbourn counters that since the estate is entailed upon an heir who cannot hear dragons, it is imperative that Miss Elizabeth marry him to ensure that a proper Keeper will remain on the estate. He charges her with neglecting her duties by leaving the estate improperly after said offer of marriage. He also claims innocence on the charge of attempting to persuade a Keeper."

Murmurs filtered through the audience.

Minister of the Court rapped his staff on the floor until the room stilled. "On the first charge, the point of law is quite clear. A Keeper may refuse a marriage as long as it does not leave the estate without a Keeper."

"Collins is dragon-deaf!" Longbourn stomped. "He cannot be a Keeper. She must marry Collins and return to my Keep."

"Is there another daughter who is not dragon-deaf?"

Mary rose, shaking as hard as Collins. "I am, sir."

The Minister of the Court looked straight at Mary. "And have you been acquainted with the estate dragon?"

"Not nearly so much as my sister, but yes."

"You have been taught the role and responsibilities of a Keeper?"

"I am not nearly so good at them as my sister."

"Her dragon friend would disagree." Elizabeth edged back to stand beside Mary. "She quite adores Mary."

"Are you willing to accept the role of Dragon Keeper?"

"Me? Sir, I ... that has always been my sister's task. Longbourn would never accept another. He adores, Lizzy, insists upon her presence regularly. He is angry and resentful that I should be there instead of her."

Longbourn roared his agreement.

"Silence, Laird Longbourn!" The Minister rapped the floor again. "That was not my question. Would you willingly accept the role?"

"I have never considered it ... But I suppose should anything happen to Lizzy, I would have to. Yes."

"Laird Longbourn, you are familiar with Miss Mary Bennet?"

Longbourn grumbled.

"In the absence of Miss Elizabeth Bennet, has she provided you with food, security, and comfort?"

"Not very well. She is fearful and clumsy. She does not know how to do many things right at all."

"The court will hear that answer as an affirmation. Longbourn's needs are met under the care of the secondary junior Keeper."

"I want Elizabeth." Longbourn roared and stomped. "Mary will not do!"

Mary wrung her hands, eyes very bright.

"This demonstration of temper supports the case against you. You seem quite capable of threatening your Keeper."

"She made me angry!"

"So, you confess?"

"I was angry. I would not have hurt her."

Uncle Gardiner stepped slightly forward, gripping the rail before him. "I witnessed the event. He lifted her in his talons, covered her with his wings and breathed venom on her. I believed she would be dead when he dropped her."

"She is my Keeper! I would not have hurt her!"

"Miss Elizabeth Bennet, were you at any time in fear for your safety or your life from Laird Longbourn?"

She squeezed her eyes shut and nodded. "Yes, sir I was, as I never had been from a dragon before."

Longbourn trumpeted, the sound rang hollowly through the huge chamber.

"And on the count of persuasion—"

"I did not persuade her!" He stomped and slapped his tail on the stone floor.

April zipped to him and hovered in front of his face. "I was with her. I heard the voice, too."

"It was not mine!" He snapped at her.

She barely buzzed away in time.

"Stop! She is a member of your Keep!" Cownt Matlock growled.

"There was a voice, sir, a dragon voice, urging me to accept Mr. Collins' proposal." Elizabeth's voice sounded so small and weak in the room full of dragons.

"It was not me!" Longbourn screamed.

"Could you definitely recognize the voice as Laird Longbourn's?" The Minister turned to Elizabeth.

"I ... I do not know." Elizabeth leaned against the rail for support. "It came from the cellars. Only a major dragon's voice could be heard at that distance. There is no one else it could have been."

"It was not me. I should know very well who I have tried to persuade and who I have not."

Voices shouted from the back of the Conclave. Others in the middle and the front answered them. The roars grew louder until Elizabeth had to cover her ears.

The Minister struck the floor gong twice. "Come to order immediately."

The Conclave took far longer to settle down this time.

"On the matter of persuasion, sufficient evidence does not exist. The court finds for Laird Longbourn."

Longbourn trumpeted and flapped his wings.

"However, the court also finds that Laird Longbourn, you are in violation of the Accords. There is no evidence Keeper Elizabeth Bennet is in dereliction of her post. She is well within her rights to withdraw if she feels threatened. No Keeper should ever feel threatened by their dragon."

The Conclave agreed. Loudly.

"She is a fool if she believes I threatened her." Longbourn flipped his wings to his back and tossed his head. He had never been gracious in defeat.

"Then you will be relieved to know that you do not need to have a fool as a Keeper. Miss Mary Bennet, are you willing to marry Mr. Collins and take on the role of Keeper of Longbourn and Guardian to the dragon-deaf?"

"Marry Miss Mary?" Collins stammered.

"Do you object to her?" The Minster of the Court glowered.

"I ... ah ... no ... I had just thought the elder sister was the more appropriate choice." He waggled his fingers at Mary.

"She has refused you, twice I believe. Miss Mary Bennet, do you object to a marriage with Mr. Collins with all the privilege and responsibility it will entail?"

"No, sir, I do not object."

A quick glance suggested not only did she not object, but she rather relished the notion.

"Then by order of this court, I declare Miss Mary Bennet betrothed to Mr. William Collins, a marriage to be conducted at the earliest possible date in her home parish of Meryton. The couple shall reside at Longbourn where Historian Bennet will take charge of Collins' instruction and official sponsorship into the Blue Order in one year's time. A cockatrix who can speak to men directly will be assigned to Longbourn to translate. Until such time of his official induction, Miss Mary Bennet, you are his official Guardian. He is not to be out of your presence in company at any time. If at any time he proves to be any kind of threat to the Blue Order or dragonkind, it is your responsibility to alert the Order. Mr. Collins, justice among dragons is swift and severe. Do you understand?"

Collins gulped and sagged into the support of the Bondsmen.

"Does the Conclave agree?"

A deafening roar filled the court room. Was it possible that the dragons were as glad to have reason not to kill him as the men were?

"Let the records show this decision."

Longbourn shrieked and flapped his wings. He bounded over the box's rails and landed just short of Elizabeth. "You would abandon me?"

She pulled her shoulders back against the trembling in her belly. "I will not be afraid of my Keep's dragon."

"And this is your final word on the matter?"

"Mary will be your Keeper now. Treat her well, and she will be glad of the appointment."

Longbourn huffed acrid breath at Mary, and she shrank back. He turned to Elizabeth. "You are no longer welcome on Longbourn estate. I will not have its shades polluted by one who abandons me. You are never to enter the house or the gardens again. I forbid it. You shall never see your family or your father again."

"It is within your right to determine who is allowed within your territory, but you cannot dictate the family's choices to see her outside your territory." The Minister of the Court called from his bench. "Speaking of your territory, your application to expand your boundaries is denied and your territory will be reduced ten percent as penalty for your transgressions against your Keeper. Keep well within the boundaries of Longbourn estate or more severe consequences will follow."

Longbourn roared and stomped. "Bennet will never see you again. I forbid my Keeper from it, and I shall persuade the others who do not hear. You have no home. You are no Keeper."

A high-pitched cry echoed from the far side of the room. Pemberley bounded out of her box and half-lunged, half-waddled to Longbourn.

"No be mean her!"

"Get away from me, you little—"

Pemberley reared back on her hind legs and huffed. A little spurt of flame singed Longbourn's nose, and he jumped back.

Elizabeth hurdled over the railing and caught Pemberley's face in her hands. "No! You must not do that. You know better than to threaten another dragon!"

"But he hurt you. He want hurt you again! Only protecting. I allowed that."

"Of course, you are, my dear. But there are many others here whose job that is. We must learn to perform our role, and let others do theirs. Now, you should apologize to Longbourn." Elizabeth pushed Pemberley's head toward Longbourn.

"I sorry." Pemberley dropped her head and muttered.

"I have no need for apologies from babies and dragonless Keepers." Longbourn stormed off down the tunnel he had come from.

"You no Keeper now?"

"It is nothing for you to worry about. Nothing has changed for you."

"Yes. Yes, it do!" Pemberley flapped and hopped like an excited fairy dragon. "You no have dragon. I be you dragon. You my Keeper."

"You already have a Keeper, dearling."

"I want two! I vikontes. I can has two, right?" She turned to Cownt Matlock. "Please, can I has two Keepers?"

Matlock rose and the Minister of the Court struck the high gong twice. "Is there any in the Conclave who doubts her imprinting now?"

Silence. Not even the scratching of talons on the stone floor.

"Let the records show this decision. I officially welcome you, Vikontes Pemberley into the Blue Order." Cownt Matlock licked the top of her head.

Pemberley licked him back, looking up at him, puzzled. "That mean I can has two?"

"Dearling, I am sorry but—"

"There is a way." Darcy laid his hand on her shoulder. He drew a deep breath and stood very tall. "Miss Elizabeth Bennet, would you consent to be my wife and Pemberley's Keeper?"

Her eyes bulged, and she grabbed for the railing behind her.

"See, you can be my Keeper!"

"No!" Lady Catherine sprang to her feet. "Absolutely not! Under no circumstances."

"On what grounds?" the Minister of the Court asked.

She looked straight at Matlock. "You well know the reasons."

"State them for the court." Had Matlock learned that glare from his dragon?

"He is engaged to my daughter. From their birth—"

"A betrothal I never agreed to—"

Pemberley squawked and flapped. "I not have that one! No, she awful! She no like me!"

"Your precious changes mean that he is not bound by his dragon's demands." Lady Catherine crossed her arms over her chest.

"But you should listen to mine." Rosings lumbered toward them. "I will tolerate the young one as my Keeper, but I will not share my territory with another dragon, even Pemberley. If the young one marries Darcy, one of us will be left without a Keeper unless they do not live together."

"An intolerable option," Darcy muttered under his breath. "I will not have Anne."

Lady Catherine whirled on him, shrieking like Cait. "But it is a spectacular match! If you refuse, I shall never see you again. You will be—"

"Enough!" Matlock stood. "Darcy is in no way obligated to marry Anne."

"But since their birth—"

"Escort her from the floor." Matlock waved several Bondsmen into motion.

Lady Catherine regained her composure enough not to be dragged away kicking and screaming—but only just.

Pemberley watched the procession then turned back to Cownt Matlock. "I can has her my Keeper?"

Sir Edward stood in the second row of the officials' gallery. "It is the opinion of the Lord Physician that the drakling would fare best with Miss Bennet's presence."

"I concur." Barwines Chudleigh lifted her head a little higher.

"And I." Rosings bellowed.

More dragons added their loud agreement.

Pemberley wrapped her neck around Elizabeth's waist tightly and stared up into her eyes to plead.

April landed on her shoulder and nipped her ear. "I shall stay with Pemberley if you do not take him!"

She glanced behind her. Uncle Gardiner nodded.

Beside him, Mr. Darcy caught her gaze. Oh! The look in his eyes! Her face flushed and it crept down her neck.

Mr. Collins had never looked at her that way.

Darcy could be taciturn and dour, ill-mannered and rude. But men like Colonel Fitzwilliam followed him, Walker trusted him, Pemberley and Georgiana adored him.

"I ... I accept."

Pemberley squealed and wrapped her neck around Elizabeth's waist.

"Let the record show that the Court approves the request of young Pemberley to be granted two Keepers and note the betrothal of Miss Elizabeth Bennet and Mr. Fitzwilliam Darcy."

Apparently, the dragons approved.

The Minister allowed the Conclave to quiet on their own.

Lord Chudleigh rose and cleared his throat. "That concludes the cases before the Blue Order Court." He gestured toward Lord Matlock.

"There remains a final matter for the Conclave to consider, one of grave concern. I have received three independent reports from Dragon Friends stationed with the militia in Hertfordshire, all pointing to the presence of an unknown dragon in that county."

Who knew silence could be every bit as frightening as dragon roars?

The Accords permitted a major dragon to kill another major dragon trespassing on its territory. But a battle of major dragons, especially ones of similar size and strength, could go on for days and would be certain to draw the attention of the local human population, threatening the secrecy of the entire dragon community. Dragon war was the most likely outcome. If a rogue dragon really existed, it had to be dealt with immediately, hopefully by bringing it into the Blue Order and under the rule of the Pendragon Accords. The alternative was unthinkable.

Matlock began reading the reports. Dragon thunder heard the night of the Netherfield ball, but two voices, not just one.

Her skin prickled. Was that possible? She closed her eyes. What had she heard that night?

Reports of thefts from the regimental supplies ... Great Heavens, Pemberley's egg might well have been hidden among the stolen supplies—was that the crux of the argument between Wickham and Darcy before the ball? That Wickham had lost the egg he had stolen?

Mary leaned forward and whispered in her ear. "Do you think it is possible that voice you heard—"

Elizabeth grabbed her hand. "I ... I think I heard it the night of Jane's betrothal at Netherfield as well."

Mary gasped. "Netherfield? Lydia!"

"What do you mean?"

"Before she went to stay at Netherfield. She was saying some very odd things. I think—Heavens! Can it be possible?—I think she might be like Aunt Gardiner!"

"You think she has started hearing dragons now?" Elizabeth chewed her knuckle.

"As I think about it now, yes, I do. If there is an unknown dragon at Netherfield, and she is speaking to it, of course she would want to be there with it, alone. It could be trying to convince her to become its Keeper."

"But Jane and Bingley—"

"Are at risk of suddenly disappearing to make way for Lydia!"

Darcy leaned toward them. "Do you think it possible that the dragon script we found at Netherfield could have been written by a dragon?"

"The last time I was there, I found paintings in the drawing room, with hidden bits of script. There was one that I did not understand, but now I think the script read 'sanctuary'—possibly a dragon taking sanctuary? Lindwyrms have been known to write and even paint—it could have been done by one."

"Whilst in Meryton, Walker thought he heard a voice—"

"That is right! He asked Longbourn about it." Why had she not paid more attention to that?

"Do you recall what he said—that there was nothing unknown in his territory? He did not actually deny its presence." Darcy bit his bottom lip.

"He has been awfully cross, could tolerating the presence of another dragon—" Mary said.

"Lord Matlock!" Darcy's voice boomed over Matlock's reading. "We have come to believe that the dragon you speak of is a lindwyrm that has possibly taken residence at Netherfield Park."

"And you failed to mention this?"

Elizabeth gulped. Actually, it was Papa who failed to mention it. He had been musing for quite some time of the possibility of an unknown dragon in the region. She thought it had been idle talk, wishful thinking of something noteworthy he might record for the Order. If it had been more than that, though, he should have brought it to the attention of the Order. Why would he not?

"It is only now that we have put all the pieces together. If it is indeed at Netherfield, it may pose a serious threat to the dragon-deaf residents there."

"Sir!" Elizabeth cried. "It is my eldest sister and her husband. Pray, allow me to go to Netherfield and investigate. Perhaps I might make contact with it and induce it to become part of the Blue Order."

"If there is any among the Order who can do such a thing, it is she." Rosings shrugged her wings and shuffled back to her place.

Barwines Chudleigh rose up and extended her wings. "I concur."

The room filled with sounds of approbation.

"Let the record show that Miss Elizabeth Bennet will go immediately to Meryton to assess this situation and make contact with this unknown dragon. Use whatever persuasion is necessary to stay at Netherfield Park and protect the dragon-deaf residents there. Keeper Mary Bennet, you and Historian Bennet will provide as much assistance as possible, while respecting Longbourn's ban on Miss Elizabeth in his territory."

"I go, too?" Pemberley asked loudly.

"No, my dear, it is far too dangerous. You must stay—"

"No leave me! No go!"

A murmur began among the dragons. Barwines Chudleigh slithered to Pemberley. "There are times all dragonsss must do what they would rather not. It is part of living under the Accordsss. Your Keepersss have a duty to dragonkind, as do you. You will ssstay here with the girl, Georgiana. Whilst they are gone, Bylock, the Ssscribe's drake, has offered to teach you to read and write. We will also help prepare the girl to be presented to the Blue Order ssso that she might have her own Dragon Friend, or one day be a Keeper herself."

"But I no want her go."

Elizabeth laid her arm over Pemberley's shoulders. "It will not be like last time, I promise. We will send letters, but not through the post. Walker and Rustle and perhaps even Cait will help us. I am your Keeper now, Pemberley and will never abandon you. I will always come back, even as I did this time."

"You did come me." Pemberley hung her head and swung it to and fro.

"That is right. She did, and she will do ssso again. Your Keepersss are trustworthy. Otherwise we would not ask this of them."

Pemberley blinked up at Chudleigh. "We have tea?"

"Yesss, we shall have tea quite regularly. I will help you learn to use your wingsss."

"You fly? I want fly."

Elizabeth patted her shoulder. "That is something I cannot teach you. Only someone with wings can do that. You should thank Barwines Chudleigh for her kind offer."

"I want learn fly. Thank you much."

"Is the matter settled then?" Matlock asked. He did not cover his annoyance well.

"I stay, learn write, and fly," Pemberley called back.

Chudleigh leaned down to Elizabeth's ear. "She is going to be a handful." With a wink, she slithered back to her place.

Lord Matlock descended from his station and stood beside Cownt Matlock who sat back on his haunches and lifted his head high above the rest. "The Conclave is adjourned."

The Minister rang the floor gong twice. Bondsmen scurried in from all sides, escorting dragons out by rank. One came for Pemberley and, after a little encouragement from Darcy and Elizabeth, was able to lead her back to Rosings and out.

Another Bondsman escorted them back upstairs to the street level rooms where a footman took over. "Tea has been prepared for you in one of the parlors, courtesy of Lord Matlock."

"How very civilized of him." Fitzwilliam laughed and offered Elizabeth his arm.

Darcy stepped between and offered his. She slipped her hand in the crook of his arm, leaning into his strength. Somehow it felt natural and right and very, very confusing.

"As territorial as a dragon!" Fitzwilliam jumped back between Mary and Uncle Gardiner. "You will join us, will you not?"

"Thank you, but perhaps I should go find Mr. Collins?" Mary glanced about.

"I would not expect him to be released for several hours yet. Lady Astrid will be tutoring him on the basics of the Accords, particularly on secrecy. Then, I imagine Aunt Catherine will wish to discuss the hiring of a curate to fill his pulpit. You might as well enjoy tea whilst you wait."

"A splendid idea." Uncle Gardiner offered Mary his arm and they followed the rest to the small parlor on the second floor.

Afternoon sun poured through the windows, bathing the room in light and warmth. After so many hours of candlelight, it seemed bright and almost garish. Thankfully, dark woods and soft blues and golds soothed her senses. A low, round table was set with tea things in the center of the room, surrounded by comfortable chairs, interspersed with dragon perches where April, Walker, and Cait were waiting for them.

Elizabeth went through the motions of serving tea, happy when the men launched upon a discussion as to how they might penetrate the poisoned room at Netherfield. The topic should have been fascinating to her. Usually it would be, but too many other things filled her mind.

"Are you well, Mary?"

Mary stared into her tea cup. "I am just so surprised by the events of the day. I never expected—"

"Are you certain you are content with being betrothed to Mr. Collins?"

"Indeed, I am. I can see you are skeptical, though. Do you think it incredible that Mr. Collins should be able to procure any woman's good opinion because he was not so happy as to succeed in securing yours? I hope you will be satisfied with what I have done. It is best for the family—for all of us."

"I would be happier knowing that the choice will not make you miserable."

"None of us can know the future, Lizzy. But I am not romantic, you know. I never was. I ask only a comfortable home, and considering Mr. Collins' character, connections, and situation in life, I am convinced that my chance of happiness with him is as fair as most people can boast on entering the marriage state. I have always been fonder of him than you have. Heather finds him quite tolerable. Truly it is the best solution for all of us. I might ask the same question of you though. I did not think Mr. Darcy—"

Rustle flew in, almost toppling the perch as he landed.

Elizabeth and Uncle jumped to their feet and steadied it.

"Heavens, catch your breath, Rustle. It is all good news! Mrs. Gardiner will be pleased." Uncle offered him tea from his own cup.

Rustle swallowed a couple of gulps. "If only I had been sent in want of news, all would be well, but that is far from the case."

"Pray tell, what is wrong?" Elizabeth sank back into her seat.

"In my satchel, there is a letter, sent express from your father." Rustle turned his back so Uncle could retrieve the letter.

He broke the seal and unfolded it. He scanned the page, color draining from his face. "Bennet writes:

"Something has occurred of a most unexpected and serious nature. An urgent message came at twelve last night, just as we were all gone to bed, from Colonel Forster, to inform us that Lydia was gone off to Scotland with one of his officers—Mr. Wickham! At first light, I went to Netherfield, hoping that perhaps they were simply sequestered there, but to no avail. Her trunk was gone. The housekeeper was unaware of her departure, saying that Lydia had kept to her room for the last two days with a sick headache.

"I would not trouble you simply over a possible elopement—as serious as that would be—but Lydia has lately been showing signs of starting to Hear dragons. I have been waiting to be sure before introducing her to dragonkind. Not long ago, April expressed concern over Mr. Wickham's excessive interest in dragons, not to mention his connections to the Pemberley affair. Should he be a Deaf-Speaker, or trying to become one, any connection to a Hearer not loyal to the Blue Order could be disastrous.

"I would go after her myself and have tried to do so. But my condition no longer permits me to ride, and even an hour in a carriage is nigh on intolerable. I must ask you, my brother, for your assistance in this matter. While it is possible this may all turn out to be naught, the risk is too great to ignore."

"Great heavens!" Uncle fell into his chair.

"Was not Mr. Wickham in Brighton?" Mary whispered.

"He was supposed to be." Darcy slammed his fist into his palm. "This is my fault. Had I only revealed what Wickham was, apprehended him when I had the opportunity—"

"You could hardly have done that until the egg was found—which I might remind you never happened. Instead, you had a new hatchling to care for, hardly a time that you could be away to negotiate with the colonel of the regiment to turn Wickham over to you in chains," Elizabeth said.

"I must find her." Uncle rose unsteadily.

"No," Darcy stood. "It was my charge first. I must complete it."

"And I will go with you. No offense, sir, but he will find the two of us more formidable." Fitzwilliam wore the sort of expression that would brook no argument.

"I can manage the matters at Netherfield myself, Mr. Darcy." Elizabeth gazed straight into his eyes, not precisely a challenge, but—

He nodded slowly. "Though I do not prefer to leave you alone to do it, I have complete faith in you. Will you consider taking the Darcy carriage to Meryton? Your sister and Collins, and you, Mr. Gardiner, if you desire to go as well, might all drive there together, and the coach would be at your disposal whilst you are there. Most important, you will have the ability to return to London whenever you should need."

"That would be most welcome." The crest of her cheeks heated. Perhaps she should have had more faith in him. "I should leave first thing in the morning."

"We should not wait even that long," Fitzwilliam said. "There is still time to cover considerable ground before nightfall."

"An hour to pack should suffice." Darcy glanced at Elizabeth, his expression difficult to read.

"I will inform Father and see you at Darcy House in an hour then." Fitzwilliam bowed to them and left.

15 Chapter

IN THE MEWS behind the Order offices, Darcy handed Elizabeth into the carriage and moved to climb up with the driver.

"Go sit with her. You are betrothed now." Walker grumbled from his perch atop the coach.

"I do not want to intrude. This has all been so abrupt—"

Walker jumped closer and stared beak to nose, directly into his eyes—never a good thing from a cockatrice. "You are betrothed to her without ever having told her of your regard. If you refuse to join her in the carriage now, you are making a very public—and very stupid—statement as to having made a match of convenience and only convenience."

"Surely she would not think such a thing."

"I cannot speak for her, but they would." He pointed with his wing toward faces in the windows watching their departure. "Rumors will begin before the coach has even turned the corner."

But what did rumors matter?

"Have you any idea what Lady Catherine will do with that sort of information? The things she will say to Georgiana and—"

Darcy climbed down and into the carriage.

Elizabeth sat on the far edge of the seat as if expecting someone to sit beside her.

Of course, she did. They were betrothed, and it was proper for him to do so now.

Damn it all, Walker was right.

As usual.

He slid onto the seat beside her, lurching ungracefully as the coach rocked into motion.

"This is not how I would have had things." He rubbed his hands together.

She slid farther into the corner of the coach. "I suppose we must now make the best of things."

He raked his hair back from his face. "That is not what I meant."

She cocked her head and peered at him. Her bewildered—or was it hurt?— gaze did nothing to help matters. Nor did it improve when she turned to regard the side glass.

Usually silence was comfortable, even pleasing to him. Why should that not be so now?

What was he supposed to do? He had tried to speak and it had hardly been successful, but this silence was even less so.

"Mr. Darcy, I am a very selfish creature, I suppose." She spoke without looking at him. "For the sake of giving relief to my own feelings, I can no longer help thanking you for your unexampled kindness to my sisters. Were it known to the rest of my family, I should not have merely my own gratitude to express, but perhaps it is best this way, as my mother's effusions might not be to your comfort. Regardless of your claim to being at fault, Lydia's behavior is my father's problem, not yours, and your willingness to—"

"If you will thank me, let it be for yourself alone. That the wish of giving happiness to you might add force to the other inducements which led me on, I shall not attempt to deny. But your family owes me nothing. Much as I respect them, I believe I thought only of you." He reached for her hands. They seemed so small between his own.

She glanced at him. Oh, the look in her eye. Was she truly so surprised?

"I can only suspect what your feelings were towards me in Meryton. You are too generous to trifle with me. If your feelings are still what they were then, tell me so at once. Regardless of your answer, my affections and wishes are unchanged—"

"Your affections, sir?"

He dragged a hand down his face. "Yes, Elizabeth, affections, of the warmest and most violent nature."

"And you have supposed me to be aware of this?"

"I had hoped. You seemed so well able to identify Walker and Cait's true intentions towards one another."

"They are dragons, sir, who are infinitely easier to understand than men."

"I know of no one else who would suggest such a thing."

She cocked her head and quirked her brow. "When men puff up, raise their frills, flutter their wings, change color and scent, posture and sharpen their talons, then I shall agree, they are as obvious as dragons."

He chuckled. "I am not so sure they do not do most of those things."

She rolled her eyes and looked away.

He released her hand. "If you find our arrangement intolerable, I promise you, I will find a way to free you without harm to your reputation."

"I do not see how that could be possible. A woman is never set free from an engagement without damage to her reputation. And I do not see Pemberley tolerating—"

"Is it what you want? To end our agreement?" He shifted around to stare directly into her eyes, his gut knotted more tightly it had been in court.

"I ... I did not say that."

"You have said nothing about what you do want." He pressed his knee against hers.

She stared at her hands. "No, I suppose I have not."

"So, tell me." Why was it so difficult to get an answer from her?

"It is strange to consider what I want—it has always been the dragons first."

"Pemberley aside, what do you want?" He leaned very close.

Perhaps that was not a good idea. Her warmth was far too pleasing.

She licked her lips. "I would like to become better acquainted with you, to have the opportunity to see the man that the dragons see in you. You have their respect, loyalty, and affection."

The tension in his belly eased. "Any man whom dragons admire you can admire as well?"

"They are very good judges of character. Walker would not sully himself with an unworthy association. You bring buttons for Quincy and treat Blanche with the deference of a young cousin. Wellsbey would do anything you asked. Even Rosings respects you—which is saying a great deal when she feels so much less toward her own Keeper."

"I must hope then that you will see in me what they do. It has always been my desire to have my wife's esteem."

She clutched her hands tightly, whispering, "Jane and I had always said we would only marry for love. I believe she has done so."

He laid his hands over hers. "I hope that you shall be able to do so."

She raised her eyes to his. "I do as well."

It was too forward, too bold, and too irresistible. He leaned in and kissed her, gently, warmly.

Pray, let there be no doubt in her mind of the ardency of his regard.

He pulled away just enough to capture her gaze.

She understood. Surely, she did.

He handed her out of the carriage at Darcy House, and they flew into a flurry of preparations only barely finished when Fitzwilliam arrived to carry him off to find Lydia. He extracted a promise that she would be mindful of her safety at Netherfield, declared he would write very often, kissed her once more, and rode away with Fitzwilliam, Walker following overhead.

Cold and numb, she instructed a maid to pack her trunks for the morning and wandered into the library.

What a fabulous room, and what beastly luck there was no possible way she could enjoy it now. She fell into a chair near the fireplace, face in her hands. How was she to explain all that was happening to Georgiana when she hardly understood it herself?

She was free from Longbourn's demands and Mr. Collins, but at what cost? Her breath caught in her throat. Never to go home again. She had no home now. If Papa was stubborn, she might never see him or Mama again. Though she would not mourn the loss of Mr. Collins from her acquaintance, she would miss Mary. And Jane, Kitty and even Lydia.

Never would she have guessed she would end this day homeless.

No, that was not true. Not exactly.

Darcy insisted she consider Darcy House and Pemberley estate her homes and instructed the staff to regard her as the mistress of his home.

Heavens above—how had it all happened?

She was betrothed to Mr. Darcy—in front of the entire Blue Order Court and Dragon Conclave no less.

What had she done?

At least he was not a dragon-hating, boorish addle-pate like Collins. No, far from that, he was an honorable, kind, respectable man who wore honor and duty like his coat and cravat. And he liked her—a great deal if his kisses were to be believed.

She pressed her hands to her cheeks. He liked her.

What ghastly, horrid, deplorable luck that the very hour she learned of it, they would be separated with no idea as to their reunion. Was it possible to miss him already?

What kind of correspondent would he be? At least his intentions were very good. That would have to be enough for now.

Georgiana took the news, all of it, tolerably well. To be sure, she was overjoyed that Elizabeth would soon be her sister. As to the rest, her trepidation was tempered by Cait's promise to carry correspondence between Meryton and Pemberley herself.

Had it been to impress Walker that she volunteered to serve as Collins' translator to Longbourn, or was it to answer her curiosity about the presence of a rogue dragon? Either way, for all her general air of self-importance, it was comforting to know she would have another Dragon Friend nearby.

April could hardly stop her flittering, far too delighted that Elizabeth had found a mate. No doubt, April would be seeking one of her own soon, too. A broody fairy dragon was just what one needed when trying to make contact with a rogue dragon. A generous cup of chamomile tea and honey eventually helped April to sleep.

Not so Elizabeth. She stared at the ceiling until nearly dawn when a rapping at her window drew her out from under the counterpane. Walker stood on the window sill.

"I cannot stay. There is a letter in my satchel. You may send your reply with me the next time I see you."

She removed the letter, buckled the satchel, and he flew off.

How had Darcy had time to write?

The letter was not even sealed—he obviously trusted Walker implicitly. And it was written in pencil—who wrote a letter in pencil?

One very determined to write under less than ideal circumstances.

Her hands trembled as she unfolded the letter.

My dear Elizabeth,

I cannot say that I am disappointed to be writing to you so soon, I only wish I had something of substance to report on the matter which concerns us both. F and I made it to a coaching inn just before the evening rainfall came in torrents. So, we are reasonably dry and fed for the evening.

She chuckled. Travels with Father had taken them to some less than comfortable places. He was politely describing a leaky roof and difficult to identify foodstuffs on a dirty plate.

In the morning, Walker will fly to Brighton. With any luck he will be able to find local dragons who may have overheard some of Wickham's conversations. F and I will make inquiries along the road. Hopefully there will be some news of them. I have faith that between these efforts and Rustle's in Meryton, we will be able to make quick work of finding them.

Did he realize that he need not be so positive for her sake? Probably not; he really did not know her that well at all. Still though, it was a kind gesture.

With so little news, I am sure you question why I have bothered sending Walker out in the middle of the night with a letter. I would not have you thinking me so inconsiderate of my Friend; I am writing this largely on his behalf.

You might wonder what possessed Cait to volunteer to go to Meryton in the service of Collins when we both know her feelings toward the man. She is not by nature such a generous being. The decision was largely a self-serving one, and of Walker's initiation. He wanted her to be near you.

He fears Cait is too proud to tell you this herself, but she will be laying her clutch in the coming weeks, and he fears her health may be at risk. The eggs of her previous clutch were especially large, and she had difficulty laying them. As eggs of subsequent clutches become larger, he fears she is at risk of becoming egg-bound.

Walker believes that you will be able to tell if Cait needs help and, more importantly, she will accept it from you. After what you have done for Pemberley, they both trust you implicitly.

As do I, my dearest, loveliest Elizabeth.

Her vision blurred. She dragged her sleeve across her eyes.

I realize you do not yet know me well enough to understand how very few people I say that of, but you can apply to F for a full accounting of the matter.

I count that among the first, but far from the only of your virtues that induced me to seek your hand. Though I hope this business will not keep us apart that long, I hope to acquaint you with all my reasons through our correspondence. Then perhaps you will be able to say that you know me.

Your sincere and loving servant, FD

He trusted her! Trusted her!

That should not mean so much, but it did. She pressed the letter to her chest. As cruel as it was that they should be separated, if he continued to write such letters, it might not be so very dreadful.

She carefully tucked the letter inside her reticule. The coach would be brought around soon, and she needed to bid Pemberley and Georgiana farewell.

During the journey she would read the notes she had transcribed about lindwyrms—the most likely species of the rogue dragon—and reread Darcy's letter. Hopefully that would be enough to distract her from the fact that she was wholly unwelcome at Longbourn.

She wrapped her arms around her waist and made her way down the grand stairs. Slate and Amber met her on her way to the cellar steps and greeted her enthusiastically, offering their congratulations and excitement over having a proper mistress in the house again as well as their hopes that she would be able to return home soon from her Blue Order business.

Home. They called Darcy House her home.

What an odd thought.

But here she was Keeper to a dragon that adored her, had a sister excited for their new relationship and new Dragon Friends who anticipated her company. Most importantly, her betrothed—a man who trusted her—invited her to call this place home. What more could "home" possibly mean?

What indeed?

If only a rogue dragon, a man who sought to be a Deaf-Speaker, and her unmanageable sister would cooperate, she might be able to discover what that kind of a home meant.

In the meantime, to Meryton.

For more dragon lore check out:
Dragon Myths of Britain
At RandomBitofFascination.com

Read the rest of the series:

Acknowledgments

So many people have helped me along the journey taking this from an idea to a reality.

Debbie, Anji, Julie, Ruth, Susanne and Raidon thank you so much for cold reading and being honest!,

And my dear friend Cathy, my biggest cheerleader, you have kept me from chickening out more than once!

And my sweet sister Gerri who believed in even those first attempts that now live in the file drawer!

Thank you!

Other Books by Maria Grace

Fine Eyes and Pert Opinions
Remember the Past
The Darcy Brothers

A Jane Austen Regency Life Series:

A Jane Austen Christmas: Regency Christmas Traditions
Courtship and Marriage in Jane Austen's World
How Jane Austen Kept her Cook: An A to Z History of
Georgian Ice Cream

Jane Austen's Dragons Series:

A Proper Introduction to Dragons
Pemberley: Mr. Darcy's Dragon
Longbourn: Dragon Entail
Netherfield:Rogue Dragon
The Dragons of Kellynch
Kellynch:Dragon Persuasion

The Queen of Rosings Park Series:

Mistaking Her Character
The Trouble to Check Her
A Less Agreeable Man

Sweet Tea Stories:

A Spot of Sweet Tea: Hopes and Beginnings (short story
anthology)
Snowbound at Hartfield
A Most Affectionate Mother
Inspiration

Available in paperback, e-book, and audiobook

On Line Exclusives at:

Bonus and deleted scenes
Regency Life Series

<u>Free e-books</u>:

- *Rising Waters: Hurricane Harvey Memoirs*
- *Lady Catherine's Cat*
- *A Gift from Rosings Park*
- *Bits of Bobbin Lace*
- *Half Agony, Half Hope: New Reflections on Persuasion*
- *Four Days in April*

✒ About the Author

Six time BRAG Medallion Honoree, #1 Best-selling Historical Fantasy author Maria Grace has her PhD in Educational Psychology and is a 16-year veteran of the university classroom where she taught courses in human growth and development, learning, test development and counseling. None of which have anything to do with her undergraduate studies in economics/sociology/managerial studies/behavior sciences.

She pretends to be a mild-mannered writer/cat-lady, but most of her vacations require helmets and waivers or historical costumes, usually not at the same time.

She writes gaslamp fantasy, historical romance and non-fiction to help justify her research addiction.

Contact Maria Grace:

author.MariaGrace@gmail.com

Facebook:
http://facebook.com/AuthorMariaGrace

On Amazon.com:
http://amazon.com/author/mariagrace

Random Bits of Fascination (http://RandomBitsof-Fascination.com)

Austen Variations (http://AustenVariations.com)

White Soup Press (http://whitesouppress.com/)

On Twitter @WriteMariaGrace

On Pinterest: http://pinterest.com/mariagrace423/